Echoes

Aralot's Keepers Book Three

Amanda Heit

Heit, Amanda.

Echoes / by Amanda Heit.

1st edition.

Paperback   978-1-949858-14-3

eBook   978-1-949858-15-0

Printed in the United States of America

October 2020

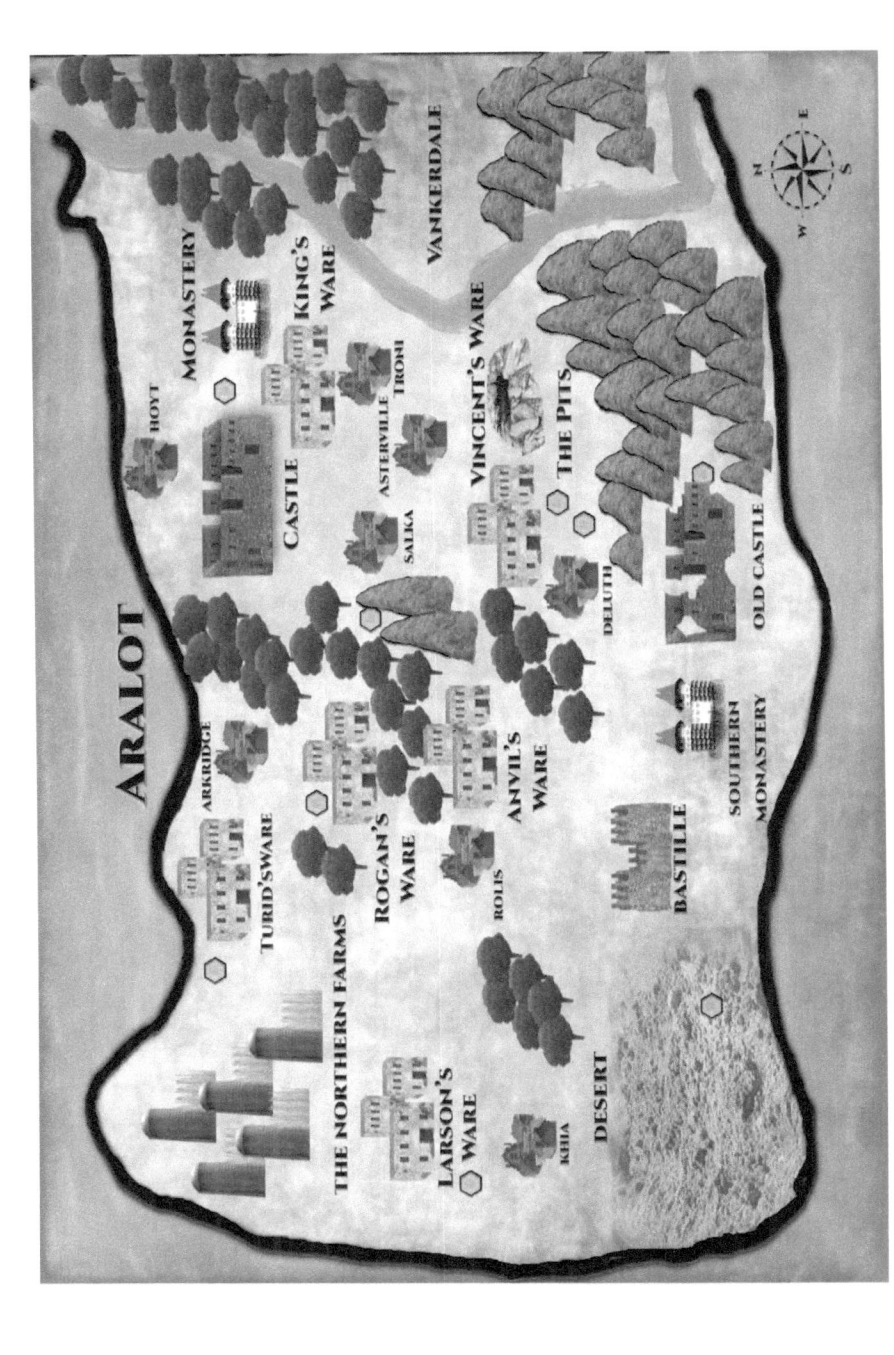

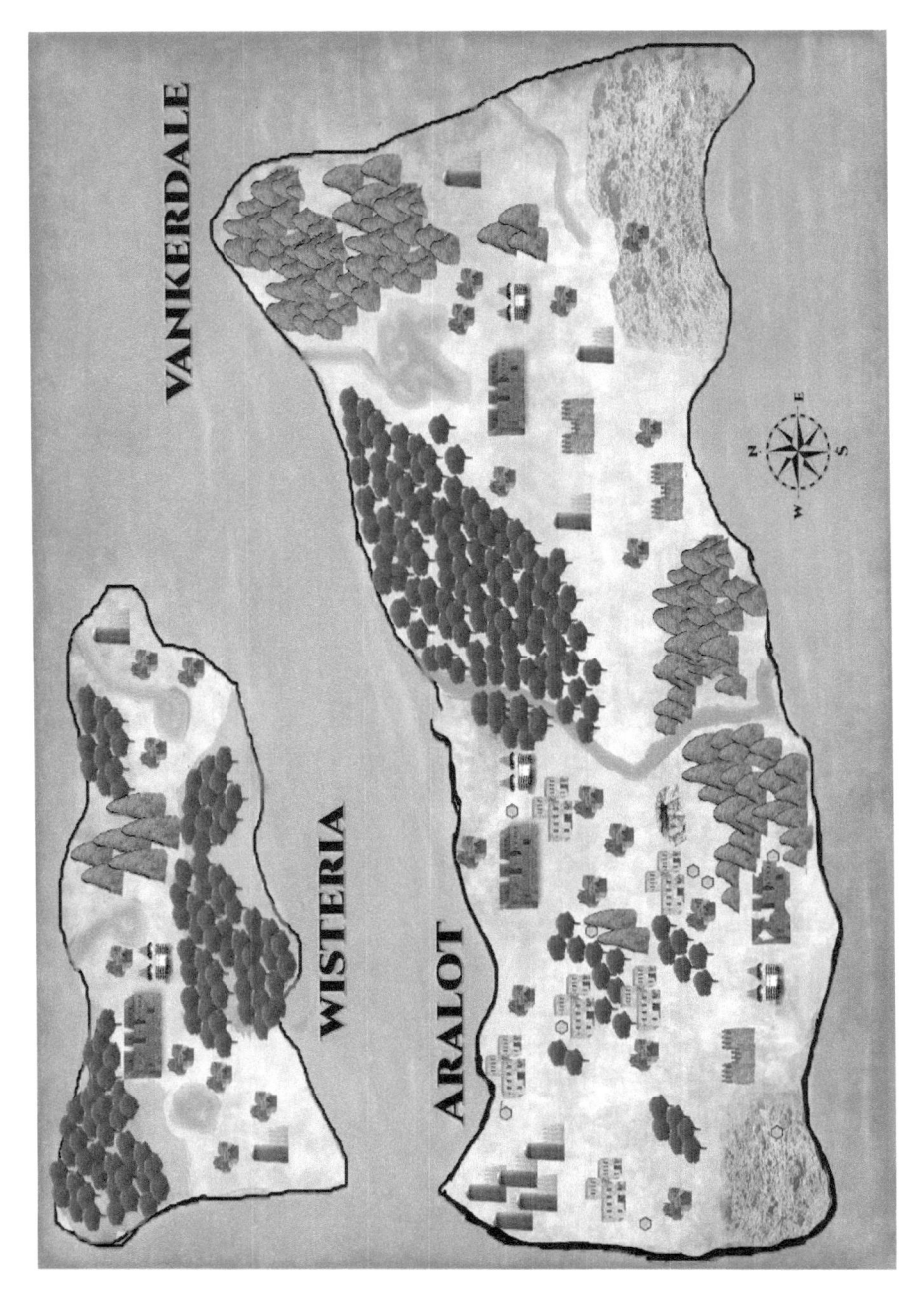

Chapters

Ring

Kayla

Snap. The sound broke against Kayla's ears alerting her to the fact that something was horribly wrong. Crunch. That sound was even worse. There was a heavy, dark creeping something really close to her, and she had one guess as to what it could be. A dragon. She had joined The King's Dragon Ware, but last she knew, she was in her bed safely tucked away in her bunkroom with spells around her to keep intruders away and her screams contained. Was this a dream? Her nightmares were getting worse lately, if such a thing was possible.

There was a time that she could easily wake herself up from them. The closer she got to turning sixteen, the harder it got to wake herself up. Now that she had passed her birthday, she'd failed to wake herself up at all. This nightmare spell was the one spell that lingered that even her magical dragon couldn't destroy. It was her last unwanted curse. There was no such thing as rest when this spell was there. There was no peace; nothing but the fear of past dragon keepers that invaded her thoughts, teaching her how to kill dragons, how to fight, how to be brutal.

Thump. Okay, that was it! She was going to wake herself up! That was a real sound. There was something inside her bunkroom coming to get her. The only people who were allowed to use magic inside of Aralot were the royal family and the steward's royal family; although, ware leaders had been given protective charms too, and a few of them actively used magic now that it had been handed to them. With the loudness of this sound, whatever was breaking things beside her had already taken down her magical protective covering. She had to wake up!

Grind. Crunch. Oh, dear. That was the sound of bones. Someone was dying inside her bunkroom! She had to get up so she could fight the person or demon off. Maybe this was the result of Prince Tristan again. Despite his earlier concessions to take down his curses, they were still fighting each other, and they both knew it.

The smell of blood hit her senses next. Kayla tried to scream. Normally she tried not to do that because she didn't want to wake up any of the other girls in her bunkroom with her nightmares. That was why she had so many spells around her when she slept to contain her sounds. The spells had failed! She had never shared a room before because she was an only child and up until now had lived with her parents at the edge of the Northern Farms. Nothing came out of her mouth, although she could feel the struggle holding down her consciousness.

Kayla returned to her old standbys that used to work when she fought herself in her sleep. She bit her tongue, tried kicking, tried reaching for the knife slid into the top of her left boot so she could cut her arm. Anything to jolt through the spells that trapped her so she could return to herself.

It wasn't working, so Kayla moved toward magic. Her nightmares gave her ample fuel for scary spells. She had just had another such dream, one that taught her a bunch of evil spells that her grandfather Herb Felding had used against her dad when they were trying to kill each other. Kayla shoved a river over her entire head. She could feel the rush of the water, feel the fear pulse through her body because she had never learned how to swim. Not being able to enter water that was deeper than her ankle had been one of her curses. She was going to die, and she was going to kill herself if she couldn't get herself to wake up!

The water vanished as if someone else was using magic around her, stopping her from waking up. Kayla heard a dragon growl. The deep throaty tone of it was one she knew well, but it also belonged in her nightmares, so she wasn't sure if she was making up the sound of the dragon or not. This was Coal. He was a special ultra-dragon king that had a hide so thick it was nearly impossible to break through to kill him. He was a jet-black night dragon with moon-shaped claws, gleaming green eyes, and fire that could get so hot it could break through other dragon scales.

Coal wasn't supposed to be scary anymore. He had only been beastly killing off people and dragons because Queen Aria was controlling him in a possession spell. Kayla had just destroyed that spell, so Coal was free to be himself now. He had bonded King Tyler of Vankerdale when Tyler gained his keeper abilities. Unlike Kayla, Tyler liked being a keeper. He enjoyed being able to hold multiple dragon's thoughts inside his head because he loved all dragons.

Being a keeper had drawbacks. Dragons gave keepers special dragon names, and when they called those, keepers felt the magic of their blood constrain against them to answer the call. It was hard to fight against the pressure to help a dragon. Keepers were supposed to be a blessing for the land. They were knowledgeable people that would care for dragons when they were wounded, and play with dragons when they got bored. In that regard, it was keepers that had first created dragon wares. It was keepers leading man and dragon to be best friends instead of worst enemies. It was keepers that were first bonded to dragons, connecting human souls to dragon ones, safeguarding hearts and sharing lives.

The dragon growl came again, along with the question asking her what she was doing. It was still Coal's voice so Kayla was really confused as she tried out a different spell on herself. She started to flatten out her lungs, feeling her body scream with the need for air.

"Fine!" Valiant screamed at her. *"Take over!"*

"Valiant! What's happening?!"

Valiant was her first bonded dragon, her gatekeeper dragon that blocked out all other dragon thoughts from her head so she wouldn't go crazy with the magic her blood gave her. Kayla had spent her entire life having him in her head, but it wasn't until very recently that he had talked to her. He had been trapped in Vankerdale, bait to bring her over to the neighboring kingdom so that Vankerdale could steal Aralot's magic. Tyler and Kayla had saved him from all of that. Now he was safely in the kingdom of Aralot where Kayla lived.

"Coal was looking for you so I brought you over. It's the first day of the week. You're supposed to be sleeping tonight."

Kayla's eyes finally opened, and she instinctively reached for weapons dropping something onto the ground in the process that she had been holding. She was not where she had put herself last. She had gone to bed in her bunkroom, but it wasn't new to her to learn that Valiant woke her up and walked her around in her sleep.

Pg. 4

Only bonded dragons could sightshare with their riders. Swapping the essence of their consciousness so that Kayla was the dragon and Valiant the human was usually only done while the dragon and rider team were both awake. Valiant was a spellbinding dragon, a rare breed of dragon that could shoot out magic. He had the unique ability to sightshare whenever he wanted. That usually meant he took over her body and had her draw pictures of dragons in her sleep.

Before Kayla knew that she had a bonded dragon, she thought that she was mentally insane for all the pictures she drew in the middle of the night. She had spent many years double checking to make sure that she wasn't possessed. She had given up on tying herself into her bed to prevent the drawing because she always broke out. Before Valiant told her that it was him drawing through her, she had checked for those pictures every morning and destroyed them. They had scared her. The images were a curse threatening her sanity. At least now Valiant was talking to her so she could explain why she moved in her sleep.

She was out in the woods that rested beside the King's dragon training ware with Coal who was standing in front of her chomping through two dead deer. That was the chomping sound and the smell of blood. Kayla let out a sigh of relief that it wasn't one of her bunkmates dying.

"Is that what woke you up?" Valiant asked her. *"I never can quite tell what makes you push against me."*

"I heard the sound of bones snapping," Kayla replied. *"That would wake up anyone."*

"Except that you were being me sleeping in my dragon form out on the field not in the woods. You shouldn't have heard a thing," Valiant complained. *"You should pick up that box you dropped. It's for you."*

"What was the water for?" Coal's deep voice asked her in dragon speech. Since Kayla had grown up swapping her human and dragon form so much, and hearing dragons talk to her all day long and all night long, she could understand any word in the dragon language. Most people couldn't. They had to resort to the few words they did know, or resort to another dragon translating things for them.

Kayla looked around, noticing how she was still soaking wet. She shook her head and checked on the state of her magical keychain hooked closely on her weapon belt. She had been the one drowning herself and Valiant the one stopping her. It was nothing but herself that had been using magic tonight. Nothing but herself that broke out of the spells in her bunkroom to be wandering around in the woods in the middle of the night. If she didn't love Valiant so much, she'd remind him that having her body move on her like this was utterly terrifying.

"You were asleep!" Valiant complained. *"And you can't expect me to stop being you. You're the other half of me. I can't stop being myself."*

Apparently.

"I'm sorry, Coal," Kayla spoke to the hulking black dragon as she put her weapons back in the weapon belt so she wasn't a threat to him. "The water was me fighting a scary thought. It got a little out of hand. You brought me a box?"

She looked down at the ground to find the object she had dropped that Valiant had her holding before. It was a small wooden

Pg. 6

box with an intarsia of a wolf face on the lid. Kayla picked it up, opened the box, and let it drop to the ground yet again.

"Shall I tell Tyler of your reaction?" Coal asked her with a short growl.

"No," Kayla replied, taking a step back and a deep breath in. The breath was filled with the smell of dead deer so she frowned. It would have been better if it was Valiant out here tonight getting this from Coal. He wouldn't have made her drop the wedding ring in the dirt. He wouldn't be making faces against the smell of Coal's dinner.

"I simply wasn't expecting…" Kayla trailed off.

"Tyler thinks that you're not coming back unless he reminds you that you agreed to marry him. You ran off on us really fast."

"I didn't forget," Kayla answered. She picked up the box again and pulled out the ring to examine it. It was beautiful for sure. All the gems were inset so she wouldn't have to worry about knocking them out when she engaged in dragon training activities. There was a large diamond in the center and two pink sapphires on each end.

"Why didn't Tyler bring this to me?" Kayla asked. Then she might have stayed asleep because she wouldn't have found herself standing alone in front of Coal who used to be one of her worst enemies. Asleep or not, her bodily instincts worked just fine, trained and honed by muscle memory and intuition. Coal had tried to bond her before, and if he had gotten away with that, she would have had so many more complications with her gatekeeper dragon Valiant and her mother's ice dragon Sparkle who claimed Kayla as one of her riders too. There was no way she could stay asleep when she was standing before this particular dragon. That's what had pushed her awake tonight.

"Maybe Tyler did come," Tyler's voice said from behind her.

Kayla's shoulders hiked uncomfortably up as she spun around. With glasses, short dark-brown hair, and a beard that framed only his chin and beneath his nose, Tyler was a rather cute person. Kayla gave him a smile so he wouldn't see the real panic that pushed through her nerves.

"It's beautiful! Thank you. I'm sorry about the dropping it part and the water part." Tyler was already privy to her troubling dragon issues, so she had no problem in explaining the one that she was dealing with tonight. "Valiant was being me. I dropped the box because it's a bit scary waking up to find myself out in the middle of the woods without knowing what I'm doing. I just became myself. I was asleep before that."

"You don't need to apologize. You have our sympathy. Coal for one understands a little too well what it is like to wake up without remembering what he had been doing. You told us that you destroyed Coal's possessed scale." Tyler told her this more as a question than a statement. Kayla had no idea that her mouth had told them that. She nodded. Coal had been possessed for quite some time and forced to tear apart dragon wares and towns around Aralot.

Technically Valiant had destroyed the stolen scale, because Kayla couldn't find a way to destroy something so indestructible. Valiant had binding magic so his worked better than hers did against ultra-dragon king scales, even if they both got their magic from the same source. They used magic from Bantin who was the only magic producing dragon between the three kingdoms of Wisteria,

Pg. 8

Vankerdale, and Aralot. Before Tyler, Vankeredale had been trying to steal Bantin away. Aralot was the only kingdom that could cast spells with a replenishable magic source. The other places cast spells very sparingly because they couldn't risk running out.

"Who was our threat?" Tyler asked.

Kayla shook her head at him, and because he was still standing there, she slipped the wedding ring onto her finger and placed the box in her pocket. She had already told Queen Aria that the woman wouldn't need to worry about the new king of Vankerdale hunting her down for using magic against Coal. Aria had been using Coal to kill off people and dragons that had been inside an infected keeper bond. Kayla had explained to Aria that only the bonded dragon in the bond would have any issues with a poisoned human, and Kayla was hoping that was good enough that the queen would stop killing living creatures that were not infected. Even though Kayla's mother, Tia, had been infected by keeper poison and subsequently cured, there were still too many people that didn't understand exactly how the poison worked. It was common practice to destroy anything that an infected keeper mind had touched.

"I took care of it, Tyler. You don't have anything to worry about anymore. Coal won't be possessed."

"I have plenty to worry about," Tyler refuted. "There's a spellcaster out there that uses magic for evil."

"I took care of it," Kayla stated again, not about to budge. Aria wasn't the only one splashing evil magic around right now. Kayla was aware of quite a few crimes that she was keeping quiet about simply because she was trying to allow the individuals a chance to repent for their deeds and make things better.

Tyler rolled his eyes when Coal snorted something at him from behind her. She had no idea what Coal thought about, but she was glad that he wasn't thinking his dragon thoughts inside *her* head. She had too much to worry about herself without adding more dragons and their problems to her life.

"I didn't forget that you mentioned that you found a person you want to teach magic," Tyler hinted. "Unknown spellcasters—"

"Tyler, that person will never be a problem," Kayla cut him off.

She hadn't meant to tell Tyler that at all, but her current section leader and teacher at the King's Ware was amazingly talented at using magic. He had cut off her spells once simply by willing the magic away. It took a really strong mind, and respect from Aralot, to make magic work so seamlessly. Caleb Andrade would be an amazing spellcaster. It was for that reason that she had given him a magical trinket that she had stolen from Tyler. She had also placed inside Caleb's trunk one of her early magic books. That was her one crime of the century, because Caleb wasn't allowed to learn magic since he wasn't royal. Even so, she couldn't help but give it to him.

He was beautiful with the stuff, as if it was embedded inside his soul. Her father, King Jack, was the kingdom's spellcaster, so Kayla knew a good magic user when she saw one. Jack hadn't been able to get magic to behave for him so quickly without undergoing an extensive study of the subject. Caleb had the potential to be better than her father, better than her, better than anyone. Magic and Caleb were like watching the sun break over the edge of her horizon. A glorious burst of color, warm, happy, and fathomless. Caleb had a white soul, and a caring, loving heart. She had checked with a spell. He was completely brilliant, and would never use magic with an ill intention.

Pg. 10

"You're probably smiling about him again," Valiant interrupted her inner monologue.

"No one but you can hear me," Kayla shrugged, and she wasn't smiling. She was keeping the emotion off her face, because she was talking to her fiancé while thinking about the guy she had a crush on. Not a good combination.

"Why is it that whenever the topic is magic that you go completely mute?" Tyler questioned. "Magic in the wrong hands worries me."

"Which is why I took care of it."

Tyler rolled his eyes at her. She wasn't going to tell *him* how to use magic, even if she had never once seen him try. Maybe Tyler would be good at it too, but she didn't want to find out. Maybe it was a pride issue that held her back, because Aralot had been keeping magic away from Vankerdale for several generations. Tyler was the king. She didn't want to feel responsible for giving him what he was after.

"There's a special luncheon on the seventeenth where you're supposed to meet all the nobles that serve as our councilors," Tyler said next. He put his hands into his pockets as if he could already guess her rejection. "I would love for you to be in attendance."

"I'll do my best to be there," Kayla answered. It was a lie. She wasn't planning on showing up.

"We will be discussing the topic of what to do about the dragons from Vankerdale that have vanished into Aralot after the border spells were taken down. We will also be discussing the start of dragon wares. Your input would be amazing."

Blast! He was trying to make her show up by pushing against her keeper nature that made her want to care for every dragon. Vankerdale didn't have any functioning wares because they were just barely stepping out of their old curses too. In a way, that made Kayla and Vankerdale remarkably similar. They were both trying to start over. Tyler would be great at helping Vankerdale do that, but it was a shame that he knew how to push her buttons. Tyler had seen through all her weaknesses before too. In his mind, that wasn't a bad thing, because he had done his best to help her overcome her limitations. However, he had also used that knowledge against her to bring her into Vankerdale twice and get them engaged.

"I will still do my best," Kayla answered, as if the topic of discussion wouldn't change her desire to show up or not. The seventeenth was going to be a rough day. She'd probably spend all of it fretting about ditching Aralot for her responsibilities in Vankerdale.

"Okay. So how are things going with Prince Tristan Cluster?"

Worst topic ever. As the steward's son, Tristan was called the Prince of Aralot. He currently had just as much authority to be the next leader of the kingdom as Kayla did. Neither of their fathers had been crowned with the real crown, because the real crown was a cursed thing that no one wanted to mess with. Legally, King Klavian and King Jack shared the throne. Magically, it was Kayla's father in charge, but that didn't change the way that Prince Tristan saw himself as the inheritor of the kingdom. It didn't change the way that her parents said she had to date him either, or the unspoken words that came along with that telling her that if she married Prince Tristan everyone would be really happy. They'd be joining the two ruling lines into one, getting rid of an age-old rivalry that her parents had mostly done away with already.

Pg. 12

"Tristan is in the process of becoming a better man."

Kayla chose her words rather carefully. Tristan had taken down the curses he had put on her and her family, but he would always love sneaking around, stealing, and hunting innocent animals and bugs. He had his own secret stash of magical ice orbs that he kept in the Desert Ware. That alone gave him more magical power than the rightful spellcaster at any given time. Tristan could magically destroy anyone that tried to kill him off, and he had the magical knowledge to do so. Most of the time he rubbed Kayla the wrong way, and she knew that she grated against him even when they tried to be civil with each other.

Tyler pulled his hands out of his pockets to rub at his eyes. "Is it just me or are you being incredibly short with me right now? You normally tell me everything that's on your mind."

Yes, wasn't that unfortunate? It was because Tyler was a keeper like herself. Another part of being a keeper was respecting and protecting all the other keepers. Most people only knew of three keepers total. There was Kayla, her mother Tia, and her Aunt Rosa. People would learn soon that Tyler was a keeper. Kayla knew of five more. Her Uncle Conner had been hiding away in Vankerdale and he had three kids named Sashi, Ruth, and Tova that were going to all be keepers. Her father had just turned himself into a keeper as well. Right before Kayla's mother ascended the throne all keepers kept themselves hidden, because the Clusters had been killing them off. King Klavian had decided to stop killing the keepers because Tia was his strongest supporter in achieving his dreams of being the king. Now everyone was friends, but keepers still felt the need to hide.

"Tyler, it's my one night to sleep. I don't feel like talking. All I want to do is go back to bed with my own body," she added so that Valiant knew she didn't want him to walk her around.

"You can use my body," Valiant whined. *"It's ever so nice to sleep inside."*

"Okay," Tyler gave her a smile and then he stepped forward to pull her into a hug. "Sorry to keep you up. If you didn't have that magic on you, I'd highly consider tying you up to take you home with me where you belong."

Kayla had to laugh at him when Tyler blushed. See! He did it too! It was like whenever they were in the wrong kingdom, they couldn't help but spurt out all the real thoughts going on deep inside.

"I would," Tyler said more resolved this time. "Kayla, I need you there. I know you said that you had a few things you needed to take care of in Aralot first. I respect your time and your commitments, but I need you to come home. Don't be too long?" he asked.

With that, he gave her a short kiss on the cheek and climbed up on the back of Coal, who had finished eating his deer. Coal backed away, and using his powerfully strong wings launched himself into the air to take Tyler back across the river that separated their two kingdoms. Kayla waited only long enough to know that Coal could no longer see her before she ripped the wedding ring off her finger and threw it back in the dirt.

Married! She was only sixteen! The only person she had ever dated was Tristan, and the only person she had ever had a crush on was Caleb. She was too young for this. Kayla curled up into a ball on the ground. It was a posture that Valiant himself adopted a lot. She wasn't sure which of them had started it. On the ground was a very familiar place for her to be, since she used to fall there all the time when any short glance at a dragon ripped her heart open and turned her sad.

Normal people who lost the bonds to their dragons experienced pounding headaches that had them falling over as they mentally missed the dragon thought they were used to. Kayla used to have no idea she was missing dragon voices since she had lost Valiant the day she was born. She never got the headache, because she was a keeper and it was impossible for her to lose dragon voices in her head. Instead, she experienced the deepest inner depression anyone could imagine by being unbonded. Valiant had just barely cured that for her by replacing their bond, but being on the ground when she was in emotional distress would always be a habit after sixteen years of being here.

"What am I going to do?" Kayla moaned. *"First, kisses shouldn't be like that. They're supposed to be awkward and flirty, not normal and comfortable."*

"You're complaining because you like Tyler?" Kayla could hear Valiant's snort all the way over here even if he was right and they were nowhere close to each other. Valiant loved Tyler. Tyler was one of Valiant's first human friends. Tyler had freed Valiant from captivity and brought him to Kayla, so Valiant would always be grateful for Tyler Valeron.

Kayla stood up from the ground to glare in the direction of her dragon. He wasn't helping! In fact, if she was feeling mean enough, she'd probably threaten to break their bond again so she could fight with him over this. She didn't want to like Tyler! She quite enjoyed having a crush on Caleb, and if she admitted that she liked her fiancé she would have to give up on Caleb. She'd only just admitted to Caleb that she had been his friend forever. He had been trying to talk to her for as long as she could remember, drawing pictures to catch her attention, standing up for her when she couldn't get off the ground. Caleb was her childhood hero, and now he was her teenage dream that would never happen.

"I think you've been watching too many nightmares. No one needs to fight their own dragon. You need sleep. Humans can't survive without sleep."

"And who was it who woke me up?!" Kayla screamed, before she realized how perfectly horrible she was being and collapsed back to the ground again. She didn't need to scream. She had made her choice over this already, and yes, she was feeling super tired and grumpy because she lacked sleep. Maybe if she shut her eyes, she could catch a few minutes of rest…

She was running at a brown-scaled dragon. Gastron by name, this was her grandfather's fourth bonded dragon. This happened to be the night that Herb Felding killed Gastron off in his own field because he was mad that the dragon came to see him. Herb was poisoned, an infected keeper, and he had been hiding the knowledge that he still engaged with dragons from everyone, even his own wife. No one knew that he was bonded after he had ditched the dragon wares and turned to farming.

Kayla wished she could shut her eyes as she was forced to jump on top of the dragon's head in the dream and stab him through the skull, after first ripping off the scales on his head. At least Herb was relatively clean when he killed off his dragons. His father, Gladius

Felding, was much worse. He tortured the dragons before he finished the deed.

Jumping past Herb, Kayla found herself being Shane Felding next. He was her great-great-grandfather, and despite Kayla wishing that he had never had family problems, he had one large fight with his dad once. This was another one of those heartbreaking moments that she hated to watch. Shane was standing in front of Troy's door. Troy Felding was Kayla's third great grandfather. This was the night that Shane set fire to his dad's house and…

"Wake up!" an unfamiliar dragon screamed at her so loudly that Kayla had no choice but to comply with the dragon's wishes as her keeper blood shoved past the spell in her way. Kayla rolled over, somehow remembering to shove the ring she had dropped into her pocket as she spun to the side to get away from the wild dragon that was screaming at her. Her hands obtained prongs, her feet the perfect posture to launch her on top of the nearby dragon so she could destroy it. Yes, she had been watching too many nightmares.

The dragon that had screamed at her wasn't engaging in battle at all. It was a dusty blue night dragon, similar to the color of Valiant, although her dragon had more gray to him than this creature. This one was pretty though, with light yellow eyes that didn't scare her one bit. Kayla put her weapons back away and groaned as another part of her keeper heritage struck at her. Similar to her mother, Kayla could tell a dragon's name just by looking at him. They were the only two keepers who could do that. Kayla normally pretended that she didn't know any of the dragons that talked to her. She had been shoving against them and herself her whole life, but she was trying to be better to accept what she was now that she wasn't broken.

"Thanks, Norber," Kayla sighed, giving the dragon a short smile for waking her up as he scrambled backward away from her. He looked at her as if her knowing his name was scarier than her holding prongs near his face. One of those was far more lethal than the other. She could kill a dragon in her sleep without trying. What if the curse on her made her do that? What if she was going to turn into a wraith that hunted down and killed dragons? The kids in Anvil's Ware used to call her a wraith behind her back.

"That was only because you walked around hiding under a hood to avoid looking at dragons, and they didn't understand," Valiant reminded her. *"You will not turn into a wraith and become a dragon killer. I swear that to you upon my grave."*

And bonded dragons couldn't lie to their riders so there was that. She wouldn't start killing dragons in her sleep. Not with her own body anyway. The infected keepers that kept coming at her still would.

"You saw another one of those nightmares?" Valiant asked. *"I'm trying to find out how to stop those nightmares. I try over and over. I cast spells on you all the time. I try to fight it with you, Kayla. I don't know what it is."*

"I know," Kayla said out loud. Then because she was still in front of Norber, she gave him another smile. "You doing all right? I didn't even hear you walk up."

He hummed at her for being concerned about his wellbeing, and then he pointed with his tail deeper into the woods.

"What?" Kayla asked glancing the way Norber pointed. "I can understand dragon speech. Just say it."

Pg. 18

Norber shook his head no and pointed more insistently. What was it? She had to admit that she was curious. She'd never engaged with a wild dragon before, and she had no idea what one of them would want to tell her if she ever did decide to talk to it.

"Is something there? It's not hurt is it?"

Norber didn't answer except to keep pointing. Kayla gave him another smile, and with an unusual feeling of trust over the strange dragon she had never met before, she turned her back on him and started to walk where he pointed. She would never do this if it was Coal directing her where to go. There was that magic again, shoving at her instincts to let her know that Coal had not belonged in Aralot. He was supposed to find Tyler and bond him. He was supposed to go into Vankerdale and start dragon wares and heal the broken dragons across the river. Knowing this only made it that much harder for Kayla to want to join him. She felt tied to Aralot. So tied. So stuck. She couldn't move away.

Kayla stopped walking on the thought. It had crossed her mind before that she'd run away from Aralot and leave her home behind her if that was her only choice left to keep away from Tristan. So what was the real desire that kept her upright and functioning? What was she supposed to do?

With gritted teeth, she plunged on until she caught sight of what Norber had been pointing out. All at once her eyes teared up, her heart flooded with gladness, and all the weariness of her bones vanished as if she was next to Valiant when he had hummed at her. Bonded dragons could transfer their happy emotions over to their riders like that. It wasn't a dragon that she was looking at. It was Ritz.

Blond, blue-eyed and bold, he was the rebel leader of the Colts, ageless, trapped in time, cunning and clever. Most people kept their distance from him, and Kayla did so most of the time too. However, the last time she had seen him, he had been risking his own life to save hers. He had tried to prevent her from being kidnapped into Vankerdale.

Kayla squealed out her glee, letting her eyes run as her legs did the same thing. Ritz, of course, knocked her off her feet before she could jump on him to hug him. He didn't engage in frivolous things like hugs. He didn't share affection. He was hard and cruel and could get inside people's minds so well that he could make them believe they were someone else. He looked down at her with his stern clear blue eyes that never revealed his age. Ritz had slapped her before, but when Kayla could get him alone like this, she took all the words he ever said to her and kept them locked up inside her heart.

"Ritz!" Kayla sang his name as she got to her feet, still smiling at him. "Anyone ever tell you that they like to be around you?" Kayla asked.

"Only when they're lying," Ritz answered, causing Kayla to smile at him even more.

"Not me. I've tried to explain it to Conner, and Tyler, and even Valiant. I can't. I happen to love you."

Ritz laughed at her. "Has Valiant told you that you start going loopy when you're exhausted?"

"No! Ritz, I'm telling you the truth. I can't help it. I may be a mess everywhere else but I know for a fact that I love you. Nothing else makes sense right now except for that."

Pg. 20

"Yup. You're losing it, Kayla." Ritz assured her. "No one loves me."

"I do," she insisted again. "You're a bit of a pain, but I like seeing you around. Thanks so much for being the one coming to save me."

"On that note, what amount of saving you am I looking at this time?"

Kayla's heart melted even more. She couldn't explain her problems to her parents, and she could hardly explain them to herself, but regardless, here was Ritz, the most cunning man of their era, offering to help her yet again. He had offered before to help her with Vankeradale, only she had no idea what kind of help she needed. It was still complicated.

"I don't know. I can't sort through any of it. I'm so confused."

"That comes along with being tired." Ritz nodded at her as if she could blame her poor decision-making skills all on her lack of sleep. "I'm going to ask you questions and you will tell me the first answer that comes to your mind. No second guessing. No backing out. Promise me. I want the truth."

"Okay," Kayla agreed. "But the truth as long as it's my truth to share."

He had once asked her for the secrets to portals. They were magical doorways that kings used to transport themselves to the far reaches of their kingdoms. Kayla knew everything there was to know about portals. She knew how to make them, destroy them, and become immune to them. She was never going to share that truth with Ritz.

"What happened in Vankerdale that you're not telling anybody?"

Kayla opened her mouth and shivered. There was a reason for her silence. A large reason for the short answers she had shared. She had given the bare minimum of words she could get away with because what she was hiding was very emotional and she had never been good at sharing her emotions with anyone. She used to get her emotions balanced out by chatting with Uncle Anvil, who was more her parent's friend then her real uncle.

She couldn't see Uncle Anvil anymore because he led the dragon ware that Tristan had cracked down on. Anvil couldn't take on any more riders, or breed any more dragons for a full season. Vermelo, the Captain of the Guard, had asked her Aunt Rosa and Kayla's Uncle Clark to take her parents off the throne and take over the kingdom. Rosa and Clark lived at Anvil's ware and Tristan thought they were getting too strong.

Similar to Ritz, Kayla usually found herself drawn to Vermelo, but she disagreed with the way he was pushing at her parents. Vermelo had wanted her mother to charge across the cursed border to free Kayla the first time she was kidnapped. Her parents hadn't sent anyone to help her because that would have mentally wounded a lot of dragons. Kayla had to rescue herself.

"I killed Prince Evan."

She had never killed anyone before. Not ever considered it. She'd not said a thing about it after the deed was done. Not hardly thought about it. Thinking about it now had her heart beating within her chest rather fast.

Pg. 22

"It was either me or Conner. I'm not quite sure. I was fighting Prince Evan with magic after he sliced Tyler's arms off and tried to kill him. I fixed the arms. Then we ran after King Peyton and killed him off too. I used magic against King Peyton, got inside his head, stopped him from casting spells at all of Conner's attacking dragons. Conner said that King Peyton killed off five of his dragons before we reached him. Conner for sure killed King Peyton, but he wouldn't have been able to without me."

Kayla took in a deep breath, waiting for Ritz to say something about her admitting to being a murderer. He didn't. He gave her a short nod of his head as if he understood what it was like to fear what she could do. Kayla gave him a short smile for that. He would understand. Ritz had been the one that killed off King Gladius when the man was too poisoned and insane to rule anymore. That's what had Ritz starting the Colts. They were the only opposition that had been able to withstand the spells that Gladius cast across the land.

Kayla had never wondered about it before, but she did now. What if Ritz hadn't liked killing off Gladius? What if he felt like there was no other choice left? No other way to stop the curses, the madness, the terror that was affecting dragon and mankind alike? What if he cried when Gladius died? What if he knew the man personally?

That's how it was for Kayla with the Peytons. She didn't know them well, but she had cried about them later. There wasn't another option left but to stop them. They were going to kill off Tyler for being a keeper. She had to protect Tyler, stop the Peyton's from warring with Aralot, and stop them from stealing dragons. They often stole dragons from Wisteria, which was how they had gotten Valiant. They refused to stop stealing dragons even after her parents had fixed their curses, so Tia had put one of those curses back on after King Peyton had forced Kayla's birth, forced Valiant's bond, and stolen him away from her.

"Anyway," Kayla said to clear her head. She had more confessions to make. "I also got engaged to Tyler Valeron and made him the king of Vankerdale."

"Why?" Ritz asked.

Such a simple question with a complicated answer. This was the part that she was still struggling with.

"Technically it's only an engagement, so it can be broken, but Vankerdale sees a royal engagement as being married already. When I'm in Vankerdale talking to Tyler I can't help but spill my secrets to him. I tell him everything as if he has a right to hear the aches of my heart. I think it's because we're both keepers. If he's over here, he says stuff too, as if we can't hide our real thoughts when on each other's soil. Sort of like—"

"The curse in Vankerdale that constrained their keepers is broken," Ritz stated. "Pyro broke the curse. I know. I also know about your dad. I know that Jack made himself a keeper, destroying the theory that all keepers are hereditary by Felding blood. They can now be created and destroyed with the use of dragon kings. The rules for being a keeper are changing. With it, you too must adapt. Explain about Tyler please."

That was one of the most helpful and annoying things about Ritz. He always seemed to know things that no one else knew. Kayla knew that her dad had turned himself into a keeper because when he had walked into the room after doing so, she had just... felt it. She felt a new devotion to him. A new love to protect him. Wait a second. It wasn't unlike the sudden burning love that she had for Ritz.

Kayla shook the thought away and went back to Tyler.

"Tyler is a fantastic friend. Valiant adores him and I think he's rather sweet, smart and perfect for Vankerdale. I would have thought that even if Pyro hadn't taken his curse off and made Tyler a keeper. I agreed to marry him for political reasons. Vankerdale had reason to attack us for the curse my mom left on them. I didn't want their bonded dragons doing that. I didn't want anyone else to be the king either. If it wasn't Tyler taking the throne, it would have been some other Peyton. Conner said that the Valeron's are the people who founded Vankerdale in the first place. It's Tyler's right to rule, only the Peyton's knocked his family out of the castle."

"The Peyton's killed off the Valerons similar to the way that the Clusters killed Feldings," Ritz agreed.

"I don't know why some people feel the need to turn on keepers when they're not infected with poison and they're just fine." Which brought Kayla around to thinking about her personal interaction with a man who attacked keepers.

"I agreed to marry Tyler so I wouldn't have to marry Tristan." There she said it. She had signed a magically binding paper with Tyler to avoid Tristan Cluster. "Tyler wouldn't be a bad choice…" She trailed off. Tyler was rather dedicated to his role of king, and he'd never hurt her. He had said as much with his pre-wedding vows.

"I promise that I will do my best to be your friend. I will pick you up when you fall, be your eyes when you can't see, your listening ear when you need to scream."

She didn't have very many friends because all her life she had spent it cursed, falling on the ground. Tyler was the first person she talked to her own age that she had told her fears and secrets. He was also the one who had rescued her dragon Valiant.

"I will defend you from your enemies instead of leave you to face them alone. I won't blink an eye when you secretly talk with Ritz."

Which was something that no one else would ever do because Ritz had a horrible reputation. Kayla didn't trust him half the time either, but she was unloading to him right now because she felt like there wasn't another option. She was so unraveled that she'd tell her sins to anyone.

"Would you rather be engaged to me or Tristan Cluster?" Tyler had asked her.

That was the part that had her scribble her consent. Not Tristan. Never Tristan. Tristan was her mortal enemy, even if there was the potential for them to be friends. Kayla could see herself learning to love him—eventually—but it would be a long, hard process. There was something in her soul that made cursing keepers one of those sins that she couldn't ever overlook. Tristan could atone all he liked, but she would never feel like marrying him.

"It can't be the worst thing I've ever done," Kayla continued. "I'm not the only keeper of my generation. I'm not the only blood heir to the throne. I know everyone thinks that I am, but I'm not. My Uncle Conner has three kids. If I marry Tyler, I won't be dooming Aralot to merge with the larger kingdom. There's still hope for everyone else, just not for me."

Kayla covered her mouth after she said that. There was no way she could reveal Conner's secret family to anyone if they were not a fellow keeper. That was a secret that she'd die to keep, because Conner wanted his kids to remain hidden. His wishes affected her soul.

Oh gosh!

Ritz was the fifth keeper of Aralot that none of them had ever been able to find before! He had to be if she couldn't hide these secrets. He was so smart and always informed about everything because he had wild dragon spies for him all over the place. He had to be a keeper. And judging from his timeline, Kayla was pretty sure she knew which one. Ritz was Gladius's younger brother Maslon. He used to be a shoemaker. Maslon never joined the dragon wares and was said to have been killed along with his whole family. Gladius had written in his journal that he cursed his younger brother. The curse? Long life until some promise or condition of the curse was fulfilled? That meant that Ritz was her granduncle. They were family.

"You miss, are grounded to the end of eternity." Ritz's words broke her out of her startled contemplation. "I told you to tell me the first thing on your mind. You're deviating. I can see it in your face. You're not telling me everything. If it was only a choice between Tristan or Tyler you wouldn't still be here. You'd be in Vankerdale rubbing it into Tristan's face that you escaped him while he stood around here laughing in glee that he won. A lot of us will be miserable if he wins," Ritz said darkly, as if he personally didn't want to see Tristan on the throne. Maybe he didn't. Ritz may have taken Gladius down, but he could still be partial to a true Felding ruling the kingdom.

"He probably has a spell on you that makes you want to give him what he's after. You're still denying him the honor, so there is something else that is holding you here. What is it? It has my intense interest."

Hers too. Now that she was finally talking through it all, it helped her to sort through things she'd not seen before. She knew what was holding her here the instant Ritz phrased his question the way he did. It wasn't Tristan or Tyler that had her caught. It wasn't dragons either. What she really really didn't want to leave, what she was clinging to harder than all of Aralot, harder than any other member of her family, was a voice that had stolen her love away before she ever realized it was gone.

She couldn't tell Ritz that her ultimate stumbling block was her desire to keep Caleb Andrade in her life, because she didn't have Caleb. They were only friends, even if Caleb had hinted that they could be more. She couldn't stop thinking about his recent words.

"I'm not leaving you. No matter what you're made to do, or where you have to go, or what man steals you away from me, I'll always be right here every time you need me."

She needed him. She just couldn't tell him that she needed him. She hadn't told anyone at all. She'd not even stated it specifically to Valiant, although they both could tell what her heart was after.

"Kayla. First thing on your mind remember?"

"Caleb Andrade," she whispered. She had to look away from Ritz because the answer felt so sensitive and so hopeless that it made her want to cry.

Pg. 28

"Oh," Ritz didn't sound as conflicted over this as she was. He even grinned about it. "I should have guessed. Everyone could see that coming ten miles away, and here we are with none of us seeing it. Well played, Kayla. You held him off so long that we all gave up on you noticing him."

"But I did notice him! I always noticed him. His is the voice in the back of my mind that tells me to stand back up when I fall down. His is the voice that defends me when I can't find the words to defend myself. He's the one that makes me feel beautiful, noticed, and needed."

"The guy loves you. He's always loved you. It took you sixteen years to notice, and now that you have, you don't want to run away from real love. I see that now. The struggle in your soul is a fight for love. It's always been that. You fought the sadness of your broken bond to keep Valiant's love. You fight your nightmares of terror in search of love. You're drawn to Anvil because he loves you more than his own kids, when he shouldn't. You're drawn to Caleb because he's not allowed to love you when he does. You've got me feeling like a fool to have not picked that out sooner, because I've known your problem for ages. I want you to stay with the person that makes you the happiest. Promise me that you will."

That was a hard promise. Kayla shook her head because she couldn't do it. There was no way that she could stay with Caleb.

"I can't!" Kayla wailed. "I finally got most of the war in my head to stop. I have no idea how to fix the war on my heart. I can't!"

"And that is where your problem is," Ritz said, as if there was a very simple solution to fix everything. There wasn't. "Promise Kayla. Don't run away from what your heart tells you."

"You told me a little over a week ago to not go looking for love because I had it all right in front of me."

"This is different. I still stand by that order. Don't go searching for warrant love. You have what you need to stay alive. It's found in the ever so attractive form of Caleb Andrade. He's the only one that can save you. Now to get everyone else seeing the same thing…"

Ritz trailed off, and the look on his face clued Kayla in that he was talking with a dragon in his thoughts. Was it Norber? The dragon had pointed out Ritz to her, sending her over to spill her secret about Vankerdale after the dragon had watched her get a ring. Yes, now that she thought about it, she was fairly certain that Norber was in Ritz's thoughts. The dragon was probably his bonded dragon. They met in secret in the middle of the night so that no one else figured this out.

"I know you're also confused about Vermelo at present, but he's still your friend," Ritz puzzled out loud. "I'll send him a nudge. As for Tyler, I've got people in Vankerdale that will be able to help on that front. Would Tyler start a war if you broke off the engagement?"

Kayla shook her head. "No. I told him to find himself some other wife and he said he would, but he's keeping my name on his list because it makes him look good, keeps the peace up, and helps me with Tristan."

"I will also work on Tristan. You won't have to worry about him smothering you with tricks and lies to steal what's not his. Your task is simple. You work on finding sleep and happiness."

Kayla laughed at him. She had told Ritz all her problems to help herself understand them. She wasn't about to stop working on them herself.

Pg. 30

"Come here," Ritz ordered, stepping to her and wrapping an arm around her shoulders in the closest thing to a hug he could manage.

Kayla looked at him in awe. This was magical and she knew magic. Ritz dropped his guard, letting himself relax into a natural instead of a rigid posture. He never got like this with anyone. So for him to be relaxed had to be his way of accepting her claim to love him.

"If I had a daughter…" Ritz trailed off, looking into the distance.

Kayla examined the side of his perfectly smooth face shocked. Ritz never said anything without meaning, and as honest as he was looking right now, he really meant it. If he had a *daughter*. He had been Maslon before he had to hide himself as Ritz. Maslon did have children that had reportedly died, but Ritz had lived so long that it was highly possible that he had more children after that point. At least one more. A son. Any child of Ritz's would have been a Colt and a keeper. There was one person she knew of that had no idea who his father was who fit all those categories rather well. Uncle Conner. He had grown up a Colt, only guessing that he was a Felding when he turned of age and his keeper blood activated so that he started to hear dragons without ever being bonded to one. She had found Conner's dad! What had started out as a horrible night was turning into a remarkable one.

"Your daughter would be a whole lot smarter than me," Kayla sighed.

She wouldn't be trapped into being married to the current king of Vankerdale in order to stay away from marrying the steward's son in Aralot. Ritz's daughter would have everything figured out already including the crazy nightmares. Actually, she wouldn't have any nightmares at all. Lucky girl.

Ritz tightened his hold and looked back at her, gazing directly into her eyes. Kayla didn't think that he trusted anyone, so to have him say what he was, trusting her with his own deepest secrets, filled her heart with excitement. Ritz trusted her! She had the respect of the leader of the Colts!

"You're comparing yourself against the unknown again. You don't have to do that. You don't need to be good enough for your parents, or the dragons and riders, or the Colts, or the nobles. You can't please everybody. No one can. Your father tried it once, and I'm pleased to say that he figured out rather quickly that being himself was good enough. At the end of the day, the person you always take with you and have to please is yourself. Don't make comparisons against everyone else, Kayla. As long as you have learned something new, made progress, even a little bit, as long as you have tried your hardest, then you're doing well."

"*Ritz acting like he trusts you makes me nervous,*" Valiant interrupted. "*Before you stopped me from talking with my friend Tyler, he was telling me that Conner thinks you are in charge of all the other keepers, because Conner spent so long trying to protect you. You get everyone's secrets because you're their leader. It's you that they all look up to, and you that they all aim to save. Funny, huh? You're younger than most of them.*"

"*And they all get way more sleep than I do,*" Kayla quipped, as she yawned. It had to be a result of her keeper blood then that gave her these nightmares of deceased keepers. That was why Valiant couldn't suck the spell off her so she could sleep. There wasn't a physical new spell that was on her. It was in her blood, in the very nature of her being. Perhaps if they could find some way to study how keepers were first created, they could figure out how to stop the dreams.

"The dreams are getting worse," Kayla sighed to Ritz.

He dropped his arm from around her shoulders and gave her a short smile. "You fight it best by holding onto anything that makes you happy. You fight it best by feeling joy. Go flirt with Caleb. What are you still doing over here?"

"Norber told me to come this way," Kayla shrugged in answer. Not to mention that Caleb was snoozing. It was the middle of the night! "Valiant was walking me around in my sleep."

"Which I find unnerving," Ritz shuddered.

"Which is something that bonded spellbinding dragons can't seem to resist I've found. It's either that or because Valiant was locked in a cage for most of his life and his only escape was to sneak out by being me."

"That one," Ritz agreed. "You're his salvation. Goodnight, Kayla. Try doing something nice for Caleb that will make you happy so you can get some rest. Fight the fear and the sadness by blasting it with love."

Kayla nodded at the Colt leader as she started to walk away. Ritz always seemed to know what he was talking about. He hadn't told her what the curse was that was on her, but if he had a possible solution to keep it at bay, she was going to try it. As a section leader, Caleb always had extra chores that needed doing. She was bound to run into something that would help him out, and yes, the thought of doing something sweet for Caleb did make her feel happy.

Adelyn
Tyler

It is a disappointing feeling to be excited for a special moment only to realize that no one else is excited. Tyler was feeling that sting as he pulled open the door to his house that he'd not been able to step inside for the last four years. Prince Evan hadn't ever let him go back home and had him working for him around the clock. Now that Tyler was the king of Vankerdale, he got to make his own rules, and he was going home. He'd been the king for nine full days and he had waited long enough for this trip.

"Hello!" Tyler cried out finding the front entryway devoid of human life. He rolled his eyes, shut the door behind him, and headed deeper into the house. Not much had changed since the last time he had been here. The pictures of boats were the same. So were the statues of happy families holding hands in circles that his mother collected. He paused at a newly framed sketch of a shadow family holding hands. He even pointed to it and looked over his shoulder ready to tell someone, anyone, that his mother had accidentally bought one of Caleb Andrade's images of the royal family in Aralot. That was totally Kayla as a little girl with her mother and her father. Tyler had seen a similar image like this that King Jack carried with him everywhere inside his rider's saddlebag. Only in Jack's picture, it showed Kayla's face while this one didn't. There was no one to share his discovery with.

"Hey!" Tyler cried out louder this time. "Is anyone here?!"

He moved past the pictures in the entryway letting his shoes clank against the wooden floor so that the people that should be here would hear him. Where was the excited rush of loving arms? The happy faces, the joy that he had finally returned home? So much for expecting a warm welcome.

"I'll kiss your face," Coal offered.

"No thanks," Tyler answered his dragon. He'd kept Coal awake to take him here. Coal was a night dragon and thrived when it was dark. He was being really nice to cart Tyler around during the day. Tyler didn't want it all to be a waste.

"Not a waste. I love listening to the excitement of your thoughts when you're flying. It makes it all worth it. You should get a better nose. Then you can smell if anyone is home."

Tyler laughed. He couldn't change his nose. He was always going to smell things the way a human did. However, it was nice that he had some encouragement to keep walking through his empty house.

Oh ho! Not empty. He could make out the sound of footsteps heading toward him. He had no idea who it was that appeared in the hallway, but the girl had him backtracking a step, making him second guess if he'd gotten the right house.

This was his house. He was pretty sure that his family hadn't moved and left all of their decorations and furniture to the gorgeous

Pg. 36

blond that was looking back at him. Her hair had natural highlights with a darker tone beneath the blond that came to play in the light brown of her eyebrows. Her eyes were green and they popped with the green blouse she was wearing that rested over her slim frame, gray pants, and black boots with rhinestones.

"Hi, Tyler," the stranger greeted him as if he had every right to be tromping through this place. Tyler glanced around looking for a familiar face yet again. The one in front of him was lovely, but not what he had come to find.

"Do I know you?"

She shook her head and then smiled at him. Oof. This girl could knock a man out. Maybe it was the light makeup around her eyes or the touch of pink on her lips, or simply the entire combination of stunning that still had him standing right where he was.

"No," she spoke again. "Well, we met once when I was in diapers and you a toddler so I doubt you remember it because I sure don't. My dad went to school with your dad and came by for a visit. Our parents are off at the market so we got left behind—"

"We?" Tyler was quick to pick up on the word. He moved closer to the cute girl so he could look past her (best not to get too distracted here), and search for anyone else he actually knew.

"Narl is here. I can't help but think that I'm left to babysit him because he won't move. His wife gave him this big dramatic sigh and somehow managed to get the last spot in the wagon because of it. I got left here instead. My dad was all like, 'Adelyn could use more rest after our trip,' and then I was stuck here."

"Adelyn!" Now he knew who she was. That was the name of Bate Peyton's daughter. Bate was indeed his father's old best friend. They wrote letters to each other monthly, so to them it didn't feel like they never got to see each other. Tyler's homecoming was overrun by the arrival of an old friend.

"We wrote letters for a bit back when I was nine and you seven," Tyler said to Adelyn.

Adelyn nodded at him. "Then you went to the castle and stopped writing."

"Oh no." Tyler moved farther past her now that he knew who she was. "I didn't stop writing. I was writing all day and night for Prince Evan. I had no time left for personal conversations. Prince Evan had me running this whole kingdom on the strokes of my writing. Where is my brother?"

Tyler still couldn't see him and he was running out of options now. Narl wasn't in the entry room. From where Tyler was standing, he could see the kitchen and the dining room. The bedroom doors were open so Tyler assumed his brother wasn't in one of those, because Narl always shut the door when he was in his bedroom.

"That must have made it easy for you to become the king then. Everyone always talks about how hard it was working for the Peyton's. Everyone likes working with you, Tyler. It's all over the place how the nobles would approach you first before going to talk to the past Prince Evan or King Peyton. It's been a little hard to not pull out our past letters and tell everyone that I knew you first."

Adelyn laughed at herself, and Tyler decided to give up on finding Narl. In truth, he had forgotten all about Adelyn. It didn't sound like she had forgotten about him. She still kept their letters, so they must have meant something to her. He had no idea what he had ever written to her, but it was probably normal kid stuff.

"What did we talk about?"

"You? Oh gosh. What didn't you talk about? You wrote about everything from the dragon that hissed at you to the mud that got splattered on your shirt. You were a very thorough kid. You'd always pick your most exciting day of the week and write it all out to me. It was like I was living out here in the big city instead of out in the middle of nowhere. I thought that I'd feel lost when we got here since you stopped writing, but I don't, because I can see all the places you wrote about. It's rather cool like stepping out of a storybook right into the pages."

Tyler couldn't stop the smile on his face. He did that? He really had forgotten all about writing to Adelyn, and all this time she was fantasizing over his words to visit the city. Her father was working as a captain in the army on the far side of Vankerdale really out in the middle of nowhere. No one ever ventured there and nothing exciting ever happened.

"You always did write too much," Narl's voice said from somewhere in the room right when Tyler had given up on him. Tyler looked around again still failing to see Narl. He sighed on his own thoughts because he was thinking that if he was Kayla, he would have already heard where his brother was at. Her ears were super.

Adelyn pointed Narl out. There he was! He was hovelled into a corner of the kitchen with a book covering his face like he was reading. He couldn't really be reading because the book was upside down.

"Gee, dude, you okay?" Tyler asked him, coming to sit down beside him along the kitchen wall. "You didn't even come see me when I walked in the house. I've not been able to get home for years and I hardly get a word out of you otherwise. Not mad at me, are you?" Tyler asked scratching at his nose. "You would have become the king too. Kayla was right there! For a moment I had everything that Vankerdale needs. I had access to magic, dragons, law, and Aralot all at the same time. It was way too hard to pass up. I had the chance to save us all."

"I am not mad at you, Tyler. I'm proud of you," Narl declared, putting the book down to look at him.

Tyler put a hand on his brothers pulled in knee because Narl looked awful. His eyes were red, his expression ashen, his skin pale. There was something going on that he wasn't talking about. Narl's brown hair was rather messy, and his face had a few days stubble.

"You're right that I would have done the same thing, although I'd never marry Kayla Brixton."

That was because Narl had it easy. He had already met the girl he was to marry back when he was younger. It was love at first sight for him. For Jess it took a little bit longer, but she came around once Narl dropped his younger voice and got his mature deep mellow tone that left her swooning.

"Between the two of us, I'm only engaged. I only have Kayla on my side as long as Prince Tristan is in her way in Aralot. I had to bully her into signing that paper. I was trying to keep her over here so she wouldn't be over there. The longer she's in Aralot, the more she dies. She has no idea of course, but she can feel it in her soul. She refused to sign to make me the king unless I promised to find some other girl to

Pg. 40

marry me. Kayla is being taken by that curse in Aralot that kills off all of Aralot's queens. So, I thought that perhaps if she wasn't there to die, she could be saved. King Jack has had me trying to find the solution to the cure for her, but I highly doubt the answer to the cure or the curse is written out over here. I've spent days and nights trying to find it and can't find a thing."

"King Jack?" Narl asked, almost rising to his feet. He moved to get up and then something made him shiver instead. His shoulders went back up protectively and he pushed back into the corner deeper like he was hiding from something.

"Yeah. Jack. Met him a time or two. Rode his dragon. You would have loved Pyro. He's such a smooth flyer, and he can write letters in the dirt, make himself go invisible, and puzzle out ancient secrets from long past dragons on our soil. Pyro is incredibly clever. It's easy to tell that he was born a dragon king."

Narl smacked his arm. "Don't get distracted by Pyro. King Jack! He really was here? It's hard to decide if the rumors were true that he was locked up in the castle or not. How could anyone lock up King Jack?"

Tyler laughed at his brother. King Peyton had Jack locked up for three months. Tyler had no idea himself until King Jack managed to break out.

"SilverWings took his magic away. Which reminds me. I need to mail Kayla her father's ring back. I finally found it."

"You're not going to send it directly to King Jack?"

Tyler shook his head and let his own back sink into the hardness of the kitchen wall. Since he was getting comfortable on the floor, Adelyn shrugged and sat down in the kitchen doorway to wait. She was probably bored. The best thing Tyler could do was take her outside and show her around the city she had dreamed about seeing.

"I need to get Kayla back over here. Do you know how hard that is? That girl is the most stubborn girl you will ever meet, particularly if you're asking her questions about magic. She won't say a thing."

"So you married her but you don't like her?" Narl questioned.

Tyler rubbed at his eyes. It was so hard to explain, but if anyone deserved the truth it was Narl. He had worked for the Peyton's right before Tyler had. He knew the struggles that had been placed on them, the difficulty with communicating with Aralot, the drain of lacking magic.

"I do like Kayla. I'd drop everything I'm doing to help her out in an instant, but I'm not in love with her."

"You like her for pity," Narl decided. "You can't stand the thought of Valiant crying when his rider dies. You're doing this for Valiant. No one else is going to understand that, Tyler. No one but the two of us ever talked to Valiant. The rest of the kingdom had never heard about him until you broke him out. Prince Evan said it was him who did that, but I know it was you. I remember all too well what it was like over there. You broke out Valiant, kidnapped Kayla twice, and broke the spells upon us. You can't cancel your engagement to Kayla. The rest of the kingdom sees that as the only reason to stand behind you instead of another Peyton."

"I know…" Tyler let out a shaky breath. He did see that. He had the support of General Reis, but apart from him, the other nobles all hailed the Peyton's as kings of the land since they had been on the throne for so long. Getting Kayla's signature was a rather strategic move on Tyler's part. However… "If I don't cancel it, I could lose all of Aralot's support."

"No. You lose only Kayla's support."

"She won't…" Tyler couldn't finish.

So hard. Tyler found himself looking at Adelyn as if she could reach into his head and explain it all for him. She couldn't of course, but she did give him an encouraging smile and that helped.

"Kayla will always support me. She's a keeper. She can't help it, particularly if she's on Vankerdale soil, because she's not the commanding keeper over here. As far as I can tell that would be me. Pyro changed the keeper laws so that Vankerdale can have keepers too now. The magic over here compels Kayla to be more agreeable to my demands. Kayla isn't the problem if only I can get her back. I'm talking about the rest of Aralot. They want Kayla on their side, naturally, because she's their princess. She's got this mandate to date Prince Tristan that she's trying to appease. Aralot wants to see her on their throne instead of ours."

"Your wife is dating some other guy?" Narl balked. "Gross, Tyler. How can you stand it?"

"We are only engaged!"

"You can't be engaged! You have to be married to be the king. If you don't claim you're married, then I'm knocking you off your seat!" Narl jumped to his feet, and Tyler found himself likewise jumping up to back away from his older brother, his blood-red eyes, the strangeness of his stance, and his anger.

All at once, Tyler knew exactly what was bothering his brother, and why Narl hadn't moved out of the kitchen corner. Narl was experiencing dragon thought! He had turned into a keeper as well, and the magic in his veins was screaming at him to get out there and protect the kingdom, only he couldn't because Tyler had gotten the throne first. Narl was at his wit's end trying to decide if he should let Tyler keep it. He'd no doubt been rather startled to start hearing dragons as well when he had no warning beforehand that it was going to happen. Coming home had never felt so tricky. Tyler hadn't expected to be fighting against his own brother.

What would it be like to face his dad? Had he turned into a keeper too? Tyler had thought that the magical blue line on his arm from King Pyro, which he still hid beneath quarter-long sleeves, had only affected him. He was wrong. All the rightful heirs to the throne in Vankerdale had been affected by Pyro breaking the curse against them. At least there weren't too many of those because the Peyton's had kept the Valeron's numbers so low.

"Okay, okay! I'm married to Kayla Brixton! I'll find a way to get her back over here. You're hearing dragons, aren't you?"

Tyler tried to shift the conversation away from his love problem by pulling back his sleeve to reveal the raised blue slash.

"Pyro did it. He broke the curse that held back keepers in Vankerdale. You're not going crazy. Us Valeron's have always been the rightful rulers of the land, only we couldn't be keepers before. Aralot's very first ultra-dragon king blocked us off. I showed Pyro the

Pg. 44

monolith, and he cut me. It came as a bit of a nasty shock when Coal started talking to me all the way from Aralot. You doing all right? What dragon is talking to you?"

"I am not going out there," Narl whispered, looking in the direction of the front door. "It's not one. It's like five of them. They won't shut up. It's driving me crazy. I can't tell Jess. I can't tell anyone. They'd think—"

"They would think that you need to get bonded fast," Tyler interrupted. "Your gatekeeper dragon blocks out all the other unwanted thoughts. You know that, Narl. What you most need is to go outside."

"No!" Narl shouted, jumping toward Tyler again, which caused Adelyn to hop to her feet and start backing away. She was watching them with her eyes wide, although her mouth was quiet. Such pretty eyes. Tyler looked away from her, because he was second guessing if he really should be the one ruling this kingdom. So he had an ultra-dragon king. Narl already had five dragons. He already had the makings of a keeper army, which was something that Tyler didn't have to support him.

"I can't get bonded! How can I pick one dragon over the others? How do you love one more than another when they've all been waiting for a bond for years and years? It would be unfair to the others."

"You just have to. Kayla said that if you don't, you go crazy. Have you seen yourself? When's the last time you slept?"

Narl shook his head, which wasn't a clear answer. He looked up into the air and glared as if he was struggling to talk with the dragons in his mind. Tyler didn't envy him at all. It had been rather hard to start hearing dragons, and Tyler only had one to worry about. He had to wait a long time before he could even reach Coal, because the dragon had been blocked off by a cursed wall on the other side of the large river that divided Aralot from Vankerdale.

"Would it help if I looked at the dragons and picked one for you?" Tyler asked.

Narl lunged for the knife block, pulled a knife, and aimed it at Tyler. Tyler caught his breath and started inching his hand toward the sword that was at his side.

"You are not touching my dragons. Go find your own," Narl hissed.

"Narl, you need to get out—"

"Nothing is making me leave this house!" Narl screamed.

Tyler backed away, found Adelyn's hand, and pulled her after him toward the front door. She went with him willingly. She even shut the front door and let out a shaky breath as she finished.

"That's what he said this morning too," she said, "although he didn't use a knife, and no one knew he was hearing dragons."

Tyler shook his head, glanced into the air to see that seven dragons, not five, were circling over the top of the house. Narl's dragons. He was hiding away from them. Given his confused conflicting nature, Tyler moved his hand away from his sword glad that it was him that was the king right now instead of his brother. They didn't need another indecisive king. What Vankerdale needed was wise decisions, the kind that would save them all from the oppression that King Peyton had put them into.

"Why don't you guys just pick one of you to bond him," Tyler called up. "Make it easy on him, huh?"

They were pretty dragons; all day dragons of various colors. Tyler had seen all of these ones before while he was at the castle. It wasn't surprising that they had become interested in his brother.

"I can hear you, Tyler!" Narl screamed from inside the house. "If you don't hold this kingdom together, I'm taking you down!"

"Let's go," Adelyn tugged on his hand. "Please," she added, inching away from the house and the looping dragons.

"Yeah," Tyler agreed. He couldn't help but keep his gaze on Narl's army. It wouldn't take Narl forever before he picked one to bond now that he understood that he was a keeper and not insane. He had been sitting around warring with his own inner nature and that war was coming at Tyler if he didn't stay married to Kayla Brixton. The last thing he wanted was to fight his own brother, but if he had to, at least he had Coal.

"I can take all of those things on. No problem," Coal assured him. *"Narl won't touch you."*

"I still have to do something about Kayla," Tyler moaned. He was talking to Coal, but Adelyn couldn't tell that so she answered him.

"Perhaps the best but most unpleasant answer would be to let her die. There's less trouble that way."

"I'm left with the same problem of being wifeless either way, and if I don't find a woman, Narl's coming at me. I never would have thought... He's my brother!"

"Everyone wants to restore Vankerdale," Adelyn told him, giving his hand a squeeze. "Narl has to think that he could do just as good of a job as you, but he can't. He wasn't the one breaking curses and betwixing the Brixtons."

"Betwixing isn't a word," Tyler grinned at her. "Regardless of curses, the Peytons with their larger numbers will form an army against us and kill us all off if I can't stand up to them. King Peyton was trying to kill me right before. They all despise keepers after Gladius."

It had not been fun realizing that King Peyton had figured him out. The king wanted him silenced because of it. Tyler had taken to hiding in corners and eating alone to avoid poison. He had stayed up nights on end writing out documents to take over the throne and prove that he had a right to do so through his keeper lineage. But he couldn't broadcast that knowledge to the rest of the kingdom at the time.

"Narl is right. Kayla's name is the only thing holding me up right now."

It was a shame that, because Kayla hadn't looked back at him when she ran off on him. She hardly wanted to talk to him at all it seemed.

"Forgot about me already did you?" Conner's voice asked from out of the shadows. Tyler turned to see Kayla's uncle leaning up against the side of a house. He was a blond man with brown eyes, strong, crafty, and he had helped to put Tyler on the throne. Conner was the first to jump in and help save Kayla from being in Vankerdale. It was him that had killed off King Peyton.

"I didn't forget about you. I just don't want to assume that you're sticking around now that the border is open again. Regardless of your wife's resistance toward Colts, your heart has always been in Aralot," Tyler said. Conner used to live over there until he and his dragon got trapped in Vankerdale from Jack's curses keeping Vankderdale dragons out of their land.

"I haven't convinced my family to move yet, so if you need me to plow over some Peytons for you, you have my help," Conner offered. "Who's the chick?"

Tyler looked over at Adelyn only to realize that he was still holding her hand as they'd walked down the street. It hadn't felt awkward at all until right then. Now Tyler wondered if Conner had shown up because of his brother's small keeper army that had been circling Tyler's head and this strange girl he was with. Having already taken on the castle with his own keeper dragons, Conner was now following Tyler. In that regard, Tyler really did have everyone who could rule Aralot on his side. Kayla, Jack, Conner, and Tia all agreed that he could do this.

He needed to find something that would get his own kingdom thinking the same thing that didn't involve Kayla, because while he would try to convince her to marry him, he had no real hope of it working out. He needed to find a girl that could love him. It wasn't like he went sauntering down streets holding girl's hands or anything. He'd been stuck in the castle, unable to break away from Prince Evan's demands. Tyler dropped Adelyn's hand while she gave him a soft smile.

"This is Adelyn Peyton from…" He trailed off and took a few steps away from her. He'd just been talking bad about her last name! They'd been talking about killing her!

"It's okay." She shrugged at him while she gave Conner a smile too. "I know you didn't mean me, and I've hardly spent any time with the other Peyton's. I get it. To be in charge of everyone you have to consider all options and what they will do."

"Peyton…" Conner trailed off while he tilted his head to look over Adelyn. For some reason that made Tyler feel defensive. He stepped between them, took his old friend's hand, and pulled her down the street again.

"Don't do that," Tyler ordered Conner.

"Not to worry. I only share my plans with you when I'm sure they will work. I'm still working on this one."

Conner had threatened him before. He'd lured Tyler into a circle of his dragons, and his dragons were the fiercest in the entire land since they had training in Aralot dragon formations. Conner was the only one who had managed to train dragons inside of Vankerdale while the dragons had been cursed to not bond humans. Many others had tried and failed.

"Want to hear my plan for today?"

"Not really," Tyler answered. He had wanted to go home and hug his mom. That's what he wanted to do today. He wasn't going to do that now that Narl was blocking off the house, and his mother out in the market. The market was a long five-hour walk, although he could fly there. That was an option. He'd take Adelyn with him and they'd spend the day spying on their parents. Maybe he would start to remember what she had written back to him.

"I was wanting a tour of the castle," Conner said.

"Nope," Tyler cut that idea down. "You're not getting close to that crown. I like you helping me from outside."

"Tyler," Conner laughed at him. "I have no interest in taking your crown. Before you argue, I didn't take the one in Aralot when I had the chance. I told you that already. You think you're walking a fine line to keep the crown, just think of how hard it would be for me. No one wants a Colt from Aralot bonded to a dragon that knew Gladius sitting on a throne. Not over here and not in Aralot."

Tyler had to constrain Adelyn's hand, because she tried to yank it away to run away from Conner's words. It was news to Tyler too. He had no idea that Tempest, Conner's bonded large green dragon, had known Gladius, but it wasn't something he was going to run from.

"Tempest was innocent of Gladius's deeds," Tyler stated. He knew that much. His own dragon had committed crimes while in Aralot that he couldn't get away from.

"Most people don't see it that way."

"Most people are not keepers," Tyler smiled at Conner, and then shifted so that the older man was beside him, not behind him. He wanted to watch Conner's hands. He trusted the man, but not completely. "What are you trying to steal from the castle?"

"Nothing," Conner answered with a straight face. Tyler didn't believe him at all, and his answer left Conner chuckling.

"Then nothing is what you shall get."

"I want your information on the Colts. Inside of King Peyton's room on his bottom shelf is a red book that has a piece of paper inside that talks about the Colts. I want that. You tell me how I can get it from you. I'll stop the Peytons uprising for you. I'll bring Kayla back for you. I'll find you a wife. Whatever."

Tyler frowned at him. He had no idea what Conner had gone through to get an exact location for a piece of paper he wanted to see, but it must have been hard. Tyler was going to read that paper first. It had to be important.

"Anything?" Tyler questioned. "Like you'll give me your entire collection of Caleb Andrade pictures?"

As a Colt, Conner prized himself on keeping a straight face, but he lost it over that question, looking stunned. Tyler grinned at him. Yeah, he knew what Conner wouldn't part with, and he was going to use that knowledge today. Conner had hardly let him see one of those pictures before and had refused to give him one earlier. He paid a lot of money for other people to steal him those pictures.

"Tyler!" Conner's face strained while he wailed. "Not that. There are some things a man can't part with. That's like asking me to give you my wife because you don't have one. I can't give you that. Take something else."

"So you won't give me a picture of Kayla, but you'll give me the actual Kayla?"

Conner shook his head and wiped at his nose, laughing again now that he could tuck his shocked emotions down. "I said I'd bring you Kayla. Not that you'd keep her. No one can keep Kayla. Not only is your wife dating Prince Tristan, but she's got a crush on this other guy at the same time. They are so cute together. You probably wouldn't think so, but everyone else thinks it. Kayla and her crush are absolutely adorable. Completely smitten with each other." Conner got a really large grin as he thought about what he had spied on. Tyler sighed.

"This is not my day," Tyler mumbled. "Who's the guy?"

"I'll tell you for that paper on Colts."

Of course. Tyler rolled his eyes at how quickly Conner had found something that Tyler would hand over sensitive information for. He needed to know what Kayla was doing over in Aralot so he could persuade her that she didn't need to be there. It was going to be much harder to make her move if she had fallen in love with some guy. Tyler told Conner that he'd think about it, which thankfully made the man jog off.

Tyler kept walking, only partly aware that he was still holding Adelyn's hand, and that other people were starting to look at him strangely for it. She didn't pull her hand away though, and he was too distracted to do much about it as he bit at his thumbnail trying to sort out what might get Kayla away from an actual lover. He didn't know her that well. She'd leave the guy if she was needed to save her dragon, but Tyler couldn't constrain Valiant. Valiant was his friend, and plus, the dragon had magic now. He'd break out of everything.

Tyler would have to find something that Kayla loved more, or perhaps just pull on her politically. After all, she *was* his wife. She had signed the paper on her own. Maybe what he needed to do was find a spell that would get Tristan tightening his tension on Kayla. Tristan was the person that had caused Kayla to sign the paper in the first place. The thought of him was enough to get her to run. If Tyler could get Tristan scaring her, she'd come back to Tyler.

"Who was that?" Adelyn asked, still looking in the direction Conner had vanished.

"Conner Felding," Tyler answered. "He's Kayla's uncle in some way. No one's really sure who his parents are, but he's a keeper, so he's a Felding. He's a Colt through and through, but he'd do anything to protect a dragon. He's currently one of my strongest supporters. Oddly enough, the Feldings and Brixtons are the only people I'm not worried about turning against me."

"I wouldn't turn against you," Adelyn said.

Tyler looked over at her. He even stopped biting his nail to notice that she was blushing at him. Adelyn. He really didn't remember much about what she had written back to him. Maybe if he was lucky his mother had saved the letters for him. He'd have to ask her to mail them over, because he wasn't going back to the house.

Tyler glanced at his old home, saw the still circling dragons watching him more than Narl inside, and felt uneasy all over again. His house was gone. He was never going to live there ever again, and it was a sad thought that he wouldn't feel welcome within the walls. Narl was claiming that place. Tyler should probably do something about that like…

"I need my brother. Think once he gets his head back on that he'll consider being a captain in the army or a counselor? I could really use him."

Pg. 54

Tyler turned his back on the dragons and started to head toward his own. Narl's dragons were listening to him with their much sharper ears. They had to be telling Narl everything that he was saying, because Narl would want to know. Tyler had to get his brother feeling included in the kingdom again instead of having this tension for being out of the loop now that he had been sent home after his term had ended to serve the Peytons. Narl had enjoyed working in the castle. It was probably hard on him to be cast off as he had been.

"You're bringing Adelyn to see me?" Coal asked. *"Still holding her hand? I want to meet her. This will be fascinating to see who you think is pretty."*

Tyler's entire face turned red and he dropped her hand again. He even wiped his hand off against his leg. It wasn't like that! Adelyn was a friend.

"A pretty friend that likes you. She's been hinting. I think this could work. You could like her and then there is one less worry in our world."

Tyler gave her a sidewise glance. She didn't look back because she was looking to the side away from him, either to see the kid playing with his dog or because she didn't want to say anything about him dropping her hand so fast. Go after Adelyn? Then he'd be just like Kayla. He'd be in love with a person he wasn't married to.

"Kayla is going to die, Tyler," Coal sighed at him. *"No queen has escaped this curse in the last four hundred years or so."*

"But it's a binding curse and she has a spellbinding dragon. There's a chance she can survive. I have to be prepared for that chance."

"Also be prepared in case she dies. What does Adelyn look like again?"

"Be quiet," Tyler blushed. He wasn't going to describe those alluring green eyes, those soft pink lips, or the wave of her blond hair. Not again.

"Are you scared of dragons?" he asked Adelyn, coming to a stop because he had been too distracted to share his idea with her so far, and it was probably better to get her used to the idea of a hulking black dragon before she saw him. Adelyn thankfully shook her head.

"Good. I thought we could ride Coal over to the market and spy on our parents. After talking with Narl, I'm going to ease my way back into the rest of my family. All but my mom have the potential to be keepers." He whispered that part at her, glancing around wondering how many of his past neighbors had been spying on him and heard what he had been talking about before.

"Is it hard having a night dragon?" Adelyn asked him. "Does Coal keep you awake?"

"I keep him awake," Tyler smiled. "I've decided that I like night dragons much better than the day sort. Valiant is a night dragon too, you know, and he was the first dragon I fell for. Night dragons are quiet during the day so that I can think things without being interrupted. It's great."

"I tend to fancy green dragons." Adelyn shrugged. "There's this really amazing green one I saw while we were traveling over here. I think it's a girl. She followed us for a while but then left. Anyway, she was beautiful." Adelyn sighed, as if missing the creature, and Tyler found himself smiling at her all over again.

Pg. 56

This could really work. It was hard being around Kayla because she'd been living with a broken bond and couldn't look at dragons without falling to the ground and crying about them. Adelyn made this whole thing easy.

"Can you show me the fish fountain in the market square? That's where you would toss all your lucky coins and wish for a dragon."

Now *that* he remembered doing. Adelyn was fun. She was like meeting a dragon that happened to know all these past moments about him that had made him happy. He could get used to that. Tyler held his hand back out giving her the choice to take it again or not. He grinned when she reached for it without hesitation. Then he questioned what she told him earlier about getting left behind.

What if Adelyn had decided to stay with Narl because she didn't want to see the market place without Tyler being the one to show her around? She had only ever seen it through his words before. She'd gotten to his house probably excited to meet him after all these years only to be reminded that he was at the castle and wasn't going to show. Or maybe she hadn't forgotten and had chosen to stay in the house to give herself time to search for things there that would remind her of him. Maybe he was thinking too much about this.

Coal was laughing at him when they reached him. Tyler flicked him on the nose which only made Coal hum at him instead of snort. Adelyn wasn't scared of Coal for one second. She was reaching out to touch him right away, something Tyler never could see Kayla doing.

"Yup. Kayla runs from me," Coal confirmed.

Tyler shook his head. He still liked Kayla. He needed to stop finding reasons not to like her, because he was still legally married to her according to Vankderdale's laws. Tyler helped Adelyn up on his dragon, determined to put Kayla out of his mind for a while. It was hard to do when he found himself holding Adelyn on, feeling guilty that he was with her instead of Kayla. He was going to have to do something about this Kayla problem. He'd been trying, but he needed to try harder.

"Don't let me fall off," Adelyn said, squeezing Tyler's arms with her own while she firmly gripped at the rope Tyler had tied around Coal's neck. He didn't think he had done it right but it was working so far. He lacked the proper way to ride a dragon. He lacked a saddle and those ware dragon guide books that Aralot had. He needed to get over there and buy some of those things before anyone in Aralot realized who they were selling them to.

"You'll be fine," Tyler assured his childhood friend. Then he forgot all about Kayla for a good long while when Coal ran and launched into the air. Adelyn cheered out her joy to be riding on a dragon and all other thoughts fled away.

Memories

Kayla

*"*Y*ou are beautiful! So beautiful!"* a dragon voice started singing into Kayla's head. *"Have I ever told you that you smell like second breakfast? Your nails may be short but your talents are endless."*

"Who is singing to me?" Kayla asked.

She had a large aversion to bringing new dragons into her thoughts. She had never wanted Riven to be there, but so far he didn't try to tell her anything from his rider, Prince Tristan, so that was fine. She hadn't wanted Bantin to be there either, but the magical ice dragon more commonly called Mr. Grumpy had helped to save her life, so she was good with him too. She could live without Sparkle being her head, but Valiant blocked all her ice dragon thoughts from reaching Kayla most of the time, so Kayla wasn't distracted by dragon jokes all day long.

Whatever dragon was singing to her must have passed some sort of unspoken test with Valiant in order for him to allow this dragon to enter Kayla's keeper bond. She had to admit that she was finding herself not upset. So far. Some dragon connections just felt absolutely right to a gatekeeper dragon allowing them to pull them in from any distance. This had to be a special dragon.

"Your hair is the red of warm flames. Your eyes the blue of a sapphire. Your skin the cream on top of milk."

"Really?" Kayla laughed. *"I could guess that we've met before, but your voice in my head doesn't sound the same as your voice entering through my ears."*

"You are taller than me if that helps."

This was a short dragon. They had passed hatching season with Kayla successfully avoiding the entire thing for yet another year in a row. She hadn't been comfortable with dragons until this summer when she got Valiant back. So she had to assume that the dragon listening to her right now was not a hatchling. All the other dragons she knew were much taller than herself except for one.

"Hello, Merlock. You didn't want to join my father's keeper bond? You wanted to talk with me instead?"

Merlock laughed at her. *"Jack already talks to me. He tells me lots of secrets. I don't need his bond for that. You, on the other hand, don't share secrets unless it's like this. I'm curious."*

So curious about her that he had allowed their heads to be linked through a magical spell. That was some strong curiosity. Well, she knew why Merlock wanted to be included, but she wasn't going to tell him every secret that she had. She knew why Valiant was taking an interest in the dwarf dragon today too. It had to do with the dream she had of him last night. The rather interesting one that also featured Indigo long before she had been bonded to the ware leader Rogan.

Kayla had been inside her great-grandfather's shoes during the events of the dream. She had watched Merlock get born. The poor tar spitting dragon had been cruelly used and abused by Gladius, because Gladius had been poisoned already by that time and it turned him mad.

Just thinking of the dream pulled Kayla right back into it. Normally she could fight the dreams off, at least think about them, without having to relive them again, but it was getting harder to prevent herself from dropping off into tortured dreams lately, especially if she was lying down, which she still was.

Gladius wore rather distinctive boots when he wanted to be noticed. Even the people who didn't put much stock into the sounds of other people's shoes knew to shiver when Gladius wore certain boots. He was wearing those boots in the dream, and since Kayla was all about the sounds of things, having used her ears to navigate since her eyes she kept sheltered under a hood, those boots made her shiver rather well. She shivered again, watching as Gladius pushed open a door with his ruby-ringed hand. They were at his ware near the Northern Farms, the one that had been abandoned after he died and revived by their only female ware leader Turid a full generation later.

The room had a party inside that had brought together dragon riders from a few different wares. They were easy to pick apart by their ware colors. Two men wore the black leather from the training ware in the west. Three men wore the mahogany leather of the more seasoned ware in the east. One man wore the red leather from the King's Ware which was probably called something else in Gladius's day, because the castle existed in the south back then. There was the light tan and dark tan leather of the middle dragon wares. Then there were four men dressed in Gladius's colors. His ware used a mixture of light and dark leather.

Before him the men were playing cards, and one of them passed Gladius his hand as he came into the room so he could join the group. Gladius scanned the contents on the table that could be won. There was a good amount of coins, a few fancy handled knives, and promises written on paper to buy the winner a drink. Gladius's eyes settled on a brown oblong rock that could fit into the palm of his hand.

"That's the thing that came in from Vankerdale right? The rock that everyone is passing off?"

"Yup," one of the men wearing mahogany leather answered. They were probably the ones passing it around because they were the closer ware to Vankerdale.

"And none of you think that it could be a dragon egg? Vankerdale steals eggs from Wisteria."

"It's a rock."

One guy picked it up to examine the thing and shook his head over the nature of the item. He set it back down. Another guy shook the rock and rolled it to Gladius to examine it for himself. Worst mistake of the night. Gladius grabbed it, put his ear to the thing to note some rather angry scratching, and ran with it out the door, ignoring the angry screams coming behind him for not winning the rock fair and square.

"It's a dwarf dragon egg! It has to be!" Gladius thought to his bonded dragon as he raced back out into the night.

"That small?" his dragon answered.

"Where are you anyway?" Gladius asked, proving that he had a poisoned mind if his bonded dragon wasn't wanting to be around him. *"Never mind. Send me some wings."*

"They're already there. Look up."

Kayla was forced to look upward as Gladius did, and her smile must have matched his, because she could feel the thrill of flight traveling through his body. Gladius was said to be one of the best dragon riders to have ever lived. Kayla had a first-hand account of his mastered skill, and it filled her with awe that he was so flawless in his dragon riding. It was the only perk to being him in these dreams.

Gladius climbed up a rope that was coming down so a scout could get off his black night dragon. Stealing the rope, Gladius swung on it until he got a good enough force to launch himself into the air and fall on the back of a blue night dragon. From there he launched upward to a brown dragon, then red, then another blue. None of these dragons were his own, and their riders complained about him hitching a ride, but he jumped between them all so seamlessly that he didn't get in their way. He stopped when he was high enough up that he could free fall for two minutes, waiting for the neck of a green dragon which slid between his legs, catching his fall.

"Whoo!" Gladius let out his exhilaration.

Kayla was right there with him. It was easy to see how Gladius had attracted the ladies so well. He had Kayla's heartbeat skipping up a mountain. He was incredible with the way he could climb upward through the air like that to get away from the men that had run from the room trying to get that egg back.

Gladius shut his eyes, shifting Kayla out of that part of his memory into the memory of a dragon. It was through dragon eyes that Kayla usually saw her nightmares. Dragons saw two-hundred and seventy degrees, and their greens and reds were more vivid. Kayla was so used to being different dragons that she was rather good at picking out the breeding of the dragon at first sight. These were the incredible eyes of a night dragon queen.

Kayla was looking at Gladius from the blue night dragon Indigo, back when she was only a year old. Indigo was one of the only dragons to escape being killed after Gladius was. She hid, started her own herd, and much much later was the mother to the dragon king Pyro, who was Kayla's father's dragon. Indigo also went on to connect her mind to Tia's keeper bond before she bonded the ware leader Rogan.

Indigo watched as the extremely fit blond man dropped to the ground still holding the egg. With her sharper ears, Kayla could hear the scratching on the inside of the egg much better than Gladius could. He put the egg up to his ear again to hear it and grinned.

"I got it!" Gladius cheered. He shifted his eyes to the dragon next to Indigo who cowered before him, having been the recipient of one of his mentally breaking moments. The red dragon's wings were black and charred where Gladius had recently burned them. He didn't care that the dragon was terrified of him, he still ordered the creature to start singing the dragon birthing song. Timidly it complied. Indigo added in her voice when Gladius looked at her coldly next.

The scratching got louder, the desire to be born increased, and several minutes later a very small brown dragon head pushed its way through the shell that rested in Gladius's hand. He laughed at the sight of the small dragon and dangled Merlock upside down by his tail, watching as the dragon, even newly born, dribbled out tar.

"We have a lot of things we need to accomplish, you and I," Gladius told Merlock. "If you do your part, I will feed you. If you cause me problems, I will cause you more problems than you could ever possibly know. You'll wish you had never been born."

"Hello baby," Indigo hummed at the miniature dragon. "If you stay close to me, I'll do my best to protect you. He's turning mad again."

"What did she say?" Gladius asked, turning to the injured dragon and demanding an answer to what Indigo had spoken in dragon speech. "Tell me what she said, you obstinate beast. Hold that."

Gladius tossed Merlock toward a sleeping bronze dragon. It didn't have time to wake up before the small Merlock landed on his snout, drippling out more tar in his fear. The bronze screamed as the tar burned. Gladius ignored it to turn to his other injured dragon with prongs in hand and anger now in his soul.

"Gladius used to be beautiful," Indigo cooed at Merlock, swiping him off the bronze with her tail. She tore up a patch of dirt that she shoved over the bronze's snout to stop the burning. "We'll find another beautiful keeper someday. You'll see. It will get better."

It had gotten worse for Merlock and Indigo before it had gotten better. Kayla flinched when Indigo did as Gladius continued to torture his bonded dragon with magic. At least Kayla didn't have to watch, but she still wanted to wake up. This dream had woken her up last night for a few blissful seconds. It didn't happen again. Kayla was tossed back into another nightmare of pain and heartache. One that she had never seen before.

Kayla was being Indigo again, and this time the dragon was pacing the castle courtyard nervously. This was Aralot's current castle that Gladius built for himself out of magic after he destroyed the castle in the south. At this point in history, he would have just killed off King Klavian's grandfather, spurring the start of the Colts, and King Virgil Cluster IV who succeeded him would spend his ruling years secretly hunting down and destroying keepers because of it.

Other dragon feet were pacing right behind Indigo, following her closely as if Indigo could stop the terror of the man who held the dragon's thoughts inside his head captive. Kayla knew the gait of those footsteps, but not from the nightmares she couldn't explain. Kayla had learned the sound of the dragon behind Indigo through dreams that Sparkle, the ice dragon, gave her of her mother's adventures. The dragon behind Indigo was Tempest. Kayla had met the real living Tempest not too long ago. He was bonded to her Uncle Conner and living in Vankerdale.

Indigo stopped pacing, causing Tempest to run into her tail and stop too. Gladius stepped out into the courtyard dragging behind him Merlock who was now at his full height reaching up to Gladius's waist. His brown scales flinched in the light of the sun, a glow that he personally abhorred.

Gladius locked Merlock's chain to a pole, and it was clear that torture was on his mind when he turned around to scream at Indigo and Tempest. He told them to scram. Indigo looked into the terrified eyes of Merlock and didn't move. Kayla didn't want to move either, although she normally would have begged to be released from the scenes of torture. These were the only three dragons that had survived after Gladius. Indigo, Tempest, and Merlock. They didn't talk to each other anymore, but at one point, they had been very good friends.

Gladius turned his back on Indigo before he could let himself notice the defiance.

"I locked up your sweetheart," Gladius told Merlock, waiting for the sound of a hiss. Merlock didn't move. He continued to stare at Indigo as if she could save him. She stared back no doubt wondering how. "Your pretty brown miss is going to die roasting alive in the desert if you don't give me tar," Gladius continued. "No one will hear her crying there. Give me the tar, Merlock. There are naughty dragons that need it."

Merlock blinked. Kayla could tell that he wasn't breathing. She imagined him trying to hold back all his thoughts so he wouldn't scream them. Since his stomach wasn't rumbling to get tar started, Kayla wondered if his sweetheart had survived or not.

"Give me that tar!" Gladius screamed, picking up a metal poker on the ground and ramming it into Merlock's side. Merlock whimpered and started churning the tar.

"That's better," Gladius stormed. He fetched a bucket for it that he fortified with magic before he slipped off his rings so he could drag over the bucket and not get his rings sticky.

Kayla caught her breath. His magical rings were off! He was standing in the courtyard unprotected, which was the very place that he was said to have died. When the first arrow struck him in his neck, Kayla knew she was watching the day that Gladius had died. His own archers had shot him to stop him from being so horrible.

Pain shot through Indigo's head so strong that her vision blacked out and she crumpled to the ground. A myriad of dragon voices shouted through her brain all at once. It was as if she was turning into the gatekeeper dragon of the group for a moment. The gatekeeper would be the dragon that was bonded to Gladius who had to hold back all the other dragon voices from reaching Gladius's brain.

"Help!"

"Ow!"

"What's happening?!"

"Save me, save me, save me!"

The dragons screamed out the pain of losing the keeper bond all at once. Indigo tried to talk back. She tried to direct her thoughts toward Merlock, and then toward Tempest, but thinking hurt too much. Her words ricocheted against her skull. The part of her brain that had responded to Gladius and the collective hive grew dark and cold as if icy hands had reached beneath her skull and were squeezing half her brain closed. It hurt! Kayla knew she was screaming just as loud as Indigo had been, only Indigo shut her mouth when an arrow pierced her tongue.

She forced herself up noticing how Tempest had rolled to his back trying to protect his wings, terrified of them being hit. Merlock was tarring through the chains that had him stuck so Indigo turned to Tempest and hit him back over with her tail.

"Run!" she cried. "Run away and don't look back. Don't be seen!"

Tempest swiped a claw at her head knocking the shaft of the arrow in half on her tongue. That hurt too, and Kayla had no idea how Indigo really got that arrow out of her mouth when she had no human hands that would help her pull it out. It could have led to an infection and killed her, but somehow, she had survived. She shoved Tempest into the air, blocking what arrows she could to protect Tempest as the pointed objects continued to rain down upon them, trying to kill off anything and everything that Gladius's infected mind had touched.

Next came the volleys of small launched throwing stars, heading up and over the castle walls as the Colts, who must have been waiting, threw everything they had against Gladius. Indigo got five stars in her wings and four lodged beneath her scales. She shoved Tempest up again, who was still shaking his head trying to bounce back from those cold hands that lingered now that his mental connection was destroyed. Merlock, now free of his chain, used his flexible tail to open up the castle door. He ran into the castle, slamming the door shut behind him. He was still there all these years later.

Tempest finally got airborne along with Indigo right as a large boulder smacked Indigo in the head knocking her down. Kayla didn't have a fear of falling, but it was the fear of falling that had her jumping out of her bed reaching for the first available weapon around, which happened to be the knife in the sheath of Junia's weapon belt.

"Covered in sweat again," her bunkmate pointed out, as she pulled out a prong and got in a stance to defend herself against Kayla. Junia's short blond hair hardly ever got as nasty as Kayla's long red-brown strands, and her freckles always gave her a rather cute look, despite the battle stance she adopted.

"Uh… Yup." Kayla turned the hilt of the stolen knife back toward Junia and let her take her weapon back, noticing how her entire bed was soaked with her sweat. It had been a rough night. What could she say?

"Sorry."

Kayla glanced at her other bunkmates, Brea, and Keran, who regarded her with concerned eyes. They had probably talked about her nighttime behaviors behind her back, but as far as Kayla knew, they hadn't taken them to anyone else yet. If any of them woke up in the night they'd get a good look at Kayla thrashing and screaming silently. Kayla had put up spells all around her bunkroom to deaden her sounds so that her teammates at least could get some sleep, even if she never could.

"Are you back?" Merlock asked her. *"Can I ask you to do a favor for me?"*

"What is it, Merlock?"

After what she had just seen, she was willing to do just about anything to forget the pain that had been inside of Indigo's head. Kayla never wanted to die and subjugate her own keeper dragons to the torment like that.

"Losing a keeper bond?" Merlock questioned. *"It's not so bad. It's a bit cold for about a month, but then it all goes away."*

A month. Kayla shivered. That was horrible.

"Not too bad in comparison to some things. Can you ask Bantin to give me a fresh magic orb? I've not seen a fresh one in some time, and I love the way they glow, so beautiful, just like you."

Pg. 70

Kayla laughed, which had her roommates turn back to getting ready for the day. She pulled off her blankets to toss them in the wash bin and found her own gear. She had to change all her clothes again, but she had gotten smart and wasn't sleeping in anything that she liked anymore. She was sleeping in dresses, the kind of frilly ones that she had bought to impress Queen Aria when she had to take princess lessons from the woman. Kayla didn't care for any of them, so she was soiling them up fast. However, she would need to wash them all today, because she'd spent the last two days learning things from Aria during her free hours. Today was her free day to act like a regular rider, although Aria had given her a lot of books to read that would fill her time.

"I will pass along the message to Bantin that you would like a new treasure," Kayla agreed to Merlock. *"Although you can just ask him yourself. You're both in my keeper bond, and I don't have a mandate to stop dragons from talking to each other."*

It was brave of him to consider adding himself to her thoughts when Merlock had gone through such a tragic early life. She was fairly certain that injured as Indigo had been and disorientated as Tempest had been, that Merlock's sweetheart dragon had indeed shriveled up in the desert all alone and died there.

"Delicate, shimmering, fleshy human, do not be sad for my past life. I have no idea how you came by that information, but Indigo once told me that I would die happy, back in my native homeland. There is gladness in my future and a task I must fulfill that will help mankind. Did you know that dragon queens can see certain points in the future, certain things that come to pass no matter what? I will get to see Wisteria one day."

Kayla hadn't known that about dragon queens. It was interesting to learn, because until now she didn't really know what sort of magical ability a dragon queen could have.

"Do you want me to help you see Wisteria?" Kayla asked Merlock, standing around too long in a state of undress. Brea couldn't help but stare at the ugly streaks on Kayla's left leg. That was the location that Valiant had bonded her. Then Sparkle had fanged her baby leg next, and her mother had carved up Kayla's flesh trying to conceal it all. Her leg was hideous. Kayla normally kept it completely hidden. She gave Brea a short smile and tugged on her red leather pants. They matched the red leather riding shirt with the engraved "K" on the shoulder that made her a part of this ware. Kayla found the clothes to be hideous.

"Finding Wisteria wouldn't be that hard," Kayla said to Merlock. *"A little guess work on my part, but it would be fun."*

She would have to mess around with portals, trying to find the right combination of numbers to tap on the linking block so she could find the entrance into Wisteria. Wisteria had to have at least one portal that reached the king's magical library because the other kingdoms did. It was a library where kings could go to study magic no doubt set up in good faith that the kings would use the room to help each other solve problems instead of create them. No one from Wisteria had shown up inside that library for a long long time. Kayla wondered where their portal was located. If she could find it, Valiant could peek into Wisteria along with Merlock. Valiant had been born there too and was curious about it.

"Yes, please," Merlock answered.

"Do you think that Indigo foresaw herself bonding Rogan?" Kayla asked.

Pg. 72

"I think she bonded him because he smells good. Have you smelled Rogan?"

"No," Kayla answered. Why would she? Now if the question was had she ever smelled Anvil, he was a ware leader she could place by sight, sound, smell, and feel anytime. She had spent many hours crying into his arms.

"You are so weird," Merlock laughed at her. *"Humans don't smell each other."*

"Yes they do," Kayla replied, as she latched on her weapon belt and considered the fact that she still smelled like sweat. Her hair was wet and sticky with it too. Every human was going to be smelling her if she didn't get herself cleaned up. Kayla stepped out of her bunkroom and took in the new day.

It was going to be a hot one. Maybe she should hold off on that shower until after she worked out some or she'd have to repeat herself.

"Are you awake, Valiant?" Kayla questioned. *"Merlock wants Bantin to give him a fresh magic orb. I said I'd pass along the request."*

Silence. *"Valiant?"* More silence. He was asleep then. She would pass along the message later. For now, she got in the line to get breakfast aware that eyes kept flickering at her and her grungy hair.

"Right here," Charles, the ware leader, pulled her to sit down beside him before she could walk past him to reach quite a different table. In this ware, the riders ate by section, and Charles was sitting among the married riders, not where Kayla wanted to be for more reasons than she would state out loud. No one had seen her get the present of her wedding ring from Coal three days ago, but a few people had seen her get a small package last night from a mail runner. It was another small box, and it contained her father's missing wedding ring from Vankerdale. Kayla had tossed it into the bottom of her trunk hoping that no one figured out that Vankerdale kept sending her rings.

"Morning, sir," Kayla smiled at him, keeping her nerves in check. He *couldn't* know that she was married.

"You did not eat dinner last night," Charles started. Kayla looked at her food and shrugged. She had eaten dinner last night. She simply hadn't eaten here. She had ditched the ware to sneak into the castle and eat with the cooks while they all listened to Vermelo talk about a race one of his champion horses had won.

"I'm fine," Kayla answered. She moved to bring her cup to her mouth only to have the cup start shaking while it glowed orange, sending particles across the room. Kayla rolled her eyes, collected the particles with a spell, and gave Charles another smile.

She had put a spell on herself to prevent the accidental digestion of swallowing keeper poison. Such poison was the bane of her past relatives as it caused them to fight against the very dragon they loved so much. It forced a keeper to act out against the nature of the magic in their blood, so Kayla made sure she could avoid the curse.

Keeper poison couldn't enter her mouth, and it glowed when it was present in her food. It had been on her food last night in the ware, so she hadn't eaten. It was back again. She had no idea who was trying to poison her. It could be anyone who was scared of keepers and wanted to kill her off. It could be anyone who was scared of Valiant, since he was a spellbinding dragon. A lot of people were scared of magic hitting them. Valiant had not cast any harmful spells, but that didn't stop the fear. If Kayla swallowed the poison, she would end up killing Valiant. Yup. Keeper poison. She dreamed about it in her sleep and she looked it in the face during the day.

"Guess I won't be having that," Kayla said. She picked up her fork and got ready to devour her breakfast strata only to have it glow orange at her as well. "Or that."

Kayla gave Charles an excusatory smile and got back in line to get new food after dumping her tray, silverware and all, into the trash. Charles was scared of keepers himself. At least he had once been scared of them, but Kayla couldn't exactly blame him for the poison that kept ending up in her food. He wasn't always around her to slip it on there. Kayla paid a lot of attention to the food she selected this time around. She kept her eyes on it the whole time, noticing how no one dumped anything into her portion.

She didn't sit down to eat so that she was far away from any hands. When she went to take a bite, it glowed on her again. At least she knew that normal riders would not get poisoned by eating this stuff. It was only her and her mother and her dad and her aunt and her uncle that would go crazy if the poison slipped beneath their tongues. The entire lot of breakfast looked poisoned today. So… field snacks. Kayla pulled out a few field snacks that she had made herself and ate one, aware of how Charles watched her the whole time.

"Try mine?"

Kayla smiled at the sound of the voice. Caleb Andrade. He had warm brown eyes, the kind that laughed and sparkled when he smiled. He was clever, compassionate, funny, and incredibly interesting. His voice washed over her like honey. He smelled like citrus not that Kayla was trying to smell him or anything, but he smelled good.

"Thinking of him again already?" Valiant asked, causing Kayla to blush right as she turned around to see Caleb holding out his tray. She didn't need to have a red face to match the sticky dampness of her hair.

"I doubt Caleb cares —" Valiant started to say.

"Shh!" Kayla ordered. She was trying to interact with Caleb without making everyone stare at her. Kayla picked up his fork and carved into his food. No poison! Nice!

"Sweet! Thanks, Caleb."

"Any time," he replied, casting daring angry eyes at anyone who looked back at him. Kayla didn't bother to tell him not to stare people down. There was no point. He had been holding back her bullies for years, and he wasn't about to stop now. It had gotten him in a lot of trouble because Kayla would usually walk away from the mean comments and ditch the poisoned food without picking instant fights. Caleb had punched a lot of people. At least he had back when he lived at Anvil's Ware before he was transferred here.

"What was wrong with your other food?" Caleb asked her, as his eyes finished sweeping the room and returned to her still red face.

"It had keeper poison. I created a spell to prevent myself from ever eating it. I refuse to fight with my bonded dragon and turn into an infection."

Caleb's eyes turned as hard as his jaw. His fists clenched along with the muscles in his neck, and Kayla found herself scooting away from him, because when he got like that, he always did something about it.

He stood up on a table and started to make an announcement. Kayla's face turned even hotter. This was so embarrassing! All she wanted to do was eat breakfast. Now everyone really was looking at her because of the man standing on the table.

"Don't you people have any common sense?!" Caleb shouted. "Poisoning a keeper is ludicrous. It creates a demon: a person who can't control urges to destroy every single dragon around that doesn't answer to their call instantly. You want your dragons slaughtered?! If I ever, ever find out who put that keeper poison in Kayla's food I'm going to—"

"Get down, Caleb," Charles cut him off. "I am aware of the situation. I will look into this accordingly. You don't need to take any further action."

"You're all trading your food with her from now on," Caleb declared, looking Charles directly in the face. "If one of you insists on slipping poison, you can eat it yourself."

Yeah, that was Caleb. He had gotten in trouble for standing up to Anvil a lot too. He would also talk back to Kayla's dad, King Jack. Nothing scared him. It was one of his defining good qualities, but it often backfired like right now.

"Sounds like he has a good plan to me," Valiant thought to her.

"This is really embarrassing."

"I will be enforcing that," Caleb assured Charles. "Enjoy your breakfast."

He finally got off the table, and instead of sitting down or getting more food himself, he spent his time patrolling up and down the aisles, scanning everyone as if he could catch them with keeper poison on their fingers. Kayla finished his breakfast for him and dashed from the mess hall.

Jet Stream

Caleb

He should probably stop staring at people, but Caleb could hardly help himself after Kayla finished eating and ran out of the room. Nothing got him madder than people picking on that girl. All she ever desired to do was learn and help the entire world around her. How anyone could hate her so much was beyond him. This was the worst hate anyone had ever ever given her. Keeper poison. They all knew what it could do to a keeper, and they all knew that the ware leaders and the castle had the cure if she got affected, but it was vile to try to turn Kayla insane, destroying the synapses of her brain and forcing her to hate dragons when her keeper blood told her to love them.

She had enough problems with dragons already without adding to it a poisoned bonded connection. She had already lived her entire life trapped in hundreds of curses. She was already the youngest rider in this ware, having chosen here to train when she couldn't get accepted at Anvil's Ware, due to Prince Tristan locking her out of that place. Kayla didn't need more pain. This was wrong. It was so wrong!

"Dump it," Mulligan's voice came across the still silent room. He was the section leader in charge of the level eight and older riders.

Caleb looked over to find him starting in on bag checks. He wasn't the only section leader that had left his seat either. Russel was standing at the door blocking off anyone from leaving, and Notley was heading into the kitchen to search the cooks. Malone was pulling Kayla's poisoned tray out of the trash, trying to decide what keeper poison might look like should they find any.

Fondness for these older men entered Caleb's heart. They were helping him. They weren't leaving him to worry about this alone, and he was ever so grateful even if Kayla was the youngest spellcaster to have ever lived, and she had taken steps to keep herself from being injured like this. It still made them all look bad to be responsible for a death threat against the king's daughter.

Caleb gave his new friends a thankful nod and started on the other end of the room searching through people's bags and pockets trying to find anything that would look suspicious. Mulligan was cracking down harder than Caleb was, which surprised him. He took just about anything that looked remotely odd including candy still in wrappers which couldn't be keeper poison.

"I think we're looking for something green," Malone declared, after smashing through all of Kayla's food and protein drink. Her tray was now a total mess but Caleb had to see this for himself. He mentally marked his spot in the mess hall and came to examine the food too. Yeah, green. She had a bunch of finely ground herbs in her food that Caleb didn't have in his this morning.

"Nice work," Caleb agreed as Charles came over and confiscated the entire tray from them. Malone gave Caleb a shake of his head as if he thought he could do a better job at this than Charles could. Malone probably could. He'd have figured out the exact ingredients used to make keeper poison. That was why Charles was taking it away.

While that happened, Russel shoved the door shut as a rider late to breakfast was denied eating anything at all. There was a howl from outside the door and banging came next, joined by several hands of latecomers. Caleb went back to his bag checks so they all could get out of there. At this point, they probably wouldn't find anything. Whoever had done this wouldn't still have traces on him or her.

"You too," Caleb declared when he reached Charles, who had taken up standing there watching everyone. Charles gave him "that look" for standing up to him. Caleb had seen it plenty of times on Anvil so he wasn't scared. Not one bit. He could take Charles on. He could take the man's dragon down as old as they both were.

"You can search me next," Caleb offered.

"Done, and I'll confiscate what I like," Charles added.

Sassy man. Charles had nothing on him but his ware keys and the usual dragon training tools. Caleb was gasping when Charles was done going through his stuff. He snagged one of Caleb's recent sketches, a picture of Kayla standing on one foot as she pulled her red hair into a ponytail for the day. He'd only sketched that yesterday. He had only recently learned that people stole his artwork and sold it across the kingdom. He was famous for his drawings long before he heard that he was. It made him mad that people tried to take Kayla from him like this. He drew for her, not for them.

"That is not keeper poison!" Caleb burst. "It's not even green. It's white… and black!"

"You're all dismissed," Charles declared to get away from his thievery.

Caleb was already in a bad mood, but now he was in a worse one for losing a picture of Kayla. His sketches were never returned. Back at Anvil's Ware he would do nothing on his off days but draw for hours, so that when Kayla came around, he had new pictures to show her trying to get her to look up from beneath her hooded gray sweater and notice that he existed. He would tape them up on the walls as she walked past. He would slide them into the bunkroom where she slept. He'd put them up on Anvil's office door because that was usually one of the first places she headed. The sketches never lasted long.

However, Kayla had finally noticed that he was alive. Even better, she had told him that she had been paying attention to him all these years, only she had no idea what he looked like until she met him here because she had never looked at him.

Caleb slumped his way out of the mess hall, the first of the section leaders to escape the commotion he had started. Kayla was simply going to put up with it. She was going to let the hate sliver up against her skin while she ignored it. She was good at ignoring everything she didn't like. Getting her attention, and getting her eyes on anything but the ground, was the real challenge.

"Is she going to be alright?" Avery asked as the rest of Caleb's class trickled out behind him.

"Let's hope so," Caleb answered.

Warner was responsible for picking Kayla's training team. She had Avery, Nick, Davis, Norrin, Junia, Keran, and Sherman as classmates. They were a fantastic team, patient and caring. More importantly, they were brave enough to handle the challenge of training with a keeper and a rare dragon. Most of the time those who trained with a keeper ended up inside that keeper's bond. These riders were willing to take the risk, and the responsibility of protecting Kayla for the rest of her life. So far, Caleb hadn't seen any of the signs that showed that the dragons or riders were linked to her thoughts. He was still watching though. He'd watch this forever.

"We are not connected," Warner, his bonded dragon, stated about his Caleb's thoughts. It was fine. There was still time to earn Kayla's trust and the trust of her dragon Valiant, who was really the one who handled all this connected thought business.

They reached the field and Caleb found himself exchanging glances with the team. Valiant was slowly turning himself in circles. Kayla was looking at the ground, mumbling to herself while she hugged her gray sweater to her chest and tried to decide if she should put it on or not. It was against the rules for her to wear it on the training field, but Caleb had let her wear it before back when she needed to shield her eyes from dragons in order to stand upright. She was bonded again, so she wouldn't fall over at the sight of dragons.

"You're right. It will make everything darker and that will make me tired and put me to sleep. Problem solved," Kayla declared, as she shoved the sweater back into her bag. "Plus, Tristan touched it. I've not washed it yet," she declared darkly.

Ah, Prince Tristan. He was the man that Kayla had to marry despite their age difference of eight years and their obvious dislike for each other. Tristan had a bronze dragon named Riven who was currently flying above Kayla's head. Riven snorted at Kayla for her words of revulsion, and cooed something sweet down to her, trying to change them.

"Riven said that Tristan washes more than she does and isn't dirty," Warner interpreted.

Caleb let himself smile before he strode forward again to reach their spot on the field. Kayla *was* looking hot and sticky already. She glanced up at Riven to stick her tongue out at him like the teenager she was. It was moments like this that Caleb lived for. So often she refused to let her thoughts out of her head. Getting a dragon was going to work wonders for her. She would have to start sharing her inner world. Valiant's snarl scared Riven off.

"We're going to warm up our muscles with rounded bag tosses," Caleb told his class.

He had added weights to his bag last night just for this class. Charles hadn't spoiled the surprise when he searched his things. The warm-up included throwing their bags to each other while their dragons flew in a circle in the air. Caleb was already excited to see the faces when these guys got his bag and found out that it was ten pounds heavier than they expected it to be.

At his words, Valiant blew warm air on Kayla and then sat down staring at her. Despite the now fixed bond, Caleb still faced the problem of getting both Kayla and Valiant working for him in class at the same time. He had thought that Valiant's reluctance to work was because he feared Kayla not loving him enough to bond him, but they had solved that problem and still the dragon was picky about when he would move. He didn't exhibit the normal characteristics of any other dragon they knew.

Pg. 84

It was Caleb's job to train these two. The back of his mind knew that Charles and his dragon Clipshire were watching every lesson, and if Caleb couldn't prove he had what it took to get Kayla trained, he was going to have to hand her over to someone else. That would be the worst thing that ever happened to him. This was the only place that he ever got Kayla to look at him.

"Come on, Valiant. I know you're a night dragon and this daytime training is hard on you, but I already scheduled you two nap times for today. Those are not right now. Get up. Time to be up in the air. All you have to do is fly in a circle. You look good at circles."

He had just been walking in circles, but flying in circles was harder, especially for a dragon that had been locked up in a dungeon for his whole life. Still, Caleb had to expect the best from both Kayla and Valiant, even if Kayla had no experience on dragons either. She could recite the textbooks so well that she could be a ware leader by word. Her physical skills had never been tested. Valiant closed his eyes and tucked his head down.

Since the dragon wasn't watching, Caleb let himself shake his head at him. Stubborn. Incredibly stubborn. Kayla could get that way too, but her stubbornness had never bothered Caleb like Valiant's was doing right now. Maybe Valiant was reacting this way because Kayla was also bonded to an ice dragon. Her soul was one-third human, one-third ice dragon, and one-third spellbinding dragon, because it was shared three ways. Ice dragons refused to listen to anyone but a handful of people, which normally was their rider and their trainer. Caleb didn't have Valiant's respect yet, even if he had spent some time chatting with him after dark.

"Ask him to join us, Kayla." Caleb smiled at her, hoping that a direct order from his rider would get the beast into class. Then he waved for the rest of the class to head up. He couldn't baby those two. He had to set clear expectations for them to follow and not back down or Valiant wouldn't see him as the person in charge.

At first, they left a gap in the circle for Valiant to slip inside until they realized that he wasn't going to be joining them. He still hadn't opened his eyes, but Kayla had her arms crossed while she waited impatiently in front of him. The class closed up the gap when Caleb gave the signal to do so. He would have to adjust his timing. He had to find the best time of the day when he could get Valiant alert. Maybe right after breakfast when he would have just stayed up all night wasn't the best of those moments. He'd try again in a little while, but he had to get Kayla warmed up, so he had the class land and included her in the bag tossing on the ground.

They went through weapon throwing next, which Kayla was surprisingly good at, but Caleb couldn't slough off the dragon riding all day long, so he tried again when they finished that. He gave the order to start flying waves. The dragons would wave up and down across the field, avoiding the other classes. It sounded simple in practice, but it was one of those things that a rider either got really sore from or got really good at. It helped practice balance and build up a lot of necessary muscles. It was a good warmup no matter what training stage a rider was at because the dragon could pick his own speed. Caleb's class climbed up on their dragons, all except for Kayla.

"Mr. Andrade," a confident older voice interrupted his thoughts on how to make this group of riders an actual team. People claimed that whoever had a keeper working for them became extraordinary. Anvil surely was the top of his game, as his ware

Pg. 86

housed Rosa and Tia's trained keeper dragons. Caleb felt anything but lacking right now.

"It's Caleb," he replied, turning around to see who was there. Standing behind him was a man who wore a red leather rider vest instead of the full red leather shirt. Doctors visit! Everyone loved to get one of those personal visits.

"I'm doing just fine," Caleb stated. The last time he'd visited the doctor had been about three years ago in Anvil's Ware when he sprained his ankle really bad. That must have been reflected on his transfer notice, so now the doctor was coming around to pick on him.

"I'm not here for you." The doctor pointed toward his class. "I have orders to check on Kayla."

She was going to love that. She was currently engaging her dragon in a staredown. Valiant had managed to open his eyes again, but at the words from the doctor, Valiant broke the eye contact to stare down the doctor. The doctor squirmed, even if the man had his own dragon. The gaze of a fire-breathing dragon felt different against the soul than the gaze of a spellbinding dragon. Charles had probably ordered this visit since Kayla hadn't gotten off the ground yet. Her face was slightly red from this morning, her hair matted, and with the keeper poison that had gotten close to her, it was best to make sure that she wasn't poisoned at all.

Caleb waved Kayla over. She wasn't looking at him, but it didn't matter. Her ears were as good as a dragon's, and her instincts toned like her fathers. She trudged toward them.

"I am not your best friend. I am Doctor Weber," the man stated, taking out a watch so he could check her pulse. "When I ask you a question you answer. When I give you medical advice you take it. Can I get a yes, sir?"

He grabbed for her arm and started to check her pulse. Kayla smirked at him along with her answer.

"I guess so."

She put up with him letting him check her temperature (hot), and her pulse (slightly fast), and her lungs which were normal. He had her write down answers relating to her personal womanly health, but Dr. Weber ran into a sharp glare when he asked to see her bonding wound—her old one. She would show him her newest one on her shoulder to prove that it wasn't getting infected, but Kayla tensed up dramatically when he asked to see the old wounds that she had gotten from Sparkle and Valiant as a baby.

"I know it's on your left leg, Kayla. That's way less intrusive than your shoulder. As your doctor, I need to see your fang wounds."

"No," Kayla snapped, and the next thing they knew Valiant shoved Dr. Weber up into the air by a magical spell that set him down far away from Kayla. Caleb didn't think the doctor would be coming back anytime soon.

Most people didn't like touching or being touched by magic. Caleb had found a personal fascination with it. He was grateful that he was a section leader and didn't have to go through his own surprise bunkroom checks, because not only had Kayla given him a magical mini fox statue recently, but he had found a book on how to understand magical spells left in his trunk too. It was probably Kayla's way of making sure that her dragon wouldn't be able to kill off his teacher, so Caleb had every intention of reading through that whole book.

"Wishing that he would go away doesn't mean you waste magic on making him go away," Kayla turned around to snap at Valiant. "I don't care. I expect you to respect other people."

"Do the fang wounds on your leg bother you?" Caleb asked, trying to keep Valiant from doing worse if he got angry.

"My mother cut them up and it's hideous," Kayla told him tersely. Her tone reflected that she didn't want to say more about it.

"Nothing about you could be anything but perfect," Caleb heard himself say, and then since he wasn't supposed to be flirting with his student, he covered it up by trying to get her back to class. "Go ride a wave."

He looked at Valiant and gave him the signal to get up in the air. Valiant surprised him. He stood up, which tricked Kayla to get on him so that he could roll over and trap her beneath an overturned wing. Kayla started screaming at him. Caleb sighed and looked at his dragon that had done nothing but sit around so far.

"I have been taking notes on the class," Warner told him. *"And I have noted that today is not a good day for those two. Can we fly?"*

They might as well. Even on a fire breathing dragon, Caleb wouldn't try to retrieve a rider from a wing lock. He didn't know how Kayla was going to get out of it, because she wouldn't want to stab her way through. Caleb took to the air and got the class swooping around each other, only to look down and lose his breath.

Kayla had made it out. Her gray sweater was thrown on the field beside her along with a knife. Valiant was curled up again, his brown eyes literal swirls of anger. Kayla must have stabbed him. She would have put on her sweater so she wouldn't look at what she was doing and she stabbed her bonded dragon!

If he didn't know that it was impossible for her to be poisoned, Caleb would be rushing himself down to Charles's office to demand the antidote. No rider stabbed their own dragon. Ice dragons were said to make tricky bonds because they could bond multiple people at the same time, as had happened to Kayla, but no one had any idea what kind of bond a spellbinding dragon could make. It was vital information like this that made teaching so hard! Was Kayla really poisoned or not? Did spellbinding dragons fight naturally with their riders or not?

Whatever the answer was, it had Kayla on her knees with her back to Valiant so she wouldn't have to see him. Her face held the same questions, but it also held something else. Defeat. She didn't think she could train with Valiant.

The look on her face was one that Caleb had seen more times than he liked on friends he grew up with at the ware who then decided that dragon training wasn't the thing for them. Those people talked about how their childhood was an empty waste. All those years learning about dragons when they were never cut out to be a rider. He'd watched people leave the ware over a look like that.

Those friends had to learn how to live outside of a ware, giving up everything they had ever known at the age of sixteen, stepping out away from friends and family, turning their backs on their whole life because of a single moment in time. Kayla couldn't do that! She already had a dragon. She couldn't give up. Caleb wouldn't let her.

Caleb leapt from Warner, causing the dragon to give a startled cry of alarm as Caleb fell toward the hard ground below without anything to catch him. He might have broken his neck if it wasn't for a sudden gust of wind that Warner shot under his body as the dragon dived with him and tried to keep him up. Caleb rolled, hearing and ignoring the crash of his bones on the ground. He shook off the impact, shook off the thought that he had left a class in a very dangerous position, diving above him without any further instructions, and ran to Kayla.

"This is not your defining moment," Caleb told her as she looked away from him, not daring to meet his eyes or even catch a glimpse of his shoes. "This is simply a hard moment, one that you've faced before and conquered. I know you think no one understands your struggle, but I try to. You've been battling the tears your whole life and every day you win. Every… single… day. You will get up from this. You will learn what to do. It might not be today or even tomorrow, but I know in my heart that Valiant is the right dragon for you. We simply don't understand all his needs yet."

Caleb glanced at Valiant because the dragon shifted. As mad as Valiant was, Caleb expected spells to start tumbling toward his head, but they didn't. Valiant sniffled and curled back up, refusing to look at him.

Boy, they made this hard. What were they all missing? He had to stop thinking like a normal teacher and try to see the problem for what it was. He was so worried about ignoring the rest of the class, that he wasn't giving his all to Kayla and Valiant. What did they need?

Kayla had stabbed him so Valiant was probably questioning if she had eaten some of that keeper poison. Perhaps the reason Valiant wasn't working was because he was scared that he couldn't trust anyone. Someone was trying to poison his rider to kill him. That was scary. Valiant was terrified, and he wasn't going to feel any better unless he realized that he had a few friends that would save him from that fate.

"I promise that I'll do everything I can to help and protect the both of you." Caleb was very sincere about that. It must have reflected in his voice, because Kayla risked looking at him even if she did still have tears in her eyes. Her crying would only keep Valiant feeling sad and scared. Caleb had to cheer her up. He had to get her feeling safe again before Valiant would feel safe again, and he had just the thing. Kayla had fallen apart in Caleb's arms once before so he knew how to start fixing this.

"You know one of the best looks in the world is Anvil at an earring counter."

Anvil was Kayla's favorite person ever, although not Caleb's, but talking about him always shifted the mood. The ware leader had to buy two earrings but could only wear one. He refused to take off his magical ruby earring that he'd gotten from Jack. Kayla snickered. When she was tired and strung out, the smallest jokes could get her laughing. Perfect!

"One of the best sounds is Sparkle when a dragon checks out her head instead of her tail."

Score! Valiant opened his eyes and coughed, trying to hold back a laugh. Ice dragons loved their tails and that was something a dragon would tease her about.

"One of the best feelings is when you start a free fall only to change your mind halfway through because you remembered that you were still tied into the rope."

That got them both laughing at him. Yes! Now to take their minds off their shared sadness and get them back to class.

"Okay. Let's take a different approach here. What is it that you would like to learn today?" Caleb asked Kayla, while the rest of the class bumbled through a formation above them with Warner guiding them and Caleb distracted.

"I want to learn how to jump up," Kayla answered him right away.

She lost the red to her face, lost her tears, and practically glowed with the thought. He waved at her to jump and she laughed.

"Not like that. Like where a person is flying on the back of a dragon and then they jump and happen to glide upwards onto the back of another dragon that is above them. Jumping up," Kayla explained.

"Jet streaming," Caleb corrected. He didn't want to tell her no, but that was best learned by using one's own dragon. Valiant wasn't getting off the ground, and Caleb could already see the spells starting to fly if he told Kayla to borrow Warner for her jumping. Valiant had shot spells at Warner before. However, with Kayla personally asking for the chance to leap to multiple other dragons, maybe Valiant would let her.

"It's done by understanding the upward wing pressure on a dragon. When they create an updraft, you ride the draft upward. It's hard. You have to get your timing perfect in order to catch another dragon above you."

"It feels like flying," Kayla smiled at him. "Gladius was good at it."

Beside her Valiant growled, which was a step backward, but at least they had taken one step forward today and stopped crying.

"Oh, he was," Kayla continued, already over being sad. "He was heart throbbingly spectacular. I know we're related and that he's dead, but oh my goodness I could get a crush on him. You should have seen it. I could stare at that guy jumping all day long. No wonder his wife married him."

Caleb wasn't the only one that could do nothing else but stare. It felt as though the entire field had suddenly stopped in their tracks. It sounded like it too. All the nearby dragons had perked their ears up on the name of the most notorious villain in all of history. Now they had stopped flying, causing their riders to ask what was wrong as they all stared at Kayla.

Gladius was so bad that they were still dealing with his curses three generations after his death. There was no way to get rid of him, and Kayla was claiming that he was a hunk. This wasn't the first time she had revealed that she had very different views pertaining to dead keepers. Her views didn't align with anyone, not even her parents. Caleb actually admired that. Kayla had this personal mission to pick out all the good qualities of past broken keepers to prove that they were really heroes so she could save them.

"He was incredible," Kayla sighed, looking dreamingly into the air. "I want to fly like that."

Pg. 94

Caleb had to admit that it was turning him a little jealous. How was he supposed to compete with a dead guy? Whatever. It wasn't a competition, and he already knew that he couldn't have Kayla, so there was nothing to be jealous about. She could admire the skills of her great-grandfather all she wanted.

"She makes me curious," Warner noted to Caleb. *"I want to see her fly like Gladius. Everyone says he was the best dragon rider of all time. Was he really or are you better?"*

Warner made him smile. Kayla wasn't going to be pulling off perfect jet streaming right away. She wasn't going to suddenly be jumping around like Gladius, and Caleb had no idea if he was comparable to Gladius or not. But on that note...

"Yeah, let us see it. Pick your jumping team, Kayla. We'll see if you can jet stream."

Kayla didn't look at Valiant. She didn't look at the dragons on her team either. She looked outward at the field, scanning her eyes over hovering dragon wing patterns that still couldn't get themselves to look away or return to their lessons if Kayla was going to try out being like Gladius. She was well on her way to being like him after stabbing her dragon. Hopefully, no one else had noticed that. Maybe Caleb should have phrased his directions a little better, because at this rate, Kayla was going to pick the dragons that had the strongest wings, and they would be the older creatures that didn't want to partake in her lesson.

"Where's Reed?" Kayla asked, glancing behind her at Valiant. "He'd be good at this. So would Mr. Grumpy, but Sparkle would scale him if I ever rode him, so don't ever let me ride Mr. Grumpy."

She had that right. Ice dragons were territorial over their riders, and since Sparkle shared part of Kayla's soul, if the girl ever rode Sparkle's father, Sparkle would attack him. Valiant gave a short hoot into the air, and then curled up further in a ball shutting his eyes to go sleep. Less than a minute later a flash of light-green scales came souring down from above them landing in front of Kayla with a happy hum and a cheerful hello that betrayed Reed's Vankerdale accent. Reed had ditched his native homeland when the border spells fell between their kingdoms. Caleb had caught sight of the dragon a few times now because Kayla liked him.

He should have thought of this! There was only a small group of dragons that Valiant trusted enough to sleep near him. One of those dragons was Reed. If Caleb needed Kayla to be in the air riding a dragon that wasn't Valiant, he was going to need to borrow one of Valiant's trusted friends.

Valiant had told Caleb just the other night that Reed couldn't find the girl he wanted to bond named Lena Sherman. Through dragon sleuthing, Reed had learned that Lena, who had gone into Aralot as a spy, had been sent into Wisteria to spy instead. None of the spies from Wisteria had made it back yet. That made Reed riderless and unbonded, so he was a great choice for today.

"I want to jet stream off the wind of your wings so that I launch into the air and fly all on my own," Kayla told Reed, spreading out her arms with her back slightly arched like she was imagining that flying sensation.

"Hooray!" Reed cheered for her, which had her smiling at him and climbing up onto his back. Caleb glanced quickly at Valiant. Not

Pg. 96

one complaint. Not one spell. Not even a peep to indicate that he wasn't asleep yet.

"You've got a half hour," Caleb instructed them. "Then I could use you both in class."

Reed shifted on his feet nervously as he looked at the other dragons that would be in his class. He didn't shoot the other dragons or riders with flame or even smoke. His inability to shoot out magical spells was nice too. He looked at each of the dragons and hooted at them, asking if they were friends. Caleb could interpret the shrugging acceptance Reed got by the tones of the dragons.

"Okay!" Reed chirped at Caleb and then took Kayla up into the air.

Caleb couldn't stop himself from looking at Valiant yet again. Still no movement.

"Reed's much better. Too bad Kayla is not bonded to him."

"Don't say that out loud," Caleb warned.

"I didn't," Warner grinned at him. *"Not at all."*

Caleb rubbed at his hair trying to come up with a solution that would get Valiant into the air too. No one had trained a spellbinding dragon before. They were unknown, untamed creatures, and there had to be some trick he wasn't seeing yet. Kayla had found a way to get herself into the air, but what they really needed was for both of them to be flying together. She could get really good learning how to fly Reed, but that wouldn't help her build her shaky relationship with her bonded dragon. Caleb had hoped that now that she was really bonded again that he wouldn't be having this problem. They were still having this problem.

"He's got my breath caught somewhere in the atmosphere," Kayla started singing as Reed leveled out and started doing his best to create large updrafts for her. "There are clouds there, but they're all fluff as far as I can care. And his eyes they stop my feet, 'cus his words have got this beat. I think I'm in love. So high in love."

"Is she singing about Gladius?!" Sherman called down from the rest of the class to Caleb, sounding stunned. Caleb threw his hands up in his own defeat on the subject.

"Hey, I got her on a dragon today. I'm calling it good."

He glanced at Valiant one more time to find that the dragon was smiling with his eyes shut. Tricky dragon, but when Caleb looked into the air at Kayla he smiled too. She was doing it! She was landing back on Reed after the jet stream. Success. All that for a few good jumps was worth it. After years of Kayla struggling to not even touch a dragon, she was making fantastic strides here. Even better, she hadn't given up today. Caleb had never drawn it before, but he was going to draw that struggle to give up, followed by that glowing desire she had to rise after she fell. Then he was going to make sure that no one took the picture from him.

Stabbing

Tristan

"Hi, *Tristan*," Riven said rather formally into his head. It was so off from the usual random comments that the dragon normally gave him that Tristan stopped cleaning his shoes right away to listen.

"Kayla was given keeper poison again at the ware. Valiant was hoping that you could help look for who caused it since you're so good at hunting for things."

Wow. Tristan had not forgotten that Riven had been added to Kayla's keeper bond, but this was the first time that they had ever been asked to do anything about it. He expected to feel angry to be asked to help, because he didn't like the way that Kayla had Riven trapped in her thoughts, but he didn't feel upset at all.

Kayla despised the way Tristan was good at hunting things, but perhaps as a dragon, Valiant didn't have the same issues. He hunted too, and he wouldn't feel like he could go hunting through Charles's ware without getting in trouble, so he was looking for outside help. Or inside help depending on how Tristan viewed it. It was impressive that Valiant even remembered him with how quiet the dragon had been in talking to Riven. As far as becoming Kayla's friend went so that she would stop treating him like an enemy, this was a fantastic step. He had the attention of her dragon.

"Mentally Valiant is very quiet to me, but I have been verbally talking to him trying to stay on his good side. I'm not sure where that good side is exactly. He was very concerned about that keeper poison because Kayla wasn't going to do anything about it. The other section leaders were running bag checks. Valiant concerns me. He won't fly in class because he's sitting around thinking about this poison. It didn't help that Kayla stabbed him when he trapped her."

She had done what?! Tristan gave up on his dirty shoes, picked a different pair, and shoved his head out the window. He wasn't the only one looking out toward the ware either. Even though he didn't have a dragon to tell him what was going on, Tristan could make out his father's head likewise looking that direction. King Klavian had the typical black hair, narrow chin, and keen gaze of a Cluster.

Stabbed Valiant? No way. It was impossible.

"It all felt wrong, and it has a lot of us worried over here, especially since Kayla was talking about how wonderful Gladius was right after that. You should have seen Valiant. When he gets really mad his eyes change color and they spin around in circles. Do you think he can still see when he does that?"

Probably. They didn't have enough information about spellbinding dragons to know what they did when they got mad. SilverWings would bow to people he wanted to impress, but they'd never seen his eyes swirl.

"You should see him when he's really happy. The silver on his wing's glow. He's not using a spell either. It just happens."

Pg. 100

"What's happening over there, Tristan?" King Klavian asked, catching sight of him from his nearby window.

"*Give me something dull,*" Tristan demanded. He was going to go over there and inspect the area for keeper poison, since he had recently learned what ingredients it took, and he didn't want his dad sticking his nose in his business.

"*Nothing dull to give you. Kayla is riding Reed instead of Valiant because Valiant won't move.*"

"Valiant is sleeping so Kayla is training with a day dragon instead," Tristan told his dad.

"What about right before that?"

The stabbing. He wasn't going to mention it. He was going to get over there and see what was going on himself. "I don't know what happened before that. I wasn't there. Think I'll go watch Reed. He's a charmer."

With that Tristan shut his window and rushed out his door. Reed must have had some special breeding in order to be the light color that he was. He stood out as the perfect color of a praying mantis. He could also be considered the color of a cricket, or perhaps a lacewing. For that reason, Tristan guessed that he had a bit of ice dragon in him.

"*People pleaser?*" Riven questioned. "*I suppose you could say that, but I thought nearly-there ice dragons were all pink.*"

"*This would be the step before a pink dragon,*" Tristen surmised. "*Reed has to be Wisterias attempt to make a magical dragon and King Peyton stole him from there like he stole all his other special dragons.*"

Tristan reached the dragon ware in record time only to get backlash right away for never being around. His name was on the ware roster, but he had passed the highest level already so what was there left to do? He for one wasn't going to sit around being bored forever waiting for his dad to send him off to a battle. His lack of practice with a coordinated team had backfired on him when Kayla had been taken into Vankerdale, but he still wasn't going to waste all his time here.

"Hey, Shirley!" Tristan called to a scout that was just getting off duty. "Did you see what Kayla did?"

"She ate Caleb's breakfast. Then the rest of us were late for class."

He was more interested in the stabbing personally, but he'd take this information too. It could all be a grand hoax. Kayla couldn't get poisoned, and if she thought that it was an outside source trying to poison her, she might be playacting with Valiant in order to trick the arsonist into coming into the open. The only problem with that thought was that Valiant was still concerned, unless....

"They had better not be blaming me!" Tristan thought to his dragon. He wasn't the one trying to kill them off, and he wasn't going to step out onto that field so that Valiant could have at him. That dragon would know all the spells that Kayla knew. What she didn't know she could make up, so Tristan wasn't putting himself in the path of that.

"Valiant will not tell me who he suspects," Riven noted.

"I'll have a look around," Tristan told Shirley, who shrugged at him and scampered off. It wasn't him, but maybe he could find a clue to the real poisoner. In the process, he might learn more about this stabbing. Tristan had tried looking before for the ill doer and not made much progress. He didn't think it was anyone here that had a bonded dragon of their own. Tristan started near the back of the ware where a few of the plants included in keeper poison were located. It was all still a bit unnerving that the King's Ware had a large supply of these deadly plants naturally growing around. Tristan was less sure what the antidote was, but he knew it wasn't as plentiful.

He tried to spot an area where the plants could have been harvested and he stepped away after finding several possible locations. Whoever was making the keeper poison was doing so locally. If it was up to him, Tristan would set up a watch to try to catch the person harvesting more. But he wasn't in charge, so he had to go tell Charles his findings. The ancient man was sitting around in the doctor's office having a heated discussion so Tristan kept the door barely open to listen before he stepped inside.

"I won't try again. You go do it. I got a spell blasted in my face when I tried."

"He might be a horrible dragon, but he does belong to a keeper, so Valiant won't physically harm you," Charles said. "That's the only saving grace we have on that creature."

"I don't care. Kayla does not control him because she doesn't know how. Nobody knows how. If you ask me, I think it's Valiant controlling her. She can't move if he doesn't want her to. The girl can hardly stand up sometimes."

"I didn't ask you for that assessment," Charles responded. "I asked you to tell me about her physical health."

"She's running a fever."

"Dr. Weber..."

"I won't be the one telling her to get off the field. You go do it."

"Is her bonding wound infected?"

"I checked that and no. She wouldn't let me see her previous marks. I only saw her most recent stabbing. Despite her ill health, she's actually doing something instead of lying on the ground right now. You'll have to send someone else to tell her to stop. I don't think she's contagious."

"I don't think she's fit to be out today. Did you hear what she did to Valiant?" Charles asked the doctor.

"As in fought him off for controlling her? Yes, I did. I personally doubt that girl is poisoned, not with parents like she has, but she does have a turbulent dragon. She wouldn't want to say anything if she was the one poisoning her own food so that she could stab at her dragon and make it look like she was going crazy instead of defending herself. We have no idea what things a spellbinding dragon can do. She's always been mentally fighting something. Now that something is in her face. I think she's doing it to herself so she has an acceptable excuse to fight him."

"Dr. Weber, I don't want you spreading these ideas. Is that clear?" Charles demanded.

Tristan slowly shut the door again as gently as he had opened it. He didn't want Charles and the doctor to know that he had overheard them. Here was the information about the stabbing that he had been waiting to find. Dr. Weber's theory wouldn't be kept as quiet

Pg. 104

as Charles would like, because it made the riders feel safe from personal attack. It was a rather interesting viewpoint that Kayla would try to trick them all by adding poison to her own food. Had anyone checked *her* bag?

"She didn't do this to herself," Riven stated. *"She wanted to eat her food, and she would never desire to stab her own dragon."*

"But she did stab him?" Tristan asked. He made his way to the ware leader's office and wrote up a note asking Charles to watch the plants in the back for further tampering.

"Valiant is being cryptic over the answer to that."

Tristan left the note in plain sight and then turned to go back to the castle. If his father had been watching out the window to see what Kayla was going to do today, Vermelo, the Captain of the Guard, would have been watching from the magic mirror where he could get both sound and a visual of what was going on. Tristan was going to ask him what he thought, even if Vermelo had sent Tristan multiple death threats before. They were not pals, but they shared a common interest in Kayla Brixton.

"Did you personally see Kayla stab Valiant?" Tristan asked when he found Vermelo in the courtyard practicing his use with a mace. Vermelo set the object down to not appear hostile at the moment. He was plenty deadly at other times and Tristan wasn't fooled.

"Did you see such a thing?" Vermelo asked back. "It takes at least four weeks before a keeper reaches the stabbing phase. Kayla is very short of that. She was, however, beneath Valiant's wing having already pulled a knife. The stabbing was unintentional. An accident."

This was a very different view from Dr. Weber, who had a dragon out on the field to tell him what had really happened. Vermelo didn't have that even if he had that mirror. To further get the truth, Tristan needed to know if Kayla was really holding a knife.

"No. I saw the whole thing. She was not holding a knife until Valiant lifted his wing. Then she threw her gray sweater and the knife in front of her and started bawling. It was right after Dr. Weber was spelled away. I have no idea what Kayla was thinking, but she did tell Valiant to behave himself. Dr. Weber's view over Kayla not containing the dragon is accurate, but she did not give herself poison. I highly doubt she wanted to stab her dragon. We're missing the mental details here that would clarify the questions."

Yup, but in order to get those details one would have to talk to Kayla. She was hard to talk to. Tristan always found himself bickering with her, and even on her better days she remained withdrawn.

"Have you considered your options if Kayla refuses to marry you?" Vermelo asked Tristan, distancing him from his questions on the stabbing. He'd have to get it out of Kayla later—somehow.

"You know the rules still state that it has to be a noble that is in charge of the kingdom. King Jack has never fit that category, and while Kayla can claim noble birth because of her mother, I still don't see her being capable of being in charge."

Not this again. Tristan crossed his arms as he looked at Vermelo. He had been saying this earlier too, only last time, he had done something rather bad about it. Vermelo had gone behind everyone's backs to ask Rosa and Clark to take over the throne. Clark was a noble and a Cluster who had married Tia's younger sister. They did have the strongest case for satisfying Aralot's rules, but they refused to rise up against Tia and Jack. At least they did so far, because

Pg. 106

Rosa hadn't let Clark see the paper from Vermelo asking him to take over being the king.

"Vermelo, we don't need your meddling," Tristan answered.

Vermelo's reasoning behind his first attack still stumped Tristan. Vermelo loved the Brixtons, even if he had hated Jack at first. After Jack got that crown, Vermelo was sold.

"Don't you see it, Tristan? This kingdom is starting to fall apart. Jack is losing his grip on magic. It won't be long before you start noticing the same thing. The spells that used to be rather strong are weakening to your will. It will take more time, more effort, more concentration on your part to make magic do anything at all. This kingdom needs a real king for the magic to be fortified. I apologize for our past confrontations, but now that this has come to my attention that Jack's power is vanishing, I must be super clear with you. I will stand behind you being the king of Aralot. It will be upon your shoulders to save the rest of us by taking the crown."

"Take the crown?!"

Did Vermelo think that he was stupid? Tristan knew that thing was cursed. That was why his dad and Jack never touched it.

"Vermelo that thing will kill off my wife."

"What wife?" Vermelo shrugged at him. "You know that Kayla will deny marrying you. You haven't answered my question yet. Have you taken into consideration who you will marry when Kayla refuses?"

It all made sense now! Vermelo hadn't changed his mind one bit over who he liked. He was still supporting the Brixtons, and that was why he was doing his best trying to get someone else to put that crown on their head. He was trying to keep Tia and Kayla from dying. Jack might consider wearing the crown if he noticed he was losing his magical authority. Vermelo was trying to get Tristan to put on the crown to suffer for the curse instead of the Brixtons. Tristan was never going to fall for it.

"As I said, I don't need your help."

It was impressive that all the other kings had let the crown sit on their brows when some of them had very good information over what it would do to them. It would cause them great heartache, and all so that they could have stronger magical spells. Vermelo had to be making this up. Jack couldn't be losing his magical touch.

But just to be on the safe side, Tristan headed away from Vermelo so he could test out a rather difficult spell and see if it happened to feel different.

"It only takes one person to save all the rest of us, Tristan. I know you can find someone brave enough. Find the girl that will save us. You are not a coward. Don't walk away from me like you've become a coward. You can repair this kingdom without needing to smash your head up against Kayla's. All you need to do is take that crown. I will make it nice and easy on you and leave it in your room."

"I won't be touching it," Tristan told him.

Why did Vermelo even have the crown? Last he heard, King Jack had hidden it away where no one would find it. Tristan kicked the ground. Knowing his bad luck, Vermelo had been watching Jack through that mirror while the guy hid the crown so he had always known exactly where it was. Tristan had to be really careful here.

Pg. 108

Vermelo was still going after him, trying to make him either miserable or dead. Nothing new there.

He reached his room and looked around not spotting anything incriminating yet. Vermelo wouldn't waste time though. That tempting crown would be sitting in Tristan's room by the end of the night, and Tristan would have to ignore it or kill off his wife. It still irked him that so many other kings had chosen to lose their wives. Why do that? Was it really for the glory of magic or something else?

No one knew the riddles surrounding the crown as well as Vermelo Cluster. That was the very reason why King Klavian had made him the Captain of the Guard in the first place. There was something lethal about that thing that was pestering Vermelo enough to cause problems all over the place. It was not a good feeling to know that the Captain of the Guard was trying to crown himself a king. His job was to protect the king, and he had changed his mind on how to do that. That right there was frightening.

Tristan looked at the empty cup left on his desk and brought magic up to his hand. It was rather difficult to change the nature of an item. Magic worked by taking energy and force from one area and moving it to another most of the time. In order to change an item, Tristan had to think of a creature that could actually transform. Creating a bunch of butterflies from rock, for example, was done by focusing on the nature of a butterfly hatching from a chrysalis. In order to change his cup into a mouse, he would have to concentrate rather well, because such things were not naturally done. It was an easy bit of advanced magic that wasn't too hard for him to do.

Tristan brought the magic up to his hand and focused on the change as he might normally do. The cup started to change. Easy.

Vermelo was blowing hot air. The mouse started to move off his desk, but then Tristan noticed the animal having metal feet. That wasn't part of the spell. He froze the mouse to study this out. Then he turned the object back into his cup. He wasn't losing his grip on magic. Vermelo must have cursed him so that magic was weaker for him. That was all. Vermelo was all about tampering with other people. Tristan was not wearing the crown even though he would be the king regardless of what Kayla did. She couldn't dictate his life. She couldn't change his future.

Citrus

Kayla

Kayla's emotions were still strung from class, but at least the shower had helped and now she was doing much better apart from the fact that everyone was staring at her like she was going to explode.

"Hey," Kayla gave a random rider a smile as the woman walked with her kid toward the mess hall. Kayla had managed to eat lunch in the kitchen to avoid problems, and she was choosing to skip dinner inside the ware yet again. Her current plan was to head out to get food and then play around with portals looking for the entrance to Wisteria.

"They think I'm crazy," she sighed to Valiant as she met another person's gaze. That person thought she was a demon or something with the way that glare could pierce a hide.

"They think you stabbed me because you did," Valiant informed her. Kayla came to a sudden halt and then tried to grab for her sweater so she could form her expressions without anyone else needing to see them. Her sweater was missing!

"Caleb has it. He's going to wash it for you."

"I didn't stab you!" Kayla panicked dumping everything out of her backpack onto the ground even though Valiant wouldn't lie to her about her sweater.

"He has your knife too. The one you stabbed me with."

"No!" Kayla screamed, and that didn't help anyone else around find her less crazy.

"Kayla, Love. Calm down. You were only trying to wake yourself up from another nightmare. I think it was the one with Troy looking out at the field of dead dragons after battling Wisteria, only to see that Bandit had died too. Anyway, you're getting more desperate to find ways to wake yourself up. Biting your tongue stopped working a long time ago. You pulled the knife to get yourself but I couldn't let you stab yourself so you stabbed my wing instead."

That was why Caleb was looking so earnest when she came to and started crying over the nightmare. He thought she was crying because she had stabbed Valiant. Oh gosh! Everyone thought she was going crazy. She was stabbing dragons in her sleep, even if Valiant had promised her that she would never ever do that. She had believed him!

"It wasn't you. I got in the way on purpose. It is not your fault." Valiant tried to soothe her. It didn't really help.

"Except now everyone thinks…" She looked at another rider who had stopped to stare at her. The man gave her a short smile as if he was concerned. At least he didn't act like he hated her. That was a plus.

"Are you tired still?" Valiant asked her. *"How about tomorrow you take a nap as me before you exert yourself in class."*

Pg. 112

She might have to. She had been super tired trying to participate in class, and it looked like it was all Valiant's fault every time he held back when he thought she wasn't ready. It was all her fault that Caleb was super strung up today.

"We have to stop that curse. It's never made me pass out during the day before." She was speaking out loud on purpose. She'd say just about anything to get people to believe that she wasn't cursed with keeper poison. Anything but that. Riders killed infected keepers. So did Colts. So did everyone because infections were scary.

"I don't know what it is!" Valiant screamed at her from the field.

"That's because I don't know what it is," Kayla answered him. "You know what I know." Which wasn't always the best. Most dragons had more time by now to explore being themselves. All Valiant had was her.

"We'll get to the bottom of this, and no, Mom, I am not poisoned," Kayla said, hearing the approaching wings of one of the dragons that had followed her around most of her life. "It was all a misunderstanding."

It was a red dragon. She knew that only from the sound of the dragon's voice and the flap of her wings. Her mother, Tia Brixton, had only let Kayla leave the house alone if she was being followed by one of Tia's many dragon spies. Kayla looked upward just to make sure that she had it right and smiled. Yup. Red female dragon. Pretty thing too. Her mother hadn't been spying on her as much now that Kayla had Valiant, but news traveled quickly around these places.

"How's my mom?" Kayla asked.

"Throwing up," the dragon answered.

Pregnant. Kayla was still a little worried about that, because Kayla knew that since Tristan dropped his curses her mother was going to keep this baby. Kayla had this strange fear that her parents would start to love it more than her and not need her anymore. She pushed the fear aside. She couldn't stay scared of that forever. They wouldn't turn against her because they had some other kid to love.

"Hope it's a boy," Kayla told the red dragon, as Kayla replaced the items in her bag and slung it across her back.

"Shoulders, men, shoulders!" The dragon spoke, causing Kayla to grin rather large. That was something that her Uncle Anvil would say to his riders all the time just so they would scramble into rows of ready warriors. He would laugh every time. It delighted him to see his men figuring out how to stand together, mixing their sections up.

"Hi, Anvil!" Kayla said as she headed toward the field and the red dragon followed her. All this for her stabbing at her nightmares. No other kid got this, but she wasn't complaining. There had to be some positives to growing up as she had. Anvil's dragon Clawson was connected in her mother's keeper bond, so Anvil could talk to Kayla if any of Tia's dragons were talking to her. "I love you and miss you like crazy. Can you send me my other gray sweater?"

She had left one at her parent's house and one at Anvil's Ware. At the rate she was getting her sweater lost and covered in sweat, a second would be wonderful. The red dragon agreed and continued to spy on her. Kayla ignored it because she just knew that Caleb was still out on the field working out his mood. She was right. There he was with a group of older dragons jet streaming.

Pg. 114

"I'm not saying anything, but I think he's trying to impress you," Valiant said as Caleb launched upward, perfectly catching the dragon above him.

"In that case, I should sit around so I can be impressed."

She joined Valiant on the field who was in the process of stretching out his legs after he had sat on them all day. His blue-gray coloring helped him blend in when it was dark outside, but since it was summer, the sun was still in the sky casting across the horizon a light shade of pink.

"You keep sleeping during the day and they might move me into a night class," Kayla teased Valiant as she climbed up on his back and then onto his head so she could balance there while she watched Caleb jumping. Valiant snorted at her. No one else wanted the stress of trying to train her so she doubted she would be moved. That, and she was worse at night. She would probably fall asleep even more. Even though she was still currently tired, she didn't want to shut her eyes. There was a new fear in her. The fear of falling asleep around her own dragon in the event that she stabbed him. She couldn't let that happen again.

"It wasn't you! It was your instincts fighting off whatever keeps dragging you down. Sleep with me all you like."

It would be nice if her instincts didn't have her hurting herself to wake up. She had to come up with something else. When Norber screamed at her, she had been able to wake up. Maybe a direct order from a dragon would pull on her keeper magic and help her escape this unknown curse. If that was the case, sleeping near Valiant was a good idea. He knew every time he lost her thoughts.

"That's the part that gets me most," Valiant complained. *"I can't hear you thinking. It's like some other dragon is hearing you instead, but it's not Sparkle. I've growled at her enough to know. You're not bonded to any other dragon but us."*

Two was plenty. Maybe the curse was a different sort of possession that she'd not explored before. Tristan had recently put a curse on Vermelo—that she had taken down—to make the Captain of the Guard loyal to him. That sort of magic could make a person do things without really wanting to do them. Something kept giving her nightmares without her wanting to see them. Maybe it was a viewing curse, and it had some strange condition to make it stop, like learning some lesson she still hadn't puzzled out yet.

"It is very conditional whatever it is," Valiant agreed.

Somehow, she kept triggering the condition that made her see the images. Well, she'd worry about it again later. She couldn't spend all her time focused on the curse and miss what was in front of her. Caleb had given up on jet streaming and had turned to flips in the air. He didn't need any help with impressing her when he was doing that. Gee! She was cringing each time he lost contact beneath his feet. He was laughing each time he landed again. Then he saw her and he stopped what he was doing so that Warner could swoop in and deposit Caleb in front her.

"Have you had dinner?" Kayla asked him.

"Are you asking me out?" Caleb wondered. He put a hand against the side of his dragon and leaned sidewise. Kayla wasn't sure if it was because he was surprised that she would ask him, or if he was trying to look cool or something. Either way, it made her laugh at him.

"No. I am only asking if you had dinner because I was going to sneak out of the ware and eat someplace else. I thought you might want to come along to make sure my food was decent."

"Don't take me anywhere sketchy," Caleb said, glancing around to see who could tell on them for leaving the ware when it wasn't an off day. All the dragons were still watching, even if they weren't looking at them. Their ears never turned off.

"So we shouldn't go into the Colt party room behind my dad's uncle's shop where you have to know the password for the day and take an oath to never reveal to anyone who else was in the room that night?" Kayla questioned.

"Yeah, that sounds a bit risky."

"It would be fun though," Kayla grinned at him as she started to walk to the edge of the ware with him following along beside her. He kept glancing around like he was going to get in trouble. Funny. Caleb had broken plenty of rules, but there were some rules that he had never broken, like this one. He didn't leave the dragon ware unless it was his special day to do so. He had been living like that all his life, but Kayla had grown up all over the entire kingdom and couldn't stay as still as Caleb could.

"So where are we going," Caleb asked when they exited the ware and no one said anything about it. One of the night scouts did write down their names though, so she was probably going to report them if they failed to return. Caleb looked behind him again.

"Would you relax? You're a section leader. You get away with all kinds of things. How long have you been a section leader by the way?"

"Can you keep a secret?" Caleb asked her, generating a nod and a smile from her because it seemed all she ever did was keep other people's secrets. She could be called the keeper of secrets and it would have a double meaning and be very true.

"I became a section leader a few days before your birthday. I'm not old enough to be one. When Anvil kicks a guy out, he kicks him out good."

"For punching Aiden?" Kayla asked. She was well aware of the things Aiden had said about her and her dad right before that fight.

"I broke his nose." Caleb shoved his hands into his pockets and looked away from her as if she would think he was horrible. That was nothing compared to helping kill off the former king and prince of Vankerdale. Kayla grabbed one of his hands to hold in her own to cheer him up.

"I bet it will look really neat when it heals, and Aiden will brag about his scar forever. I mean, think about it. Who else has such a personal signature from Caleb Andrade? That mark won't ever leave his face. You made him famous."

"You are so bad," Caleb laughed. "I am not signing any of my pictures. It makes me mad that people are selling them off. Your attention isn't bought like that."

Realizing what he said, he looked sharply away again, blushing. Cute!

"And you're making me just as bad as you," Caleb declared looking around again.

He was ever so amusing. It wasn't like they were doing anything illegal. Besides, Kayla could hear everyone that was around them since they left the ware, and there wasn't that much to worry about. There was only her mother's still spying red dragon, two of her uncles, about eight Colts, five nobles, and the town lamplighter. They were only surrounded by people who would tell the world that she was holding Caleb's hand as fast as their mouths could travel. She dropped it.

"You should close your eyes. That way it will be an even better surprise when we get there."

"I have my guesses. Louie's Bistro, the sandwich shop on the corner, or the castle."

"Don't spoil it!"

"I've not been to any of those so I can't spoil it."

"Close your eyes," Kayla told him again.

"I'm not you. If you're not holding my hand, I'll run into a wall and you'll start laughing."

She was already laughing. Around Tristan, she had to work to come up with clever lines in order to hold her own ground. She had not planned this out at all, and here was a grand excuse to be holding Caleb's hand again.

"I rest my case," Caleb said, glancing behind him yet again when he sensed the presence of her Uncle Fenix getting closer. Kayla doubted that Caleb could hear the guy, but her Uncle Fenix was a Colt through and through. He was crafty and he despised riders.

She reached over and covered Caleb's eyes so she could lead him to the castle. If she didn't show up there, Vermelo was going to hunt her down with all the talk of her being poisoned today. She didn't need him coming to the ware, and since she wanted to explain what had really happened to both Caleb and Vermelo, having them in the same room would make this go faster. It would also be a whole lot more fun.

"Is this safe?" Caleb whispered as he gripped her hand. "I'm fairly certain that your mother is watching."

"You're a dragon rider! Nothing you do is safe," Kayla answered, shaking her head at him. He really must have washed up earlier in the day because he still smelled like citrus. It was a good thing that she wasn't a dragon like Merlock. She would have been tempted to rub her head all over him just so she could keep smelling *that*.

"You were just doing flips making me hold my breath."

"It was worth it to get you to hold my hand. Stop looking at me."

How could he tell? She was only staring at him examining every single spec of his face now that he couldn't catch her at it. He shoved at her head still with his eyes closed.

"Stop."

"You stop!" Kayla blushed.

"That's hard to do when I finally get to see the real you."

He tugged her hand off his eyes and smiled at her. At least now she had gotten washed up and didn't smell so bad. It was making her wonder what kind of smell Caleb would be most interested in, which didn't help her do anything but get that red face back for wondering. Oh, she was hopeless. Merlock would never stop laughing at her if he could hear her right now.

"The real me? As opposed to what? The fake me?" Kayla asked.

"The you that hides underneath that gray sweater."

"But…" She loved that sweater! So much that she had three copies of it so she could always have it with her. "That sweater is the real me."

"It's hot." Caleb shook his head, pulling a face against wearing a sweater in the heat. "Never mind. You're right. Hot is the real you."

"Hey!" Kayla squealed looking away as her face got brighter yet again. No one made her do this except for Caleb. He was a bad influence on her. Too bad she was loving it.

"Right. Sorry, commander. I shall close my eyes, hold on, and not crash." He wrapped his arms around her, holding on, and Kayla wished that there was a class she could take that would tell her what to do when a guy flirted with her this much.

"Caleb. Two of my uncles are watching!" she hissed at him, hearing them both step in closer again. That was worse than her mom watching. Kayla didn't think her mom would do anything at all for watching, but her uncles would tease her forever.

"On your mom's side?"

She elbowed him. Caleb knew very well that the only uncles she had around here were Colts from her dad's side. Her other uncles, all except for Uncle Conner whom no one talked about, were all farmers, and lived in the Northern Farms. They were also only related to her mother through adoption.

"Woah," Caleb protested the elbow. "You were the one saying that I live for danger. I've got to live up to your expectations."

"Then you'd better try harder because I expect to get dinner."

"Yes, sir," Caleb saluted her. "Lead the way. I hope it smells good."

She was not going to say anything back about smelling good. The comment in her head would embarrass her greatly.

"I hope it looks good too like you."

Nope. She was not going to comment back to that one either. She was going to walk forward to the castle, ignoring everything that Caleb said to her so she wouldn't be blushing like mad when she reached it.

"You know that pink sweater that you used to wear when you were five?"

"Seven," Kayla corrected, already forgetting that she wasn't going to talk.

"Five! It's framed along with your first pair of baby shoes in that dragon gear shop near Anvil's Ware. You know, the shop you don't like to go in."

"It is not!" Kayla protested spinning around. "I have gone in there. I fetch Anvil's order of muscle cream all the time."

"Made you look at me," Caleb whispered, upturning his smile to match the shine in his eyes.

Why had she never looked at him until recently? Never mind. She knew why. Caleb was dangerous, and she didn't live in danger all the time. Kayla shut her eyes and turned away walking the path to the castle by memory. Even that made her blush, because Caleb was determined to embarrass her today. That's all there was to it.

"I did not think my plan would work out so well. Now you can't see me when I stare at how beautiful you are."

She ran to the castle, and he was quick enough to keep up. Kayla had been training herself for a long time to be a fast runner, because she had this secret goal of being better than her Uncle Conner and beat him in a race one day. She was going to need to try harder. She hadn't been measuring herself up against anyone as she trained, and Caleb was pulling ahead of her. Uh! The guy was too good. She had to open her eyes to make sure she wasn't going to crash, because while she knew the path by heart, she didn't know it by running.

By the time they reached the castle, the castle guards had already spotted them, opened the door for them, and set up dinner in the west dining room. Kayla's face was red from running so she hadn't managed to not look like a mess when she reached the castle, but she did manage to cover up the blushing.

"Such royal service," Caleb remarked, as he cast his eyes around the boring gray walls of the castle. Aria had tried to redecorate it once, but her pictures kept vanishing, so she gave up. Tristan tried to add things to the walls too, but they never stayed for long either. That was probably a good thing because his additions included knives that he wanted to hide behind pictures.

"And you even have your own nametag, Princess."

Kayla sucked in her breath. Caleb pointed to a table setting that had her name on a card pinned to her napkin. The food probably had the cure to keeper poison in it even if she wasn't poisoned. Eating it wouldn't do a single thing to help with her problem. However, she was still holding her breath and her section leader noticed.

"What is it?" he asked, circling around the table and eyeing up the guards that were watching. There was always someone watching her. She had lost the dragon guard at the door but there was no way to lose everyone.

"You just called me the princess." That's what it was that had her holding her breath. Caleb hadn't called her a queen. She liked the sound of princess much better, although she was living a lie pretending that nothing had happened in Vankerdale. The simple word had her on edge.

"Is that bad?"

Grr. She had to come up with something to say to hide her reaction. She wasn't ready to admit anything, especially not right now. Admitting that she was married would make Caleb back away from her. She would never get her chance to know him better. How about a different sort of truth that wouldn't stop her dinner plans?

"I guess it was just the way you said it like being a princess is alright instead of the absolute worst thing that could have ever happened to me."

It was nice when she hadn't known she was royal. Life was easier and simpler.

"Huh." Caleb picked a seat and sat down, which only had her smiling at him all over again because sitting down before the queen was breaking the rules. Plus, there were three plates, so they were still waiting for someone else to come into the room. Oh well. Kayla sat down, scooting her plate over so she could be beside Caleb.

She wanted to groan when she recognized the footsteps coming toward the room, but she sat up taller instead and started to shift her head into dealing with Tristan. He no doubt would ruin the fun-filled breezy evening with Caleb. Tristan slipped into the room glancing over his shoulder as if he was trying to outpace someone—most likely Vermelo. He wasn't wearing leather gear which testified that he had not been training as hard as she had wanted to do today. He had on a green shirt that was rumpled and curled upward so that part of his belly was showing.

"Jump through your bedroom window again?" Kayla asked him.

He looked down to see why she was asking and fixed his shirt, only to look up at her annoyed. "You should try it. It's great practice for doing the limbo."

"You'd probably knock me over if I came through your window." That would not be pleasant. Besides, she had looked inside his room before, and he didn't have anything in there of interest that would ever make her want to go there again.

"I would. Then I'd trap you beneath me where you belong."

There was a really long pause in which Kayla reached over to take Caleb's hand underneath the table so he wouldn't be able to jump on the prince and punch him. He squeezed her hand back really hard.

"I didn't mean it like that. Gosh, Kayla! Why can't I ever say anything nice to you? You show up and I simply snap. I didn't mean that."

"Is Vermelo coming?" she asked to change the topic. This wasn't anything new. They would never ever get along. She couldn't marry him, which meant that she only had one choice to be married to King Tyler. Kayla held in the wail and squeezed Caleb's hand again.

"Vermelo is coming. My mom's out. She's pestering people trying to persuade them to sneak into Wisteria so we can learn about your dragon's properties. My dad's hunting through the old books as usual. I don't think he can learn anything new. He's got to have all those memorized by now."

Thankfully Vermelo walked into the room and ignored Tristan to sit down at the third plate. Tristan sat down without an invitation.

"I'm not poisoned," Kayla told everyone. "I didn't even know that I'd stabbed Valiant until everyone started looking at me weird and Valiant told me why. I was really tired and I fell asleep on the field so Valiant shielded me. Then I reacted to my nightmare and sort of stabbed him. I'm not poisoned."

Pg. 126

"Eat it anyway," Vermelo said, and pointed to her food. No problems there. Kayla untangled her fingers from Caleb's and started eating. She was really hungry.

"How does one *sort of* stab their own dragon?" Tristan asked, while Vermelo slowly ate his food and Caleb picked through his. Kayla started to slow down because once she finished eating no one else was allowed to keep eating and they were all eating slower than her. No. She couldn't slow down! She wasn't the queen and that wasn't a rule for the princess. She sped up again.

"Kayla?" Tristan demanded her attention. "Why did you not go to sleep so you could function on the field? What's up with the random nightmare?"

"I don't know. If I ever find out that it's another curse from you, you will see it vanish along with something else that you wouldn't want to lose."

She had no idea what, but the threat just came from her mouth anyway. Ugh. She was just like Tristan. She didn't try to say mean things to him all the time either, but she couldn't help it. Maybe it was a curse!

Tristan rolled his eyes at her. "I have not cursed you for over a week."

"Gee thanks."

"Quite welcome," he gripped back at her, crossing his arms like he would love to put a curse on her again, only he didn't want to do it now that Riven was in her head.

"It's not a curse from Tristan," Vermelo agreed.

Tristan looked at him like the man had lost his mind. That didn't make Caleb feel better. He found Kayla's knee under the table and held on. She really wanted to explain to Caleb that Vermelo and Tristan had never gotten along. If Vermelo said something that made Tristan look innocent, he questioned the man's intentions. She couldn't say all that though, so she picked the easier solution of looking at Caleb and giving him a smile.

"Valiant and I are still trying to figure it out. It's nothing new. I've had nightmares my whole life, only not this bad. I used to get some sleep. Now I can't seem to rest unless I'm being Valiant."

"You sightshare with your dragon all night?!" Tristan smashed himself into the back of his chair at the announcement. Caleb simply took a bite of food and chewed it rather loud.

"Yes."

"And that is why sightsharing for you is as easy as breathing. Have you flown him?" Caleb asked her, sounding like her teacher again instead of the flirtatious friend.

"Yes, I have."

"And?" Caleb stopped eating to look at her. She gave him a shrug. It wasn't so bad except for when she couldn't figure out how to block out the sun since Valiant couldn't squint.

"He's a night dragon. The sun looks strange."

"If you sightshared with him could you get him to participate in class?"

Kayla nodded. Caleb had no idea that she had considered being Valiant before in every single class just so she could participate. Valiant was fine. He would be great in class. It was her that was horrible at it.

"He's not as stubborn as you think," she ventured.

"I think he's complicated. Even if you weren't tired, I don't think he'd be as willing to work for me as Reed. But I'll never give up on trying. He's got to come around eventually."

Vermelo pulled out a watch and checked the time, looking intently at the amount of food she had eaten.

"I'm not poisoned!" Kayla insisted. "The food won't affect me at all. I was slashing a nightmare. Honestly."

"You may go when you're done then," Vermelo agreed, putting away the watch. "If you ever see the nightmare of the—"

"I remember," Kayla cut him off. If she saw the nightmare of walking through the corridors of the ruined castle, she was to tell him right away.

She shoveled the rest of her food into her mouth as fast as she could so she could leave. It was getting late, and she would rather get Caleb back to the ware so she could spend some time testing portals before she had to face sleeping again.

"Kayla, have you seen it?" Vermelo asked her, rubbing at his nose before he clenched his hand into a fist because he didn't like to talk about this around Tristan. The prince knew something was up. He was looking between them trying to figure it out.

"You didn't answer right away. I'm taking that as a yes. You didn't tell me. Why didn't you tell me?"

"Maybe I'd already seen it before you asked." She shrugged at him. "What's it matter anyway? That dream isn't scary. I don't mind that one."

"What's the dream?" Tristan demanded to know, reaching for the cuff of his shirt where he had to have a gem that would force Vermelo to answer him if he didn't talk. It was always force. Always this urge to make people comply with him. Tristan was always going to make her recoil.

"Kayla is dreaming about Gladius's destroyed castle," Vermelo answered, and they all noticed that he was starting to cry.

"So it's a curse from Gladius then?" Tristan asked.

Maybe. Kayla didn't know, but it was an interesting question. If she could go to the castle and look around, maybe she would find the answer to what curse Gladius had left behind for his great-great-granddaughter. The curse was pestering Vermelo, and he wasn't the one who had to watch it all.

"Is it the same as what your mom gets?" Caleb asked her. "She gets flashbacks from her dad and Gladius's journal."

How did he know that? Caleb was really good at paying attention to her family more than she had realized. Her mother's flashbacks occurred when she was doing something similar to what Herb or Gladius had been doing, such as flying through a particular portal or walking a certain path. She didn't get very many of them, and

Tia usually only talked about them when trying to avoid the topic of how many keepers existed.

Anvil had a theory that there had to be five keepers alive at one time. Only the three girls were being visible keepers. Magical law stated that the king of the land had to be a keeper as well as a noble. Once Kayla had heard that, she wondered why her Uncle Conner wasn't taking over the ruling of the kingdom. He had refused it yet again when she brought it up. Ritz was a secret keeper as well, capable of taking over everything, but he had never stepped up to the task either. Now her dad was trying to fulfill that role by being a keeper king. It was forbidden to betray other keepers, so Kayla told a white lie instead.

"My mom's flashbacks aren't the same. She has a theory that since we don't have five keepers in the land that a few memories linger to make up for the missing two. Besides, my mom only hears voices. It's nothing like what I get. I get actual dreams instead of words of past written text." Not to mention that Kayla *saw* these people through large reptilian eyes. Dragon eyes. It wasn't the same at all.

"I'm heading out," Kayla declared. She had things to do and didn't want to sit around watching Vermelo cry while Tristan badgered him. Poor guy. Vermelo could take care of himself. On that note, so could Caleb. She was ditching him, too, even if he did give the two other people in the room a more polite farewell before taking off after her.

"You fell asleep on the field? Neither you or Valiant ever sleep?"

Kayla didn't answer. She kept moving through the castle, only to hear Caleb stop behind her and get excited because he recognized one of the guards. It was some old childhood friend that had left the dragon wares and lost contact with Caleb. He let her get ahead so they could chat.

Kayla ran. And ran. The fear that she had to do everything as quickly as she could pounded in the back of her mind. Vermelo never cried like that. There was something he wasn't telling her. She could feel it, and it scared her more than anything. She knew that he would save her if possible, but what if there was something he couldn't save her from? What if she never could stop the nightmares and her body gave out because it couldn't rest?

"I will hold you together with spells," Valiant adamantly declared.

Nice of him, but costly. He would have to replenish the spell frequently, and she would feel like a walking zombie. Thinking of walking, Kayla pulled to a stop, curious and surprised over the new boots that the shoe shop owner had imagined. One was standing right up, and the other was lying beside it in the window displaying the grip. Most of the time boots came in a solid leather color to match the rider uniforms, or came in the standard black. This pair deviated from that greatly, featuring multiple colors of leather stitched together like a quilt. It was a patchwork boot with a thin layer of fur around the top of the opening.

The bottom of standard boots came in different thicknesses with different spacing for wide scaled dragons and narrow scaled dragons so that a rider could pick a pair and get the best grip once he or she bonded. These boot soles didn't have the typical universal spacing either. The grooves alternated large and small so that a rider could get a fantastic hold on any type of scaled dragon. Incredible.

It was the most amazing boot she had ever seen. It was probably designed to draw in Kayla's mother, since everyone knew that Tia rode so many different dragons all the time. This boot would be a favorite. Instead, it had snagged the woman's daughter. Kayla smiled at the boots, noted that there was no price tag on the display window, and glanced up to find that the shoemaker was watching her reaction.

She didn't have a reaction! She wasn't going to be thinking of those boots every time she rode a different dragon that wasn't Valiant or every time he shifted his size which changed her grip on him. Kayla tugged on the straps of her backpack and dashed off.

The portal. She had to reach the portal so she could find the way into Wisteria. The closest portal around here was located down a tunnel that was blocked off inside of the best concealment spell of all time. Hundreds had walked past this location and hundreds more would do so, because it looked like a solid rock instead of a cave.

Kayla dashed inside it and made her way to the back of the cave past the location where her mother was hiding Gladius's journals. Past the location where her father had once hidden the crown of Aralot. Past the spot where Troy had left the puzzle that his first child had loved most before she had died. Past the hole where Shane had shoved his first purchased wedding ring. He had purchased it the day before his engagement broke apart. This cave was full of history, but the only part Kayla wanted to reach was the portal.

She used her keychain to light up the stone slab as she started to consider the hexagonal bricks. They had to mean something. Touching the left hexagon at the bottom corner with magic was the way to turn on the portal, but the hexagons were not consistent across each portal even though they were instrumental to their creation. What if no one had gotten into Wisteria because it required activating the portal from the right side or the middle? What if she needed to hold the magic against the stone longer instead of tapping? To reach other portals across the kingdom, even those inside of Vankerdale, she had to tap the correct corresponding number on the activating block before stepping through.

Trial and error could take a while so Kayla got started in her experiments, climbing up the stone face of the portal to reach the higher hexagons that no one else usually bothered with. It took her hours. She found five portals that went into Vankerdale before she came across a place that she couldn't enter. She stepped into the portal and couldn't get out of it due to a large black tar covered wall being in her way. That had to be why Wisteria couldn't get through either. There was a dwarf dragon in the way, one that had probably set up the wall as a means to trap out Gladius.

"I found Wisteria," Kayla thought to Merlock. "You'll have to burn your way in or whatever you do when you move walls of tar."

"Right now?" Merlock questioned. "I'm pestering the monks. They are so fun to pester."

"When you find the time," Kayla answered laughing at Merlock. The monks had never enjoyed the same pestering. They were scared of him and the tar he could fling into their perfect monastery. "I'll have Valiant tell you how to reach it."

Kayla yawned and that was the last thing she remembered for the rest of the night.

Tyler

Tyler had spent the last three hours on the ground feeling like his stomach was burning *outside* of his body. The rest of his body couldn't feel anything at all. He greatly wanted to collapse and stop breathing, only he was already collapsed. He couldn't tell if he was breathing. Going through a portal without the antidote for it was the absolute worst experience he had ever had in his life.

It was a shame that King Peyton hadn't left any mention of what the antidote was. The only way Tyler had learned the location of the portal that could get him into the magical library was because Flare, a rather charming bronze dragon, had joined his thoughts this morning and told him.

Flare had watched King Peyton enter and exit this building loads of times chatting to his eagerly waiting spellbinding dragon about the nature of a new spell he had learned. When King Peyton went through the portals, he didn't spend hours down on the ground feeling like he was going to die. Some magic was just bad magic, and this portal stuff was the worst.

"Helpful though," Coal spoke up. *"It doesn't hurt dragons any."*

Dragons couldn't fit into the library unless they happened to be like Valiant and could learn a spell that would shrink them down to enter. Even then Valiant didn't have hands to turn the pages of the books. Tyler rolled onto his back having just come back out of the library. He really wanted to install quite a different kind of door on the place.

"Hi," Flare chirped at him. It was one of the words that Tyler knew rather well. He gave the dragon a wave and simply enjoyed watching the clouds move over his head that could not make him feel sick or kill him.

Now Tyler knew that the entire structure of the king's magical library was a physical place inside of Vankerdale and not Aralot. It was his building. His magic books that Aralot kept breaking in to read. He didn't think they had the right to know so much and not tell him about it, but he was pretty sure that he wasn't going to convince them of the same thing.

He hadn't seen any of Aralot's rulers inside the library when he was there, and they had five of them that could enter: Tia, Jack, Kayla, Klavian, and Tristan. That was five spellcasters against his one. He had to get better at his spells. So far, he could do one.

"Did you wait for me this whole time?" Tyler asked Flare.

"Yes," Flare chirped back to his question.

He rolled over to see her. He knew that he appreciated night dragons more than the day sort, but he had to admit that having a helping dragon around that was awake when he was, was equally nice. Coal probably hadn't met her yet.

Pg. 136

"Silly human. You can't bring a dragon into your bond without me knowing. I woke up when you tried it and let it go through. We have been chatting while you were sick on the ground."

"Sorry to wake you up, pal."

He had been in the library as long as he could because he hadn't enjoyed the thought of coming back through that portal. Also, those spells had been going over his head. Maybe he was just picking up all the wrong books. He really needed Kayla to give him an overview of magic, only she hadn't shown up to the counselor's meeting. Tyler had to pretend like it didn't bother him at all. She probably hadn't given him a single thought. He couldn't keep doing this. He was going to write to Aralot and demand that she come back. She was the one trying to get away from Tristan, only she wasn't leaving the fool.

Tyler had mailed her her father's wedding ring, and she had to have gotten it by now because the mail runner had returned with a confirmation signature of the delivery. Kayla had two wedding rings. She probably wasn't wearing hers. Aggravating girl.

If writing to her parents didn't work, Tyler was going to have to try something more than pulling on her politically. After all, she *was* his wife. She had signed the paper on her own. Maybe what he needed to do was find a spell that would get Tristan tightening his tension on Kayla. Tristan was the person that had caused Kayla to sign the paper in the first place. The thought of him was enough to get her to run. If Tyler could get Tristan scaring her, she'd come back to Tyler.

"Do you want me to pick you up or do you want Flare to bring you home?" Coal asked him.

Neither. Tyler sat up and found the bag he had left beside the portal door before he went inside. He wasn't sure what he would find so he hadn't taken his stuff. Now he wished he had because he couldn't take books out of the library with him. He had tried. The only way to keep spells was to write them down while in there or memorize them.

"I tried learning a few," Coal told him.

Tyler wrote down what he could remember, and then started in on a letter to Kayla's parents. He had sent out the statement that he was the new king of Vankerdale pretty much as soon as it had happened. Wisteria had responded to him asking questions, wondering if they would keep trade and such the same. It was all the same there. He'd not been personally in charge of the orders to Wisteria, but he knew them all. They were fine, and if they had enough time to respond, surely Aralot had enough time. Trying to not make himself sound pathetic, he sealed the letter and looked at Flare again.

"Mail runner?" he asked.

Flare hummed at him so he climbed back up on her and went searching.

"*Good luck,*" Coal thought to him.

"*You get your rest in,*" Tyler answered. "*I've got a feeling that I'll be up late tonight.*"

"*My favorite thing.*"

It wasn't his favorite thing. He was going to be fretting about Aralot as every other king had done before him.

Contest

Caleb

Caleb moved to toss his gear onto the bed so he had space to change and paused. Someone had drawn him a picture. He hastily unlocked his trunk and rummaged through the contents, desperately trying to remember how many images he had stuffed in there in case someone had stolen one of his drawings to sell it off and had left him this other image as a replacement.

He knew this was coming. He had transferred away from Anvil's Ware and stopped leaving his pictures taped to the walls of the buildings, so those who collected his work to sell it in their underground market had lost their easy profits. He refused to give up his images of Kayla now that he knew what other people did with them.

"I think you need two trunks," Notley, the level seven section leader, laughed at him as the mess got larger and larger. Maybe what Caleb should do was mail some of his stuff back home. He'd gotten a letter from his folks today and it was tucked into his pocket. He wondered if they had said anything to him about Kayla being at the King's Ware where he was. He'd not told them that she was in his class or that he was her section leader. He'd not told them anything yet because it felt like bragging. He had been sent away from home for wanting to be with Kayla, and he still managed to get her anyway.

Well sort of. Her body had joined them all for class this morning, but Caleb guessed that it was really Valiant instead of her. Even if Caleb had asked for her to switch places with her dragon, it felt weird knowing that Valiant sleeping was really Kayla while Valiant was the one riding Reed. The lack of mental coordination showed. Valiant did pretty well sneakily adding in questions that would improve his own flying, but his mannerism just wasn't the same as Kayla's.

Caleb couldn't tell if he had lost any pictures from his trunk or not, so he sighed, stuffed the notebooks back, and looked at the pictures that had been left on his bed. The first one had him laughing. It was a stick figure of him holding up a whip that spelled out his name in sloppy waves. It totally looked like whoever left this had done so with the intent to hide their own handwriting from him. The second one had very precise box letters to hide the same thing and claimed that it was better than the first. It wasn't a stick figure. The picture was him standing in front of Warner posed as if he was about to start directing his class. It was indeed better, but in all honesty, he liked the stick figure more.

"Presents?" Notley asked him. Caleb passed over both pictures and listened to him laugh too. "You got a new fan. Love this one. It's got you down exactly right, all skin and bones with no skills with your whip."

Caleb laughed at it again. Whoever had left these wasn't trying to steal from him. Someone was teasing him for spending too much time drawing Kayla and Valiant. He knew how everyone else saw it.

Pg. 140

They all thought he was hopelessly in love with the girl, and they were right, even if he claimed that it was all because he was her largest supporter and they were only friends instead.

"I like that one too," Caleb voiced.

"You should frame it," Notley chuckled passing it back to him so that Caleb got a good look at the man's burn wound on his arm. Caleb took the pictures and changed out of his really sweaty shirt for a clean one. It was hot out there today and everyone was turning sticky except for Kayla. No matter how hard she worked, she stayed perfectly cool. Since she wasn't one to waste magic on trivial things like that, it had to be Valiant who had decided he didn't like the way his rider was turning smelly. Valiant couldn't help but shoot out random spells periodically throughout the day even if he was being Kayla when he did it.

"Want to help with the CJ4?" Notley asked.

Caleb was glad that he was looking away from the older more experienced section leader when he asked him this so he couldn't see Caleb's face flinch. That was one of the hardest formations in the entire history of wares. It was something that had to be passed in order to advance out of level eight. It was something that had to be passed to be made a section leader or even a teacher. Caleb hadn't passed it, not even gotten close to being included in such a formation. There was no way he could teach it.

"Nah, that's okay," he said feeling the sweat spreading through his clean shirt too. He should at least read over the level eight training book. He'd not done that. Anvil had bumped him up quite a bit when he sought to jettison him from his ware for brawling. He gave Caleb an offer that he couldn't refuse, mostly because there was no choice to refuse it.

"You don't find the formation fun?" Notley laughed. "I thought you of all people would revel in the added challenge."

"So fun," Caleb replied. "But here's the thing. You don't regularly teach a class for most of the day. I took on Kayla's class before I realized how time consuming being a section leader actually was. You have tons of time to get your other duties taken care of because you have other teachers instructing your classes. I'm falling behind on those other things. I need to go catch up."

Everyone had two hours of free time in the middle of the day. It was the time that Valiant himself should be sleeping. Caleb wondered if Kayla's body had taken a nap yet.

"Nope," Warner answered him. *"She's still doing homework, but I think it's actually her now and Valiant is the one asleep. He scooted away from everyone before he would lay down which isn't what Kayla did this morning."*

It was so nice to have Warner on his side all the time. He absolutely loved his dragon. However, Warner wasn't small enough to help with the supply sheds. Caleb had noticed that their supply of smoke bombs was running low after the level seven class had been practicing with those two days ago. It was his job to keep the supply sheds in order and restocked.

He ran through his other duties. The weapons were getting dull which was a recipe for injury. He'd not had a crew clearing his portion of the field of dragon dung since he took over this job. It was looking nasty out there. He'd not conducted any bunkroom checks since he got here, and he still didn't know all the rider's names on his side that had to listen to him. Then there was the paperwork he had not turned in.

The bunkroom door opened up again. This time it was Mulligan poking his head in. "Slowpoke," he called to Notley. "You're the last one. Charles wants you in his office, Caleb."

The door shut again and Caleb gave Notley a shrug. He was out of it! He didn't have to help with the formation. That was a close one. He really needed to step up his game where those advanced levels counted. Caleb grabbed his gear off his bed in a rush, accidentally scooping up his fan drawings in the process, and dashed outside to go see Charles.

He was a really old guy. The oldest guy alive it seemed. His hair was bright white, his teeth yellow from age, his skin sagging from the sun, but his mind was still good, and he hadn't given up being a ware leader even if it brought a lot of stress. He used his section leaders heavily, which was why the other men thought they were the ones in charge. Caleb was too new to think the same thing, but he had sure acted like it earlier. Maybe Charles was going to tell him not to stand on any more tables.

"Just this. Then you can go." Charles nodded down to a strange yellow envelope on his desk as he pried off a pair of gloves. The envelope was open from Charles's prying eyes. There was no return address and no forwarding address. It simply read, "Caleb Andrade." Caleb thought it looked weird too, and if Charles wasn't going to touch it, he wasn't going to touch it until he had a professional verify it was safe. He pulled out his own gloves, put them on, and picked up the envelope.

"Thanks, I think," Caleb replied. "You don't happen to have an extra level eight book laying around, do you?"

"Third supply shed," Charles answered.

"And can I use anything I need to replenish my sections smoke bombs?"

"You can use the stuff in the first supply shed for that. I think you're out though. You'll need to go gathering ingredients. If you need to buy anything in town you can fill it out on this form to have the ware pay for it." Charles pulled out a slip of paper and passed it to him. "Also, Caleb, the Captain of the Guard stopped by to personally ask me for an assessment of your class's skill level. Do remember to turn in your teacher reports. I had to make stuff up."

"Right. Sorry, sir." Caleb took his items and then backed from the room. He had never met the Captain of the Guard before until last night. Now the man was onto him. Vermelo Cluster was a noble by birth and used to make his money off of breeding and selling champion horses. Now he protected the king, and according to King Jack, was one step short of being the king himself with all the information he was privy to. It was annoying that Vermelo wanted a report of Caleb's class. If the man wanted to spy on Kayla's progress, he could look out the castle window and see it for himself. Caleb wasn't sure what Vermelo was after in the first place because Kayla had already told him that she wasn't poisoned.

Holding more papers than he had been before, Caleb dashed back across the ware to reach the field and Kayla Brixton.

"Oh, master of odd and mysterious objects." Caleb gave Kayla a low bow as she sat on the ground near her teammates and reviewed the homework for the night. He paid particular attention to her eyes to see if she was sightsharing. Her eyes would turn yellow when she was, but Valiant had been hiding the color with a spell. Her eyes still looked blue.

"What is this?" he asked, tossing the yellow envelope down to her.

Kayla glanced at his name on the top noticing the lack of address as well. She waved a spell over it and then turned it over, touching it with her bare hands. It had to be safe whatever it was, so Caleb pulled his gloves back off and crouched in front of her. As he did so, she noticed his fan art and snatched it from him.

"His is better?" Kayla asked, looking at the drawing of Caleb with the box letters. She glanced at Valiant and laughed. "The stinker!" She passed the pictures back, not bothering to look at the stick figure one. It was from her and Valiant then. Instead of feeling uneasy about the fan art, Caleb grinned. She was teasing him! It had been so fun last night until Tristan showed up. He didn't even care that her mother or uncles were watching. He'd do it all over again just as soon as he could.

"You draw?" Caleb asked, looking again at the stick figure. "I personally love this one. Notley thought it was great too. You have a bright future ahead of you."

"I don't draw. I used to but I stopped years ago when Valiant picked it up. He draws. For your information, Valiant claims that he has been able to sightshare with me since we were one. He learned to walk when I walked, talk when I talked, write when I wrote. He thinks he can make me do anything, but I let him draw alone. If I draw anything it turns out frightening."

"Frightening like…"

"Dragons squishing people." Kayla shrugged. "I don't draw anymore. That's as good you get."

Kayla turned back to his strange yellow envelope, but he wasn't about to give up on this. Kayla could draw! He wanted to see it. His desire to see her draw was so deep that his pocket that sheltered his magic started to glow.

"What are you doing?" Kayla asked him reaching for her magical keychain and no doubt sorting through all the spells she had already slipped to him so she could guess the answer.

"Nothing. I just really wanted to see you draw. That's all. I'll make this stop."

He smacked at his pocket but the blue glow only got brighter and got stuck to his hand instead. He really hoped that from far away it looked like Kayla was the one casting the spell, because all her teammates were staring at him knowing the truth.

"Okay, how do I make it stop?" Caleb hissed at her.

"You stop wishing," Kayla hissed back.

"How?" he whispered again, dropping his other papers and using both hands on the magic while Kayla laughed at him for being such a beginner. There wasn't a way to stop wishing for her to draw him a picture. He really wanted to see it. Kayla reached up into the field of the magic and frowned at it as she too tried to make it all go away. She pulled back frowning, and looked to the ground at the papers he had dropped.

Pg. 146

"Fine," she snapped. "I'll draw you a picture, but I'm not going to look at it, and it won't be pretty."

"I don't want you mad," Caleb replied, still trying to get the magic to go away. He pulled out the fox carving which was the cause of all of this, and tried to shove the magic back into its sapphire blue eyes.

"It won't work, Caleb. The resolve of your heart is too strong." Kayla sighed as she shut her eyes and continued her drawing on her stick figure paper.

"But…" Caleb protested and the magic vanished off his hands since she was now drawing for him. "That was weird."

Strange indeed, but Kayla could only laugh at him again, and the smile on her lips told him that she wasn't really mad. She was more intrigued by her inability to make his magic move than anything else. He wasn't. It was his magic! If he couldn't make it move when he wanted it to, who else could make it move?

"It was working from your heart, she said," Warner pointed out. *"You have a very strong heart. You should be proud of that."*

He wasn't because the images that Kayla drew were indeed not pleasant ones. Even more unsettling he had a good guess over what she was drawing. Junia, and Avery, who were sitting next to her, were staring with their mouths wide open at the very realistic rendition of past keepers and the first dragon each of them had ever killed. The dragons lay on the ground, eyes shut, pain their last expression.

Kayla was trying to not think about what she was doing so she was rambling about the good things while she drew the bad ones. Troy and Bandit had this unspoken mission to help the poor and they would leave roasted meat for the hungry even when they were in battle. Shane and Tang adopted a bunch of orphaned kids. Gladius was always out of money for handing it over to everyone who looked like they needed it. Herb, Kayla's grandfather, donated half the profits of his farm to the monks every year. Arvid, Herb's brother, had started a school fund that was still in use, and Maslon, who was Gladius's younger brother, would care for any stray dragon, animal, or person he came across. He didn't get a face though and his dragon was a blur.

"Did he not have a dragon?" Caleb asked unable to look away. This felt like really dark magic that he was watching. He didn't understand it at all, but Kayla couldn't—despite her own will—draw anything but this. No wonder she had stopped drawing.

"Maslon? He had a dragon. He just didn't ever kill it," Kayla answered. Then she dropped the pencil and shoved the picture away from her before she would open her eyes. "I burn all my pictures, Caleb. I advise you do the same with these. They are creepy. Troy never killed his bonded dragon and neither did Shane. They just fought a long war with Wisteria so they killed those dragons. The Clusters didn't start combining keeper poison until Gladius killed off Klavian's dad. Anyway," Kayla was about to change the subject but she happened to catch a glimpse of what she had drawn.

She lunged for it and Caleb found himself shoving her away so he could put her drawing into his backpack. Despite the dragons, these were drawings of keepers. No one knew what those other keepers looked like anymore, and having Maslon completely scribbled out was eerie. It didn't sound like Kayla had anything against him at all. Maybe she couldn't draw him because he had never been evil.

Pg. 148

"Give it back!" Kayla shouted at him blasting him with some sort of spell that did absolutely nothing. He had never thought that magic had a will of its own before, but boy, it did. Magic came out of his fox yet again and turned Kayla's spell into the wind. It vanished and brought a grumpy teenager.

"Why do you have *that* protective spell?" Kayla wailed. "Maybe that thing was made by an ultra-dragon king. You can't have the picture, Caleb. I put a map on there."

She did? "Of what?" he asked. He had watched her draw the whole thing, and he didn't see any maps.

"It's in the negative space between all the other pictures. It's the path through Gladius's castle that I take in my nightmares. Give it back, Caleb."

He shook his head and instead of giving her back her artwork, he kicked his yellow envelope toward her. Nobody else had the path to her nightmares either, and if she couldn't help but draw it, it had to mean something important too. He was going to keep it. He was going to fold up that picture and keep it right next to the fox in his pocket, where nothing would be able to take it from him. Not even Kayla.

"I'll destroy it for you. I want to see it again," he said. This had to be the first time he had ever lied to her. There was no way he could destroy this.

"You better destroy it."

"Kayla, honey." He couldn't help but look her in the eyes because it was obvious that she hated this spell on her. "I don't know why you have to see the bad in order to find the good, but you're awfully skilled at it. You look through the gruesome and frightening and find the true heart of these people. I'm not as quick to destroy your influence to rescue them. I'm going to help you save them."

And if that wasn't the largest desire of his heart all of a sudden, he didn't know what was. He had pictures of keepers. He could take those images and draw the men any way he liked. Perhaps he would show Bandit and Troy roasting food for the hungry and Gladius tossing coins to a beggar. He could get his pictures everywhere without even trying.

"You see that smudge here," Kayla pointed out a dirty fingerprint smear in the corner of the yellow envelope so she could change the subject—another thing she was good at. "That and this blue line." She traced the line across the bottom of the envelope, "indicate that this was shipped from across the ocean. That's how Wisteria marks their documents. I have no idea who would be writing to you from Wisteria."

He had no idea either so he shrugged at her and then smiled when she shrugged back. "I suppose you want me to open it. It looks already open."

"Charles opened it before he would give it to me," Caleb told her.

Kayla reached inside and pulled out a rather beautiful flier. It was done all in ink and the letters were calligraphic and fancy. Kayla's mouth upturned at the sight of it before she passed it to him. Caleb read it over a few times and wasn't sure what to do. It was a notice for an art contest that would give the winner a sum of money, a tour of the Wisterian castle, and dinner with the king.

"You think it's a joke?" Caleb asked. How had anyone heard about him in Wisteria? His pictures had gone that far? This was ridiculous. What would he say eating dinner with the king of Wisteria?

"I don't even know who the king of Wisteria is!" he cried out. "This has to be a scheme because someone wants one of my pictures. A good one."

Kayla chuckled at him. "Maybe, but it would be fun to go there. Valiant's always been interested in that place. He was born there. You could see if Wisteria has any other spellbinding dragons that they're hiding. You'd be the first person to get past those coastal guards. They don't let anyone touch their shore. If you won that, you'd be amazing. But you're right. It was probably sent to you by someone who wants to see how the lost spellbinding dragon is doing. They must have heard about where Valiant is and speculated that you'd draw him. Wisteria has spies too, you know."

Caleb looked down at the flier, still not sure if he was going to enter or not. There was a deadline, and he didn't have vacation days saved up so he couldn't leave the ware if he won. However, if Charles had given it to him maybe he didn't mind giving Caleb a break a little early. Charles would know all this stuff about how hard it was to get into Wisteria, even if it was Turid's Ware that guarded the coastline instead of this one.

"Wisteria's king is Anthony Nolteman. He has a son named Lester, and word has it that they really love their hunting dogs. They decorate with dogs everywhere. Their portraits show them being tall men with black hair. Wisteria is mostly composed of jungle, so if you went over there, you'd find that our heat today is nothing to complain about. They still utilize the old type of dragon ware with dragon doctors that care for diseases and injuries. Most of their dragons don't actively train to fight, but they have a few competitive dragon tournaments throughout the year. Their dragons that bond live in their own family pods with ample room to stash away hidden treasures. You probably don't care to know all of this though."

"Uh…" Caleb answered. He was still looking at the ink and contemplating how he hadn't drawn anything in ink in a while. "Would you do this?" He tried to pass the flier back to Kayla before he talked himself into drawing for a contest. He had never drawn to win a prize before, at least not a prize other than Kayla Brixton.

"I'd try for it in a heartbeat," Kayla replied, although in her case she'd have to have Valiant draw for her with the way her images turned out, "but my life is highly political so creating a good impression with Wisteria is always on the back of my thoughts. However, there's the fine print. That invitation isn't transferrable."

He'd missed that. He looked over the words again and then turned the paper sidewise to see that Kayla was right. In the corner of the page was a message claiming it was a single-entry ticket and it had his name written right there.

"You think King Anthony sent this to me?" Caleb asked, looking up at her startled.

"Well, probably not him personally. It would have been done by one of his counselors, which in Wisteria means one of his relatives, since all the counselors over there are nobles and related to the king unlike over here."

"I'd have no idea how to address the king of Wisteria. It's not the same as talking to your dad. Your dad is just weird. Most of the time no one even calls him King Brixton."

Kayla cringed on the name and then shook her head. "Yeah, just call him Jack. But you don't need to worry about that other stuff. I can teach you what to do. Bowing in Wisteria is rather fun. You bring your arm up to your forehead like a soldier and then curl over." She showed him to do this properly and then burst into giggles.

"It makes me laugh every time, but it's super easy," Kayla remarked, standing back up. "I advise you don't start laughing like me. I can write up a list of manners that they'd expect, which would be a breeze for you to follow because you're so naturally charming anyway. You won't need to worry about taking a slow ship over. My Aunt Rosa would be really interested in this. She'd lend you her water dragon, Pewter, and he can fly across the ocean in about four days. He's fast. Straight smooth sailing without needing to stop."

"You're really encouraging this, aren't you?" Caleb asked. This wasn't what he had expected. He didn't feel like he should be responsible for meeting the king of Wisteria all for drawing a picture.

"Caleb, it's the first thing Wisteria has sent over in the last two generations that proves that they're not scared of us. Well, not scared of some of us. I don't think I would ever get a personal invitation to go over there."

"It could be a trap. What if they rig the contest so that I win and then they trap me over there and never let me leave?"

"Yeah…" Kayla trailed off and then grinned. "That's the sort of thing that would happen to me. Not you though. If you get stuck, they'll meet with my wrath. How about that?"

"I've never seen you stay angry for long," Caleb said, as he put the flier into his backpack so he could think on this later. Kayla was encouraging him to enter. What if it wasn't a contest at all, and only one person had ever gotten an invitation? There was no way to know because none of them could get into Wisteria to tell.

"If it makes you feel better, you can go ask Ian and August what they think."

It took Caleb a minute before he could figure out who Kayla was talking about. He did his best to know the people that she cared about, but this was one of those things that had him drawing a blank before he realized that the answer was rather easy.

"The treasure hunters?" he questioned. Ian and August didn't interact directly with Kayla, but were rather King Jack's friends. They located and hid ancient treasures around Aralot. They were particularly knowledgeable about all the things Gladius had left behind.

"They came from Wisteria," Kayla informed him. "They'd at least be able to tell you if this is a new contest or something that's done all the time. I think Wisteria just likes your artwork, Caleb. You create something and it's like the viewer is standing right beside you. Your work has that soft pull to it."

"Well, I've got to do room checks and sharpen up the tool shed and find ingredients for smoke bombs while you do your homework," he claimed, as he started to back away so he could put her keeper picture in a safer place.

She used to hide from his pictures and refused to look at them. She would ignore them as if they were vile, but here she was claiming that she had a soft spot for his drawings. She had even drawn him a stick figure on her own, and after seeing the result of what happened when she drew, that stick figure held more meaning. She was diving into something that terrified her to tease him because she knew that he liked drawing.

Kayla held up a finger to stop him from leaving. She scribbled over her assignment filling in all the answers, and then passed it to him in under five minutes.

"My parents had me do that one last summer. I can handle the tool sheds and get started on smoke bombs," she offered before he could protest. Since she was walking in the direction he needed to go, Caleb found himself following her while her classmates rolled their eyes about how much smarter she was than them. She was smarter on paper, but she hadn't practiced the information she knew, so she still needed a lot of work when it came to riding dragons.

"Hey, explain the CJ4 in your own words," Caleb asked, even if he knew what the formation called for. He still had never tried it and needed tips.

Kayla nicknamed it the cold jumping forever formation. It was wickedly hard on dragons. They formed two lines in the air and had to drop their weight from the sky and fling themselves to the side beneath the dragon that used to be flying beside them. For an ice dragon that sort of wing pressure was easy. Not so much for everyone else.

As if shifting so suddenly wasn't hard enough on the dragon, the rider had to jump from the dropping dragon onto the one beside it while that dragon was taking the place of the one that had just moved. It was indeed a measure of cold jumping upward and hoping that one wouldn't miss the oncoming dragon, resulting in a deadly fall. The result when done right was a loop. The really good people would pull off the CJ5 which included two loops side by side moving around and around as riders and dragons exchanged places. It was pretty when viewed from below. It was exhausting for those in the formation and designed to confuse an enemy as the riders tossed a precious object between them as they jumped. That was where it got even harder. Caleb didn't want to say this out loud, but he didn't think Warner would be able to do it.

"Some dragons never pass level eight even if their riders manage to do so," Warner answered his thoughts. *"But if I had spent a year practicing jumping sidewise and pushing myself with my wings, I could probably get it."*

"Maybe you should start trying it out discreetly," Caleb advised. *"We're supposed to be able to do this."*

"Good idea. Next time I run off to hunt, I'll come back with sore wings."

Caleb shrugged. It was what they had to do. He wasn't always going to be lucky enough to avoid participating in the harder formations. He split with Kayla as they reached the ware buildings. She went to examine the supply sheds, and he started in on bunkroom checks feeling grateful that he wasn't trying to handle everything all on his own today. He pulled out the letter from home and read it as he skimmed over rider rooms for neatness.

Pg. 156

Things sounded normal at home with the exception that Anvil had told everyone that he was banned from taking transfers and they couldn't breed any dragons next year due to castle orders. Caleb had heard a few more details about it from Kayla. She claimed the restriction was all Prince Tristan's doing, which had been agreed upon by his father and signed by all the counselors so that Jack and Tia couldn't go against it. His family was upset, but otherwise doing fine.

As part of the room checks, Caleb was also in charge of confiscating illegal items of which he found more than he expected. He had to evacuate a poisonous snake and a tied-up pet squirrel. He dragged out an oversized teddy bear, tossed more than a few bottles, and took away an assortment of flying objects that they couldn't have at a ware. Then he had to write up citations for all the offenses, although he was still confused over who had brought in the pet squirrel. He gave the entire bunkroom the chore to clear the field of dragon dung and left it at that for now. He'd have to watch that room and start moving people if they kept up with their illegal activities.

By the time he was done with that, he went to check the supply sheds and smiled over the clean nature of the room and the list of needed supplies that Kayla had left for him to find. She was fantastic. She even wrote down for him where to find everything in town, knowing that he wasn't familiar with this area.

Since she had made it so easy, Caleb was able to pass off his list to the general store owner who offered to have it all shipped over. Even better, the man told him that Ian and August were in town. He even provided directions to their location, so Caleb set off again in order to meet two men that Kayla knew.

It felt like his day was destined to plop everything in place. Ian and August could have been anywhere across the kingdom instead of local. This was the sort of random luck that King Jack usually got.

The two men were on the exact hill that the shop owner had mentioned. Both of them were poking around a fire pit with a metal pole that should be used to hold up the tent they hadn't set up yet behind them. They had an odd lumpy shaped bag beside them. One of the men was dressed all in black, and may have at one time had black hair as well, but it was all gray now so Caleb wasn't sure. From listening in to conversations that Caleb shouldn't have heard at Anvil's Ware, this man was August. The other one had holes in the knees of his pants and a hatchet hanging from his belt. His hair was still brown. He was Ian. Ian looked up first and smiled at him so Caleb walked in closer.

"Evening, Caleb Andrade," Ian said pleasantly. "Here to ask us who keeps buying all your pictures?"

"Don't say that." August came around the fire to elbow his best friend. "He'll expect an answer. Plus, it's just rude to use everyone's names all the time when you've never met as if you know everybody."

"I do know most everybody," Ian claimed, "and you can't tell me that Caleb doesn't expect it. Who doesn't know Caleb? He's like Jack, only Jack's face was everywhere on his wanted poster, and Caleb's face is everywhere on stolen artwork. The result is the same. Everyone has seen Caleb and knows who he is."

"I'm August," August pointed to his face and then ruffled Ian's hair. "This is Booger. What brings you by?"

Pg. 158

"Kayla said you could help me decide something," Caleb replied ignoring how Ian punched his friend in the side. It was a little strange to hear the two treasure hunters compare him to Jack. Jack knew he had wanted posters up back in the day, but Caleb had only just learned that his pictures had made him famous. He pulled out the conflicting art invitation and held it out.

"Is this legitimate? Kayla said that you used to live in Wisteria so you might know."

Ian took it from him and gave out a loud "ho ho!" August read it and rubbed his hands together.

"You got invited to the royal drawing!" August exclaimed, like it was a real event that happened in Wisteria and not some plot to make Caleb ship free artwork. "If you win this, I'm upping my prices."

"No one will buy from you if you do," Ian warned. "They think your copies are fake because they are."

"Not the one with Rosa telling Pewter to stop spraying Kayla with water. That picture isn't fake," August said.

"Do they rig that thing?" Caleb wanted to know, feeling awkward. He was probably standing in front of the two people who sold off his stuff the most. "What do they do with the pictures afterward? I can't help but think that someone wants a free picture that they'll turn around and sell for some large sum that I'll never see any part of."

Ian and August both looked at each other, and then true to the tales of them being remarkably strange, August tossed him a bag of coins that Caleb didn't pick up. He wasn't going to collect money for his past work because he wasn't supporting the underground market. He left the bag alone.

"All the pictures go on display in the holy monastery for two days," Ian told him. "People flock there for a sacred pilgrimage, and when they arrive, they present tokens of gratitude to the Holy One in the sky. Then they wander about and vote on the pictures, along with a bunch of other contests that are taking place. My favorite scene was the fortune tellers. You could pocket a great number of coins from their flowing robes."

August nudged Ian again. "They don't rig the contest," August told him. "The pictures are guarded rather well, and the votes strictly monitored because of the final prize to meet with the king. At the end of the contest, the winning picture is framed and added to the wall of royal drawing winners. That wall is kept in the museum, although it's more than just one wall since it's a longstanding tradition. A lot of artists go there to gain inspiration from the ages. The pictures that don't win are given back."

"Do you have to be on that pilgrimage to know if you've won?" Caleb questioned. He felt even more hesitant to enter this contest now. He would be going up against an entire kingdom's finest artisans. Surely there had to be somebody better than he was.

"You draw from the heart with the intention to touch other hearts," Warner reminded him. *"It doesn't matter if anyone else is better. Art is all about communicating a feeling through an image."*

It wasn't all the time, but that's usually how he drew. He kept thinking about how strange it was for someone royal in Wisteria to have come across a drawing of his and decided to invite him to a kingdom that he didn't belong inside.

Pg. 160

"Most of the artists stick around, but I think that Wisteria would send you a letter instead," Ian provided. "They don't take kindly to visitors much."

"No entry is accepted if any name is visible," August added. "The people there vote against anonymous artists, so it's really all based on skill. I think you should do it."

Kayla had thought so too. August took the invitation from Ian and passed it back to him. Everybody thought he should send something back. Caleb still wasn't convinced. He thanked the two men for their time, left the money where it sat, and walked off, only to find himself scaling the roof of a random house and sitting on the top so he could see the world from above. The part he was really hung up on was knowingly sending out a picture of Kayla to share with the world. She was special to him, and he didn't like other people saying mean things about her.

"Well you won't be there to hear what comments people make," Warner reminded him. *"Caleb, I think you should draw that picture and get it over with. You'll agonize over it otherwise. Just send it and wash your fears clean. What's wrong with the world learning that Kayla and Valiant are happy? Spread joy. Spread gladness. Spread her ability to stand up after falling down. Spread the resolve to never give up, to reach for dreams even if the world is crumbling. This world needs people like you."*

Caleb nodded and pulled out his sketchbook, but instead of drawing Kayla for once, he found himself making rough sketches of keepers he had never met once in his life. They made him groan, because he really hoped that Kayla's curse wasn't spreading to him. He said he wanted to help her with keepers, but he didn't mean all the time.

Caleb pulled out the picture that Kayla had drawn for him so he could see this "map" that she had created. She had been really quick to spot it out between the other images of dead dragons so it had to be a path she was very familiar with.

Caleb traced the path with his eyes and his skin crawled. The negative space ended at Kayla's stick figure holding that whip calling his name as if the magic that had pushed her to start the drawing was the same magic summoning him toward the unknown finish. No wonder she destroyed all her artwork like this. Maybe if he got out positive pictures of keepers, he would be able to break the curse. If he could take away those nightmares, it would help out everybody.

It took about sixteen sketches before he found that he could start drawing Kayla again. Even then, he wasn't getting anything good enough to send in for a contest. He drew a few lines and tore up the page. Tried again. Stared at the sky, switched to ink pens and sketched. Tore it up. He was really starting to believe he'd acquired that curse thing when he realized that he had surpassed his two-hour mark and hadn't made it back to teach his class.

"Don't worry. Kayla wrote up all your teacher reports and submitted them for you," Warner told him. "I dictated and she wrote. Then she passed along tomorrows cleaning assignments, laughed at a few jokes that Mulligan aimed at her, and finished deciding on next week's food menu since it was your turn to approve it all. She's not flying, but she can stand on the ground and dictate a class. She's got you covered. Take your time."

Caleb shut his eyes and softly smiled. Her teaching a class of dragons would be one of the best sights in the world. She hadn't said anything to him about all the small jobs she kept picking up for him.

Pg. 162

She was the one sprinkling gladness, like a little fairy secretly picking up the broken world around her, changing it from confusing and frustrating to orderly and stunning. Trailing behind her was Valiant, mesmerized by Kayla's inner glow, as he provided her with encouragement to keep helping.

If there was one message he could send over to Wisteria, it would be the one to keep helping each other. He'd cast Valiant into a starless sky with his wings shimmering, and put Kayla holding onto his tail like she was flying beside him sprinkling out magical peace onto a frustrated world below her that turned into something beautiful wherever her light touched. It was going to be a rather dark composition with splashes of color that made the fear of darkness retreat. He was going to use colored ink and real flecks of silver on Valiant's wings. Hopefully, no one really needed him for the rest of the night, because he had to go buy some additional supplies for this, and it was going to take some time.

Tristan

Tristan could have the strongest resolve to be nice to Kayla but the things that he said would have made his mother wash his mouth out with soap if she had heard him.

"Be nice to Kayla," she had always told him. Kayla was synonymous with impossible. He tried and he couldn't! He kept himself from saying anything about spotting her taking noble lessons with his mother, and then moving the room they were inside when guards mentioned he was around. His mother must have decided that he would never be invited to those classes. Tristan had decided that his mother would never be invited on his dates. He could be nice to Kayla from a distance, but up close the mistrust was back, the desire to win out against her always present. He had to be better, had to feel like he came out on top of every verbal battle. Which was why he had broken his goodness streak and cast a spell on her tonight.

He wanted to know what she was thinking because she wouldn't say it all to his face. She could get out the snappy words too, but there had to be a hundred other things she was really thinking. He was going to read her mind across the back wall of the diner, and he didn't care who else read it with him. This wasn't about them, only about what was going on with Kayla.

She sat in the chair which was the trigger to his spell starting up. He kept his face straight as her words flashed along the wall. The other people in the room were not as kind. They noticed the scrolling words and had to look over as one to read them.

"I hate eating. Maybe if I eat really fast, I can make Tristan starve when he has to stop eating as I finish before him. That is such a dumb rule. Who came up with that rule anyway? On that note why did I even ask Aria to teach me all these rules when not one of them has helped to save me yet? I think I'll be like my mom and ignore every single one of them."

The other diners in the room turned their heads toward Tristan, figuring out who had cast the spell on the wall and what it was. So Kayla made her thoughts rather obvious, but she hadn't noticed the spell yet so it was going to continue. Tristan held up his menu pretending to pick something to eat. Kayla picked her food way faster than him. One glance down, her item was already selected and displayed on the wall. Tristan heard the order get whispered out behind him as the cooks started to get it ready. Kayla looked in the direction of the kitchen and grinned as if they knew her well enough to know what she would request. They had a little help.

"If it comes not poisoned, I will have a good evening," Kayla's thoughts displayed on the wall. *"You can tell my mom that I don't want to learn one new thing about Tristan. Is there anything new to learn about him? Can I tell her that he got a haircut finally and call it good?"*

The smirk on Kayla's face had Tristan pretend to look at his menu even harder. This was fun. His mom was always badgering him before and after dates too. Kayla had it worse. Her mom was in her head the whole time. Mothers. Theirs could get a little overbearing.

"Not let Tristan know that I find him boring?" Kayla asked, trying really hard not to laugh. And here it came. She was going to start making fun of him so she could survive through dinner. Did they have to always be at odds with each other?

"Serious? You're not casting spells, are you? I'm not cheating. I happen to have eyes everywhere. Also, you're predictable."

Kayla sniggered again and had to cover her eyes.

"Stop! Tristan will think that I'm laughing at him and I'll have nothing good to say back because I am."

Lovely wasn't it when things were translucent like this. Seeing it from this perspective had him strangely not offended. If Kayla had said this out loud, he would have come up with some retort to make her mad.

"Actually, so far it's going great. We've not said a word to each other and the evening is the most relaxing we've had so far. Thanks for asking. Can't wait for him to say something. Should I come up with a reply or stare at him until he stops talking?"

Tristan laughed at her, wondering why it couldn't always be like this. That was the ticket right there. They would be perfectly fine with each other as long as they didn't have to talk. It made for a horrible relationship in the long run, but it was working. The drawback to this idea was that if he never said anything at all, neither one of them would eat. He was like Kayla and hoped her food came out safe. He hadn't made any progress in finding her poisoner, and Charles hadn't found anyone picking around in the fields. The evil doer probably already had a large enough supply.

"Know what you want to eat yet?" Tristan asked, grinning when the answer on the wall didn't match her words. Her thoughts revealed that she had known two months ago. Her answer was a simple yes. She went back to the far more exciting conversation in her head.

"You know when I told you to be yourself tonight instead of me, I didn't mean with spells. Pick a different part of yourself to be. That is not charming. She won't be amused," Kayla's thoughts declared while she fought with herself to stop laughing. Whatever Valiant was doing had her bent over with the giggles.

"He is turning the field into a flower patch every time Sparkle tries to land so that she changes her mind because she just can't squish such beautiful colors," Riven told Tristan. "In other words, he's flirting with the ice dragon. How long until Kayla gets mad at you for breaking into her bond like this?"

"I'm already in her bond. Shush." Tristan told his dragon.

"How about you stop pestering me?" Kayla asked Valiant. "I can't ignore him all night even if it would be fun." The words scrolled across the wall right as a Colt in the corner clumsily crashed his chair into the wall as he stood up. He did it on purpose! The abrupt change in sound had Kayla looking behind her and she noticed the spell.

"Tristan!" she rounded on him. "Couldn't hold off, could you? You had to add more entertainment to your life because you can't find it anywhere else."

With that his spell on her was broken. She waved her hands and took it off which was a downright shame.

Pg. 168

"I was enjoying it, yes. We'd not said anything mean to each other yet. Your idea of a completely silent evening had its merits."

"Does it? Well then take down a few of your protective spells and I'll keep your mouth quiet for a good long time."

See, now they were fighting with each other.

"The spells are staying up, although your pride could come down a few notches. I have way more fun in my life than you do."

Nope, that was an insult. He held up his hand to prevent her reply so he could fix his own. "Sorry. I'm trying really hard not to insult you."

"Looks difficult for you. Maybe if you tried to not utter insults as hard as you try to steal other people's cash you might achieve your goal one day."

Kayla looked at his annoyed face and started laughing again. Tristan set his menu down and sighed. He couldn't tell if she was laughing at him or laughing at her dragon. His spell had been really helpful! Maybe he should go back to that silent evening idea. Or try out her approach of completely ignoring her so he could get some food. He glanced at the menu again and then waved the waiter over, who had been neglecting everyone else to watch their date. Yeah. They had some great dates. They always made Tristan wish he was with someone else.

Kayla verbalized her order as well, even if it wasn't necessary, and when she looked back at him, he knew he had her attention, which wasn't what he wanted at all.

"So tell me one new thing about you so I can satisfy my mother," Kayla demanded.

It shouldn't have been such a hard question, especially since he saw it coming, but he was drawing a blank. Having read her other thoughts wasn't helping. He didn't want to say anything lame so that she continued to find him boring. What did she find exciting? Did she like anything at all besides rock climbing and her gray sweater, which she wasn't wearing? She had decided on a long pink dress without any decorations, although she had put on a necklace which was new for her.

"Riven and I spotted a rather cute dragon that snuck over from Vankerdale."

"Yeah… no. That has more to do with Riven than you. Try again."

"I don't know!" Tristan floundered. "You already know everything about me." And what she didn't know could be learned by her asking his dragon. Riven would tell her anything.

"Not true," Riven replied. *"I can lie to her because we're not exactly bonded. She hasn't asked me anything though."*

"Do you have anything new?" Tristan asked, and the blank stare he got back was answer enough that she was going to try out staring at him to make him stop talking. Either that or she didn't want to answer.

"You can't tell Sparkle or Mr. Grumpy because they would be offended, but I have decided that I don't like ice dragon wings."

Pg. 170

Okay, so she wasn't picking the silence option. It was him that was stunned into silence. Who didn't like ice dragon wings?! They were the best wings out of any dragon ever. Ice dragons could not only rise to a full flight from a standing position, but the dragons could fly upside down!

"I have a fancy for spellbinding dragon wings," Kayla said with a short smile over his silence. "They change color when they get happy. Sparkle is not going to want to return home ever again. So, I have decided that when my mom shows up demanding that her dragon leave that you can be the one getting in trouble for it. You're the one who asked me out tonight so that I'm too distracted to tell Valiant to stop."

He crossed his arms shaking his head. That wasn't going to work, but it did make him laugh at her. "How many things have you talked your way out of over the years? Your reasoning is horrible. Not even your best angel face will make that pass."

"That's what makes it work though," Kayla laughed back at him. "I can't change up my act now or everyone would see right through me."

He was laughing again. She was really bad at hiding her emotions, unless she hid them under her hood. Everyone *did* see right through her. His reaction to that was new though. The fact normally had him annoyed instead of laughing. It was like they had finally both decided that hating each other was only going to make them both miserable, so now they could be happy about it instead.

"Everyone says that you could pass the test to be a Colt, but really sometimes I think that people just like to lie. You can't talk your way out of anything."

"You know if you thought about it just a little bit harder, you'd see that I've already won tonight."

"No, you haven't."

"Yes, I have."

"Have not."

"Have too."

He wasn't going to think about it harder. Thinking about it harder would make him come up with excuses for her for how she could be winning. She was trying to psyche him out and it was rather amusing.

"Does it always have to be a contest?"

"No," Kayla said. "There's no contest when I've already won."

"Ha ha. I see what you did there."

She was back to laughing at him. At least this way she was going to enjoy her evening rather well. Tristan would too, but he might not enjoy it later if all the Colts in the room thought that Kayla was winning this date thing. How was the date a contest? Grr.

"He's distracted!" Kayla hissed at him, causing Tristan to look around the room trying to figure out who she was talking about.

"Not in here! Valiant. He's distracted." Kayla scooted her chair away from her side of the table and came to sit directly next to him. Tristan wasn't sure what was going on, but he was pretty sure that Kayla had never chosen to be beside him like this before.

"What do you know about time magic, Tristan? Is it only something that spellbinding dragons can do? Valiant has locked a town in time before and you guys needed him to bring the town back. What do you think?"

He was thinking that he no longer had to think harder. Kayla had been rather easy to convince to join him tonight. He thought it was because she wanted to eat food around a person that could protect her, but this was the real reason. She was scheming. It must have been her that asked Sparkle to visit Valiant so that he was distracted and she could talk about Valiant without him realizing it. There were not very many other ways to get a dragon out of a rider's head otherwise. Maybe Dr. Weber had something here. She was against her own dragon.

"I can't talk about time magic where everyone can hear us," Tristan told her, glancing around the room again. There were way too many Colts in here.

"So cast a spell to block the sound," Kayla advised. She was looking at him so earnestly that he did just that. "Do you know anything?" She asked again when he finished. "I keep seeing things in the past that could be related to time. It's hard to not think of the time concept around Valiant because what if he gets mad at me? He claims the nightmares are not his fault, but how many other people are bonded to a spellbinding dragon? Merlock was telling me that dragon queens can see instances in the future, like large events that are meant to happen, which would indicate that time is fixed instead of changeable. What do you think?"

He thought that this was hard. If time was fixed then Valiant couldn't have locked a town in time. So that had to prove that time was changeable. "Dragon queens can't see the future," he said.

Kayla shrugged at him. "That's what Merlock said. He could have been lying to me, but I don't see why he would. He was talking about an event in his life that has given him hope in the future for all these years, and seeing as he's not dead yet, it can still happen. Can people alter time? Have you ever read anything about it?"

"Only once," Tristan replied. It was such a long time ago that he wasn't sure where he had read it or when. He hoped he could remember it well enough. "I read that time is as mystical as the mystique. At least I think that's how it was phrased."

"The flower on our kingdom flag?" Kayla asked, and he felt stupid for bringing that up until she nodded and pointed something out to him that he had never noticed. "If you take the inside shape of Valiant's tail, multiply it and put it in a circle, it forms that flower."

"Wait like Aralot was made on the back of time?"

"I don't know. I was asking you. Would it be the back of time or the front of time? Why that flower? What does it mean?"

He was saved from answering when the door to the diner burst open and the spell around them vanished. In its place was his father, looking greatly upset. Tristan rose to his feet ready to charge outside with his dad to stop whatever catastrophe had come up. He hoped it wasn't caused by Valiant playing around.

"We were informed at the castle that there were people messing around with magic in here." Klavian shook his head and

Tristan didn't know what to say to defend himself. "Magic isn't a toy, Tristan. What kind of spells have you done that would disrupt the peace of our inhabitants? You need to take their needs into consideration before you start casting spells."

He was getting a lecture in front of his date. Sure, it was only Kayla, and she used magic too, but his face was turning hot. Talk about him taking the blame for her craftiness of the evening. It was her that got them all distracted so she could talk about time, and he was the one getting in trouble for it.

"You do realize that most people see magic as a threat to their general wellbeing. It is only to be used in case of an emergency to solve problems that otherwise could not be solved. It's a special privilege to be using magic and you've been getting incredibly lax with it lately."

Oh no. His dad couldn't ban him from magic! That would be the absolute worst punishment he could ever get. He had used magic before in an attempt to save his father's life and this was where it was all leading to. Every time he tried to do something good, it led to something disastrous. His dad had claimed similar instances had happened to him as if the magic in the land didn't really want to listen to the wishes of Clusters. It did horrible things like the time Klavian had turned Kayla's mother into a ghost. Tristan couldn't lose magic. It was such a large part of him!

"Can you tell Aria that I won't be coming up to the castle tomorrow for lunch?" Kayla interrupted. "And also tell her, because I know she will ask, that Tristan has been quite wonderful tonight. He wasn't misusing anything, although I suppose from a nonmagical person's point of view it would have looked like it. Terribly sorry about that. Did you hear the news about Wisteria asking Caleb to submit a piece of artwork to their annual contest? I really hope he does it. This is like the first time they have tried to include us in anything in a long time. I find that remarkable."

Kayla was saving his hide. Tristan found *that* remarkable. When his father didn't say anything back to her right away, she provided him with a bunch of details about how Charles had received the invitation for Caleb before passing it to him, and what the thing said. She even got into the exact colors of the flier. By the time she was done, King Klavian was all lectured out.

"We'll continue this later," he told his son. Hopefully, he would forget it later now that he was heading off to think about Wisteria.

"You know," Tristan sighed as his dad left. "Time is also a feeling. Like right now I feel a whole lot younger."

Kayla laughed at him. She was such a stinker! She was the one asking him to use magic even though the spell that had probably gotten him in trouble was the one where he broke into her head. It was a good thing that their food came so they could eat in near silence without bothering anyone else. Their next date would need to be more private. Maybe up at the castle, or a picnic on a hill or something. He didn't need to repeat tonight's performance.

They parted at the door with Kayla heading back to the ware to tell Sparkle to go home while he headed up to the castle to think about time magic. They really needed to get into Wisteria to get the goods on spellbinding dragons. Kayla had a valid point that there could be something time related to her current nightmare curse.

"Come on, Tristan," King Klavian called from around the block.

He was waiting for him? Tristan slumped his shoulders, because he had really hoped that Kayla's distraction had worked well enough to get him out of the rest of that lecture. Well, he'd have to come up with something to convince his dad that he wasn't being irresponsible. It was those Colts that just wanted to pick on him and ruin his date that sent a secret message out the window and told someone to go crying up to the castle. There had to be a Colt laughing at him for all of that tonight.

Tristan turned toward the corner, finding that his shoes became stuck. Mud or dirt or… tar! What was tar doing here? His shoes were sinking into the soft surface and he was going to have to leave them because the tar was hot! He bent down and started to frantically pull off his laces. Sticky searing heat poured down on top of his head causing him to scream with the pain.

"Wait! There's someone down there!" a man screamed from on top of the roof where the tar was being dumped. Why was it even being dumped from up there!

"Didn't you see the sign?" another voice screamed, worried.

His protections weren't working! It had to be because no one was trying to kill him. They were dumping the tar without seeing him there, so the fact that his clothes were burning wouldn't trigger his protective spells. This had better not be Vermelo's doing for him refusing that crown! None of his spells were saving him. Tristan cut off the shoes and ripped off his clothes that continued to burn into him. Jumping out of the way, burning and shameful, it was only now that he saw a sign warning people away. There was no sign before! He could swear to that.

A wild dragon's stray fire blast came down upon him next, and he dodged just in time realizing that without his clothes he didn't have any magic on him to protect him at all. He kept his gems sewn into his clothes. If he lost all his clothes at once, he was magically defenseless.

"Kayla!" Tristan screamed. She always had great hearing, and she didn't disappoint him. She came running around the corner, avoiding the tar and the sign that really hadn't been there before.

"What...?"

"Don't gawk. Get me clothes and get me my magic back!"

He pointed to his wasted clothing feeling the burns on his entire body. He had to be a horrible sight straight out of a nightmare, but Kayla didn't hesitate. Her quickness was a blessing. She healed his wounds, crafted him some clothes from a nearby flag of Aralot, and summoned up all his gems that were roasting in that tar. Tristan was still trying to figure out what just happened as he gripped his gems in both hands.

He had nearly died! Someone was trying to kill him just as someone had been trying to kill Kayla, only she got poison that she could avoid, and he got tarred and flamed. He couldn't claim that it was his dad, but that was the voice he had heard. He could swear it. As for that wild dragon, he was going to hunt it down later.

"It wasn't trying to get you," Riven told him. *"That was an accident. It got mad at that other dragon for calling him names. When the wild dragon tried to flame the name caller, the name caller dodged and the fire came down at you instead."*

Two accidents right in a row? No way. Tristan took off at a run in the direction that the voice had come from. Whoever had called him couldn't have gotten too far. He made a mental note of everyone that was in the area, and then ran to the castle to ask after his dad. Vermelo always knew where his father was.

It didn't take long to hear the captain's voice so Tristan ran into the conference room and skid to a stop seeing both his parents along with Vermelo.

"What are you wearing?" Queen Aria asked, looking at the odd clothes that Kayla had made up. She wasn't the best seamstress. He was stitched into the flag like he was in a white, yellow, and blue jumper, and he was going to have to cut his way out of this. He'd never be caught dead looking like a cloth lump, and he could picture hundreds of people laughing about it, but that wasn't the point right now.

"Did you come straight back here after the diner?" Tristan asked his dad.

"You were not wearing that at the diner. I thought I said to not play around with—"

"Tristan!" Kayla's voice was saving him again. She came tumbling into the room looking out of breath.

"Not done gawking?" he asked, before he could stop himself.

"Oh please." She rolled her eyes at him and held out the bear medallion that he had dug up from Vladimir's grave. He had to wash the entire southern ware for that. He'd almost lost it tonight and it had slipped from his mind that he had left it in his pocket.

"I decided to check to see if there was anything else that you might need, and that came up but you ran off on me. Are you okay?"

"Are you tearing up?" It was a stupid question, because she was starting to cry. She tried wiping the tears away but more came out.

"It's just that… Well, I have this unrealistic view that you're invincible so if you were to die that would totally ruin pretty much half of everything…"

The sweetheart. She liked him even if they did hate each other on occasion. But what did she mean by *half* of everything? They were going to share the kingdom? He must be getting through to her. Perhaps nearly dying wasn't the worst thing that could have happened. Tristan pulled Kayla into a hug as he took the coin back from her.

"Death isn't supposed to be in the present. It only belongs in the past," she whimpered.

"It's going to be okay," he found himself tell her, as he held her in close.

He'd never held her before so it surprised him by how easy it was to do. She might be eight years younger than him, and her maturity and dragon skill level could improve, but they could really make it work if they tried hard enough. Tonight had proved that. If they were sharing a common goal, then they weren't competing against each other. Talking about time magic hadn't caused either of them to pick on each other. All they needed to do was share the common goal of running the kingdom and their problems would be solved. Was it too soon to ask her to marry him?

Pg. 180

"I'm fine," Tristan assured her again. "Are you going to be okay?"

She nodded into his flag covered chest and then started to pull away so he kissed her on the cheek.

"Thanks. I guess your angel halo came in handy tonight. You really do save everybody."

She smiled at him and he smiled back, taking in the blue of her eyes, the red of her hair, and the pink of her face.

"What happened?" his father asked spoiling the moment.

"Nearly died," Tristan answered. Someone was trying to kill him. He had to figure out who because it could be the same person that was also trying to kill Kayla. On that note, he looked over at Vermelo. Nah. Vermelo would never go after Kayla. They couldn't have the same attacker if it was him.

"How?" Vermelo asked next.

That spoiled the mood even more. Kayla pushed away and headed to the door without saying goodbye. Tristan looked over at his mother to see what comments she had and wished he hadn't. She was shifting her eyes back over to him after watching Kayla walk off, and her face wasn't hiding her shock over their hug.

"Mooom."

"Sorry. I just didn't expect to see that look on your face so soon."

"It's your fault." He glared at her for being able to read his expressions. Considering asking Kayla to marry him *was* his parent's fault. He never would have come up with the idea on his own.

"I know," Aria replied. "I was just surprised that's all. Are you hurt?"

"Nothing more than my pride," Tristan answered as he left the room too.

He had to get back out there and figure out who had used his father's voice. He knew what he had heard. It couldn't have been Jack using magic to mimic the sound. Jack would never kill him, and he certainly wouldn't be poisoning his own daughter. Could it be Kayla? Surely not. She had come to save him, and even as crafty as she was, death wasn't something she wanted. She was just crying about it. Was this a group effort or an individual effort? Why was the road getting tar right then anyway? He had to get back out there and find the answers.

Spider shot
Kayla

"**D**oing alright, Sugar?" Caleb asked her as Kayla made her way to the field very late for class. The reason for that was because she hadn't had a single nightmare last night. Not one. She had slept the sleep of the dead and no one had woken her up when it was time to get up. She was late, but she felt incredible.

"I overslept, which is a fact that I am rather proud of."

Caleb laughed at her and showed her what they were facing today. She could already tell what it was and it left her scared. It was days like this that she wanted to go back to the beginner classes that she had skipped so she wasn't charging out into death.

They had the spider shot set out. It was a device that would grab at dragon legs and trap them so that riders could group around a dragon to bring it down and kill it or capture it.

"It's only scary if you get stuck in there with the wrong people on the other end," Caleb said, looking at Valiant as if he had been having this conversation for a while. Valiant was crouched low, staring at the evil device like he wanted to tear it apart. "I promise. Only Kayla will aim it at you and you'll try to dodge it for practice while she tries to catch you for practice. If you never practice, you won't be able to escape it if it ever comes at you for real. It's not scary. It's battle training. Davis and Summit, it's your turn."

Summit, a bronze dragon, bravely shot into the air and got in a location where Davis could shoot him. Davis took over the controls with his customary go-first attitude, adjusting his aim and swiveling around the shot trying to find a good opening around his dragon who could hear his thoughts and change up where he was at. That made it a bit tricky, but the whole point was to dodge anyway so it was fine.

"I think we should volunteer Reed," Valiant thought to Kayla, making her shake her head at him. She couldn't default to Reed. He wasn't her dragon. He was Lena Sherman's, and the mystery rider wouldn't appreciate Kayla trying to shoot her dragon down.

"How do you think I feel about it?" Valiant protested.

Scared. Terrified. With all the nightmares Kayla went through she expected herself to be rather good at anything that would injure a dragon. It came instinctively to her, since she spent so much time practicing these things in her sleep. Jet streaming like Gladius had done hadn't been hard to figure out, because she had already jumped those same jumps before.

"Exactly," Valiant shivered. *"You're going to snag my leg and bring me down. You're going to hurt me."*

"It's not supposed to hurt," Kayla answered Valiant.

"How about you aim at Riven? He won't mind," Valiant tried next. *"Then it will be real practice for you. It's not like in real life you would be aiming at me. I'd have already disintegrated that thing with a spell so practicing on me isn't real practice."*

Norrin, who had a dragon tattoo on the side of his neck, bumped Davis right at the last second so that the balled trap zipped out into the air and actually caught Summit. The bronze dragon screamed as all the riders put their shoulders to the handles and started turning them to drag him down to the ground. Summit fought back, making it very realistic practice. Once he was down, they would release him, but on a dragon they were trying to catch, he would be lashed down in chains next. Valiant shivered and cast himself in a spell so that he started shrinking below the normal size of a dragon.

"He's not having it, is he?" Caleb asked her. "If you're up for it, Warner will try to dodge you."

It was going to have to be Warner then. The one day that Kayla was alert enough to handle class without it looking like Valiant was holding her back was the day Valiant had decided class wasn't the thing for him.

"If I go up there, I am blowing that spider shot up."

Thinking of blowing up... Looking at Tristan after he had been tarred last night was an image that was stuck in her brain. He had been bleeding with black goo on him. It had to hurt horribly, and he had lost all his clothes and all his magic. She had never found him to be so mortal. Tristan simply didn't die. He never got hurt at all. He had so many magical charms on him that it should have been impossible for the tar to catch him, but somehow his spells hadn't worked.

Then he had hugged her and kissed her face. She hadn't forgotten that part. First Tyler, now Tristan. The result had been pretty much the same as Tyler's kiss. It felt all too normal. It wasn't anything exciting, and it didn't make her heart jump. It didn't make her want to gaze into Tristan's eyes and spend the rest of her life with him. It had felt kind of boring, and it was somewhat depressing to think that her first two kisses hadn't felt like much. Maybe she was destined to be bad at kissing.

"How are you thinking about kissing when Summit is trapped?!" Valiant asked her, giving her a short growl along with his question.

Because Summit was just fine that's how. The riders were going to release him. Caleb was already walking them through how to do it. She should be over there helping, but she still hadn't moved that far away from Valiant yet. He was scared, and she wanted to help.

Summit was released. He blew affectionate air over his rider before he walked out of the way so they could practice again on the next person. Caleb looked at her. Kayla glanced at Valiant before she slowly walked forward nervous. At least she wouldn't be shooting at her own dragon. He could remain where he was, shrunken and small, on a large field. She used to be able to get away with hiding from everything, but she had to stop cowering and practice in case she ever needed this skill one day. It was better to be over prepared than not prepared at all. Things like this could help her escape future kidnapping attempts. She didn't expect Tyler to send another one at her anytime soon, but she wasn't sure how long he could last before he was here asking her to come back to him.

"You know how to use it?" Caleb asked her when she reached the large wooden frame that had been spiked into the ground with nails larger than she was wide. This thing always left huge holes in the field that riders had to fill back in before anyone tripped in the gaps.

"You look through the sight to aim and then pull the lever," Kayla responded.

Pg. 186

"The faster the better. It's all about timing," Caleb told her as he took a step back so he could keep an eye on Valiant while Warner jumped to the air for her to shoot him.

All about timing. Tristan hadn't been all that helpful when she brought up her timing problem last night. She would have thought that he'd know a little bit more about time magic than he did. His quote that time was as mystical as the mystique was rather laughable. That was saying that the mystery of time was a mystery. He called her logic bad, but his was just as stretched.

If she compared time again to Aralot's flag, she could claim that all of Aralot was a mystery too. It was. It was confusing her. If keepers had been created by ultra-dragon kings and then placed in Aralot and kept out of Vankerdale until a certain time, what did that say for when the time came that Vankerdale got keepers again? What if it didn't mean anything at all and time was all a random dice game that everyone played. Sometimes the dice bonked together and that created frozen moments in time.

It was strange then that Indigo could claim that she knew the future. How could she see the dice? Did she see all the dice or only the ones that would crash the hardest? Nothing had prepared them for when Valiant froze the town and kidnapped Kayla the first time, so Indigo probably hadn't seen that moment. Why would she see Merlock in Wisteria? Did she only see moments in time that related to dragons or did she see people too?

"You talked with Tristan about time magic?" Valiant questioned. Kayla did her best not to think anything back to that. *"Sparkle tells me that Indigo told her that she only sees dragons that have been part of her herd. She saw Pyro heading after Tia and saw him bonding Jack long before it*

happened, but she didn't see herself helping Tia get Misty back when your mother's first dragon was kidnapped."

Bummer. Then Indigo couldn't see if Kayla was going to marry Tyler or not.

"Aiming is the most important part." Caleb's voice drew her out of her contemplation, and Kayla cast him a sheepish grin for not paying any attention to what she was doing. It might come naturally, but not *that* naturally.

She looked through the sight and started to aim toward Warner, waiting until he got in a spot where he would shift his weight to head back the other direction away from her so she could trick him and catch his leg right as he turned. He started to turn and she shot, watching as the chain attached to the balls soared upward. It would have worked, except that Valiant was suddenly there shoving Warner out of the way. Back at his full height again, he caught the balls in his claws to prevent them from wrapping around anything. Then he yanked upward as hard as he could, and since the balls and chain were connected to the spider shot on the ground, his yanking pulled the spider shot upward.

Kayla jumped from the structure along with her teammates as it was pulled from beneath their feet. The metal spikes creaked, not coming all the way out of the ground, but getting pretty close. Valiant dropped the balls, letting the chain slink back to the earth along with the spider shot that landed with a heavy thud.

"Yes, Valiant! Nice job!" Caleb cheered at the same time that he ran forward to make sure none of them were hurt. "That's exactly what you do with it! I knew you had it in you!"

Pg. 188

She didn't. She had no idea that he was going to participate and defeat the machine the right way. He hadn't used a spell. What had spurred that change in his attitude?

"It was time to impress you," Valiant claimed. Although his impressing had caused her to need to jump out of the way of a rather heavy contraption, but yes, she was impressed.

"You like time, Valiant?" Kayla asked him.

He flew a few circles in the air before shooting straight up and diving back down practicing—finally—his wave pattern flying. Who would have thought that thinking about time would get him to participate? Now if only every class was like this, they might be able to make more progress with the time that they had left in Aralot.

Fate

Caleb

Blue flashes from the ground clued Caleb into another attack by Valiant. Last night they had had a one-sided conversation where Caleb expressed to Valiant why both he and his rider should participate in class. Kayla had great knowledge, but not technique. Training made her safer so that she could stay alive easier and remain with him.

Apparently, Caleb's speech hadn't hit the mark, because along with the rain making it impossible to see anything at all, Valiant was adding to the chaos, shooting spells at the other dragons and people on the team. Kayla was trying to get up into the air, but Valiant had held her back each time, and there was no way that Kayla could claim he wasn't to blame. Not today. The only thing they were doing was flying the easiest basic formations. At least his class was. Caleb was practicing his own skills, having Warner dive and swoop between everyone, so they could both get better at the advanced level they had skipped.

Avery screamed and tried to escape the blue flash. It hit him anyway and Caleb wiped the water from his face with a sigh. Having unknown spells shot at you was enough to make anyone faint. Not trusting the caster of the spell was enough to make them wet their pants. At least in Caleb's case, he trusted that Kayla could undo anything that her testy dragon dished out.

Caleb tried to spot Kayla through the haze to ask her to help so they wouldn't all end up falling off their dragons with broken bones. What he found was the nature of the spell as it hit him in the face and shoved the water off his eyes. Water repellant! Caleb scanned his class, finding everyone staring at him instead of at Valiant and Kayla who were both remarkably up in the air with them. He'd expected to find Kayla on the ground sitting in a puddle of mud. Here she was looking for instruction. Remarkable. Maybe the talk last night had been worth it.

The rain wasn't blinding him as it continued to pour down over the field making for sloppy classes in every direction. Caleb's class continued to look at him, some calm, others still feeling the pinch of panic that they had been touched by magic. It was up to him to teach the riders which reaction they should go for here.

"Best thing ever!" Caleb cheered. It really was. They had a spellbinding dragon on their side, for once encouraging training. Caleb had been keeping class easy, but if Kayla could participate, he was going to step it up and get her doing something that could, in fact, save her life.

"Brilliant, Valiant!" Caleb gave the dragon his best smile and waved his hands through the air changing up the formation. Instead of looking like the worst class on the field, they looked like the best one, even when Caleb had to signal them to land so he could shout out his instructions when the rain got even worse.

Right as they landed, an angry roar erupted across the entire field. Caleb looked over just in time to see a large green dragon flame the hide of a younger brown animal. If he was at Anvil's Ware he would have been able to judge if this was something that happened a lot. He would have known if the flaming dragon was more aggressive than most and if the attack was called for, but he wasn't, and he had nothing but questions and fear as he watched the dragon break ware code. No flaming inside the ware toward riders outside of practice during class. This didn't look like a class demonstration. This looked like war.

The brown dragon turned, roaring back as its tail came up and its mouth administered her own jet of flame. The brown dragon didn't stand alone. Its fellow classmates joined in the battle, causing the green dragon to scream in fury and the tension to escalate. Caleb tried to judge if the battle was close enough to the invisible line of his section that he was supposed to provide leadership over. It probably didn't matter. He couldn't make out any other section leader, and he hadn't heard anyone else blowing any whistles. He raised up the whistle and blew out two warnings. One was for the dragons to cut it out. The other was for the riders to clear the area.

The green dragon was screaming about murder, so Warner interpreted, and he didn't look like he was going to calm down soon. This was going to get ugly because as the other riders ran from the field through the mud, the dragons didn't. Those who knew the green dragon were getting closer, taking up his side. More flame was bursting out into the air.

Oh gosh! He had to do something! Stand down! Stand down! He blew on the whistle as he spun around to count the heads of his class. Most people had run already, but his class was standing there behind him watching calm and collected. Yes, that's what he needed to be. He needed to think. The quickest way to get the commotion to stop was to send in a team of dragons that would pull out the green dragon that had started it. He turned around again to see who he could send noticing that Valiant was standing upright again, tight and on edge. Kayla wasn't anywhere to be seen.

"Where's Kayla?" he asked, as he signaled for the containment drill to be carried out. Now was not the best time for her to be skipping away from class. There was a dragon war going on. More than his class of dragons launched into the air at the sight of the signal. He hoped he wasn't asking for more trouble as he shouted his demands. "Get the green out of there and stop that flaming!"

"*I don't know if you'll stop it,*" Warner said as he shot toward the commotion himself. "*He's mad. He clearly thinks someone got trampled.*"

"Good gracious," Caleb breathed, trying his best to count heads while he fought with himself to spot who might have been killed. He blew on the whistle for the riders to all line up. He couldn't count heads with them scattered all over the place, and even if he still didn't know everyone, a missing rider would be spotted by a friend when they grouped all together. The riders ran toward him as they cast worried glances over their shoulders toward the continuous war.

"Who is missing?" Caleb asked, letting the riders count themselves so he could watch the fight. Now that he knew a little more about what the green dragon was screaming about, he didn't think that the creature was normally this hostile.

"Whose dragon is that?" he wanted to know as he watched the first pass of the containment drill fail. The green dragon was rather outnumbered, but he was fighting for life and slashing his tail all over the place, refusing to back down from beating up that younger brown.

Pg. 194

"I can't remember the girl's name, but the dragon's rider is currently in the doctor's office because she went into labor with her second child last night," one of the other class teachers answered him. "That brown is not from our side. That dragon should be in Notley's section. And I hate to tell this, Caleb, but as far as I can tell, the only person that is missing is Kayla."

Caleb tore his eyes away from the fight to search the rider heads. What he saw was a mix of concerned fury, along with the ache to get in there and fight with their dragons. One man was holding his mouth and trembling, probably the rider of the brown dragon that the green one was trying to pick on. No Kayla. Caleb's eyes yanked to Valiant again. The dragon stood staring into the watery flames and if that was where he was staring, that was probably where Kayla had gone.

"Dear no," Caleb couldn't help but fret. He looked back into the fray. The one time Valiant wasn't stopping Kayla from jumping into a mess was when it was the worst one. There was a group of twelve dragons on the ground with the brown one running and stomping and flaming. Kayla hadn't passed her dragon evasion test. She had not proved that she could dash through a field of stomping dragons. She hadn't proven that she could rush through a line of flame. There was a team of eighteen dragons in the air swooping, and likewise getting agitated. If he didn't get this stopped soon, he was going to get an earful from Charles if his heart didn't shatter first.

"Valiant, tell me that she's not in there."

Valiant didn't say anything. As his name suggested, he remained steadfast in his staring. How did Kayla even get in there? She was right in front of him until that dragon screamed. It should have been impossible for her to run that fast. Even more confusing was that the green dragon's rider was reported to be safe in the doctor's office, so whose death was he screaming about?

The containment drill wasn't working. Caleb needed to try something else, but he was scared to call for a large group huddle on top of that mad green dragon because if Kayla was between all those feet, she wouldn't survive.

Valiant hooted into the air causing more than just Caleb to jump.

"She's out!" Warner interpreted.

"Huddle him down!" Caleb screamed, and watched as the dragons, now certain that they wouldn't also smash Kayla, jumped as one at the green dragon, smashing all together in a large dragon heap. Caleb had seen such a mess before but it had been a long time. He was a child back then, and he hadn't been able to stand around and watch as riders rushed the field trying to break up the fight. He glanced behind him waiting for the riders to rush the field but none of them did. A few of them were looking a little ill, which meant that he was missing something that Warner wasn't saying.

"Sorry. I'm a little squished at the moment. Kayla is carrying the wounded person out."

She was crazy insane to have run into the middle of the mess to begin with, but now that the dragons had stopped thrashing all over the place, he could make out Kayla rounding out from behind the pile, carrying a small child in her arms. The little boy was clinging to her for dear life shivering, trembling, and wailing.

Pg. 196

"Babysitting," Caleb mused. The green dragon had been babysitting and had lost his riders first child into a dangerous situation. He charged in trying to get the brown dragon away from the kid that the dragon hadn't noticed. Then the fight had started up. Perhaps the child was wounded, but he was clearly alive, and as his sounds picked up, the dragon sounds died down to listen. Above the eerie silence of the halted battle a melody was moving through the air. Even sweeter, the song came from Kayla as she consoled the kid.

That's when the riders broke the lines and ran forward. Caleb wanted to be among them, but he waited. Kayla didn't like being the center of attention. The dragons were rolling off each other now that the green babysitter could hear that his kid was alive. Kayla passed the child off to the first person who reached her. There were a lot of joyous shouts with the tradeoff as the riders screamed about the kid being fine. They cheered on Kayla too, but she was very good at dodging people, and she nodded to them as she kept walking forward, not letting anyone stop her from reaching her destination.

There were many things that keepers did that terrified normal people. Jumping into the middle of a flaming dragon stampede was one of those things. Two or three dragons, sure. In a controlled class setting where the dragons weren't trying to hurt anyone, okay. But heading into a zone where thirty dragons didn't care what they smashed, absolutely not. Man, she was amazing. Caleb wanted to tell her that. He wanted to pull her into his arms as she got closer and tell her how his heart had panicked. He wanted to tell her that he loved her, congratulate her on being braver than him. Perhaps the kid had made it out fine, but Kayla was bleeding from several locations. Valiant shot her with a spell as he noticed the same thing.

"Thank you," Kayla said as she passed by Caleb and met her dragon. Valiant hummed short and sweet before he gave her a growl, swiped her into him with his tail, and clamped her to his side, covering her over with a wing. Caleb smiled at the dragon himself as Kayla mumbled to him from the inside of the trap to let her out. She wasn't thanking Valiant for healing her, but rather for letting her go out there to save the kid.

"Kayla, you had me going for a moment there. Nice save. Beautiful rescue. Don't cling too hard, Valiant. That girl of yours has got the moves!"

He left it at that as he whistled for everyone to return to their classes now that the disaster had been stopped. It could have been so much worse. They could have lost a child today. Things like that had happened before. He knew a few kids that had wandered too far from safety and never made it back to their bunkroom that night. Kayla would have heard of those same cases. Dragon training was a dangerous trade. Not everyone survived it. Not everyone that was ware born decided to stay.

They needed something gentle after that for today. Tomorrow, though, he was going to have the dragon's blindfolded in every class while they walked easy drills so they focused more on hearing where people were around them. He didn't want his section causing anything like that.

Charles himself came out and whistled for everyone to clear the field due to the horrible training conditions. Riders rushed off to get dry, which put most of them in their bunkrooms. Caleb debated between going in there to read his spellbook or heading to the mess hall to interact with others. He chose the mess hall and was very glad that he had when Kayla beat him to the door and held it open for him.

"What's something that I don't know about you?" Kayla asked him letting him go inside first.

There had to be lots of things, because she had done her downright best to ignore him before and she had succeeded very well. It was probably better to start at the beginning though.

"My full name is Caleb Jace Andrade because my mom decided that she was going to have four kids and one of them would be a boy that she could name with the initials of the CJ4 formation. However, when I was born, she already had Mikka, and she wasn't sure if she would be getting another boy later down the road. She didn't want to lose her idea so I got the name even if I was the second born son instead of the fourth born. She had four boys. Grant should have been me."

"No one can be you. Are you good at that formation?" Kayla asked him.

He gave her a shrug. He still had never tried it out even once. It was a lot to live up to being named after one of the hardest formations, like he was going to be the best of the best. Every rider wanted to be the best they could possibly be, but he'd never know where he sat until he got the courage to admit to the other section leaders that he didn't know the formation.

"My dad named me," Kayla told him, "and my mom found out through Sparkle before he ever said a thing. Did you ever… I don't know… not like having a sibling?"

Caleb let his wet shoes and clothes leave puddles on the ground as he slipped onto a bench near the edge of the room. A lot of other riders had chosen to come here too, and more would trickle inside to play games and take advantage of the extra free time, so it was only going to get more crowded. Normally he'd be in the middle of that crowd, but since he was with Kayla he was going to pick the back.

"I love my brothers," Caleb replied. "Mikka is older than me and Brandon and Grant are both younger."

"You didn't ever worry that your parents loved them more than you?"

Caleb leaned forward, putting his elbows on the table to study the beautiful soaking girl beside him. Clearly, this was coming from somewhere and leading up to something else. Perhaps she was missing her parents because this was the first time she had been away from home where she didn't get to see them every day. It was the same for him. He had always lived close to his parents, but it hadn't bothered him that he was leaving them. He'd only been upset that he had moved away from Kayla.

"Are you suggesting that you want more of your mother spying on you instead of less?" he asked. "Having a parent distracted by another kid is fabulous. You can make all kinds of faces behind their back that way."

She chuckled at him and leaned against the table too. The way that she could smile felt like the sun had come out, even if it was still pouring out there. He had it easy being able to slip inside a building. Warner was going to be struggling to find a spot among the trees.

Pg. 200

"You just made it all better," Kayla told him, even though he wasn't sure what he had helped with. "My mom's going to have a baby and she won't miscarry it this time. I'll have my first sibling and I've not known what to think about it."

"Siblings are fantastic. They're like having a best friend you can fight with that can't get away from you. When you're done fighting you just love each other again because you're siblings. You'll make a great sister, Kayla. Have you ever been to the southern monastery? What's it like?" he asked her, curious to hear more about the world from her perspective.

She had great views, and he wasn't the only one listening to her fantastic storytelling skills. Riders hushed their conversations so they could overhear. When new people came in, they were instantly drawn to the topics, curious and enlightened. Kayla was fascinating and he would have loved to see her teaching a class on kingdom unity because she had it all. Kayla talked about the monks in such a way that he started appreciating their lifestyle. The same thing happened when she talked about farmers and then Colts.

All of a sudden Caleb was being opened up to the details of people's lives he had never known before. The entire kingdom became relatable when Kayla spoke. It was such a shame that she had kept quiet until now. Several of the riders were frantically writing down her stories to share for later. Brea couldn't get close enough to them. She snuck behind Kayla and started braiding her wet hair in order to get the best seat available.

It was when Brea was just about done that Caleb saw something he had not ever wanted to see. Kayla would be perfect for ruling them all. She had stepped into the lives of everyone, worked beside them, struggled beside them, lived beside them. In her own way, Kayla's love for everyone around her was what held up all of Aralot. He could sense it, and it made him a bit sad, because when she claimed her throne to continue spreading her peace, he was going to have to slip farther away from her again.

Kayla didn't head back to her bunkroom when everyone else was ready to leave for the night. The rain had finally stopped so the night dragons could get a good class in, but the rest of them were done for the day. Caleb expected Kayla to turn toward her room, but instead she ran toward the exit. That girl just couldn't stay still. It put him in such a tricky position, making him want to give her trouble for breaking the ware rules all the time. He was going to have to start doing something. She couldn't leave *every* night.

Caleb walked in the direction she had taken, looking out past the ware toward the dark wet woods. His eyes caught a man leaning up against a tree. Ritz. The ageless man had sharp eyes perfect for spying on Kayla. Caleb had seen this guy spying on Kayla back when she was twelve. She hadn't noticed at the time, but since she spent quite a lot of time rock climbing in her youth to reach the portal at Anvil's Ware, Ritz watched her too trying to learn her secrets.

Back then Caleb had identified Ritz as the leader of the Colts right away. He had a distinctive quality about him that made a man sense he was up to no good. Ritz had scampered up the cliff face after the young Kayla until he got too close to the portal scouts. Then he had turned before they caught him, but he had noticed that Caleb had already figured him out.

Pg. 202

"Caleb Andrade!" The blond man had correctly named him as Caleb had hovered on Warner, likewise spying on the young princess of Aralot.

Ritz made no indication that he was scared of Warner at all. Caleb found that to be interesting because Colts were known to have a large fear of dragons, even after Jack proved that a Colt could bond one.

"Ritz," Caleb had called down, drawing a smile to the man's face over Caleb's own recognition.

"You make a man wonder. Will your fascination ever phase out? You realize that Kayla looks at Colts. If you became a Colt, she would look at you."

Caleb was only sixteen, but the thought of Kayla looking at him even then was something he tried to achieve constantly. There was Ritz giving him a way to gain his desires, but it came at a huge cost. Colts didn't have dragons, and he had just bonded Warner. If he hadn't, he might have thought harder about this invitation.

Caleb wasn't sure how often the renegade ringleader asked riders to join his personal team, but he had guessed that it wasn't often. Caleb had told Ritz that he was perfectly fine and flown off on him.

This time when their eyes met, Ritz didn't smile. He wiggled a finger at Caleb, asking him to draw in closer. Caleb did so, but it wasn't without caution and alerting Warner to the man being around.

"You're a little close to the ware tonight," Caleb told him.

"Never close enough. Has she slept?"

"Who?" Caleb asked, not about to let on that he knew what Ritz was talking about.

"You could lose her before you ever get her. There's more than one prince hanging out of her pocket," Ritz said next.

Caleb didn't think there was a person alive that liked talking to the Colt ringleader. Ritz was known to manipulate people to get what he wanted. He was also known to have a large interest in the affairs of those who sat on the throne. Caleb was well aware that he had already lost Kayla, but recently it hadn't felt like it. It felt like he had won her over. To hear Ritz remind him otherwise dampened his spirits in the already humid air.

"Don't talk about her like she leads people on."

Ritz laughed at him. Caleb wanted to charge at him, prove that he had what it took to be important to Kayla, but that was a very bad idea given who he was talking to. What he should do was walk away.

"She doesn't lead people on. Kayla is a rock climber. She leads them up and then lets them drop all on their own."

"My dragon will stop me from the splatter," Caleb claimed.

Ritz rolled his eyes at him. "I'm not talking about you, but I can if you want. Have you ever noticed how you have the habit of being around when Kayla hits her lowest points? A little nudge here. A little nudge there. Always behind her, the voice of encouragement. Kayla spends all her time listening to voices. Yours has got to be stuck with her by now."

He was so confused. If Ritz wasn't trying to tell him to stay away from Kayla what was he trying to say?

"One day you will understand the difference between fate and magic. Until then, enjoy your evening."

"What's the difference?" Caleb asked as Ritz turned his back on him and started to head off.

"In this current moment, there isn't one. Given Aralot's will, your heart will shatter. When it does… well. You can always come see me. I've been there before. There's still room for you among the Colts. Anytime."

Ritz sort of made sense but he really didn't. It was strange that he would ask Caleb to join the Colts for a second time in his life. Strange that he talked to Caleb about shattering and losing people Ritz personally cared about when he had no relationship for a conversation like this. Strange that he thought Kayla was going to drop people down a mountainside. Caleb watched him walk away and then shook his head.

The guy had won! Caleb was supposed to report it when Colts got this close to the ware, and he hadn't done anything of the sort, because he stood there being too confused to say anything. Caleb chuckled over how Ritz confused everyone around him. That's all that conversation was—a way to get himself out of trouble. Caleb had fallen for it big time. He had nothing to worry about where Kayla was concerned. Things were finally looking up for her. She had a dragon. She was away from her mother's constant watch. She had him. No matter what happened with all the politics, he wasn't going to leave her.

Textbooks

Tyler

As much as he wanted to take Coal with him into Aralot, the dragon was too easy to recognize. Everyone in Aralot knew him. So this was a new experience for both him and Flare. He had taken a while to find a bookstore, and she had been rambling things to him about Kayla all day long as she spied on the girl from up above. Kayla and Valiant had moved through various states of class participation all day.

No wedding ring on Kayla. No mention of Tyler. The people in the bookshop didn't seem to know who Tyler was, so his picture hadn't made it out to the masses in Aralot. He was guessing that Kayla was blocking his letters, but she shouldn't have been able to block the one that had gone right to the castle. The Aralot kings were going to learn that Kayla had signed a binding document and then ditched him. Tyler had sent Jack a personal letter as well. Instead of helping Tyler, Kayla was helping everyone else.

Flare had told him that Kayla had fetched a knee brace for a rider that twisted his knee. She had brought allergy medication and distracted a teacher so that a rider could use the bathroom and not be seen late to class.

"Here's one through six," the shopkeeper told Tyler as if he didn't trust the reason why Tyler wanted to buy these books. The man probably thought he was a spy. He practically was one today.

"All of them," Tyler stated again.

"How many ware books should I be getting?" he asked Coal.

"At least eight," Coal answered, even if he was supposed to be asleep. He got woken up a lot and Tyler knew that it didn't bother him, but he was always going to feel slightly guilty about it.

"Stop already. I love spending time with you even when we are apart. Toss the man some more coins and ask for eight."

He pulled out a few more coins but it wasn't the shopkeeper reaching for them. Some thief of a kid reached up to grab his stuff. Tyler barely managed to hang on to his coin sack while he shoved the kid out of the way.

"I can get you them all," the kid declared. "In exchange for that."

"Scram," the shopkeeper ordered.

Tyler put his coins back in his pocket and followed the kid outside. The shopkeeper had already lost his money by not providing those two other books. Maybe the kid knew something.

"You can get me all eight books?" Tyler asked him. He wasn't a scrawny kid, but he was rather dirty. The kid nodded and then ran off. Not wanting to stand around like he was waiting for a kid, Tyler wandered, looking through the other shops, finding himself rather opinionated on the financial state of Aralot. They were doing great.

"Here!"

The kid found him again while Tyler was looking into a rather good-smelling bistro. The books the kid had fetched were not new. They were dogeared and written on with smudges and a few blood stains, but they had the words he needed. The added notes from past instructors were only a bonus. This was better than a new set. The front of each book claimed that they were the property of Brandon Sloan and they looked rather stolen.

"Hide them quick. If the rider finds you with them, he'll beat you up. Riders don't like their things being stolen," Coal advised.

"Thanks a lot, kid." Tyler stashed the books away and passed over the coins, aware that he was being watched by quite a few older individuals. The kid dashed away with one woman calling after him that she was going to tell his mother what he had been up to. Tyler thought he was a fine kid. He quite liked him.

"You'll give those books back," an unfriendly voice demanded.

Tyler spun around, taking in the muscles of the rider wearing red. If Tyler could settle this in a fencing contest, he might be able to get out of it, but he wasn't so sure he could get away from this guy otherwise.

"I bought them," Tyler smiled right before he was knocked off his feet by a dragon that shoved into his back and jumped toward the rider snarling. Valiant! He was in a shrunken form, come to save him! Flare hadn't told him that Valiant had run off.

"That's because he only just did it. He's fast. All I had to say was that he had a friend in town and off he went."

"Many thanks, Flare."

He couldn't hold off this rider or all these townsfolk all at the same time. He wasn't a wimp by a long shot, but these people were trained warriors. He would have been knocked about if it wasn't for Valiant coming to his rescue.

"Get you little…" the rider glared at Valiant as Tyler got back up to his feet.

"Is Kayla going to come too?" Tyler asked hopefully.

Valiant rambled something to the rider that had him shaking his head, but the unlucky man took his glare with him and blessedly left. Tyler might not be a scary force, but Valiant sure was.

"No," Valiant answered Tyler's question as he turned around and blew Tyler with warm air. He hummed at him next and pressed his small head into Tyler's stomach so that Tyler could rub his nose.

"Never?" Tyler questioned. "I need to see her. Did you remind her to show up for the meeting because she wasn't there."

Valiant looked into Tyler's eyes and then curled up on the ground. He did that whenever he was facing something he didn't like.

"Nice," Tyler huffed. "When Valiant? I'm not waiting around forever. Tell her to come see me."

"No," Valiant told him again. He even opened up his eyes to say it. It looked like even Valiant was trying to keep her away from him. That made it all harder.

"And why exactly am I left waiting?"

Pg. 210

Valiant gave him an answer that he couldn't understand. Tyler looked into the air wondering if Flare was close enough to hear the dragon speech to translate for him, but he couldn't see her.

"And that means…"

"It means you'd better get out of here soon before Brandon comes back with his team," the woman who had screamed at the kid advised. "He'll do it too. You'd better hurry."

That wasn't what Valiant had said, but Tyler did get the message that he needed to leave. He had gotten what he had come for, and he didn't want to lose it. He looked in the direction that Brandon Sloan had run off and made a face. He needed these books. He had an entire kingdom counting on him to provide information on how to interact with the dragons in their heads.

"I will see you both later. Do remind her that she forgot about me," Tyler said, as he took off in a direction away from the ware where he could meet up with Flare again.

Valiant's snort behind him wasn't helpful. Tyler couldn't hear Valiant's thoughts, but he did know that Kayla had not forgotten about him by a sound like that. She didn't want to see him, even if Valiant didn't mind. The girl had cold feet. Not that he could blame her really. They didn't have dragon wares in Vankerdale. She couldn't train Valiant there because they had no teachers.

If only he had more time, he would have risked going into the ware and talking to Kayla himself. Perhaps she knew of a teacher that he could hire. Maybe she had built up a team at the ware that would follow her across the border. She probably thought it best to pass her classes before losing all this knowledge too.

"*How many years would that take her?*" Tyler asked Coal.

"*The King's Ware starts at level six so between two and three more years.*"

Way too long. If he didn't have a team of angry riders after him, he'd really head into the ware for Kayla's answers. He couldn't risk it now though. He had to get out of here. He was no match against a team of Aralot. The books he now carried would go a long way to helping him change that. Maybe if Tyler could meet Conner again, the man would volunteer to teach Kayla the dragon skills she was ditching Tyler to learn.

Night Class

Caleb

"Goodnight, CJ4!" Kayla called to him as she headed into her room for once instead of sneaking out of the ware.

"Night, Princess," he hollered back, suddenly loving the name his mom picked for him. He'd always hated the name Caleb because he thought it should belong to Grant. Now he wouldn't trade his name for anything. Kayla had given it to him as a nickname, and it was the sweetest part of his day so far.

"So… whenever you're ready. I've got all night," Caleb told Valiant who was watching Kayla walk off. She could head out with a smile even if her dragon hadn't been in a working mood again today. Caleb had been trying to get Valiant to do one thing and one thing only for most of the day. Caleb wasn't changing his mind. The dragon was going to get up there and practice side-by-side flying. Instead of flying today he had rolled around, ran off, slept, and cheekily grinned at them while he did nothing. It was frustrating to wait, but it had taken sixteen years for Kayla to start talking to him. It couldn't take Valiant that long to agree to fly beside another dragon in unison.

Caleb had at least come prepared for his extended stay. During the two-hour rest break, he had put the magic book from Kayla into his backpack. He took it out now and started reading from where he had left off. As much as he liked reading about magic his mind was wandering. Tomorrow was his classes day for scout duties, so they were going to be up in the air most of the day watching everyone else. Constant flying was harder on dragons than people, so Caleb had worked the people rather well today and been lax on the dragons.

Valiant couldn't participate in scout duties tomorrow unless he was going to fly beside another dragon. Caleb didn't know what he was going to do with him. What he really wanted to do was leave him on the ground and take Kayla up on Warner instead. Then he'd get a full day just him and her as they watched over the ware.

"Hello," Valiant chirped at him.

"Hi," Caleb replied slowly, because it was ever so hard to tell if he was talking with Valiant or Kayla. He didn't want Kayla being the one flying the route tomorrow. He wanted Valiant to do it for himself. The dragon rambled off something to him so Caleb looked over at Warner who was up in the air practicing drops again.

"He asked you if you were going to draw Kayla so he could watch."

"I'm not drawing. I'm waiting for you to fly beside another dragon."

Valiant snorted out his disappointment, but at least it was a good indication that it was really him. Kayla wouldn't ask him to draw.

The soft sound of a dragon landed behind Caleb followed by icy air that shot over him and onto Valiant. Caleb spun around to tell Sparkle that Valiant couldn't play with her tonight until he did his homework, but it wasn't her. It was Mr. Grumpy instead. This was going to mess up his plans, because he felt uncomfortable telling the giant magic producing dragon to leave.

Valiant didn't say anything verbal to Mr. Grumpy, but the two rose to the sky together so Caleb slid his book back into his bag to watch. Side-by-side flying. Valiant was being really picky, but he was up there now that it was evening and his friend had come to call.

"Okay, Valiant scout duties tomorrow will be a long loop. You'll start low and then gradually get higher as you trade places with the other scout teams. You'll need to match your speed with the dragon beside you. This is not a race."

It looked remarkably easy since it was Mr. Grumpy matching himself more to Valiant's pace than the other way around. Caleb didn't think that Mr. Grumpy would be around tomorrow, since he was rather unpredictable, but for now Valiant had passed. Hazaah! It hadn't taken all night.

Caleb looked back down from the air to find that Vermelo Cluster was standing at the edge of the field looking up watching the flight. It made Caleb wonder how long the man had been there, because Caleb had turned in his most recent reports. Well, Kayla had turned them in for him, so if Vermelo was after Kayla's riding skills again, Charles wouldn't need to make anything up.

Then again, maybe Vermelo was watching to see how Valiant's skills were coming along. It was rather unusual to see Vermelo in the ware, so other riders were finding excuses to lean against buildings and watch as if something exciting was happening. Caleb wasn't sure if anything exciting was supposed to happen, but Reed made an appearance next. He came charging through a gap in the current scout's flight pattern entering easily since it was now well known that Kayla flew him. His light green coloring made him easy to spot, and while he came alone, he was followed. Two other dragons dove down behind him chirping out words to the scouts as they came.

"They said that they are friends with Valiant," Warner provided. *"I've never seen them before."*

Caleb hadn't either. One of the dragons was a mature wild blue night dragon and the other was a brown dragon with unusual blue eyes. Warner flew in closer as Valiant started talking to them and managed to learn the dragon's names. The night dragon was Norber and the brown dragon was Halfax. Kayla was the one who was supposed to know them, and it was hard to argue against that since she wasn't there. Valiant didn't have a problem with them flying near him though, so Caleb shifted his way across the field and took a chance.

"Can we run the triangle formation?" he asked.

It was an attack formation used to split up tight groups of other dragons in the air. Caleb expected Mr. Grumpy to not acknowledge that Caleb existed, since ice dragons would only take orders from one to five people in their entire lives, but Mr. Grumpy was the first one leaving Valiant's side to create the front point of the triangle. If they were handling this formation in a real attack that was exactly where Caleb would place him so he could ice bomb everyone. To see the uncontrollable ice dragon responding to him so quickly left Caleb smiling. One to five people. Was he one of the five that an ice dragon would respect? That was remarkable.

Valiant tried to sneak into the back of the triangle. Caleb laughed at him and placed him on the side where his spells wouldn't

Pg. 216

hit his fellow dragons in front of him as he shot them out. He had Reed on the other side and the two wild dragons in the back. Caleb glanced toward Vermelo again who still had his eyes in the air. Caleb was feeling rather good about Valiant's current progress. He was actually listening right now.

Mr. Grumpy was trying to go slow to not outpace the others and they were trying to go fast as they charged at the invisible air blockade. Crash. This was exactly why Valiant needed to practice flying with a team. Knowing how to fly a formation in theory wasn't the same as doing it in real life. Caleb got Warner to join him and he had the dragon's fly it again. Caleb called out corrections to the dragons in the air as he hovered on Warner. He hesitated giving direct orders to Mr. Grumpy because ice dragons were known to blast at people who told them directly what to do. He had to risk it though when Mr. Grumpy needed to hold his tail higher. The dragon had passed his required years of training, but that had been ages ago, and he had been locked up for years afterward and then left wild after that. He was getting lax on his tail work.

"I wouldn't tell this to just anybody, but Mr. Grumpy's real name is Bantin. If you use his name, he's more prone to do what you ask," Warner told him. *"Whisper it though. He doesn't like people knowing."*

Caleb smiled at the expert dragon tip and whispered his instructions. "Don't take this the wrong way, Bantin, but your tail needs to be up! You've got a forty-five-degree angle there. I need to see sixty-five. As Shilo would say it, spear that sun."

Shilo had been the dragon's trainer and the only person in the world that Mr. Grumpy was reported to have listened to. Bantin growled at Caleb for his correction, but he didn't shoot ice in his direction. He sent Caleb a burst of icy frost instead, and then got his tail where it needed to be. Not bad. Not bad at all for correcting a beast like that.

The lesson continued with Caleb directing the dragons in formations that Valiant had been ignoring for quite some time. Riven joined their team, evening out the numbers, and while Caleb didn't like leading a class that included Prince Tristan's dragon, he was more concerned with the two wild dragons in the back. Norber and Halfax listened to him too easily. It was like they were used to taking human orders, which wasn't characteristic of a wild dragon. If he ventured a guess here, these two were dragons that Kayla knew from a secretly bonded Colt, which meant that he was teaching a Colt somewhere how to pull off level six formations. At least he was until Valiant decided he was done learning and dropped to the ground, laughing at all the others who were still willing to work.

"Come on, Pal. I just need one good night out of you," Caleb complained while Valiant hummed at something inside his head and ignored them. Kayla. What was she doing? She was supposed to be asleep. If Valiant was laughing, Caleb was guessing that she wasn't anywhere close to being asleep, even if she should be tired. Caleb lowered to the ground too, and climbed off Warner to get directly in Valiant's face.

"Ignore Kayla. She's a buzz in your head. She's not the only thing in there. I need you to focus, Valiant."

Valiant still wasn't having it. He wasn't curled up into a ball, but he had stopped listening again. His features were alert, but only alert to what Kayla was up to and nothing else. He didn't blink at Caleb at all. Bantin gave him an icy blast of air trying to get him to pay attention. It did absolutely nothing but give Caleb chills. Valiant dug his claws into the ground and hummed again. Caleb scanned the area.

He was still being watched by Vermelo. There were still a few riders out that should have been in bed hours ago. Caleb looked up into the air trying to keep his own focus. He was currently training a Colt or two, the prince's dragon, the only magical ice dragon, and a dragon from Vankerdale. It was a rather impressive group. This was the most unique training group Caleb had ever heard of.

Blue flashes. Valiant wasn't training because Kayla was reading up on some new spell and the thought of it was more enticing than listen to Caleb. It was a rather fancy spell too. From out of nowhere appeared a very alert and rather startled waist-high dark-brown dwarf dragon beside Valiant.

He was adorable! With a wide face, clear yellow eyes, and a smooth coiled tail, the dragon looked like a hatchling. Caleb knew Merlock instantly, but he had never met him. The only people who had ever seen this dragon were those that were allowed inside the castle.

Caleb had heard from his lessons that dwarf dragons spat tar, only respected you if you smelled good to them, and never got larger than the size of a newborn. Their tails were like snake coils, so flexible that they could turn door handles, and so strong that they could snap you in half.

Merlock scuttled around in a full circle to see where he had landed. As a lover of the dark himself, he rarely venturing out into the open. He hissed at Valiant for bringing him there and then hummed at Caleb. Caleb had no idea what to do with a dwarf dragon. The animal butted his head into the side of Caleb's shins. Merlock proceeded to rub his head on his legs returning again and again to Caleb's pocket where the magical fox statue that Kayla had given him rested.

Caleb shoved Merlock's head away when he felt brave enough to do so, all too aware that most human and dragon life around him was staring at him, watching the rare sight of the dwarf dragon. This whole thing was mind boggling. *No one* trained dragons like this. Why did Valiant think Caleb was good enough to train rare breeds? Here he was with three rare dragons all at once.

"Not for you," Caleb stated, clamping a hand over his pocket to keep Merlock away from it. Merlock tilted his head to the side and let out a very deep hum, the kind that was only used around mating season. Caleb felt rather confused.

"My best guess is that Merlock loves the smell of magic," Warner thought to him.

Excellent guess. That would mean that he would absolutely love working with two other magical dragons. However, Caleb had been told that Merlock couldn't fly, so they would have to learn a formation on the ground, where Valiant currently was refusing to fly.

"Okay, fine," Caleb relented.

He looked back out at the waiting dragon group in the air and rolled his eyes on Valiant's smirk. It was just too tempting to try to find a formation with three rare breeds. As far as he knew, Merlock had never trained at anything at all.

"We'll run a ground formation." This was probably a bad idea, but Caleb really wanted to see that dwarf dragon tail in action. "You'll have to listen to everything I say." He glanced at Mr. Grumpy who surprised him with a smile. Maybe none of them could avoid the temptation of playing with Merlock.

Caleb leaned over and whispered his instructions to Merlock, who agreed to participate if Caleb would give him a snack. Caleb had to laugh at the way that Merlock communicated his wishes. He was very clear and agreeable, making him the best thing that Caleb could use to throw up against a team of otherwise very clever dragons. Caleb agreed to provide Merlock with a snack, and the small critter shot away from him to say hello to the dragons he was going to be secretly knocking over. It was particularly interesting to watch Merlock reach Bantin. Not a single snarl came at the ice dragon. The beastly dragon turned all shades of loveable as he hummed at the smaller but older dragon rubbing around his legs.

"That's remarkable," Caleb voiced. There were a lot of dragons that Bantin refused to work with. The same as Valiant, but here was a team that could coordinate themselves together with a little time and become something rather impressive.

Caleb gave his signal to Merlock to loop around, guessing that since the old dragon had worked with King Gladius that he would be well aware of basic hand signals. Merlock was, but he wasn't the only one taking on the signal as if it was for him. All the dragons instantly understood the sign and rotated, causing Caleb to laugh. These dragons knew way more than he was giving them credit for, even the Colt bonded dragons. That meant that he could push them into complicated formations because they would be able to handle anything he shouted or signed at them.

With a large grin, he dove all in now that Valiant was done testing out his new spell and had his head back in the lesson. Caleb had the team running switchbacks through each other, trying to avoid stepping on Merlock who couldn't help but laugh every time his tail snagged their legs and toppled them over.

When they got better at avoiding Merlock on the ground, Caleb had them run through some of the hardest formations in existence, and then sent them up to the air to practice. Merlock wasn't left out. Caleb had the small dragon jumping between dragon backs in place of a human rider. It was the perfect solution for him. Merlock loved it, and if one of the dragons messed up and missed catching him, Merlock was fine spreading out his wings and gliding back down to the ground without injury. He jumped around thrilled out of his scales to be flying.

"On behalf of that little guy, I thank you," Vermelo said, coming up to stand beside Caleb. "I don't think he's been able to fly for over fifty years. You just made his dreams come true."

Caleb hadn't forgotten that Vermelo was around, but it was still strange to see his onlookers and stranger still that Vermelo thought he could step onto a training field during a class and interrupt the instructor.

"Merlock's loving it isn't he? I'm still a little hesitant over those wild dragons."

Vermelo looked at Reed, which Caleb supposed could be the more deadly dragon, given that Reed was hanging around until his missing rider turned up. Reed was the one dragon who couldn't understand the hand signals as quickly, but the other dragons chirped the answers to him, and once learned, it was always learned. It was those Colt dragons that had Caleb curious. He didn't feel as threatened by the dragon from Vankerdale. Reed was acting on his own. Norber and Halfax had been sent in by some clever scheming Colts who realized that Valiant would stick up for them.

"The important part about tonight is that there are dragons willing to put their differences aside to work together," Caleb said. "There are a lot of ware born dragons that would refuse to fly beside a wild born one. These dragons respect each other and all of them seem to adore Merlock."

"King Klavian doesn't. Merlock gives him nightmares, but you didn't hear that from me," Vermelo whispered. "What do you think about Mr. Grumpy?"

"I'm honestly surprised that he showed up, and even more amazed that he listened to me."

"I'm not," Vermelo told him. "There are some people that have all the makings of being a legendary dragon trainer. Dragons can sense the extraordinary. You look at any group of dragons, Caleb, and you know exactly what to tell them. You may be in your early years yet, but I swear that you're going to revolutionize the world."

"That's a bit much," Caleb laughed. "My end goal is to train Valiant. He thrives on the new and novel."

"Name one other person that successfully trained a spellbinding dragon. There aren't any. And ice dragons? They will only work for the best. As for dwarf dragons, no one has ever gotten Merlock to join a class before. Trust me, Jack has tried plenty of times."

"It's crazy tonight, I know." Caleb rubbed the back of his neck and then laughed when that caused the flying dragons to nearly crash into each other, trying to interpret his signal. He gave them a real signal and had them mix up their positions so that Reed was beside Norber, Valiant beside Halfax, and Mr. Grumpy beside Riven. Merlock ran to the tip of Riven's tail and jumped onto Norber's back, still happily singing that he was up in the air. Caleb was going to have to draw this. No one would believe it otherwise. He was training three rare dragons tonight as if he could pick out how to make them all happy.

He watched them pass each other. Merlock jumped across on the new dive, and then Caleb called them down to land before the dragons got too tired. Half the team was composed of day dragons after all. They were awake past their bedtime, and the other half would be woken up multiple times during the day for additional work. He didn't want to tire them out so badly that they didn't come back to work with him again. If every night could be as amazing, he would feel like he was doing a great job as a section leader.

Despite his hesitations over what he was really training, he was loving this class as much as all those smiling dragon faces out there. No teacher got wing work like this out of a dragon unless the dragon was confident that his bonded rider could handle the pressure of what he was learning. That's why it was important that riders and dragons trained together, but in these dragon's cases, they couldn't.

He knew in his gut that not all of these dragons were linked to Kayla. She was responsible for keeping Valiant in a good enough mood to listen, but that's where Caleb drew the line on that. All the other dragons had been rambling to somebody else about how thrilled they were to get a direct class in a ware.

Caleb looked over all of them yet again trying to pick out which dragons looked the most distracted. Riven for sure. He was looking toward the castle, humming at something that Tristan thought to him. Reed was sitting down sulking as a result, because he wasn't bonded. Merlock was rolling over Reed trying to cheer him up, so those two didn't have bonds. Norber and Halfax were trickier. They had come in together, already a team, so Caleb wasn't sure if it was a pair of Colt siblings that had been bonded or perhaps a married couple. The dragons were bonded though. He could tell by the way they both paused to listen before chirping to Valiant and taking off together to leave and meet their secret riders.

Mr. Grumpy likewise had thoughts running through his head—positive ones. The dragon was back to smiling, pleased with his efforts to work in the class, which meant that Mr. Grumpy hadn't really been listening to Caleb tell him what to do. He had been obeying the voice in his head telling him to listen. Caleb shifted on his feet uneasy. Bantin didn't have fangs to bond. Something creepy was going on here. Someone very close to him was right now thinking to the ice dragon, having watched this class. He didn't think it was Kayla because she was totally talking to Valiant.

Valiant went down in his huddle, hiding his wingtips. He only curled up in that particular posture when his wings were glowing and he didn't want others to know. He would flash them at Kayla to make her smile at him. Without her being around, he wouldn't show anyone his joy. He was a blocked off world without Kayla. On that note, Caleb had never gotten Valiant to work so well for him before.

"You going to bed?" Vermelo asked him.

"No way. Kayla's coming back. That summoning spell that brought Merlock out tonight had to be a new spell," Caleb remarked.

As her section leader, Caleb was supposed to get Kayla in trouble for sneaking out so much. He just couldn't do it. Kayla had figured out how to get Valiant happy enough to work. If his mind was entertained enough with a new spell, he would participate. Caleb logged that information away, because if he could find something to entertain the dragon with, or even an older spell that could make him laugh, he could get this spellbinding dragon working.

Mr. Grumpy shifted his head to follow an invisible figure. Totally Kayla, because Valiant was refusing to give her away by looking at her, but he was already humming at the thought of her coming to see him. Merlock could smell her too. He rolled off Reed and jumped along behind her, chattering incessantly to her in dragon speech. Kayla's voice chattered back in the dragon language and soon she was holding a conversation with Merlock, Reed, Mr. Grumpy and Valiant that human brains couldn't interpret.

"Got the goods on what she's saying?" Caleb asked, looking behind him to Warner, but his dragon was fast asleep and wouldn't be able to interpret anything at all. Caleb looked back at the dragon huddle just in time. Kayla dropped her invisible spell, which had Merlock grabbing at her legs with his tail. He wrapped himself around her as much as he could and sat there humming at her like he would never let her go. Valiant snorted at him, but he was incredibly patient with other dragons claiming his rider like this. In that way, he was the opposite of an ice dragon.

Kayla looked at Vermelo, letting her words shift into recognizable sounds again. "I'll make sure Merlock gets back to the castle if you want to head off to bed," she offered.

"I appreciate everything you do," Vermelo replied, giving her a nod.

Mr. Grumpy made a chirp of agreeance and that's when it all clicked. Vermelo! Mr. Grumpy was bonded to Vermelo! That was illegal. All ice dragons belonged to the king by right, although Tia got away with having one because she was the rightful heir to the throne. Kayla had to know this already for Valiant to agree to train with him. She caught the realization of the bond run across Caleb's face. She put a finger to her mouth to ask him to keep quiet, and winked at Caleb after Vermelo turned his back.

"Loved class tonight," Kayla spoke to him. "Wish I had seen it firsthand. You are a fabulous dragon trainer."

"Wish you'd tell me who I'm training," he spoke back. She had to know the rider of every one of those dragons that Valiant had accepted. He received things that Kayla accepted. Unfortunately, Kayla would only give him a shrug. Then she fell back to her classic distraction technique by reminding him that he owed Merlock a snack. At the mention of the distraction, Merlock dashed away from her toward the kitchens in anticipation. It was easy to see why Jack loved this small dragon so much. He was always so agreeable. It was a shame that he hadn't joined a training group until now.

Caleb started for the kitchen to grab a meat lovers snack thinking about how everything had gone over. He couldn't see the end result of his efforts, but he had just as much blind faith in Kayla as all those dragons. They'd follow her directions anywhere, and it was up to him to teach them the right way to defend her. Behind every keeper stood a dedicated teacher. Perhaps Vermelo was right. He would revolutionize the way dragons were trained, because he got the opportunity to bask in the company of rare dragons.

Jungle
Kayla

*"Y*ou are the funniest human in the world!"* Valiant laughed at her for messing up her own class today. She had finally figured out how to get Valiant in the mood to fly. All she had to do was teach him a new spell, and he could be in the mood for all sorts of things. Today they were both ready to be in class, except that Kayla was going to mess it all up because of what she had found last night in the magical library.

It had been rather startling to step into the room and find a new human within. The man was a mess of sobs, and she didn't really blame him since he was burned with tar as well. The conversation had been remarkable.

"Can I help you?" Kayla had asked.

"I'm going to die," he had responded.

"Actually, you went through a portal and those make everyone feel that way, but you're going to live."

"No. I'm going to die. I can't go back and face…" The stranger broke off and sobbed.

"You're from Wisteria, aren't you? You don't look old enough to be King Anthony, so I'm assuming that you're Prince Lester. You found the entrance to the library really fast. I only just sent our dwarf dragon to get the entrance back open for you."

"Aralot. Get away from me."

That was as far as the conversation had gotten because Prince Lester was still crying his heart out. Kayla had silently healed his wounds with a spell. She had gone to check on the portal that she had told Merlock to look into, and found that the tar was indeed out of the way. In its place was a bunch of dwarf dragon eyes, blinking at her in the dark, along with a mangled body that those dragons were eating. Kayla hadn't stayed too long after seeing that.

She had spent her time trying to find a spell that would get Prince Lester back home without needing to risk heading through the dwarf dragon herd in his way a second time. Valiant had tested out the summoning spell she had found on Merlock, and claimed that it would work, so all Kayla needed to do was get Valiant into the magical library to send the prince home. He had lost whoever came with him. She wasn't sure who that was, but it was obvious that the prince was very distraught about it. Kayla wanted to get back into the library before anyone else realized who had been left in there.

On that note, Valiant blasted her with a spell that froze her feet, earning a glare from Caleb while the dragon continued to laugh hysterically at Kayla's plan.

"Bad dragon," Caleb expressed, putting his hands on his hips. "I didn't ask you to do anything at all. I need Kayla to perform scout duties."

The other dragons in the class were already up in the air flying around. As lazy as Valiant appeared to be most of the time, this was a perfect duty to get him to skip. Valiant couldn't help himself. He rolled over from laughing so hard, and since he was laughing, Kayla was starting to pick up the giggles too.

"Don't you encourage him," Caleb moaned at her. "You need to be able to scout! Get him in a better mood, will you? Think of a spell that will—"

Kayla missed the rest of the words, because Valiant rolled back over and hit her with the transporting spell. It worked! She could picture Caleb on the field getting frustrated with Valiant for sending her away, but she was thrilled about it. Valiant had placed her right in front of the cave to the secret library portal. All she needed to do now was go inside and check to see if the Wisterian prince was still there while she waited for Valiant to show up. Valiant had to act up just a little bit more so he could escape.

"Act? Please. All I have to do is curl into a ball and Caleb will turn his back on me. Then I will disappear. It's perfect! Let's ditch class tomorrow too!"

"No. We can't do this all the time, and we won't be gone forever. I just need to take care of that crying prince!"

"Why you?" Valiant grumbled.

"Because everyone else would start asking him political questions and turn his appearance into some impromptu business meeting. I doubt he wants to deal with that when he's already feeling so sad."

"Ah. Protector of the heartbroken as always," Valiant responded. *"Just tell me when and I shall join you. Although no one has proven that a dragon can fit in there, and if I were to stay, I would like to borrow your fingers to peruse books, please."*

Kayla shook her head as she entered the library again. It still struck her as completely weird to swap herself with Valiant, even if she had grown up with the idea of it happening her entire life. For most riders, it was the occasional swap in order for a rider to spy better. It wasn't anything like what she had going on in her life.

"How are you doing now?" Kayla asked, spotting Prince Lester again. It didn't look like anyone else had noticed him in there yet because he glanced up at her, holding a book in his hand and a worried expression on his face. Now that he was in a better frame of mind, she could see him for who he was. Prince Lester had wavy short black hair, deep-set eyes, and an ache in his soul that Kayla could make out without even trying.

"I snuck out of class to come check on you. I brought you breakfast, and an idea to help you get back home when you're ready to leave. Do you need a tour of the room? I can give you a rundown of the sections to help you find the spell that you're looking for."

"What are you? The bookkeeper?" Prince Lester asked her. He looked down at the book in his hand and tossed it to her as if she would put it away for him. Kayla caught it and set it on the floor, not about to find its place. The room had rows of books stacked up to the ceiling with golden ladders that could slide around the sections to help people reach the higher books. There were too many possibilities.

"The books put themselves away. They can't leave the library either so don't bother trying. I'm Kayla Brixton. There isn't a bookkeeper. Only rulers of a kingdom can enter the library."

She pulled out a breakfast sandwich that she had made this morning and handed it over, smiling when he took it and hungrily took a bite.

"It's your first time in the library so is there anything I can help you find? I tend to find that those who have to work really hard to get in here have a really strong reason to find a particular spell."

"How about a spell that restores to me something that I have lost?"

Kayla pointed to the right section and then shook her head glancing at the portal. "It won't restore your lost friend that the dwarf dragons ate."

"No idea what you're talking about," Prince Lester claimed, moving in the direction she had given him. Kayla frowned at his back. Here she was trying to make a good impression and help him out and he was being prissy. Maybe it was just denial. He didn't want to admit what he had lost getting into here.

"Was it hard to get in? It looked hard. I'm sorry that our dwarf dragon wasn't around when you tried to enter. Merlock would have helped you. He knew King Gladius, who gave him torture, so now he's a big sweetheart unless he's protecting something that people shouldn't touch. Then he gets a little bit pushy, but he'd never have hurt you. Maybe those other dwarf dragons thought that they had to protect this location."

"This is a forbidden room only for those who wish to lose their souls to the forces of evil."

The way that King Lester said that was so harsh that Kayla gave him a shrug and stepped away from him. He clearly thought that he had made the worst choice of his life to come here. No wonder Wisteria was never seen in this room.

"You obviously risked a great deal then, sacrificing your life and soul in order to help your subjects. What's bothering you?"

"You at the moment. Everything about you," King Lester snapped back. "You personally have everything I am after."

"Which is...?"

"Another one of those sandwiches."

Yeah right. "All out, but you can have this." Kayla passed him a field snack, which he took just as fast as the sandwich. She gave him a few more just in case, and then tried to make out his thoughts. She failed so she tried again.

"What sort of thing have you lost? I can narrow down your search for you. If it's abstract like your mind or a memory—"

"Miss Brixton," the prince cut her off. "I am not willing to make myself eviler than I currently am. Stop trying to make me use you against yourself. You will see it as a betrayal and your evil will turn itself upon my kingdom in a rage that we can't afford to face. You use magic like it is part of the air, heedless of the damage you are inflicting upon your soul for doing so. Leave me alone. I will find the answer on my own without you."

He was very charming. Kayla rolled her eyes at him. "I am very aware of which spells will damage a soul. I have studied that sort of thing in detail before. I don't use those kinds of spells. Are you trying to cast a spell at Aralot? We will figure it out and stop you."

"That's exactly what I'm talking about. I've heard all about you. You are the worst human alive. You were born from magic and you live inside curses all day long as they control your actions and eat at your soul. Anything you speak and think can be used against a man, and you tear down your enemies like they're old posters on the wall."

"I beg your pardon! I do not!" Kayla took a few steps backward. She had never been good at confrontations like this. The Colts would testify of that to anyone who asked. It looked like some Wisterian spy had passed along her news. Only it was all wrong and spun around like she was an evil sorcerer. She already felt bad enough about the Peytons on her own without help from the Wisterian prince. He had a very negative view about the use of magic. Maybe that was why Wisteria had been blocked off from the entrance of the library to begin with. The only thing any of those rulers would be looking for if they came looking was a curse. They thought all magic was evil.

Aralot didn't need their curses. Kayla crossed her arms at the prince, giving up on being nice back to him and cast a spell at him. He froze and glanced down at his body trying to figure out how she was damaging his soul.

"The only thing I did was put a spell on you to tell the truth," Kayla told him. "Are you trying to curse Aralot?"

"No," he answered right away making her frown at him even more.

"Then what curse are you trying to find?"

"A spell to regain all the lost dragons from Wisteria," he answered. "Now take your curse off me. I don't need a damaged soul as shattered as your own."

She wasn't broken, but it didn't look like he was going to believe her even if she believed him now. She didn't like the spell he was looking for. It would be a conditional spell, and depending on the condition, it could make her lose Valiant. Prince Lester could demand back all the dragons that had ever been born inside of Wisteria, regardless of where they had grown up or where they wanted to currently live. There was no way she was going to hand that spell over to him, because yes, she would be very mad at him for taking her dragon away. The best way to handle this was scoot Prince Lester back out of the library so he could continue to rule across the ocean far away from her. Then she could pretend to be nice to him while she wanted to flick him on the nose.

"The only way to get your cooperation is to entreat your very limited small pool of friends for help so that they can work around your vileness and restore order to the world you have broken by existing," Prince Lester continued. "You entice toward yourself the very thing Wisteria needs."

Her dragon. She needed to take that truth spell off him quick. His honesty was a bit much. There was no way she would ever get a personal invitation to enter Wisteria. Everyone there thought she was a disease. Better distract him.

"Who was it who died to the dwarf dragons?"

"My father," Prince Lester answered, before he shut his eyes pained.

Kayla took her spell down and stood there in silence. King Anthony was dead, chomped by a horde of dwarf dragons who were trying to keep him out of this library. Somehow Prince Lester survived, and the man would probably have nightmares about it forever. Maybe his father had sacrificed himself at the last moment. Kayla thought it was stupid for them both to have tried to gain entrance to the library at the same time if they knew it could damage them. They risked everything to get a spell to bring back dragons. Were they so low on dragons that other predators were terrorizing villagers without dragons to maintain a population control?

"Look. I'm sorry, King Lester. I am pained over your grief. The Peyton's were just stopped from stealing dragons. I can't have you start up dragon theft now."

"Those dragons should be ours!" he screamed at her. "It was the Peyton's who stole them all! They refuse to give them back, and I am very well aware that you will be the same."

"Because you've asked me?" Kayla shook her head at him. "King Lester, I am around dragons all day long, and for some of them it would be very hard for them to travel back across the ocean without an adequate surface area to land on and rest. I'll tell you what I will do to help you and then I will send you home."

"Do not touch me. You leave me alone!"

"I am going to cast a spell," Kayla said, ignoring his fears, "that makes it so that any dragon that wants to return to Wisteria has the necessary wing strength to make the flight. I shall start having the dragons pass the word along that those who would like to return to their native homeland may do so. In this way, you won't need to stain your soul for using magic yourself, and it gives the dragons a choice and a means to accomplish your wish. Forcing them back is evil magic that I will not cast for you."

"You are a witch. A vile vile witch. Action shall be taken to reclaim—"

Kayla wasn't listening. She stepped through the portal into Wisteria so that she could get her plan ready to send Prince Lester home. She was going to have Valiant do this part so he could see his old home, but after learning what the prince was after, she was changing her mind. Valiant could stay safely where he was, and she would step out into the unknown jungle. To do that, she was going to have to get past all those dwarf dragon eyes. They were still staring at the portal in the dark just waiting.

"Did you have to eat King Anthony?" Kayla asked them in dragon speech. "Now you've got Prince Lester a nervous wreck. I am taking him home, and you won't be getting in my way or you'll be sorry. I need to see the start of this cave."

She took a step forward, holding a ball of magic in her hand for light and protection against the nasty nature of these dragons. She was just about to cast a spell to stick them all to the wall with their mouths shut when one of the dragons answered her.

"The kings of Wisteria have only ever sought after magic to do evil. Eating King Anthony was necessary. We missed the prince, but we shall get him too before he can misuse magic. We are the guardians of the glow, miss. What do you think you're going to do with that force?"

"Send the prince home away from the temptation of doing evil," Kayla answered. "Maybe I'll put up a spell that will stop future kings from entering your home if they have harmful intentions."

"But I like eating kings," one of the dwarf dragons admitted.

"King Anthony was disgusting," another one spoke.

Kayla shook her head at them, and took a few more cautious steps forward, looking around at the black tarred tunnels they had created. She could navigate Merlock's lair without a problem so she was hoping she could navigate this place too. She headed in the direction that would feel more like the exit to dwarf dragons. The family of small dragons didn't bother to send tar at her, but the floor was very sticky with it already. Her boots were going to need a good scrubbing after this.

"Don't put up a spell to stop them!" a dragon pled and then shrank away from her when she glanced in the dragon's direction. It had to be a really long time since these dragons had seen anyone use magic, and the last person to have done so would have been Gladius as he stole away Merlock's mate and killed her off. That was a very sad thought, so Kayla pushed it aside and kept walking.

"How about a spell that will warn them of physical death if they are coming in search of a curse?"

"No! We will eat them all! They come in here to kill us. They toss in poison to sour our stomachs. They were killing us off for months before they came down, thinking that we were all dead. All kings of Wisteria shall be eaten!"

It was a good thing that she wasn't a king of Wisteria then. Kayla located a hole to climb up through and found herself an exit. She was in Wisteria! She had traveled across the ocean and was standing on foreign land. All around her were thick wide trees with branches covering the sky. Beside her was a marker on the top of the ground warning of danger for all who fell into the dark hole. Yeah, they had enough of a warning. Maybe she didn't need to cast any additional spells if they knew what they were getting into already. She probably shouldn't be helping Wisteria, but she knew what it was like to be missing a dragon, so she was going to stick to her plan regardless of King Lester's bad attitude.

One of the dwarf dragons climbed up out of the hole after her. The black creature looked at her hand as if mesmerized by the blue glow that remained in her hand. It hummed at the sight, which caused some other dragon hidden from view nearby to chirp out a curious sound and start creeping closer.

"I have to be able to visualize or see the location I am sending Prince Lester to in order for this spell to work," Kayla told the mini black dragon. She couldn't send the new king back to Wisteria if she had never seen any part of it, so here she was.

There was a good grouping of trees that looked safe enough to send the new king, so she picked that. However, she needed to use more magic than she could hold, so Valiant would be needed to shift into her form so he could see the trees and then cast the spell from afar.

"They failed," a male voice spoke from behind her before she could ask Valiant to swap. Kayla spun around as a group of camouflaged soldiers popped up from the ground and the larger dragon came into view. It was a green dragon, perfect for hiding inside

Pg. 240

the humid jungle that surrounded her. On the dragon's back was a man wearing thick camouflaged layers including a green hat, but the light blue eyes of the man could be seen as well as the wrinkles on his worried face. Kayla used the magic on her hand to pull up a shield, causing the black dragon at her legs to hum again.

"Hello," Kayla said, eyeing all the arrows that could be sent at her in a rather unpleasant way. "Your rulers didn't completely fail. I am of the understanding that King Anthony didn't make it, but Prince Lester did, so I cured him of his wounds, gave him breakfast, and will be sending him back to you even though he's a bit snappy. Very opinionated person, your new King Lester. He said that you were looking for a way to regain a few lost dragons, so as proof that I am not an evil witch, I am going to grant Wisterian dragons the wing strength needed to cross back over the ocean and return to you, right after I free up King Lester."

"It's true then? You control Wisteria's lost spellbinding dragon and you keep him trapped to your side at all times?" the man riding on the dragon asked her. He even got cocky enough to slip off his dragon—he landed poorly—to step up close to her protective spell even if the tar shooting dragon by her feet could still shoot tar through her spell.

"Across the ocean we use the word bonded, not trapped. I don't confine him at all. I don't believe in the stealing or trapping of dragons, unless of course they are being horrible and harming things they shouldn't be destroying. Then maybe I'd trap a dragon to remove him from the area, but that's not the same thing."

"If she kept the spellbinding dragon at her side all the time the dragon would be here right now and our goal would be achieved," the voice of the first soldier spoke back.

Maybe he was a general. In any case, she wasn't going to stand around here all day chatting. She had to get back to class. It sounded like Wisteria's goal wasn't only to regain lost dragons, but Valiant, who would probably entice Bantin to come with him so Valiant could keep his magic source. There was no way she was moving to Wisteria when she was already stuck enough between Aralot and Vankderale. What Wisteria was after was the same thing that Vankerdale had been after. They were trying to take magic away from Aralot. They were never going to succeed.

"Would you like a view?" Kayla asked Valiant.

"A short one. I don't think you should stay there long. They will trap you to reach me. I could never turn on my kingdom like that."

Kayla shrugged. She didn't realize that Valiant had a fondness for Aralot at all, since he had hinted before that he didn't mind Vankerdale and being with King Tyler.

"Home is wherever you are," Valiant told her, and then he shifted their forms so that Kayla found herself looking at the frustrated face of Caleb. To a dragon nose, Caleb didn't smell like citrus. He smelled like minerals; the sort that would be found in a cave full of treasure. Yes, that was it. Caleb smelled like treasure. The thought caused her to hum at him while he glared at her even more.

"Where did you put her? If you don't bring her back in the next two minutes, I'm giving you chores. Don't tell me you can't do them either. You're going to get the ware sparkling clean, wash all the buildings, clean up all the dung—"

Kayla became herself again.

"He's giving out ultimatums. It's chores for you, Pal," Kayla informed him.

"Stop Kayla! You're making me laugh again! I can't cast a spell if I'm laughing this hard! Why is it you that comes up with the plans and everyone else getting in trouble for them? You are so funny!"

It was nice to see that he was still in a good mood. Kayla turned her back on the Wisterian's and dropped back down the tunnel, ignoring the men calling for her to come back and send home their lost dragons. She was already doing that, just without the force they wanted. She ran back through the tunnels hoping that Caleb's two minutes would stretch a bit. Maybe if he saw Valiant casting spells, he would think that he was bringing her back instead of sending King Lester away.

Kayla reentered the magical library and grabbed at King Lester's arm while he screamed and hit at her, unable to break free of her sudden grip or hurt her through the protections. She pulled him back through the portal into his own land, and once he was out of the magical library, Valiant's magical spell converged around him and sent him blissfully away from the guardian dwarf dragons and back onto the surface where he belonged.

"You'll have to walk back. That was exhausting. I'm taking a nap," Valiant declared. *"When I wake up, you're doing chores."*

Hooray for her. If Valiant didn't get the ware clean with spells, she was going to be sore tomorrow as he used her arms to do all the work during the night. It was worth it though. She had successfully saved and put back the king of Wisteria. They were going to need to watch those people. Those Wisterians were up to something.

Snares

Tristan

The answer was clear that it was none of the Brixtons that had turned on him. Tristan had never had such connections before, but Riven could now ask Valiant to ask Sparkle or Pyro where their riders had been during his tar attack. He had gotten locations for Rosa and Anvil and Clark and all the ware leaders by having his dragon ask follow-up questions, all without needing to go around himself to pester people. It was fabulous, or would have been if Tristan wasn't still trying to figure out who was trying to kill him.

Tristan rubbed at one of his eyes that were starting to get blurry from all the late nights he had been pulling. He still didn't believe that the deathtrap had been an accident even if it still looked that way, so he was currently en route to check out the locations of a few Colts who had never liked him. His shoes moved quietly through the woods; Riven trailed behind him flying in the sky.

Tristan had checked the location of his own parents and Vermelo and all the guards in the castle. He had gone through the riders in the ware verifying their claims of where they had been, and it was none of them either. Tristan was left with the result that the perpetrator had to be a Colt. No other person would be able to sound like his dad or devise plans around what could kill him so effectively.

Since the best of the Colts was Ritz himself, a man who had never liked him, Tristan now had Ritz on his radar as a person that could be out to kill him. The only part of this idea that didn't match up was that Ritz would never try to kill Kayla. However, he was cruel enough to try out keeper poison in order to kill off her dragon. Tristan could see that playing out if the man had decided that spellbinding dragons should not be in Aralot or bonded to the princess.

What if Ritz knew about the nightmares and blamed the dragon too? All that talk about time magic from Kayla had Tristan looking into the subject further. The only thing he could find was that time had to be bound and locked in order to mess with it or it would change naturally. Therefore, the curse on Kayla was given to her by some dragon. It didn't necessarily have to be Valiant though. Wisteria wouldn't let anyone into their kingdom. They could have another spellbinding dragon that the past King Peyton had not stolen away from them, and that beast could be smashing Kayla back through time in retribution for her having a dragon she shouldn't have.

It was on those lines that Tristan could see Ritz turning on her to get rid of her dragon. That would make Wisteria ease up on her. Valiant had to be careful. So far nothing more than Sparkle had come at him, but Sparkle could be tricked into creating another dragon deathmatch if Ritz planned it out carefully. He was a very patient killer, not needing to worry about time constraints, because he himself was ageless—another point against him in this spellbinding dragon theory. When had Ritz run into a spellbinding dragon that locked him in time? Valiant was the only dragon of his sort, unless Ritz had been around when SilverWings was born, or perhaps if Ritz had been to Wisteria.

On the day of the incident, the tar in town had gotten a large crack in it, making it necessary to pour in a new stream to fix the hole. That was why it was being dumped from the roof, but the timing, and that dragon battle over his head had been a bit much. No one had been able to explain why the tar got a hole in it in the first place. The only dragon that could have done something like that was Merlock. Merlock didn't usually walk through the town at all. He stayed hidden in his tunnels beneath the castle but those did stretch beneath the town. It was possible that some remodeling below had caused the movement above. Perhaps an intruder had entered Merlock's home and left a torch lit or something, causing him to rage beneath the ground and smash things to put it out. That was Tristan's best guess of that part of the "accident."

Tristan sighed, because he didn't want to go through Merlock's tunnels to ask the dragon why he had been messing up the road. Merlock had a thing against Clusters. He didn't particularly like any of them, and Tristan was included in that dislike. He couldn't go trekking through the dragon's home without getting tar spat in his direction. Merlock wouldn't tell him why he broke up the road, and Tristan didn't believe the event was an accident in the first place. That was why he was out here looking for Colts.

Snap. A rope wrapped around his ankle and then he was being pulled off his feet. He grabbed at a knife to cut off the rope, only to find his arm get snagged in a trap next. This one had metal teeth that dug into his flesh, making him want to pry off that trap first. Snap, snap, snap. He was going through a minefield of traps pulled through them all by that blasted rope on his ankle!

"Can I help?!" Riven screamed at him winging his way closer.

Tristan could hear his dragon speeding up to reach him, but with all the metal snapping on him, he wouldn't want his dragon to step down here and get his feet caught in this too. What he needed to do was slice off the rope so he could stop dragging through all of this. Whoever had set this up, knew what he was doing. A person could kill a dragon like this, or perhaps just Tristan, because before he reached that rope again, he was plunged into a pool of water and a net shoved him below holding him down.

"Tristan!"

Riven was frantically screaming at him, probably trying to figure out how to reach him, because the pond had trees in the way that would prevent a landing, and the traps were horrible. Tristan squirmed trying to hold his breath as he cut. He got the rope off his ankle finally and started in on the net only to feel his center of gravity start to wobble because he hadn't expected the water. He hadn't taken in enough air before he was tossed into the pond. He felt like gasping, and his instincts had him doing just that as he felt a dragon tail slash through the water, snapping apart the net that held him down.

"I'll get you," Riven promised, but his tail was getting snagged, and Tristan could hear Riven's feet getting caught in traps as Tristan's vision started to blur. He blacked out for a moment feeling like every part of him was being suffocated. Riven screamed. Tristan found himself falling on a wooden floor as the traps dug deeper into him.

"Tristan!" Kayla was screaming his name next and it took a moment to orientate himself and figure out why. It wasn't Riven that had told her he was in trouble, even though the dragon could have done so. No, Tristan was currently in the Kings Ware mess hall where he had placed the second half of his bear medallion last night. Charles had caught him putting it on the floor where the King would sit if he came to visit. Hardly anyone used this chair, so Tristan had decided to set up camp to alert him whenever Kayla was getting poison thrown at her so that he could catch the evil-doer in the act. He had saved himself by having someone else attack Kayla. Kayla splashed magic on him to break off the traps as he gasped for air.

"You're safe!" Riven cheered, even if the dragon wasn't. Riven would put himself in the way of anything to save him just as Tristan would put himself in the way to save his dragon's life too. This second death attempt was another close one, and he didn't like it.

"What was it this time or is that a stupid question?" Kayla asked him.

No time for that right now. He was dripping wet with metal traps at his feet, but he jumped up and looked around the room trying to find who could be adding poison to Kayla's food. Caleb had everyone trading trays with her so…

"Who did you just trade with?" he asked.

All the riders were staring at him for suddenly appearing before them, looking like the drowned bait that he was. Maybe the coin idea wasn't his best when he would scare off the poisoner, but he asked his question again. Kayla looked over at a tray she had ditched on the floor in order to run to him. She pointed to a rider that she probably didn't know, but Tristan knew rather well. This man would never do anything to harm a dragon or rider. He was a doctor, and his whole life was spent trying to stop the evils of dragon disease. Somebody must have placed the poison before the man passed over his tray. Tristan would have to do more digging, but he couldn't leave his dragon stuck as he was.

"Can you help Riven?" he asked, turning to Kayla as she crouched by her food waving her hand over it to make it glow orange and discover the poison for herself.

She looked up at him startled as she found out where Riven currently was, and then she ran for the door to go save his dragon. Tristan turned to the tray of food, and then the doctor, and started in on his questions again.

People were going to get tired of him doing this. He could already see the annoyed but compliant looks from all corners of the room. Who was doing this? Kayla was keeping way too quiet about it. She didn't go about raging down everyone's backs as he was doing, but he couldn't let it continue. These threats had to stop. Someone wanted them both gone, and he couldn't place the blame on anyone who would directly benefit from succeeding.

Caleb

Charles plopped the letter down beside Caleb on the breakfast table, and then waited impatiently for Caleb to look over and see what it was. Since the address was missing and the envelope only contained his name, Caleb was guessing that this was the reply from Wisteria about his artwork. He flipped over the envelope noticing how this time Charles hadn't already opened it, and it was stamped with the Wisterian seal. While Aralot used the mythical flower of the mystique, and Vankerdale used the head of a dragon, Wisteria used a set of open bird wings.

It felt like he had just sent off his reply to the contest, but it had been six days ago. It was supposed to take four days for his reply to arrive and another four to send back a response. It looked like Kayla had been right that her Aunt Rosa took an interest in this letter. She must have cast a speed flying spell on Pewter, or had Anvil or even Jack do that, in order to cut the timing of the trip nearly in half.

Caleb glanced behind him at Charles's face. Had he won or was this a notice to tell him that his artwork had been stolen before it could be displayed? Caleb broke open the red seal imagining walking around a city set in the middle of a jungle, entering a holy monastery across the ocean, and bowing to a king. There would be so much to see, so many new pictures to draw and faces to scan. The architecture would be as exotic as the air, and the sounds as exciting as a holiday.

He read the paper as Charles read over one of his shoulders. Mulligan, who had also been passing out the mail today, came to stand behind him and read over his shoulder, curious to see what had Charles's interest. Caleb rubbed at his stubbly face. He wasn't going to get his painting back, and it wasn't because anyone had stolen it. It was because he had won. Him! Against all the greatest artists in Wisteria it was his image that had gotten the most votes. He was rather impressed by that. The paper detailed how the votes had been cast on the anonymously submitted painting just as Ian and August had described. The people over there voted blindly, not knowing that the winner was from out of the kingdom.

Caleb didn't like the hidden catch. If he wanted to collect the prize money, the tour of the castle, and dinner with the king, he had to show up to collect it by tomorrow. There was no way he would be able to do that, even if he did what the paper directed and used the spellbinding dragon in his drawing to bring him.

He knew that there'd be a trap to all of this, and it was right here. Wisteria was trying to get at Valiant. Included in the envelope was a paper for him to write his reply as to whether he was going to show up or not, claiming that no other paper would be accepted. If he didn't send back a correspondence, the king was going to assume that this message had never reached him and would send out an army of dragons to hunt him down. Charles frowned and gave out a short grunt after reading the same thing. Mulligan sat down beside Caleb instead and handed Charles the rest of the mail to pass out giving up on helping him complete the task.

Pg. 252

"Super awesome," Caleb shook his head. "Admit that I won't bring them Kayla's dragon and start a war with Wisteria. This has worked out well, you think?"

"Uh…" Mulligan stared at the words again. "You gave them a picture? I don't think it's a wise thing to start wars, Caleb. You're not…"

"The king?" he asked with a shrug. He knew that, but this was Aralot and its spells hammered down against people who could be used like this. Wisteria had to know that too, so they were picking on him knowing that he interacted with the dragon they were interested in. Caleb slid out the extra piece of paper and wrote his reply.

"I am honored that your kingdom enjoyed my artwork. It was composed with the intention to remind others that even in the darkest of moments there are those around us that still spread light. I regret to inform you that I will not be able to make your deadline to collect the concessional prize, and since the composition was sent as a gesture of peace, you have no reason at all to send over an army. I have received your letters without any hassle involved. Thank you for considering me to participate in your yearly celebrations — Caleb."

He signed his name rather fancy and then glanced up at Charles for his opinion over the whole thing.

"I would have loved to see what you submitted," Charles answered. "It must have been amazing. Congratulations, and if I may say so, Wisteria's ploy was weak."

With that, he turned and walked away. Caleb looked back down at the paper, debating how to address the return envelope when the paper suddenly changed on him.

"The army is still necessary if the dragon is not returned home."

The sentence appeared on the page, causing Mulligan to swear, and Caleb to rapidly scan the room for Kayla before he remembered she was out dining with the queen this morning having skipped quite a few days of princess lessons due to Aria being distracted by whatever it was she worked on in the castle.

"What do I do?" Caleb whispered to Mulligan. Mulligan made a point of locating Tristan who was sitting in the king's chair as if he owned it. He pulled Caleb's paper off the table and onto Caleb's lap as if Tristan's eyes could stretch that far.

"I think you should hide this before Tristan blames you for starting a war," Mulligan whispered. "He'd find some way to make it look like your fault. You should give this to Jack."

The riders that were nearby all glanced over at them before acting suspiciously nonchalant. If Tristan looked over, he was going to know something was up. Caleb slowly slid from the mess hall toward his room with Mulligan trailing behind him. He wasn't supposed to be the one making these kinds of decisions, but he wasn't going to let anyone take Kayla's dragon away from her again. She'd just barely gotten him in her life! They were still working out their kinks and learning how to live with each other. This paper was talking to him right now. He didn't want to wait around for Jack. Caleb was answering this thing. He flung open his bunkroom door, and sat on his bed hastily straightening his blankets and pillow as Mulligan sat down beside him still interested in the outcome.

"The dragon is already home. He is bonded and happy and will not be moving away," Caleb wrote back.

Pg. 254

"Apologies," the paper started to talk to him again.

He was talking to a magical paper! He had no idea who he was even writing to, and this was rather creepy. He found his left hand reaching for the magical fox carving in his pocket as the words continued to scribble out before him.

"I forgot to consider that you would not be privy to all the details of this request. We have written over and over again to the King of Aralot requesting that the spellbinding dragon be returned home for a visit to help with the nature of a complicated spell. Just like with our requests to Vankerdale when the dragon was there, no return message has ever been sent. We can only assume that the request has been denied or that the letters are being stolen by spies. We do not seek to keep the dragon, only borrow him. We have no choice left but to send over an army to collect the dragon if you refuse to send him over on our behalf."

"Magic." Mulligan shivered. "It's always a war over magic. What do you think they'll have Valiant do? Curse us?"

"Hold on," Caleb whispered to him, unsure why he was even whispering because no one else was in the room with them. "I've got this."

"What is the nature of the spell that you need help with? Spells do not need close proximity to work. I could help you with the spell from here, assuming you're not being an evil snot."

"Caleb!" Mulligan tugged on his arm. "You can't write that! You could be talking with the King of Wisteria!"

"And he's being an evil snot," Caleb shrugged. Whoever this was had tricked him into sending out a picture so that he or she could reach Valiant through him. This only proved that Wisteria knew he was teaching the dragon. Some spy had been blabbing really loud.

"Unfortunately, the spell that needs to be broken can only be done with close proximity. Send the dragon home."

"No," Caleb spoke out loud. He turned the creepy magical page over and looked at Mulligan. "I think we should write a letter to Turid informing her that Wisteria plans to send over an army."

"I think you should tell the actual king," Mulligan advised again.

"Or maybe just have Kayla take a look at this," Caleb considered.

He wasn't sure what Jack would do, and uncertainty filled his thoughts. Jack had gone into Vankerdale to find Valiant for Kayla, but he might allow the dragon to cross the ocean to prevent a war. Jack would think that he'd be able to stand up to whatever traps Wisteria had for Valiant over there. What if he wrong?

Caleb flipped the paper back over watching for more words to appear. In some secluded place inside of Wisteria there was another person doing this exact same thing. That person gave up on waiting first.

"I understand that you do not want to lose such a magnificent dragon when the creature brings your land hope and joy, but he is needed to resolve two curses."

It was getting larger. Wisteria thought they had a listening ear and they were going to keep bringing up issues.

Pg. 256

"The first one could be solved on your end. There is a magical pull in the air that takes all rare bred dragons and sends them into Aralot. You may have noticed how Aralot has claim to the ice dragons, the ultra-dragon kings, the dragon kings, the loyalty of dwarf dragons, the water dragons, and now the spellbinding dragons. That dragon hoarding spell was cast during the reign of King Gladius. If you find it and destroy that curse, we would be grateful.

"The second spell requires Valiant. In order to thwart King Gladius, our spellbinding dragon of the time cast a curse on the land that can only be altered by another spellbinding dragon. We would consider it a gesture of peace if your spellbinding dragon—that should have been ours—is returned to us for that purpose. Please do not send Kayla. You can keep your cursed witch."

"I don't feel like I have the authority to write anything back anymore," Caleb said, glaring at the insult over Kayla. Their spies needed to do a bit more talking if they had failed to point out that insulting Kayla around him would make him mad. Kayla was not a witch. She was an inspiring angel who lived to bring assistance to the hopeless. Caleb tossed the paper into his trunk so that he could pretend that he had never seen it as he told Mulligan a lie.

"I'll give it to Kayla. She'll know what to do with it."

"She will probably tell you that you shouldn't have called the king an evil snot," Mulligan pointed out.

Caleb shrugged. She wasn't going to see it, because Caleb didn't want her feeling obligated to help Wisteria at all. She had more important things to do. The odds of Wisteria breaking past Turid's Ware were slim, and even if they did make it past there, they had Rogan's Ware in the way too. Charles was right. The plan was weak. It

Pg. 257

was never going to work, so he didn't need to make everyone else worry about it.

Visiting
Tyler

"Hi, Adelyn what are you doing here?" There she stood, brought in by a guard along with the claim that she had a special delivery for Tyler. She had been searched for weapons and magical devices beforehand and the only thing she was carrying was a letter.

Adelyn looked to both her sides, giving Tyler a great view of her fabulous hair and profile before she looked back at him with the largest confused face.

"I don't really know actually."

Tyler started to reach for his magical bracelet (he hadn't made a ring yet), but Adelyn kept talking making him think that possession wasn't the cause of her confusion. She had been tricked into coming.

"We were going home and then this merchant stopped the wagon and had these great deals about things we could buy. I have no idea what happened, but all of a sudden there I was as the requirement for all the goods that we bought."

"Come again?" Tyler asked.

"That's how I felt about it except I didn't really mind because the only thing I had to do was deliver a letter to you in the castle. The merchant said that he couldn't do it."

Merchant. Tyler had not been able to find Conner anywhere. This sounded like the kind of scheme he might think up since Conner had seen Adelyn with Tyler once before. Tyler and Adelyn had spent a wonderful stress-free day together that had been the best vacation he had had in years.

"Was this guy Conner?" Tyler questioned.

He had right now a picture of Conner in his pocket that he had just gotten back from General Reis. The general was using it to show to the guards to teach them that talking to Conner was mostly fine, but he wasn't allowed inside. Conner was helpful, and had helped make Tyler the king, but there was no way to fully trust the guy. Seeing Adelyn here with a strange letter made Tyler guess that Conner had perfected that plan he had been working on. Probably that one to get information about the Colts.

"Uh... I don't think so. Here's the letter." Adelyn held it out.

Tyler reached for it not trusting her reaction. Conner had a closet full of disguises that he wore all the time. He could make himself look like somebody else, but his actions were always going to be the same. He wanted into the castle. That had mostly been so he could get Valiant out of it and bring the dragon back to Kayla, but it looked like his goals hadn't changed too much.

"I do have a problem. Dad had to report to his job by a certain date and they couldn't wait for me, so I'm kind of without a ride home now. They bought the supplies and kept going. I got left behind."

Pg. 260

"I can get you home," Tyler assured as he opened the letter.

It might not have been written in Conner's handwriting, but the letter was all about Narl bonding a dragon, as if someone else had been paying real close attention to the oddity of so many of them flying over Tyler's old childhood home. Narl had picked a red one, and he still had a lot of those other dragons nearby forming his army. Tyler was up to two dragons now with Coal and Flare, and his brother's seven still sounded formidable.

"So do I have to go home right away or can I see where you live?" Adelyn asked, crossing her legs over each other still looking nervous.

Something was up more than just this letter. Tyler didn't think he was going to get it out of her while she was still jittery about the merchant's visit. Perhaps a tour would help calm her down enough to start talking. Or even better, he grinned, the tour would give him a great excuse to spend tons of time with Adelyn.

Boots

Caleb

"Shopping for yourself or Kayla?" the shoemaker asked as Caleb stepped into the shop with his obviously busted shoe in his hand. He was walking with one foot barefoot and the guy was asking him about Kayla? Caleb had to laugh about that. The world often felt small with how many people knew he liked her. Other times it felt too large with how all the important people, namely her parents and Anvil, ignored his interest, calling it a phase. How could his love be a phase if the feelings had never left? Nope. He was never going to get over Kayla.

"I busted this one," Caleb tossed the shoe with the separated sole onto the counter and watched as the shoemaker inspected the stitching and glue. Even to Caleb, it looked like someone had taken a thin blade to it and helped it break.

"You didn't get this here so I'll give you a better one."

The shoemaker tossed onto the counter a rather unique pair of patchwork boots that begged to be called high class and super cute. The outside stitching was so good that it was hard to tell it was even there. The inside lining was soft and breathable with a tuft of fur around the opening. The laces were smooth, the hooks perfect, and the spacing on the soles nothing that Caleb had ever seen before.

"Wow!" Caleb remarked as he ran his hands over the creation. It wasn't anything he would ever wear as it looked far too feminine, but he knew a few girls who would declare an emergency holiday if they knew these were here so that they could come hackle down the price over them. "Those are a bit small for me."

Caleb started to pass the boots back, but the shoemaker stopped the return with a firm hand holding them on the counter. "They're Kayla's, and they're paid for already. I've been waiting for her to come in for them, but she never has. You'll do."

"I can't imagine Kayla ever asking for this," Caleb shook his head. They were too flashy. She hadn't worn anything distinctly vibrant since she was seven. She used to wear a bright pink hooded sweater and looked absolutely adorable. She had been hiding her charm for years, although she still looked impressive in a dress.

"She didn't ask for it. You can keep a secret, right?" The shoemaker looked to the front door to make sure that no one else was going to walk in and then he leaned forward. "Ritz brought them in for Kayla. I had the same first reaction, but Ritz tossed them into a display window right before she came running past, and I kid you not, Kayla stopped cold and stared at those boots for a good two minutes before running off."

Okay, he was sold. Kayla didn't stare at anything unless she loved it. Caleb wondered if Ritz had experienced the fluttering heart and the strong satisfaction that came along with things Kayla looked at. Caleb knew every single picture he had drawn that her eyes had touched. They weren't many.

Pg. 264

He also knew the exact locations on his face that her eyes often lingered. It made him grin. He nodded and tucked the boots under an arm before pointing out the problem he had come in with.

"You don't find it odd that Ritz is trying to get Kayla boots?" the shoemaker asked, as he looked at Caleb's shoe size, and sole grip, and started to find items that would match on a wall.

"Not at all. Ritz has been following the girl around her whole life. He's kind of like…" How was he to put this? It wasn't anything that anyone had told him, and the notion certainly hadn't come from Jack. Caleb had heard Jack warn his daughter to stay away from the Colt leader before. Caleb didn't think that Kayla did so. She wandered too much. She was on her own too much, and she probably knew every hiding place Ritz would ever stand in to spy on the rest of the world, because she would have stood in the same places.

"Eh, Ritz is like another one of Kayla's odd uncles," Caleb decided. "Not that Ritz would feel that way," he added, because it wouldn't do Caleb good for that to get out, "but he'd know how Kayla thinks of him."

"And use it to his advantage," the shoemaker quipped. "What do you think he's trying to get from those boots?"

Caleb shrugged, even if he already knew the real answer. A smile and some information. That was all Ritz wanted from those boots. People and dragons would go a long way to get a smile out of Kayla. They would do a lot to get her thoughts too.

Caleb paid for his new pair of boots, feeling as though it was Ritz who had brought him in here by messing up his shoes. It was just his style to use others to do his work for him. He could have met Kayla out in the woods and given her the boots himself, but that was just too much effort. He wanted to see her smile from afar. Or maybe he wasn't trying to see her at all but simply make her happy as if they were friends. It was just like Kayla to be friends with a guy that everyone else feared. That was her style to a precise point.

Thinking of style, Caleb found himself pausing in front of the dress shop next. When Kayla went up to the castle, she put on long dresses that got in the way of running. She tossed them off her as fast as she could, but wouldn't it be nice if he could find a dress that she actually liked? After that doctor's visit, he understood her choice in wearing the longer items. She didn't want the scar on her left leg to be visible. Her scars made her feel insecure, and he wanted her to feel brave. There were other workarounds to hiding legs like tights or even leggings. Yeah. He'd just slip inside and see if he could find something that would match with these boots.

Caleb entered the dress shop, instantly catching the attention of two girls that were already in there. They snickered about him calling him by name. Colts probably. They didn't look like they were nobles, and they looked like they were browsing more than anything. The shopkeeper was idly standing around watching them, but gave Caleb a smile.

"You pick. I'll get you the correct size," the lady told him already assuming before he said anything at all who he might be there for. "I can give you a recommendation."

"No thanks. I'll know it if I see it."

"I can custom sew her anything. I keep Kayla's measurements on hand."

Pg. 266

Caleb gave the seamstress a nod of his head and started looking around trying to ignore her. She really did know who he had come in here for. It was a conspiracy. Everyone knew him and who he was in love with. The Colts tried to give him tips next, holding up dresses and attempting to make him pick what they thought was good. He wasn't sure if they were trying to be helpful or trying to make him buy something Kayla wouldn't like.

"Ladies, I am capable of spotting—"

That one. It was a dark blue, so something that Kayla would wear without feeling like she was standing out too much. It had a false corseted bodice with a gray ribbon lacing up the front. Gray lace hugged the neckline. The hem had extra lace frilling outward and it was utterly adorable.

"Not to break your hopes, but that is too large for Kayla and she would never wear it. I can adjust the length—"

"No," Caleb cut off the seamstress. "That's why I like it."

"She won't wear it."

It was rather irritating that everyone thought they knew better than him. He'd show them. She would wear it. She was going to love it.

"What would look better underneath? Tights or leggings?" he asked. "She only wears long dresses, but then she can't move so she hates them. She'd be able to move in that. You can adjust it to fit her right?"

"This one," one of the Colts in the room came over holding a gray pair of leggings. She modeled it beneath the dress for him, and since it matched the color of the lace and the ribbon he nodded. That outfit with the fur-lined boots and she was going to be too adorable for words.

"Okay," the seamstress agreed. "I'll put in a few tucks and have it right out for you."

She didn't sound convinced yet, but she took the dress into the back and started to sew on it. After a few minutes the dress was packaged for him and he was on his way out the door nervous but excited. He'd never once given Kayla a present, but she had given him one, the magical fox statue that he kept in his pocket. Now that he was about to give something to her, he was second guessing himself.

What if those ladies were right and Kayla wouldn't wear the dress? What if she threw it in her trunk and never looked at it again? Perhaps this was how Ritz felt too, which was why he hadn't given Kayla the boots himself. Caleb was dancing on his toes as his riders showed up to class when he reached the field again. He decided to start with Ritz. Let him have the first blunt reaction to his gift.

"This is a secret so naturally everyone is going to know," Caleb started. His riders looked at him curiously, all except for Kayla who probably knew more secrets about Aralot and the people within than anyone. She might know more than Ritz did, since she lived within both rider and Colt worlds.

"Ritz is gifting out boots."

Caleb tossed one of the bags in his hand to Kayla. She stood there, not touching it for the longest time before she decided that the bag wasn't going to hurt her. What if she did that to his gift? What if she looked at it blankly and left it on the ground? Oh, he was so nervous!

However, when her eyes spotted the boots the instant smile on her face said it all. She really did like them. She had no doubt stared at them before just as the shoemaker claimed.

"He's gifting boots, or he made the boots, or he noticed me look at the boots?" Kayla questioned, still smiling as she pulled them out.

"I was told directly that he brought in the boots for you to notice. Only you're a little late in picking them up."

She ran her fingers along the fascinating grip and then the stitching before she tore off her old boots that were oddly black on the bottom from tar and put on the new ones. Valiant started sniffing at the new boots, probably testing to see if they had any magic that would get his rider since the sender was an unusual source. Caleb had never heard of Ritz giving anyone a present before unless it was a nasty one. All the same, he wasn't worried that the boots came from Ritz. Whatever the man's angle was in gifting them, Kayla would hold out against it while she looked fabulous.

"That's for you too," Caleb said, tossing over the next bag and squirming so much that Kayla laughed at him, no doubt picking up that it wasn't from Ritz. Oh, he hoped that she liked it.

"It'd be so much easier to move in, and I know you've never considered leggings before, and I'm not the most fashionable of people, but you could give it a try…"

He was rambling like a school kid, and his entire class was laughing about it snickering at his display of gift giving. This was all new to him. He had never been invited to any of Kayla's birthday parties. He'd never been able to give her a present, and she was reaching into the bag slightly uncertain herself.

Valiant snorted against Kayla's thoughts and she grinned even larger as she pulled out the present. Then she stared at it smiling, and Caleb squirmed again, still waiting to know what she was thinking. She was starting to get teary which could be a bad sign. Man! He should have left it to those boots. Ritz was much better at figuring out what Kayla would like.

"I have never gotten anything more personally thoughtful," Kayla said, looking up at him. "Not once. Thank you so much!"

With that, she flung herself at him, easing the tension in his chest. Ritz wasn't getting a hug like this. It was a really good hug, with the perfect amount of squeezing and heart fluttering and social awkwardness.

"Where's my present?" Davis asked, reminding Caleb that he had a class to teach still.

"Your present is in an easy warm-up," Caleb told him. He had to pry Kayla's fingers off him to get her to let go. He wasn't going to say it out loud, but that right there made giving her a present even better. He'd have to wait to see her wear it, but he didn't have to wait to see the boots. Those looked like they had always been on Kayla's feet. They brought out her natural charm as if they had been, and they probably were, made especially for her. His compliments to the shoemaker.

"Balance poses this morning," Caleb directed.

He led them through the whole class, and by the end, Kayla's patchwork boots felt like another extension of her. It was totally her style, cute, charming, a collection of every rider ware with an exquisite gripping sole. She was going to be more fabulous when she put that dress on.

Gladius

Kayla

Sneaking out at night was fine, but it was so much easier sneaking out during the middle of the day when she didn't have to worry about being too tired to function. Kayla had never done this before, but all she had to do was put on that dress that Caleb had given her and start walking in the direction of the castle. Everyone thought she was heading over to see Queen Aria and left her alone. Brilliant! The only drawbacks to her plan were that she couldn't take her rider gear with her and she couldn't take Valiant. She didn't expect to need either where she was going so she wasn't worried about it.

Caleb had whistled at her on her way past him, and it was all she could do to block him out by putting her hands next to her face as a barrier to hide her ever-increasing blush. She loved this outfit already. He had no idea the freedom he had just given her, both by finding a way for her legs to move and lending her an excuse to escape the ware. Had he known what she was using it for, he might have decided to take the present away for a time.

She was having one of those good days where she didn't walk around feeling completely exhausted, so she had to take advantage of it. She wasn't finding anything on how keepers were created in Aralot, and she wasn't going to go into Vankerdale to find the monolith where the answer would be, so she was giving up on the idea that being a keeper caused her nightmares. No other keeper had these nightmares. Kayla was going to search through Gladius's old place for clues, even if the ancient, gutted castle had been searched hundreds of times before by stray, curious visitors. Her nightmares could be the result of something that Gladius had left behind.

The only way to find answers was by looking through his old home. Gladius must have torn the place down for something. That was a nightmare that she had never seen, but one that she found she wanted to. What spurred the anger that broke where he lived? Why move away from the mountain's feet of safety putting his new castle a whole lot closer to Vankerdale when he didn't trust them? Gladius had moved his new place as far away from his old one as possible. There had to be a reason. Keeper rage was targeted at dragons, not castles. The broken castle had to contain a secret and it was probably located at the end of the path that her nightmares and drawings led.

Kayla slipped through the portal coming out inside the cave that looked outward at the broken stone walls. She had not been this south in ages, and the only times she came here she passed the castle up quickly to head to the town or the monastery off in the distance. All these years later the old castle was still empty and full of ghosts from Gladius's memories that Kayla wished to see. If only she was Caleb, with his strong pull on magic, wishing to see the memories might actually work. Too bad she wasn't him.

Kayla walked out of the cave and stood before the most intact castle wall. It was this wall that had been in the nightmares of anyone who handled Gladius's cursed flower necklace. All this time later and the necklace still gave out the nightmare that sent a dragon with red eyes at whoever held the pendant. That sort of long-lasting spell had to be binding. It was so strange that Gladius had the power of binding magic when none of the rest of them could figure out anything about it. Maybe he had memorized all the theories on the subject and promptly destroyed them. Kayla shrugged since she couldn't go into the past to ask him any questions. The best she got was seeing his greatest fears and defeats in her dreams.

"So what was it then?" she asked, stepping around the wall to look at the rest of the place. What had made this castle fall? She could picture the castle in its glory days standing out proud and tall. Here was a castle that used to have beautiful fretwork on its walls, gold inlays on its doors, and hand-stitched curtains. It was a place for kings, loved and beautiful, unlike the castle they had right now. Kayla cast a spell to make the room before her match the room in her dreams and smiled.

"And you got mad at this why? It was so beautiful!"

"Just like you," Ritz's voice came from behind a wall so Kayla had to take her spell down to see him standing there.

"How did you get here so fast?" she asked him blinking in surprise.

She expected Ritz to be near Charles's Ware waiting for her to get those boots. She had not told him the antidote for traveling through portals, so even if he stepped through the portal after her, he'd have to spend at least three to five hours on the ground moaning in pain. He wasn't on the ground moaning. There was no possible way that he could have reached this castle right after she had. Plus, he was in front of her. Even if he could walk quietly, she would have seen him walk right in front of her. Maybe it wasn't him?

"Are you real?" Kayla asked, taking a step toward him and watching his feet to find that he was indeed standing on the ground and not floating above it like a ghost. He had to be real. He took a few steps backward to either confirm this for her or prevent her from poking him with a finger to find out. His footsteps sounded real. He looked perfectly solid. It could not have been a portal that brought him over here, so she had to assume that he had not been near the ware in the last week because he was flying here. If he had come here right after leaving the boots in the storefront window then the time frame could work out.

"He didn't," Valiant told her. *"Ritz was spotted talking to Caleb four days after you saw the boots."*

Which was still enough time to reach the old castle if he flew on a fast dragon. It was only a five-day flight. Maybe he was here to secretly take care of a dragon where no one else ventured and would notice. Kayla looked around in search of a dragon not seeing any that were close. If he was taking care of a dragon, he would have been farther away hiding up near the mountain cliffs, concealed. He wouldn't be inside the castle because Ian and August, the treasure hunters, lingered around this place. It would not hide his interaction with dragons. Ritz suddenly standing here didn't make sense. He had not been there before, and her dragon caretaker theory wasn't working.

"You haven't found some kind of token that can transport you to another location instead of using a portal, have you?" Kayla asked Ritz.

"Is there such a token?" Ritz grinned at her. "What's it look like?"

Pg. 276

"Never mind," Kayla shrugged at him. She wasn't going to tell him what Tristan had found, and she doubted that there was another such item in existence anyway. Those medallions had been crafted by an ultra-dragon king ages ago.

"You're thinking too hard about this," Ritz told her, reading the confusion on her face. "Sometimes the easiest answer is the one you overlook. Not all magic needs a portal to move things."

Okay. So he had used some kind of spell that brought him here, only she had no idea what it could be. In all her years of learning, she had never found a spell that would function as a portal. If Ritz had, then he had to be using some rather ancient magic, and if he understood ancient magic, he might very well know about the spell that gave her those nightmares.

"What's at the end of the path, Ritz?" Kayla asked him.

His eyes hardened, his hands reached for something in his pocket, and his voice was his lethal one. If Kayla got him too mad, he was going to charge her.

"You may be in a dress, but I will take you down harder than ever," Ritz confirmed, losing any sparkle of warmth in his blue eyes. "I won't hold back, Kayla. I told you not to go looking."

Yes, he had, but looking for what? And if he was blocking off the thing at the end of the path, that made him a guardian to that thing. She had guessed before that Ritz was trapped ageless in a curse to protect an old artifact. He wouldn't be released until the condition of the curse was met.

He could be guarding an artifact inside of Gladius's old castle! After all, it was written in both Gladius's and Maslon's journals that Maslon had gotten a curse. Since Kayla had already guessed that Ritz was a keeper, and therefore the still living Maslon, this all added up. Gladius had Ritz stuck inside a conditional guardian curse that made him appear at the castle every time someone either got close or had the intention of finding what he was protecting.

"Guarding something are you?" Kayla asked him trying to make him confirm her guesses. "That's as far as I can puzzle out anyway. I absolutely love the shoes!"

"Your distractions won't work on me. I taught them to you."

She laughed at him. So he had. "I'm not trying to find what you're guarding. I was hoping for answers about my nightmares. They lead here."

She hadn't even finished her sentence before her ears picked up the sounds of eight wild dragons heading toward her as fast as they could. Kayla spun around to watch them wishing she had at least a prong with her. Ritz was super serious about this. He'd had enough time to mentally call for backup. His curse pulled him here to fight her, and she was more unprepared to face him than any other time in her life. At least that would be what he would want her to think. She had to keep herself prepared.

The dragons screeched at her, flew over her, and landed themselves right in the way of where her path would take her if she followed that maze through the castle to the end. Kayla tilted her head looking at the blocking dragons. They had narrowed eyes ready to fight her until she either died or gave up.

Pg. 278

"Kayla..." Valiant whimpered at her.

"Not to worry. I'm not stupid."

"I've never trusted Ritz as you do," Valiant told her. *"Those dragons are in his thoughts. They will kill you."*

No, they wouldn't. She wasn't going to run at them and get charred to death. She could figure out her nightmares without touching the thing Ritz was guarding. Hopefully.

"I wasn't going to look at the end of the path." Kayla smiled at Ritz. "It was just a question. I'm rather more curious about why Gladius leveled this castle in the first place. And those objects from him that still work, that has to be binding magic. Where did he find information on binding magic?"

"Honestly, your tricks don't work on me," Ritz told her again, causing her to smile and laugh at him. She glanced down at her outfit, still loving it even if she would have done better to bring her weapon belt.

"I'm right, aren't I? You are really Maslon who was a shoemaker, and your older brother Gladius cursed you to guard something that he left inside this castle. I can't see how you'd get here so quickly otherwise. I came looking and that triggered the condition of the spell to bring you. Your son is my uncle Conner, and you have no choice but to stop me."

Now that she said it out loud, Ritz being the one to stop her sounded even more unpleasant. He had watched her grow up. He would know what to say to make her tremble.

"I have plenty of choices," Ritz spoke back. "I have the choice to kill you right now for spurting out all those lies you just said."

Kayla shrugged because there wasn't a Colt alive that had discovered his secret. No one could figure out who Ritz really was. Despite his claim that he would kill her for knowing, she wasn't worried. With Ritz, the thing that got him calm was time. So she was going to give him lots of time to stop wanting her dead while she tried harder to disarm him.

"It's okay. You are the only person who understands all the risks and benefits. Whatever it is that has you here, I trust that you'll do the right thing. I know you will."

He glared at her, probably thinking that she was lying to him. Ritz had been a guardian for nearly three generations. He would know which curious people to confront and which to leave alone. Judging that he was revealing himself as a keeper in the middle of the day, and still set to attack her, Kayla was guessing that he saw her as one of the worst threats to this area. With his additional forces today, she couldn't reach the end of the maze in her dreams. That location was for another time, or perhaps for another person. It didn't mean that she couldn't go poking around in other places of the castle though.

"Where are you?" Kayla asked, spinning in a circle while she ignored Ritz's breathing pick up and the fact that he pulled a knife against her. He'd be even better than her dad with that thing, able to strike her down before she could start reaching for her magic to save her.

"Come on Gladius," Kayla continued walking toward a place in the room he had paced a lot. This was what she had really come for. She wanted to see inside his thoughts to better understand if it was

Pg. 280

him that caused the nightmares. What if Ritz had been charged by Gladius to keep people away from some cursed object that Gladius had blamed for his madness? After all, Gladius never knew that it was poison that destroyed his dragon bonds. He could have speculated it was something else. If that was the case, had he seen these nightmares too?

"What was the goal of your life that kept you sane. The righteous desire that made you cry at night when the poison had you turning against yourself? What were you trying to accomplish before it all broke down? Where have you gone?"

"You are going to explain what you did to my castle!" Gladius's rather clear voice had her jumping. He appeared in front of her, looking rather solid, and Kayla didn't think that anyone else around could possibly cast a spell to make him show up except for her and Ritz. Neither of them had used magic. No blue glow was tingling up her fingers and Ritz was likewise surprised.

"What have you done?" Ritz hissed at her, jumping to her side and putting her behind him to protect her from the image of Gladius. This proved that Ritz didn't really want to hurt her if he was now protecting her. She hoped she hadn't triggered an even worse spell for asking her questions.

"I didn't do anything," Kayla answered peeking around Ritz to see Gladius. He was absolutely perfect and wearing his not scary boots she might add. His blond hair shifted with the slight wind, and his blue eyes were sparkling. Kayla could picture him jumping those dragons again, and the only thing she could do was stare at him in awe. Everyone else would probably be running away already.

"You must have done something," Ritz hissed at her. "This has never happened before. Figure out what you did and fix it!"

"But it couldn't have been me! I'm not strong enough to wish up anyone."

"You're strong enough to do anything. Make him go away!"

"Good to see you too, Mo," Gladius rolled his eyes at his younger brother Maslon as he scowled at the broken castle and then raised his eyebrows at Kayla for an explanation. "What is this? Did you pull me through time for a joke?"

"This is a nightmare. You are sleeping and having a bad time of it," Ritz answered, causing Gladius to laugh at him.

"No. With all the walls tumbled like this, I can make out the erosion quite well. You pulled me through time. Why?"

"Where did you hide all your information on binding magic?" Kayla burst, dying to know the answer. "You have objects that still work. The magic has to be bound to them. How did you do it? Also, what was your motivation in life?"

Gladius was standing before her! No one ever got to talk to him anymore because he was long dead. She hoped that he was willing to answer her questions. If he did, this would be the most remarkable day of her life!

"My motivation? Why? Did I do something stupid? Mo, what is this? Who is she?" Gladius asked, crossing his arms and giving his brother a special "spill it" look.

Pg. 282

"She is your great-granddaughter born from your twin son Herb who had a daughter named Tia who had a daughter named Kayla. Just forget it. It's all a dream. Kayla will make you go away."

Ritz gave Kayla a nasty glare that she could only shrug at. She still had no explanation for why Gladius was there, but she could hear him breathing. She threw a rock at him to see if it would go through him, and he knocked it away with an arm like he was perfectly there. Amazing! He rolled his eyes at her further expression of awe.

"I have twin sons?" Gladius asked. "Who did I marry? Why did I do that? I was going to stay single forever. We had this discussion. Mo, please tell me that I didn't get married. I was going to hold out against her forever. I was never going to fail."

This was really early in his timeline if he wasn't married yet. Hold out against who? His wife Jean? Ritz put down his knife and with his other arm trembling reached a hand toward Gladius trying to decide if he was real or not.

"Maybe you should tell me what this is," Ritz asked as he poked his brother and jumped away from him scared.

"I already told you my guess. I fail. You win. You're the one that succeeds in being the worst lover."

"Will you stop!" Ritz screamed back. "Kayla doesn't know and you can't tell her! How are you here?"

"Time magic," Kayla voiced, stepping to the side of Ritz so she could get closer to Gladius too. "That's so cool. You think that you came forward through time. Are you going to remember this for the rest of your life?"

"This is not time magic." Gladius shook his head at her. "You are both messing around with heart magic. It's even stronger. Heart magic uses your very souls. You should be careful because one ill wish and you're doomed. It's worse than blood magic even. Very risky. It can only take place inside this castle. There's a reason why the castle was placed right here. It looks like Maslon decided to destroy the place later on."

Neither Kayla nor Ritz answered him. Gladius had busted the building apart not Ritz. Maybe Gladius was trying to prevent further heart magic. So he did remember this later, and Kayla could be the reason why he blew up his castle!

"It feels like summer. With the sun still high, two hearts looked to the past in search of their salvation, and the combined earnest desires brought to them the face of redemption."

"Don't quote scripture at me!" Ritz demanded. "I was never one to believe it all."

"Even though you've clearly fulfilled the prophecy. Here I am come to redeem you of something. My motivation you want? To be the worst lover in all of history. Only it looks like I fail at that. Maslon is the one who wins. He's the one still standing. I knew that I loved you more than you loved me."

Gladius sighed sadly at his brother and Ritz started to cry. This had to really hard on him to see his brother after all these years, knowing what was to come when Gladius had no clue. It made Kayla tear up too. If it wasn't for that poison, Gladius would have been a fantastic soul.

"Why do you need to be a bad lover?" Kayla asked.

Pg. 284

"You know how to make me go away, Mo. You have to turn your heart against me. It's going to be rough."

Ritz shook his head and started to back away, causing Gladius to grin at him. "Or you can do that. Step out of the castle and watch me vanish. It only works if Kayla believes she has gotten her redemptive answer. You're a sweet guy, you know that?" Gladius continued as Ritz turned and fled outside the castle walls. Instead of vanishing Gladius remained just as he said he might.

He shook his head looking at her. "Blood oath. I won't explain my choice to be the worst lover in all of history. I'm sorry, miss. You'll have to get your answer some other way."

"Kayla get out of the castle!" Ritz screamed at her.

"I'm going to bring you a box of assorted cheeses tonight," Gladius told his brother, watching as Ritz's face paled. "I did it didn't I? Only you won't have any idea what sparked my visit and you won't learn why I came by until I have a great-granddaughter. Funny things hearts. They love around time. Time holds no boundaries for the strongest of hearts."

"Get out, Kayla!" Ritz screamed at her again.

She couldn't leave him! This was Gladius! She'd never heard anything about heart magic before. She'd heard about blood magic and time magic, and Gladius looked like he had used both, but to hear him quote that scripture would indicate that while he was hated by everyone after his death, he was really everyone's greatest savior. What had he saved them from?

Gladius smiled at her as if he could see her thoughts through her eyes. Ritz was able to do that. Maybe Ritz had learned if from his older brother because Gladius nodded at her like he understood her amazement. He stepped forward and gave her a hug.

"Punch him in the face. I feel very uncomfortable right now and my head is bursting!" Valiant claimed.

Magic flashed up from her keychain right into Gladius's hand. It was then that she remembered that even in his best of times, Gladius was still scary. Kayla rolled out of the way to defend her keychain of magic as she put up a shield to block his spell. Unfortunately, the shield was what he was hoping for. His spell connected with her shield and shoved her out of the castle causing him to disappear.

Kayla landed on her back and struggled for breath. It was him! It was really him! She had met Gladius!

"Your parents would kill me if they knew what you'd just done! Stop it, Kayla! Go away. Get as far away from this place as you can. Run. Gladius is not your savior. He's not your anything. He can take any line and twist it inside of your head to make you believe what he wants you to believe. He is a demon with scripture quotes. What you failed to notice was that he was wearing his wedding ring. He knows that he got married. He knows that he fails because he's already done it. He didn't bring me a box of cheese until after he had lost track of his twins. That was one of the nights that he tried to kill me. He went on and on about how my heart was twisted and ugly. Now I know why. It was because of you. Just go!"

Kayla sat back up and looked at the castle, not wanting to look at Ritz and his tears. She didn't want to go. These people were keepers. It felt like her responsibility to make them happy again. They were

Pg. 286

very sad men. She wanted to understand the reason that these two competed against each other for being the worst lover. If Ritz was correct and Gladius was already married, then both Maslon and Gladius were married with children to care for. Maslon had not been the worst lover at all. It was Gladius that got married last. It couldn't be the love of family that they were talking about. Was it the love of dragons? Did they not like being keepers? That made her ache for them.

"I can't go," Kayla teared up. "You were both tormented. There's something that you're guarding that tormented you. I can't just leave that alone, Ritz. I'm going to save you."

She ran back into the castle again with Ritz screaming at her. He knocked her down right as she reached the castle wall. Her hand connected and Gladius's voice was back again.

"Same day for you I take it?" he asked, moving closer to them with his thick-soled boots, the ones that brought out fear because it testified of his foul mood. The fear sliced through Kayla right away. Ritz was right. She should have left it all alone. These were spells that she didn't understand and Gladius did. She was bringing him through time. He could do anything with that, like make himself stuck here in the present. Could that happen? It hadn't happened before. Gladius didn't vanish. He had died.

"I've been waiting for you two. You and your ripped hearts bound into a time tangle that you can't get out of. What is it that makes her love me so, Mo? I've done my best to only write nasty things down for my posterity, and it hasn't changed a thing. She's still here!"

His journal. Gladius really did only write down the worst in his journal. He had done it for her. This was messing with her head! How much had she influenced his actions by refusing to see him as evil?

"My vote? See him as evil, Kayla. Do it now," Valiant frantically thought to her. *"Every time he's here my head hurts!"*

"Kayla was bonded to a male spellbinding dragon upon birth. She has no idea what she's doing," Ritz answered. "You don't either. Step away and leave her alone."

Ritz yanked her hand away from the castle wall, but it was too late. Gladius was already back and Kayla wasn't so sure she believed all this heart magic stuff. Gladius started laughing his hysterical laugh, the one he went to right before he tortured something. Kayla shoved Ritz off her and got into a battle stance. She felt no love for Gladius when he had that laugh. There was only one thing on her mind, to send him away, and if it was her heart controlling the wishes, he should have vanished. Instead, he just laughed harder while Ritz got into a defensive posture beside her.

"There's no *way* to avoid that binding love interest!" Gladius giggled. "Oh, she's going to die. I hope you brought her here to die. Death to all of Aralot's lovers!" Gladius screamed, flipping away from laughter into his madness.

He shot a spell at her, and Kayla had no idea which one it might be so her only choice was to make up a spell from her rather strong will to not get hit by the magic. It was her will against Gladius's. Their spells clashed in the air and started pushing each other, neither one making much progress. Kayla blinked at it, but Gladius had already moved on. He came at her again with a red death spell that she knew how to stop.

Pg. 288

He was trying to kill her! Gladius was in the present trying to make her die for loving what he couldn't, since he had been poisoned to hate dragons. This was the most horrible thing that she had ever seen.

"There he is," Gladius glared cruelly as he blasted her off her feet with some spell she didn't know. Kayla scrambled back upright because Gladius was talking about Valiant. He was bursting through the portal coming to save her. Couldn't he just stay away?! Gladius tortured dragons!

"I know. So he will be focused on me and you can stay safe," Valiant thought back.

"No!" Kayla screamed as Gladius turned his back on her and ran toward her dragon. He had killed way too many dragons. He might not have gone up against a spellbinding one, but that didn't mean that he didn't know how. She had to stop him. Kayla shot out a spell toward him, but it didn't do anything. Gladius was one step ahead of her. Her entire world inverted and she found herself falling upward toward the sky as her spell went that way too. It was just the sort of evil thing he would think up to make Valiant move to catch her so he could get a good shot at her dragon.

"Don't come for me!" Kayla frantically screamed.

Valiant didn't. He sent a missile load of curses down at Gladius while one of Ritz's dragons abandoned his guard post and came toward her. The dragon didn't make it. One spell from Gladius had the dragon's eyes shoved into the back of his head, killing him and sending him crashing to the ground! Kayla's breathing became frantic as she continued to fling upward toward the clouds feet first. This was the stuff of her nightmares. Just like when she had seen Tristan hurt, this stuff shouldn't be happening in real life. She wasn't prepared enough for this!

"Focus!" Ritz screamed at her, not even flinching that his dragon had died. "If you tell yourself that he's won, you let him win! You can do this! Change your focus, Kayla! I promise that you can outsmart Gladius at *any* time. Change your hearts focus to this: Find and destroy the spell that Gladius left here. You do that and you will win!"

"You're going to die next, old man!" Gladius screeched at his brother. Kayla could barely hear them with how far away she was getting to everything.

"Oh no, I won't. I've had years to figure out why I'm still alive. You can't touch me!"

Ritz pulled out of his pocket a shrunken glowing ball. It looked like a magical ice dragon sphere only it could fit into the size of his hand. That would take a really strong spell to condense magic like that. Kayla had never seen Ritz use magic, but he could use it. He started casting spells at Gladius too, and with Gladius being shot at from two directions, Kayla took in a deep breath and looked away from the fight.

She had to clear her head of the fear and get herself back down on the ground. Ritz had seen this before, so he had to know what condition it would take for her to defeat it. She needed to only focus on finding the spell that Gladius had left behind. If that was how to outsmart Gladius, then she had to do that. There was some spell here that could be harming her. Some spell that caused Gladius to appear to take down anyone who might be looking to destroy what he had hidden.

Pg. 290

That's probably all this was. There wasn't heart magic because she really hadn't used magic herself when Gladius showed up. She had seen real heart magic before from Caleb. If it wasn't for him, she would be more prone to accept Gladius's flawed logic. Caleb was her savior. Ritz was her savior. Gladius was still dead, and the only reason why he was here was that Kayla had triggered his protective spell by wanting to find his secrets. It was probably the same trigger that had brought Ritz over.

The spell that was attacking them was exactly what Ritz had figured out already: protections designed to get inside her head to make her leave Gladius's spell alone. It had done a fantastic job making her believe that Gladius was here from the past. She had come here to discover if Gladius was to be blamed for her nightmares, and found that he had left behind items that Ian and August had not been able to move and relocate. The treasure hunters had crawled all around this castle. They had probably triggered the Gladius spell at some point, which meant that Ritz had lied to her. He had seen this before. He did know why Gladius had shown up. He just lacked the knowledge to know how to take down a triggered protective spell, so he was pretending that he didn't know what it was so that she would be more inclined to get rid of it.

With another strong breath in, Kayla cleared her head enough to put herself back on the ground. She changed the direction of the force acting upon her so that gravity could work again. She landed poorly, but she wasn't hurt.

Kayla cast a locating spell trying to discover where Gladius's cursed object was hiding. Before she could finish, a gaping black hole started to widen in front of her. Dragon claws were coming up from the deep. Black dragon claws attached to a black dragon body as if the demon was tunneling out from the inky depths of purgatory. A formidable dragon head followed with red glowing eyes. The dragon fixed its gaze on her and then got its fifteen-foot-tall body out of the hole that vanished as it fully materialized. Kayla had already forgotten what spell she was trying to cast as that dragon stared her down and then started to open its mouth. Oh no. Dragons like this triggered her most primal fears. She wasn't falling to her knees, but she was considering it. No dragon that large crawled up from the ground. It couldn't be real!

"Don't be distrac—" Valiant started to warn her.

He didn't finish talking, because he ended up screaming instead. Kayla jerked her eyes away from the demon in front of her to find her dragon. Gladius's fake body threw a curse at Valiant that shattered a few of his scales, trapped Ritz inside a bubble that started to suffocate him, and turned back onto Kayla as she rolled out of the way of the black dragon's flame. If Caleb could see her right now, he would be able to mark it down on her chart that she could dodge a flaming dragon.

"I'll keep Ritz safe. You focus on yourself," Valiant told her as he blasted through the spell that was taking away the guardian's air. Ritz came out of it gasping with a short nod of thanks toward her dragon as Valiant healed himself.

Kayla hardly had any time to focus on them at all, because Gladius was shooting at her again. He was wickedly fast, and the spells had her completely busy as she blocked them. She also had to counter the black dragon that could shoot out fire, ice, and wind. It couldn't be a real dragon. This was supposed to terrify her away from her goal and it was doing a good job.

Pg. 292

Kayla realized that she would have been very dead already if she wasn't super aware of the kinds of spells that a crazy-minded Gladius would send in her direction. Her nightmares had prepared her to act against her internal organs collapsing, and her bones shattering from the inside out. They prepared her to escape the swiping of dragon tails and claws and explosive forces that came from their mouths.

This was way worse than fighting against Prince Evan. The spells were going to continue against her as long as she had the desire to find what Gladius had hidden around here. She couldn't use the same tricks on Gladius that she had used on Prince Evan. She couldn't distance him from magic and confuse him because Gladius's spell saw all her intentions. Ritz had told her to focus on finding the spell to defeat it, but she couldn't do that and succeed. She had to change up her desires. Once she stopped wanting to defeat Gladius, he would go away, but she couldn't just stop wanting to defend herself when he was still shooting.

Valiant screaming forced Kayla's gaze to him again to notice a defeated white-scaled dragon with a separated head before him. It looked like Sparkle…

"Hey what are you doing?" Kayla thought to Sparkle as she dodged yet another attack from the black dragon trying to stab her with his spiked tail and deflected four more of Gladius's curses. Her clothes were getting very dusty, but at least Caleb was right. She could still move in this dress.

"I'm trying to decide if Valiant likes sitting on his tail or hiding his wings better. I can't have both of those things missing from my ice sculpture."

"Tail," Kayla answered.

Sparkle was fine. The image of the dragon before Valiant was only an image.

"It's not her!" Kayla called out, glancing at Valiant as he screamed again, this time because it was Merlock looking shriveled in his path.

"I know!" Valiant screamed at her. "This spell is trying to kill off everything that I love. I'm taking it down!"

"But we have to desire not to take it down in order to take it down," Kayla pointed out.

She rolled and glanced at Valiant better to notice that he was facing his own personal Gladius. So was Ritz. All three of them were fighting the same spell on their own terms. Valiant was being forced to fight against the very dragons that he loved. Ritz was facing Gladius in his absolute most crazy state. She had to outsmart this spell. How had Ritz dealt with it in the past? He had probably missed a spell and gotten plowed over, but he couldn't die, so for him, that final spell wouldn't be fatal. Once he was down, the spell would stop because he gave up. That was it!

Kayla ran over to Ritz and pulled him in front of her as she dropped all her defenses. He took the blunt force of the spell that had been coming at her. It put his whole body on fire, but he stopped the spell with one of his own and nodded to her since one of the Gladius's and the creepy black dragon was now gone. Ritz's personal Gladius had followed him, but Kayla was free of the spell as long as she could keep herself from wanting to find anything. So *she* didn't want to find anything. She wanted Ritz to find it.

"If you can find the object that is triggering the condition of this spell, then I can find a way to help you with it," Kayla said. "I can't desire to locate the thing myself."

"I have to spell it out for you?" Ritz growled as he was blasted with a curse that deformed his face and legs. "It's a purple orb inside that black hole."

There see? That was much easier. He had already gotten close enough to the object in the past to tell her that much. Now Kayla could get around her desire to find the thing because she already knew where it was. All she wanted to do was *peek* at it.

Kayla rushed out from behind Ritz carefully listening and watching for curses that might come after her. Nothing shot out from either of the Gladius figures, but Ritz's trailed behind.

"That hole messes with emotions. It's nothing you can't handle though. Emotions are your specialty."

Emotions. She fought against emotions all the time, even after getting her bond fixed, it seemed. She could overcome this thing. She moved toward the hole, noticing how she felt like running away or at least leaving the hole alone. Emotion number one.

She got closer only to find herself feeling really confused about why she going this way. She felt like she was forgetting something that she needed to get back to right away. Emotions two and three. Kayla ignored them and kept pressing forward.

It was a beautiful day. She felt like hosting a party or in the very least dancing for joy. She didn't do either. It would have been nice if this hole was the sort that was deceptive and got larger as she got closer, but it wasn't. She was going to need to slide down this thing on her belly. There were a lot of people who wouldn't jump face-first into anything that Gladius had left, but Kayla wasn't one of those people. She cast a spell to clear out debris, dead bugs, and cobwebs before she slipped down.

"Kayla stop! Stop!" Valiant's voice shouted at her from outside.

"Why?" she thought back to him not trusting the sound of his voice unless it came to her in her head.

"This is killing me!" he screamed at her again.

"Why?" Valiant's thoughts answered.

The sound of his voice had to be a spell. That's all it was. The spell was trying to make her turn around and flee.

"I meant why are you asking why?" Valiant insisted. *"This hurts. Get out of there!"*

But… but she couldn't. There had to be a spell left down here designed to make people flee. Valiant was a spellbinding dragon. He could fix himself. No other person had that assurance as they headed down into the hole. Hearing their dragon scream would be enough to make them quit.

She shimmied down further and came up against feelings that she was all too familiar with. Despair. Defeat. She felt like she couldn't emotionally keep going, so keep going is what she did. Her tears were falling, her heart was aching, but this was the sort of thing she fought all the time. If she didn't know that her tears had come from being unbonded to Valiant, she would have guessed that it was a curse that Gladius had left behind for her.

Pg. 296

The hole dipped, sending her sprawling out onto the cold ground in the pitch dark. With a bit more room to move, Kayla created a magical glow with shaking arms from feeling so sad. The pressure pushed against her harder to ask for a rope and climb away. There was nothing in the hole, only a dead end, and starvation if she didn't get out. Kayla didn't believe the feelings at all. There was something in the hole. It was a rock. It didn't look important, but it was the only thing in here, so it had to be something.

She shoved it out of the way with a spell only to find that the rock was hollow. When she got a closer look, she found herself gazing upon a purple orb. Ritz was right. There was a spell down here. Purple magic was conditional, so Kayla grabbed at the object, ignoring Valiant's continued screams, and climbed back out shimming her way into the light. It wouldn't do her any good to try to destroy the orb in the dark, not to mention that she couldn't desire to destroy it at all. She had to get around the condition of the orb by outsmarting it. The only way to tell if what she was doing was working, was to see if her actions changed what Valiant and Ritz were battling.

She wanted to *modify* the orb's nature. That was the best way to handle a curse like this when it was triggered by intentions. She'd keep modifying it until the spell "worked" better.

Now out of the hole, Kayla checked on Valiant and gulped. He was still sending out counter spells to what was flinging at him, but he no longer had his legs or his wings. He had both Gladius and a flying angry Bantin attacking him while he couldn't move. He met her gaze only briefly before quickly looking away, waiting for her to do her part to put an end to his torture. Ritz was dealing with images of people she assumed were former Colts coming to attack him. He had a mob trying to take him down.

Kayla cast up a shield around herself in case her desires happened to accidentally weaken and she got attacked again herself. The first spell she sent at the orb took away the use of dragons. Gladius didn't like dragons. His spell couldn't use dragons as a defensive force. Kayla's magic swirled around the purple orb, and worked! The fake Bantin that Valiant had been facing vanished. He was left with facing something even harder for him—her. Nasty.

"It's not me," Kayla shouted as she watched herself try to shred his claws.

"I know it's not you. I can hear you thinking. You keep thinking. I'll keep distracting."

The next thing she modified was the type of spell that the fake Gladius could cast. Gladius was a fan of hot things. He often burned his dragons and used tar on them. Heat was the only attack that this spell could use. It got remarkably hotter around her as fireballs came down from the sky, tearing up everything they touched. Ritz was dodging them as best as he could, and so was the rolling Valiant as he also faced Gladius sending blue hot dragon king fire at him.

She was getting so close! She could make the spell change to her wishes so she thought up something that would stop it for good. Gladius was dead. The spell could only work if he was alive. Boom. The fire stopped. The images of Gladius disappeared, but Gladius had expected something like this because it wasn't really over.

Rain started pelting down on top of her, followed by hail as large as her fist. Drat! Gladius had added a condition that if his spell stopped there would be nasty weather. With the building all torn up as it was, there was nothing for Kayla to hide inside. She had to keep up her magical shield while she tried to come up with a way to fix the sky.

Pg. 298

"I'll get it," Valiant declared, *"and tonight I am taking your keychain to visit Bantin so we can refill that thing."*

Well good. If Valiant was going to focus on the sky, she could finally focus on getting rid of the thing that Gladius had hidden. Without the curses in the way, Kayla could figure out what the purpose of the orb was so she could take it down. She cast several revealing spells at it until she understood the nature of the object in her hands.

This thing cast out a magical pull on dragons. It was the pressure that the water dragons, dragon kings, and spellbinding dragons felt, making them love the kingdom. King Lester had been asking after this spell. If Kayla got rid of it, they were going to lose water dragons to Wisteria. They were going to lose dragon kings to Vankerdale. Ice dragons could be born in any kingdom giving others the ability to use magic. There was a chance that Valiant wouldn't feel as secure here, especially since he had an interest in visiting Wisteria. There was a chance that Merlock would leave the castle and never return. She could be messing up a lot of Aralot's greatness by taking down this orb.

"I've already told you that my home is wherever you are," Valiant reminded. *"And do hurry up in your choice. I want my wings and legs back."*

Right. She might be taking away what helped Aralot stand stronger than the other kingdoms, but she'd be making it fair again at the same time. If she ended up living in Vankerdale, she didn't want Valiant feeling the pressure to be living in Aralot without her. She had to let dragons make their own choices. She had to allow them their free will again. After all, she knew what it felt like to be living inside a curse that took away part of her freedom. It was miserable.

Kayla blasted the purple orb into shatters. It was done!

She glanced around to find that the foul weather had stopped as had the other curses that were around them. Added to the ruins were charred marks from their spells along with more rubble. She hoped that no one would notice that a magical battle had taken place here, even if it was fairly obvious.

"Did you get rid of the spell for good?" Ritz asked her as he glanced first at his dragons and then at Valiant. He chose to take a step toward Valiant, maybe so he could avoid the thought of the dead dragon on the ground.

"No. I modified it until it couldn't be harmful. Then I imposed the condition that it couldn't work if Gladius is dead which he is."

"You put a new condition on it," Ritz nodded.

"You know, you're really good at using magic for not having studied the books my parents did."

"Who says I never figured out how to get into your house to study them?" Ritz grinned at her. Then he scowled because he remembered that he was supposed to be getting in her way.

Kayla rushed toward Valiant. He wasn't crying, but he looked so tortured that Kayla burst into sobs right away still so close to her own feelings of sadness to ignore them.

"He's not bleeding. He'll live," Ritz consoled as he cast a spell at her dragon. "It's conditional whatever the spell is. It's not to make

Pg. 300

him flightless or immobile. It's not to make him feel torture. I need to think like Gladius."

Ritz closed his eyes and tried to think while Kayla cried. She had put her dragon in a position to be hurt worse than anything he had ever gone through before.

"Not to worry. I have every intention of casting a spell on myself to make me believe that this was one of your fabulous nightmares so I don't believe that it really happened at all," Valiant told her. *"I don't want to have nightmares about this moment. You're the expert on Gladius's nasty work. What might the spell be, Kayla? Where are my wings and legs?"*

That was probably the best question to ask. Gladius and his spells had all been one larger overreaching spell. In the event that a dragon came to destroy the orb, he would have devised some kind of spell to stop the creature so that the real Gladius could show up later and gloat over the beast's failure. Valiant's legs had to be someplace nearby like part of the ground or the air. The spell they needed to cast at him wasn't one to undo a curse, but rather to restore what was lost. It was all in the wording.

"Great," Valiant agreed with her thinking. He tried out a few spells and then hummed when his legs and wings came back. *"I found them! They were sitting on my back. That's why everything felt so heavy. I thought it was because I didn't have legs to hold me up."*

Ritz opened his eyes at the hum and then shook his head at her for coming here. Kayla didn't know what to say to him. Ritz had suffered for this more than she had. His dead dragon didn't have spells to defend himself.

"I take it that you've learned your lesson. When I tell you to leave somewhere, you leave. Now get out of here. I don't want to see you here ever again."

Kayla's eyes teared up all over again. Ritz still had seven other dragons blocking her off from the endpoint of her dreams. Whatever that other buried object was would be far worse. It was best not to take the blockade lightly. Now that the fear of Gladius was gone, Kayla could see exactly how it was that Ritz had tricked her. He had led her to find the orb while he kept her away from that other curse.

"Let's go," Valiant begged. "I don't like this place. It smells bad like time gone sour. Come on, Kayla. I want to go."

"But..." Kayla looked toward Ritz's fallen dragon and then back at him. "I'm really sorry. I know that the words don't help—"

"Get out of here!" Ritz commanded. "I can take care of that. I'm more than capable of taking care of a dragon. It's taking care of you that drives everyone insane. Get out! You already won. You shattered the orb that draws in rare dragons to Aralot. Now Coal won't feel any pressure at all to stay here when he travels between here and Vankerdale. Had you broken it when SilverWings was alive, you would have saved him from the pressure too. You were the hero of one story. Get out of here before you become the tragedy of another."

Kayla didn't move. All she wanted to do was hug Ritz and save him from having to bury his own dragon. That was the keeper part of her wanting to take away everyone's hardest burdens, but Valiant was ready to run. He sucked her up with a spell and dashed off ready to put that whole castle behind him.

Kayla had told Ritz that she trusted him to do the right thing regarding his guardian calling, and she normally did, but what if in this case, he couldn't? He was trapped in a conditional spell that forced him to keep her away. Ritz had no choice but to distract her from what he was guarding by leading her toward another equally distracting artifact that she had destroyed. She had failed against him and not reached the end path in her dreams. That's all she could think about as Valiant led her away.

What Ritz still guarded with his wild dragons had to be the source of her problems if her dreams led her right to that spot. She should gather an army together and defeat his dragons and tie him up so she could win the race to the finish line. Her main problem with that was that Ritz was a keeper. Keepers didn't attack each other unless they were incredibly poisoned.

On that note, Kayla's eyes prickled. She hoped that it wasn't Ritz trying to get her keeper poison so that she had the means to turn against him. He might think it his job to torment her so that she could break past the spells that had him stuck and ageless. That was so depressing. She had to figure out who was really giving her poison so she could tell herself that it wasn't Ritz.

Maybe if she focused on similarities with nightmare spells that would help her find the source of her problem. She did know of a nightmare spell. Gladius had left behind that cursed flower necklace.

She hadn't done anything at all to affect a binding spell like the necklace used. What she had destroyed had not used the same power as the cursed nightmare necklace. It if did, then Valiant would have been the only one that could modify the orb until it was so weak that he could destroy it. It had been her casting spells at it, not him.

Pg. 303

She had done what Ritz had told her to do. She had changed her focus to find the spell—a singular spell—that Gladius had left here. This meant that if her focus had been on Gladius himself, then the other spell, the one that was at the end of her nightmares wasn't a spell that Gladius had left behind. Perhaps he destroyed his castle trying to defeat it. Perhaps Gladius's reason to keep diving into magic as hard as he had was that he was trying to find a way to stop the same spell that was now attacking Kayla.

It wasn't from him. Realizing that, made Kayla want to wail. He had been an amazing spellcaster! If he couldn't solve the problem of that curse, would she ever be able to? He could have created that nightmare necklace trying to understand the spell that he hadn't been able to stop. The spell against her could be binding and have some really strange condition to it. Kayla sighed. She had to find the answer because she would love a full week of restful sleep.

Valiant set her down right in the middle of the field at the King's Ware, cast his spells on himself to forget that their adventure was all real, and then curled up into a ball to hide. Kayla stood there feeling stuck. It wasn't that she was in shock still, she just simply couldn't get it out of her head that while she had destroyed the orb and rescued rare dragons, she had failed to save a keeper. It felt like her job somehow. Save them all. While she was one step closer to figuring out what had Ritz trapped, she felt rather far away, since Ritz was going to prevent her from reaching that one spell with his very life.

"It was all a nightmare, Kayla. Will you please stop. I'm exhausted," Valiant rambled at her as he peeked at her with one eye and then shut it again.

Pg. 304

"You know, you don't roll in the dirt at the castle," Caleb remarked, as he came over to her taking in her dirty, damp, and singed new clothes. He shook his head at her and looked at Valiant as if the dragon would provide an answer to what they had been doing.

"What do you do when you feel like you've failed the one thing your heart tells you to protect?" Kayla asked Caleb as he came around behind her probably to remind her that she had work to do and that she needed to change.

"You cry a little," he answered. "Then you find someone you trust and give them a really big hug. What happened? Your dress is a mess. Did you fight invisible demons again?"

"It was…" Kayla looked at Valiant who was trying to get to sleep and chose to answer carefully for his sake. "A nightmare that felt way too real. I thought for a moment that I had brought Gladius back to life. He came at me with his charm, making me think he was there to save me, and then he tried to kill me before he went after Valiant and…"

She wasn't going to bring up Ritz. Her actions helped out rare dragons in the present and future, but it had cost a life today. It was a battle of will and mind. It was a battle of magic, her against Gladius, and while she was glad that Gladius wasn't traveling through time with heart magic, she was still sad.

"*Ritz died?*" Valiant asked her popping up both his eyes to gaze at her alarmed.

"*One of his dragons,*" Kayla answered. Gee, Valiant's spell had worked on himself well if he didn't remember that part. She wasn't going to be the one to take his spell off. He wanted it that way. He blinked at her confused, shrugged accepting her verdict, and then closed his eyes again.

"Did you need a hug?" Caleb asked.

Kayla didn't turn around to see his extended arms. She sat herself down on the ground and stared at the dirt. She had not stopped the nightmares. That had been her goal in going to the castle in the first place and Ritz had turned her toward a different fight instead.

"Maybe Gladius isn't responsible for the nightmares," Valiant offered. *"That whole thing was a bad dream, right?"*

Kayla ignored the question. Ritz and Gladius were running from love. That was the one part of their lies that she still believed. They competed to be the worst lover, even if it was Ritz who had told her to stay with the guy that would make her the happiest. If she ever left Caleb, she was going to end up being exactly like they were. Maybe that's what the cursed object was that Ritz was hiding her from. It was something that pushed at keepers to try to make them miserable.

Her mother had almost married King Klavian. Kayla was pushed into nearly marrying King Tyler. Many of the keeper's families were troubled like this, thrown toward marriages that they didn't want. If she could hold out against this curse, she just might make it. Maybe she didn't need to destroy it to win. All she needed to do was trust what Ritz told her. Stay in Aralot. Stay with Caleb. The curse would stop.

"Have I ever told you about the time that I dived headfirst into a pile of dragon dung to escape my dad catching me ditching class?" Caleb asked her as he sat down beside her.

Pg. 306

She couldn't help it. Kayla shook her head at him the smile already creeping onto her face. He put his arm around her and proceeded to make her laugh until she felt ready enough to change her clothes and join the class. Ritz was right. She had everything she needed right here without needing to go look for it.

Secrets

Tristan

Tristan checked over his shoulder for the fourth time looking horribly suspicious as he headed toward Vermelo's bedroom, but he couldn't help it. If his dad caught him, Klavian would stop his progress or worse claim that Tristan was abusing magic again. He had cast a spell on himself to be invisible to the guards, and while that same spell applied to both Vermelo and his dad, Tristan couldn't help but feel like someone was still watching him. He got that feeling a lot around the castle. He could never quite tell if it was because Vermelo was spying on him through that secret mirror or if someone was actually watching him. Maybe they could hear him. He glanced at the nearest guard who wasn't looking his direction and then crept on past to the foot of the stairs that led up to Vermelo's tower.

Vermelo chose to sleep closer to his guards than any of the Clusters inside the castle. He made frequent trips into town to visit his family, but he'd not gone home to sleep for quite some time. Yesterday should have been the day he went home for a visit. Vermelo hadn't budged as if he needed to stay around and keep an eye on things. Since he was sticking too close, Tristan was searching the Captain of the Guard's things even if Tristan had already ruled Vermelo out for being both his and Kayla's killer. The man knew something. Something he didn't want to revealed, and if Tristan could find it, he might be able to gain a clue to who was after Kayla.

Tristan was certain of Vermelo's knowledge with the way the man had teared up about Kayla's nightmares. He had watched her walk from the castle as long as he could. While Tristan hadn't spotted Vermelo sticking his head out the castle window to spy on her, he couldn't locate the magical mirror. That was proof right there that Vermelo was keeping the object close to him so he wouldn't miss a thing.

Tristan picked the lock on Vermelo's door and stepped inside the empty room to get started. He disregarded the horse trophies, the letters from the man's kids, the dirty clothes on the floor. He searched drawers, wall panels, and pictures, gathering his evidence on the bed in a heap before he sat down with a glance at the door and started in on looking over what he had found.

Vermelo was hiding letters from Vankerdale. They clearly stated that they were to be sent to the rulers of the kingdom. Tristan hadn't heard anything about these, so he opened up the first one to make out King Tyler's handwriting. The guy had a rather neat script and he didn't attempt to confuse Aralot with fancy words and hidden threats as King Peyton had done. If anything, King Tyler was trying to take away all the guesswork.

"Dear esteemed Aralot,

This is my third attempt in asking for your acknowledgment that I have acquired the throne in Vankerdale by becoming the next king. As you are aware, the rules in Vankerdale state that upon taking the throne the king must be married to a noble. In my case, I chose the option of being engaged, but I
Pg. 310

would appreciate you telling my wife to return home. There are duties that Queen Kayla needs to fulfill. Please remind her of such."

"What?!"

Tristan glanced at the door to make sure the no one had heard him. Vermelo often kept guards near his door. It was strange that they were not in the way for Tristan to spell away. It felt like Vermelo wanted him to come into his room and discover this. It was just the sort of thing that Vermelo would do to make Tristan decide that Kayla was off-limits. Vermelo was all about trying to convince Tristan to take the crown. The object had been in Tristan's room for two days. Now it had been moved into here. Tristan had noticed the crown's box beneath Vermelo's bed during his search. He still wasn't touching that.

Tristan put the letter back into the envelope and pulled out the next one. It was rather similar, asking for Kayla to be sent back. Tristan moved to the envelope with the earliest date and pulled out not a letter, but a legal document that proved Tyler was the new king. The paper should be stored in the castle's records room not in here. At the bottom of the page was Kayla's signature. Vermelo was hiding from everyone that Kayla was already lost to Aralot, and Kayla was hiding the same thing. She was the worst! The absolute worst! Tristan had been dating her this whole time only to find out that she had never been dating *him*. He had just started to like her!

"How could she do this?" Tristan asked Riven.

This happened to him every single time! He'd get close to a girl only to find that she was running off with some other guy. Maybe it was a curse he didn't know about cast upon him until he could get rid of Kayla Brixton!

"Are you turning on her again?" Riven asked him. *"It was nice when we were friends."*

"She is married," Tristan informed, tucking the letters back where they came from even if he wanted to slam them into their locations and wrinkle the lot.

Actually, this was really good news. With Kayla gone, he was going to get the throne. He would wait for Kayla to go back to Vankerdale, no need to push the girl when she had no other choice, and he could stop worrying about how they would get along forever. He didn't have to date her any longer. He didn't have to bend himself trying to guess at her moods or see into her mind. He had no obligation to her at all. It was rather relieving. He was free of Kayla Brixton! If he wasn't still in Vermelo's room, he'd do a cartwheel.

"We are still in her keeper bond," Riven stated.

"That hardly matters," Tristan answered, spinning himself in a full circle to add to his joy. *"She's like her mother. Kayla won't ever ask us to do anything unless it's a life or death matter, and by then, we should be doing something about it anyway. Freedom! I can date who I want. I can like who I want. I can talk as I want, and I can glare at her all I want!"*

"Perhaps try to keep the glaring down to a minimum," Riven advised. *"She's not told anyone yet. Our subjects still see you two as a couple."*

"No one sees us as a couple," Tristan answered as he opened the door and took the stairs down three at a time.

The Colts all made fun of him. The nobles kept their mouths strictly shut. The riders all recoiled. The only ones who cared would be

Pg. 312

their parents. Kayla was probably really glad about this too. Tristan could picture her jumping for joy that they didn't have to get married because she was already married.

"Are you going to tell your mom?" Riven asked causing Tristan to stop skipping giving away his invisible position.

The guards were looking over at him now and glancing at each other wondering if they needed to do something about the sound of invisible footprints. The thought of telling his mom wasn't very pleasant. No. He would leave that to Kayla. Tyler would find a way to get around Vermelo obstructing his mail, and when that happened, Kayla was going to be taking the blame for her own actions. It wasn't going to be Tristan getting the lecture this time. It was going to be her.

"Who's there?" one of the guards called out.

As fun as it would be to have them all scrambling around, it was best to not cause himself trouble with his parents. Tristan took his invisible spell off telling the guards that he was testing it out and then he ran back into the castle.

Vermelo was cleared yet again. He was hanging around waiting for the moment that Kayla got in trouble, because he didn't want to be the one breaking the bad news either. He was probably in denial that she was gone and trying to cling to her as long as possible.

Tristan still needed to worry about who was trying to kill them though. Back to that. Even if Kayla moved to another kingdom she could be poisoned. That could be the reason why she hadn't left yet. There wasn't anyone in Vankerdale that she trusted that could give her the cure if she started to go mad. Kayla was waiting around for the poisoner to make a mistake and show up. Maybe once Tristan found out who the coward was, Kayla would leave and finally be gone!

If only he could blame Valiant for his attacks, he would be getting somewhere. Tristan had once feared that Valiant would send nasty spells at everyone, and there was the possibility that Valiant was trying to kill Tristan off if the dragon feared that it was Tristan sending the poison at him. However, this theory sank into the dust because Valiant would never harm a member of his own keeper bond so it couldn't be him.

From the way the attacks had been, Tristan was left with Ritz as his last suspect. Ritz would be able to use his dad's voice. Ritz could want him dead, but why now instead of before? What had he done that got Ritz mad at him? Nothing. Tristan clicked his tongue together and then nodded.

It had to be Ritz! Ritz had used his spies to learn that Kayla was married in Vankerdale. He couldn't have Kayla on the throne, so he was going to kill off Tristan before anyone got the idea that Tristan should keep the spot. After all, both Tia and Rosa were expecting. Ritz would love to see a Felding in the castle instead of a Cluster. It wasn't like the next Felding king would be poisoned like Gladius had been. There was no reason to not support him. Ritz was trying to kill off Tristan before anyone else realized that Tristan was one step closer to being the king.

Turning on Ritz was going to be tough. No one had been able to kill him off before. The man had outlived his own life several times over and he was known for taking down anyone that stood against him, even those that held magic. Still, there had to be a way to take Ritz down. What Tristan needed to find was the condition of the spell that was keeping Ritz alive. If he destroyed that, he could destroy Ritz before his killer found another clever way to defeat him.

Theft

Tyler

Jack was doing it again! He was breaking into the castle and lurking around the hallways until Tyler just happened to walk past. With a full guard calmly walking in his wake, Tyler crossed his arms at the sight of King Jack sitting in the light of a window on the *inside* of his castle.

"Nothing new yet," Tyler told him before the man could ask.

"Oh, I beg to differ. The last time I was here you weren't secretly married to my daughter."

Nice. That news had finally reached Jack. It had taken long enough! Tyler had sent Jack that personal letter days ago!

"I have never kept that a secret. Maybe you should ask your daughter why she is keeping it a secret in Aralot. I didn't force her to marry me, Jack. I asked her and she said yes. I've sent her a ring. I sent her your wedding ring too that King Peyton had stolen from you. I asked Valiant to bring her by. Nothing. I have done nothing but keep my word over here while your daughter runs around playing tricks on me."

Jack shook his head keeping his expression otherwise placid so Tyler wasn't sure just how mad he really was. When Jack decided to skip over the topic, Tyler guessed that it made him too mad to want to discuss it further.

"Also, the last time I was here you hadn't ventured onto my land, spied on my subjects, and bought a set of ware books. I do know what you've been doing, Tyler."

"I need those things." Tyler wanted to shrug but his last visit with Jack replayed through his mind.

Jack had asked him to locate information on what kind of a spell a spellbinding dragon couldn't take away, and when Tyler asked what was in it for him, Jack had told him that he'd let him stay a keeper. Since it was Jack's dragon that had given Tyler the ability to hear his dragon, it was a very dirty threat to first grant him mental communication and then steal it all away. Tyler had to remain calm and in control here. He still held by his statement that the Brixtons and Feldings were his strongest supporters, and knowing how weak that support was sometimes made him want to shake in his shoes.

He could do this. For Vankerdale. For all the people who had lived cursed their whole lives. He was going to give them a better life.

"We need the training, Jack. Most of us have no idea how to properly mount our own dragons. With us able to bond again that's going to get us all hurt. I have to provide my people with a list of safety measures and understandable techniques they can use to stay on their dragons."

"Nothing new about that nightmare thing?"

Tyler shook his head and looked down the hallway where General Reis had arrived at a jog. Seeing Jack, the general gave a signal to Tyler instead of hollering his message. He waved his fingers around like they were a group of dragons flying in the air. After reading through the ware books, Tyler had decided to make a few signals of his own, and he was glad for this silent one. Conner was here. Jack looked over at the general not guessing what the secret message was, and looked back at Tyler anxiously.

"I'm really sorry, Jack. I've scoured every inch of everywhere looking for more. What you are looking for is not in Vankerdale. I'd suggest Wisteria if they weren't still shut off to the both of us."

"Our spies haven't been returning from Wisteria," Jack mumbled. "For that matter, neither have yours. We took some of yours, bribed them to our side. Well not me personally, I think it was Aria who did that, but they've not come back either."

Jack frowned at him as if he hadn't wanted to tell Tyler that. It was the same way with Kayla when she was here. She rambled off things like this too. It was odd that Jack did it, but perhaps it was a result of a spell on the inside of the castle. Unless of course, Jack had turned himself into a keeper.

"So the spies learned something," Tyler pointed out. "It'd be nice to get them back."

"Maybe I'll work on it," Jack shrugged at him.

Jack had been trying to find a way into Wisteria for years already and hadn't come up with anything yet. Tyler wished him luck and then excused himself to follow General Reis while he left a few of the guards to see that Jack was escorted out the back.

The general led him to the side of the courtyard looking more worried than finding Jack in the castle. Tyler considered alerting Coal in case this was a new threat, but he held off in case his dragon was sleeping. If there was a real threat, he'd have Coal waking up anyway with his troubled thoughts.

The general pulled Tyler to a sudden stop against a wall. From here Tyler could make out Adelyn with her back to them talking to someone. Conner? Tyler just knew that she'd met him again. Adelyn was shifting on her feet nervous, yet engaged.

"You got it?" Conner asked. "You figured out the message?"

"Yes, I figured out the hidden Colt message," Adelyn answered.

Tyler frowned. Despite feeling that Adelyn would never intentionally harm him Tyler felt cold hearing her talking. She'd knowingly betrayed his trust to get Conner the information he was after.

There was only one Colt message that Conner wanted. It was the one from that book in King Peyton's room. It hadn't looked remarkable at all to Tyler so he hadn't ever handed it over. Conner had turned to someone else, and Tyler wished the man hadn't picked Adelyn, because now he was feeling mad at her.

"So here." Adelyn passed over a jade carving of a dragon that had sat in dust in the throne room for years. "Let my family go now, please."

She had lied to him! Conner hadn't promised her family a bunch of supplies in exchange for Adelyn delivering a letter. He had captured them all, no doubt with his dragon horde, and used Adelyn to get the object he was after. Poor Adelyn. She had to be incredibly nervous. Conner's dragon team was the greatest coordinated force that Tyler had ever seen, even after venturing into Aralot and spying on the wares for a bit. Conner's dragons had years of practice working together.

"They are fine. I'll get your family back home safe and sound. There's nothing to worry about anymore. Thank you for this. You told Tyler that he needed to send you back?"

Adelyn nodded as she stepped away from Conner looking scared of him. He pocketed the jade dragon and walked off. Tyler caught a few guards looking at him waiting for him to give the signal to knock Conner over and take back the trinket, but he didn't. Adelyn's family was at stake, so he let the man take what he wanted. Her father was a captain in his army as well as a Peyton noble. His life was more important than a jade dragon.

"Have him followed," Tyler whispered to General Reis. "See that he releases his hostages. I can't afford to lose support from the living Peytons right now."

"Pst!" Tyler hissed causing Adelyn to spin around and shrink away from him next.

"Tyler, I..." Adelyn trembled, noticing the guards that had closed in for her stealing from the castle. Tyler could have her locked up for the rest of her life, but that would hurt him personally so he didn't.

"Don't worry about it. Conner is fantastic, but only if he's on your side at the moment. When he's not, he's terrifying. I get it. What is that thing? What was the code? It was clever of you to find it. He asked me for the letter before and I didn't see anything of note."

"It's... Oh, Tyler!" Adelyn flung herself into his arms and clung to him, not wanting to talk, but he really needed to know, so he gave her a quick squeeze and held her at arm's length staring her down.

"It's a way to destroy the Colts. That's what the secret message said. It was written by Gladius when he was raving mad and it said that the jade dragon could defeat the Colts, so he was sending it to Vankerdale to keep it safe for him so they didn't fall. It made no sense at all. Wasn't it the Colts that killed Gladius? Why was he trying to save them if they killed him off?"

"I have no idea," Tyler answered.

Gladius was one complicated mess of a man. Perhaps the reason why Tyler couldn't read anything important on the paper himself was because the paper didn't work if it was a king reading it. Gladius did things like that. King Peyton had probably asked others what the message said before. He kept around the jade dragon since it had a curse for Aralot. That was the sort of thing that King Peyton would enjoy.

Tyler looked in the direction of the border and sighed. As if Aralot didn't have enough to worry about, Conner was trying to destroy the Colts while everything else exploded. They were going to lose their princess and their claim on the renegades.

"We will just have to trust that Conner knows what he's doing," Tyler said pulling Adelyn back in. As a Colt himself maybe he was safeguarding the jade dragon, or moving it away from Tyler so that Tyler couldn't hurt it. It could be a defensive instead of an offensive gesture on Conner's end. However, his way of obtaining what he wanted made him a continuous threat to Vankerdale. Conner was a hard person to trust, even when Tyler wanted to trust him. Dealing with fellow keepers was hard.

"Your family will be fine. Conner works for the glory of Aralot, so it must be something he needs to do if he came after you when I didn't help him."

"I feel horrible," Adelyn wailed. "I lied to you and then stole from the throne room—"

"And you did the right thing," Tyler told her. "Just try to do the right thing differently next time, huh?"

Fired

Caleb

It was hard to believe that it had already been eight days since he had started training Valiant's special night class. The evening training made such a large difference. Valiant wasn't as stubborn to participate in the day class, both because Kayla kept sneaking out at night to teach him new spells, and because if her mental dialogue didn't work, Caleb would sneak in words from the magic book he had been reading into his class instructions. That always made Valiant look at him and pay attention, even if that attention was simply to laugh at him for how slowly he was reading the book. It was a major improvement to see Valiant's eyes instead of his body curled up into a lump.

Caleb scanned over the field trying to decide what he was going to have his class do tonight. Most of the dragons hadn't arrived yet. He caught sight of Kayla checking over Valiant's scales and claws before she snuck out for the night. Three days ago, she had come back having dusted her new dress from him rather well. While Valiant was improving, it was a shame that Kayla was not. Instead of Valiant sleeping on the field during the day, it was Kayla falling down taking up to half an hour to wake back up sometimes. When she was down,

Valiant wouldn't work. He stood over her protectively, sometimes snarling into air at no one in particular.

When Kayla was awake, she was often too tired to do much. She had him incredibly worried. Caleb would have started consulting numerous doctors about this if it wasn't that he knew she was alert when it was dark. He hoped that she was simply adjusting to having a night dragon instead of falling worse for a curse. Her body would figure out a better rhythm soon, and Caleb wouldn't have to fret so much that she couldn't stay awake when the sun was out. Maybe he should encourage her to learn a spell that helped her to read faster. That way she could satisfy her dragon without needing to stay awake too long.

Caleb walked closer to Kayla, glancing into the air as Halfax, Norber, and Reed arrived on the field. That was four out seven dragons. He was only missing Bantin, Riven, and Merlock. Merlock took his sweet time in arriving, so Caleb usually started without him.

"He's here already," Warner informed him. *"Merlock has been staring at the top of the flag pole. Charles's dragon has asked him not to tar the pole three times already causing Merlock to laugh."*

His class was getting into trouble. Speaking of trouble, more of it came winging his direction. Riven was next to arrive, unfortunately with Tristan on his back. Tristan flipped from his dragon before the beast landed so that he could thud down next to Kayla. Caleb could already see Kayla's defenses rising. She hadn't been wearing her sweater before, but she pulled it on and tugged down the hood now that Tristan was here.

Caleb increased his speed so that he was close enough to order the prince to get out of his class should he need to. Just the look on Tristan's face said he was up to something.

"I think that we should marry," Tristan declared, crossing his arms like he knew Kayla wanted to avoid this topic.

Please avoid the topic. Caleb wasn't ready for this. He'd not even gotten a full month of Kayla being his friend before he was facing losing her. Caleb waited for her to use a classic redirection strategy, but she didn't.

"I think that we should not," Kayla answered.

Had he heard that right? Caleb took another step closer just to be sure, unable to stop the smile that was slowly starting to come. She said no! She went on all those dates with the prince and turned him down! Caleb wouldn't have to spend the rest of his life trailing in Tristan's shadow trying to hide that he still loved the girl. Tristan was nothing like Jack. If he married Kayla, Caleb's life wouldn't look anything like Anvil's.

Caleb glanced around at anyone else that may have heard this. There were a lot of riders out on the field right now, and every eye he met was paying attention to this refusal. They were free of Tristan! He watched a collective relieved sigh run through the onlookers, but they may have been premature.

"Your mom is going to be so mad at you," Tristan laughed. He uncrossed his arms and angled himself closer to Kayla peering beneath that hood of hers. Caleb hoped that she was scowling at him. The way he said that next sentence made it sound like he knew something about royal marriage vows that the rest of them didn't. Could Kayla not refuse? She had to be able to refuse!

"Want to know my favorite dragon word?" Kayla had asked him. "It's stop."

That word had never made Caleb laugh, but it caused Tristan to laugh so hard that he had to place his hands on his knees. There was really something else going on here. Caleb was even more certain of that when Tristan asked if Kayla had seen Ritz around. How was Ritz connected to wedding vows?

"Ritz is only seen when he wants to be," Kayla answered. "And so am I."

With that, she flashed her invisibility spell and stalked away. Tristan made some mental comment that led his dragon to snort at him. Caleb grinned at Riven as Tristan left next. Even creatures bonded to him found him to be aggravating. Now that was something he might laugh at if he wasn't still trying to figure out what Tristan hadn't said.

Perhaps there was some odd law that said that Tristan had to get married before her or something. If that was the case, Caleb could see him claiming the throne as his own long before Kayla could ever say the same thing.

"I've never heard of that rule, Caleb," Warner told him. *"That can't be it."*

Well, it was something, and since Caleb was still stuck on the subject, he was scratching his head over who Tristan would marry if it wasn't Kayla. He was glad that it wasn't going to be Kayla, but the prince would need to find a wife somewhere.

"Riven can I get your opinion?" Caleb asked. "What kind of a person would Tristan happily marry?"

Warner was a great help in translating the answer before he tucked down to sleep. Tristan liked smart girls who were pretty and funny. Having a dragon was a must. It had to be someone who enjoyed expensive gifts and was clever and charming. Caleb tried to decide if he knew anyone that fit all of that, because he had to add to the wanted list. The girl would also need to have a tendency to fall for troublesome guys who took humor out of picking pockets.

The harder Caleb thought about it, the harder it became. There wasn't a rider around that didn't feel some desire to hide their pockets from Tristan when he came by. At least not at the King's Ware. Tristan had visited all the other wares too, and he had dated several girls there, but according to his dragon, whenever Tristan thought he was making progress, the girls found some excuse to back away from him, usually by instantly dating someone else.

This was a hard call. The only kind of person Caleb could think of that would laugh at the same things Tristan did was another Colt. Finding one of those with a secret dragon was a hard task. He knew he was training two Colt dragons right now, but he had no idea if their riders were female or not, and he doubted the dragons would ever tell him. That would betray their deepest bonded oath to never betray their rider.

Bantin landing with a loud thud and calling for Merlock to leave the flagpole alone, had Caleb putting his thoughts on hold to pay attention to his class.

"What have you been getting into?" Caleb asked the brown Halfax. He had green sludge all along the back of his tail. Halfax tried to wipe it off on the dirt as Caleb shook his head at him. He could clean that tail off, or he could look over at Valiant expectantly and… Ha! Valiant cast a spell that took care of the problem right away.

Merlock arrived, still the last to class even if he had been early, and gave Caleb a toothy smile waiting for his nightly workout. Caleb returned the smile and came up with what they should work on tonight. They had been going over flight patterns, which were useful, but the dragons needed a fun night every now and then. Tonight was it. He was going to have them work on utilizing their talented stomachs. Dragons enjoyed the rare chance to flame or ice or tar inside a ware.

It showed a lot of faith in the dragons he was training if he was already willing to let them belt out harmful substances, but he did already trust this group to do as he asked and to keep things relatively safe. Bantin was going to be shooting out ice—short blasts, not the wall wrecking kind that Bantin was capable of. The other dragons could learn how to dodge that. Then they could learn how to avoid tar from Merlock. Valiant could patch back up whatever mess they made, and he no doubt would add strange things to the mix to amuse himself.

Sometimes he would have strong wind blow against Bantin to slow him down. He had made Norber's tail extra heavy before. Halfax's talons had gotten too large for him to land, so Bantin had given him a snow pile to crash into instead. Reed had found himself flying upside down. Riven had turned orange. It was never a dull class, and his spectators had only increased if anything.

Pg. 330

Caleb glanced around noticing the lounging riders that hadn't been shooed off to bed yet and the ones on the field waiting for their own night classes to start up. They still had plenty of room to work in, so Caleb signaled for them to start their warmup. The dragons rose to the air along with Merlock to warm up their wings.

"That was remarkable, Caleb," Charles said, a little out of breath, as he stepped up behind him. "What was that sound you taught them?"

It took Caleb a minute to even remember what sound he had just given. He was sort of training reflexively, as if this was the most normal thing he could be doing, coordinating three rare dragons and three fire-breathing dragons.

"I don't know if the dragon sound has a name to it, sir," Caleb answered looking over his shoulder to see that Charles was looking a little pale while he sweated in the heat. Charles had been the ware leader here forever, but tonight his hair looked whiter than snow, and his eyes looked a bit yellow as if he was contemplating sightsharing but not quite doing it.

"I don't even know what the dragon sound means," Caleb admitted. "Valiant chirped it out and it lines them all up perfectly. It felt like the right word to use. These guys are really smart. They're getting down formations in a few tries."

"They have a good teacher," Charles smiled at him still sounding breathless as he rubbed a spot on his arm. "I've watched many section leaders in my life. You're one of the best, Caleb. I wanted you to know that since I've not told you. Anvil insisted when he sent you that I wouldn't be disappointed and he was right. I…"

"Thank you, sir," Caleb replied, feeling the compliment flood through his chest. Caleb might not be old enough to be doing this, but Charles believed he was capable, and he had watched the best of the best his whole life. This was a grand compliment indeed.

"Sir?" Caleb asked because Charles's eyes went wide. When his knees buckled underneath him and he started to fall Caleb panicked.

"Get the doctor!" Caleb shouted at Warner effectively waking his dragon back up and cutting off the class. Warner belted his dragon voice across the field. True to their intuitive natures, the dragons in his class stopped and landed on the field, all except for Reed who looked outward toward the ocean, as if he had the inner worry that his rider was hurt someplace.

At Warner's shrill cry for the doctor, the ware sprung to action. The scout dragons changed their formation. One dashed off to bring a doctor in case he wasn't already rushing out his door. Two more dragons dashed over to Warner searching for the source of distress so that they dropped down beside Caleb when prompted.

"He just…I don't know…" Caleb told the older riders. It was moments like this that Caleb felt his youth. He had studied basic medical training, but he had never gotten too deep into that area. These scouts would have far more experience than he did and he was supposed to be teaching them.

"He's not breathing," the night scout told Caleb in a voice that was far too calm.

Pg. 332

Charles wasn't breathing?! Couldn't they do anything?

Charles's eyes were still wide. He reached into his pocket and pulled out his ware leader key. This he passed to Caleb. Caleb stared at it in his hand for a few seconds before Charles's dragon screamed out the cry of death.

"No!" Caleb screamed next.

The other night scout grabbed Charles limp form from him. That was a wise decision since Caleb was looking around for something to hit. He should have been able to do something! This couldn't have happened right in front of him. If he had been paying more attention or had more training or actually been the section leader that Charles claimed him to be, he could have done something!

"It's Charles," the night scout told the running doctor. Dr. Weber stopped running toward them at the news.

"Oh," he replied with the attitude of a shrug that had Caleb wanting to scream at him. Charles was dead. They had to do something!

"Not to break it to you, but even Valiant can't spell back the dead," Warner told him.

Then Valiant should have done something before Charles stopped breathing. Caleb looked at the spellbinding dragon to express his frustrated thoughts only to have Valiant give him a sad sound and curl up on the ground. Caleb stomped his feet. Once Valiant got in that pose there was no getting him out of it. Class was canceled tonight.

"Caleb, don't take it so hard," Dr. Weber put a firm hand on his shoulder. "Charles's heart has been stopping lately. He knew this was coming. There wasn't much anyone could do. He was getting old. You had better step back. He wanted his dragon to do the honors as soon as life failed him."

They all jumped back as Charles's dragon landed between them and turned his rider to ashes. Then Clipshire jumped back into the air and left without looking back. Caleb stared after the dragon with thoughts of death running through his head. What would his dragon do when he died?

"We're dying together," Warner told him.

Caleb teared up as he stared at the ashes. He didn't want his dragon dying at all!

"It's another stage of life, Caleb. Don't be sad. Charles is still alive in the soul of his dragon, and when Clipshire dies, their souls shall be able to play together again."

But it was all so sudden, so out of the blue, that Caleb didn't know what to do about it. All that was left of Charles were some ashes that were cleared away by Dr. Weber who scooped them into a bucket and went to go dump them. It just felt wrong.

"Are you going to tell us who Charles designated as the next ware leader?" the night scout asked Caleb, indicating the key that he held in his hand.

Caleb snapped back to himself. He couldn't stand there staring at the empty ground. At the moment, he had the ware key. He was suddenly the ware leader. Did Charles know that he was going to die right then? He had walked over to the first section leader he found and passed over his role.

"I'll go look at his paperwork and see what he left behind," Caleb offered.

He turned to go to the office, noticing how Reed chirped down to the other dragons in the class asking them if they were going to practice some more. Bantin's voice answered and it must have been because they wanted to know who was in charge next that caused Reed to land and wait.

Gosh. A lot of things changed when getting a new ware leader. What if the new ware leader figured out the connection with the Colt dragons and forbade Caleb from teaching them? This could completely ruin this whole unauthorized class he had going on.

Caleb cracked open the cabinets and started searching the office. He found progress reports and important deadlines. The ware was scheduled for a surprise holiday next month when a touring singer's group would be in town. That was nice of Charles. Caleb found rule books and formations and the schedule for scout duties written out for the next half year. It wasn't until he looked in Charles's desk that he found what he was looking for.

Right on the top were instructions to follow for when Charles died. Charles wanted the included letter to be mailed to his family while his belongings were to be donated to those in need. He had a speech written up to be read to the ware, but the part that had Caleb groaning was the part that told him to deliver the ware key to the king.

King Jack wasn't here, and while he could be summoned easily enough through Valiant telling Sparkle telling Pyro to send Jack, Caleb wanted to be more prepared for when he told everyone what Charles had left behind. If it wasn't the king leading the King's Ware, then it was the most seasoned warrior. Caleb read through the records again, picking out a few names for the next oldest person, trying to decide if any of them would accept being the next ware leader when he had no idea who these people were at all.

He was interrupted by a short knock on the door, and before he could move to open it, Tristan came in, followed by his dad and Vermelo.

"Got the news," Vermelo stated. "Sorry for your loss. I heard it came as a bit of a shock to you since you were talking to Charles at the time. How are you doing now?"

"Keeping busy," Caleb answered honestly.

Part of him still felt horribly inadequate to have not saved Charles. He was going to be reading through his books on medical care tonight and then checking out the section on magical cures.

"Charles didn't pick anyone. He said to give the key to the king, so I've gone through the names and found people who could —"

"I never liked the idea that our strongest ware should be led by the weakest oldest man. Charles was a fantastic ware leader, but I'd calculated that he would die about eight years ago and have already modified the ware law accordingly," King Klavian interrupted.

"So we… what? Hold a competition for ware leader?" Caleb asked. That would be a grand thing to see everyone fighting to prove they were the best in the ware so that they could be in charge.

"Of course not," King Klavian replied. "In the absence of the king not being in charge of his own ware, the position can be filled by the next eligible and trained kin. In this case, Prince Tristan is our only option."

Pg. 336

Caleb jerked his head toward Tristan who wasn't laughing about this. King Klavian was serious. He was putting his son in charge of the ware. Caleb found himself turning his pocket away from Tristan so the guy couldn't take the key from him. Tristan. He was going to have to do what Tristan said. This was going to be horrible.

"Try to look on the bright side," Warner thought, attempting to find a positive. *"Riven is in our night class, so Tristan won't disband it."*

There was that, but Caleb still didn't like this. Tristan held his hand out for the ware key, and Caleb highly considered running with it for a second. He didn't though. It would accomplish him nothing but make Tristan mad at him for not accepting his authority.

"Charles left behind an already completed schedule for half a year out," Caleb said as he put the key on the desk next to the papers, instead of in the prince's outstretched hand. Things were already in place. Tristan wouldn't need to change anything since it was working just fine.

"Charles was like that," Tristan nodded. "I've read through all his papers before when I was bored. He was very good at dictating tasks to his section leaders and believed firmly that a good leader directs more than controls. Just a second," Tristan said as he walked over and pocketed the key before he opened the office door looking outward. "I asked Riven to wake up the other section leaders as this is something they need to know."

Caleb glanced out the open door to see the other men running toward the office as fast as their legs could carry them. They scrambled through the door in various states of alertness and anxiety. Caleb felt calm in comparison to their faces, until Tristan moved to the cabinet that Caleb had just been looking inside and pulled out Caleb's personal file.

"To catch all of you up," Tristan told Notley, Malone, Russel, and Mulligan, "Charles had his final heart attack and died tonight. In the event that the king is not around to lead his ware, it is the prince that shall be taking over. In the event that I am away, it shall be Mulligan in charge. I need to address one more change in position. Charles was bribed to ignore Caleb's skill level by Anvil. I am not capable of being bribed in the same way."

Tristan tossed Caleb's file onto the desk causing Notley to glance at Caleb confused before skimming the report. He groaned and rubbed his eyes at the sight of the first new change to their ware. Caleb found himself holding his breath. He wanted to challenge Tristan over this. Could he get away with that in front of King Klavian and the Captain of the Guard?

"Caleb only just reached level six after finishing two levels per year since he was sixteen. If you want to know, he's only nineteen. He does not have the qualifications to be a section leader." Tristan reported what Notley had decided to remain silent about.

"Charles just said I was good teacher," Caleb declared, taking a step toward Tristan ready to fight it out regardless of who else was watching.

This was not happening. Tristan had used his Colt skills to be the ultimate snoop so he could learn how to humiliate everyone around him. This was only the start of the battle. If Tristan knocked Caleb down, there went everything he had built with Kayla and Valiant. It was all going to crash apart. Either that or Caleb would hope that it did so that he didn't feel horrible that Valiant was listening to some other person other than him.

"What?" Malone cried. He grabbed at the report to see for himself, and even if they hadn't talked much since Malone always had the night shift, the man still defended him. "Caleb is a great section leader."

"So he is," Tristan agreed. "And he will be an even better section leader after completing his own training. This is not negotiable. I know you all think I'm evil right now, but Caleb can't teach what he hasn't learned. It just doesn't happen with anyone no matter how fast he has completed his other levels. Anvil was simply desperate to find a legal way to transfer Caleb when it wasn't transfer season. Caleb was forced to take a position that he wasn't qualified for. He can stay at the King's Ware, but he won't be a section leader anymore."

"Tristan, I can do this," Caleb assured him.

He'd already been doing it for almost four weeks already and he was fine. So he had a few moments where he didn't know what to do with certain injuries, and he couldn't help teach the CJ4, but other than those parts, he had been able to handle everything else.

"Can we leave him in charge of Valiant?" Mulligan asked. "Nobody else wants that dragon. The creature shoots spells all day long. They could be anything."

"Not negotiable," Tristan said again. "Tomorrow Caleb will be joining the level seven class with Notley. Russel is in charge of finding a new place for Kayla."

"I don't want Caleb!" Notley protested.

Perhaps he was trying to be nice, but it didn't help Caleb's mood any. This was a royal disaster. Charles died and Caleb suddenly lost everything that had made him happy in the same minute. He knew he had a bad feeling about all of this. Being Kayla's teacher had brought to him the best days of his life, and now it was all gone.

"You have to be kidding!" Russel shouted next. "We put a lot of thought into who should be in Kayla's class when she got here. We are not breaking up that team right when they are starting to work together."

"So keep her class," Tristan shrugged. "But you'll need to find it a new teacher. Caleb will be busy. You are all dismissed. I expect you to clear this office without further argument."

They cleared the office, but they took the argument with them.

"I could flame him," Mulligan declared once he shut the door. "All I need is a match and some tinder and I'd light him up."

"Nobody cares that Caleb is underage," Notley agreed. "They all like him. He cares for others, and he's not scared to do what needs to be done. I was enjoying not needing to micromanage his side of the field any longer."

"There is no way we can find another teacher for Valiant," Russel whined.

"It's going to be you, Russel," Malone stated. "I'm going to go... fly something."

He stomped back to the field that he was supposed to be watching. Caleb wanted to stomp along with him and start telling people what to do just to spite Tristan for taking away his job.

Pg. 340

"Keep the whistle," Mulligan whispered to Caleb. "And you can still bunk with us. Section seven is full anyway."

Mulligan walked off next, followed by Notley grumbling under his breath.

"Well, what kind of disaster am I looking at tomorrow?" Russel asked Caleb. "I have no idea what to do with your class."

Caleb shook his head not wanting to hand it over. It was *his* class! If he could get away with defying the new ware leader's orders he would highly do so. The only problem with turning on Tristan was that the rest of the ware wouldn't. It would be Caleb up against the best teams of the ages and there was no way he could get out of all of that without getting hurt. It wasn't fair to Warner to ask him to stand in Caleb's defiance. He had already made Warner lose his home once.

Caleb looked out to the field toward his special class to find that they had all left. His spot in the field was empty except for the head-tucked Valiant. Tristan must have told Riven to break it all up. The only dragon left was Merlock on his way back to the castle. He chirped at Caleb and ran toward him since they were so close.

Russel took a step back from Merlock, and shifted himself to not be near his head. Caleb had no problem with rubbing the dwarf dragon's head and then hugging his face when Merlock sent him a series of sympathetic sounds before he clamped his tail around Caleb's legs and curled onto his feet.

"That thing is not in your class right?" Russel asked.

"He's in my night class," Caleb said through gritted teeth. "Russel this isn't fair!"

"Actually, it is. You don't have *any* qualifications to be teaching. I'm not saying that you've done a bad job, but even if it wasn't Tristan taking over, any other ware leader would have sent you back to class."

"Jack wouldn't," Caleb protested.

"Really? You think he'd find you capable of teaching his daughter through all of her courses if you have no idea how to do any advanced formations? Jack would put her with a teacher that knows what he's doing. Tell me what I'm looking at tomorrow with your class. When you're done learning your own lessons, I'll put in a good word for you to teach again."

Caleb pulled out a knife and threw it into the ground really hard. Merlock didn't flinch a bit even if the weapon whizzed right past him. That was trust right there. He had these dragon's trust, but he couldn't get past all the blocking riders. Stupid riders!

"It won't take too long," Warner tried to ease. *"We advance quickly. I'll give it everything I have."*

It would still take a full year, perhaps more, because level eight was the hardest thing anyone could ever do, and he still had to get through level seven first.

"When we finish, we will be better at helping Kayla. There's still time to talk with Valiant in the evening before we're shuttled off to bed."

Caleb groaned loudly next. Bed. He was going to be back to following all the rules, not allowed to wander around where he felt like going. Not allowed to skip into town to buy supplies. Not allowed to stay up late and talk with Valiant or his team that had abandoned him.

"Are you going to tell Russel what to do or will you watch as he destroys everything we've built?" Warner questioned. *"It's our team. Don't let anyone destroy it. We're going back to it as soon as we can."*

Oh, gosh. No one was going to like what Caleb had to say. He glanced at the sleeping Valiant trying to decide where to start.

"Valiant is asleep. He tucks his head when he's out. Actually…" Caleb tilted his head to the side and then shook it as his ideas kept coming together figuring this spellbinding dragon thing out. He wasn't done deciphering it, and he hated passing it along.

"Kayla tucks his head when he's out. That's her asleep on the field. Valiant is being Kayla right now. That's the first thing you need to know. They can sightshare at any point during the day or night and they will. Kayla doesn't get a headache from this and Valiant spells her so her eyes stay blue. You'll have to learn how to pick out their behaviors, because there are certain clues that they give so you can tell who you're really talking to."

This had to mean that Kayla didn't really sleep when she went to bed and she would become mentally exhausted if it wasn't for Valiant trapping her inside his own body to let her rest. That was a rather amazing yet disturbing realization at the same time. Valiant was so tired all the time because he slept for two beings. If he was working in class then Kayla couldn't.

"Uh…" Russel glanced at Valiant and then looked back at Caleb, a bit terrified already. Caleb was only getting started.

"When Kayla sneaks out of the ware at night and learns new spells, the next day is when Valiant will participate in class. You have to let her break out."

"That's illegal," Russel crossed his arms as he glanced toward Malone who had been allowing Kayla her nightly procedures as well. He'd not told his scouts to stop her ever.

"It's the only way we've found for her to get her dragon to participate. Valiant needs something new to entice his brain, make him laugh and keep him entertained, or he will curl up and refuse to move. If he does that watch out. He will start shooting spells. He will also sit down if he gets scared. He is a very emotional based dragon in that regard. He doesn't work if Kayla is in a bad mood or if he's in one."

"That is dragon dung," Russel claimed. "We can't cater to a dragon's emotions all day long."

"Then he will shoot you with spells," Caleb shrugged. "He really likes the one that freezes people in place, and the one that sucks Kayla back to him if he doesn't want her to head away. He is overprotective and scared, but there have been beautiful moments where he overcomes that and surprises us all by doing everything right that the other dragons in his class haven't figured out yet.

"Sometimes he shrinks his size and runs away. Just let him go. Even Kayla can't get him back when he's set on being a pain. If Kayla is without a dragon during the day, we've gotten through class by having her ask Reed to participate. I was still working on getting Valiant to trust my judgment enough to work for me all the time without needing to resort to that, but he works well in the evenings when he can pick his own team of dragons. The last few days have

Pg. 344

been good ones where he participates," Caleb sighed knowing it was all going to be ruined.

"I already need a vacation," Russel claimed. "This is way too much. Do you ever focus on anyone else but Valiant during your class?"

"Oh sure. I ignore Valiant most of the time and let Kayla work things out with him, unless she's a crying mess too. In that case, you need to find a way to cheer her up fast. Jokes work well. Brush up on a few good ones or even bad ones really. She can laugh just as easy as she can cry."

This was why he didn't like giving all of this up. Russel already had a resistance to doing what needed to be done and figuring out the unknown to help Kayla and her unique dragon. Caleb really hoped that this wasn't dooming her to sure failure.

"Okay, so there are a few tale-tell signs for when Valiant might shoot a spell. His stomach expands a bit, and he often digs his nails into the ground if he's standing. If he's sitting, I don't have a cue for that yet. If he's flying, his wings straighten out more often than not. I bet he would love to have a spell shooting session so I can figure this out," Caleb said, thinking over how fun that would be. No one else would see it as fun, but Valiant could help him practice magic while Caleb figured out what signs to look for. If only he didn't have to give it all up!

"You know what?" Russel said throwing his hands up. "Mulligan is in charge if Tristan is goofing around. I'm giving this class to him. Mulligan can handle the whole spell thing. It makes me uncomfortable. I don't know how you stand it."

"I love it," Caleb sighed as he rubbed Merlock's head again.

"When you can move, go to bed," Russel directed. He looked down at Merlock and then left Caleb to his misery all on his own. Bed time. He was already told to go to bed again.

"They're funny sometimes, huh?" Caleb asked the small dragon. "The bravest men, and spells make them shake."

Merlock gave a shudder as if spells could make him shake too. Then he ran off after leaving Caleb with a loud hum. Caleb glanced over toward Malone and then up at the night scouts. It didn't look like Malone had spread the word about what changes had been made to the ware. He was going to let everyone find out at the same time tomorrow. Caleb gave the man a short smile as he walked the perimeter of the field at night one last time. He hadn't realized how much he loved being a section leader before. Back at Anvil's Ware, he was always getting in trouble for skipping class when Kayla showed up so he could go spy on her. He got in trouble for wandering, for following his heart more often than his head.

Being a section leader had given him everything he had most wanted. Freedom, purpose, Kayla, and the right to take on impossible challenges because he could. If Valiant felt comfortable with adding more dragons, Caleb wouldn't turn any of them away. He'd train Colt dragons, Vankerdale dragons, wild dragons, or Wisterian dragons. He had no prejudice against where a dragon was born or who the dragon loved.

He could work with the dragon not having a visible rider. Through a lot of the blocking formations all a rider needed to do was hold on anyway. It was those ones that Caleb had been focused on with his night class, and it didn't make the team any weaker knowing

Pg. 346

these dragons might not show up the next day. Each lesson was one where they could help save others. It made him feel like Kayla's accomplice. She was often all about saving the people, and he was all about the dragons. Between the two of them, they were perfect.

Caleb rubbed at his eyes again as Warner joined a dragon huddle to go back to sleep. Valiant slept alone for a while until Reed came flopping in to join him. Reed gave a short snort and glare toward the woods as if he hadn't been able to get to sleep over there before humming at Valiant and falling asleep beside him—or rather beside Kayla. She didn't flinch at all or even take in a deep breath to smell who had landed beside her, because she was a really deep sleeper.

Kayla appeared a few hours later and started to fiddle with Valiant's headgear. When Caleb drew in closer, he noted that it wasn't really Kayla yet, but Valiant decorating his own leather with colorful stones that had probably come from Kayla's rock collection back at home. It made Caleb wonder if Jack and Tia had noticed the infiltrating dragon into their home that night.

Caleb circled the field again before moving off to fill in a few potholes. Then he found his mind going over all the things he had left undone so he went to straighten up the supply shed, check on the water levels, patched a few holes in the walls from riders stabbing through the mortar to climb buildings, and generally hung onto what he had always wanted for as long as he could.

He wasn't excited when day broke, but he was the first to reach breakfast since he was super hungry again. He was on seconds when the mess hall filled to its usual large volume.

"How'd he do?" Notley whispered to Malone on their way past him to their prospective seats. Caleb was slumped into the seventh-year table, not meeting anyone's gaze, just waiting for the announcement to go public that he had been sacked. He was sitting where he now belonged and it made him moody.

"He didn't sleep at all. He was pacing all night," Malone answered. "I doubt that he'll be fit to function well for you today."

They were talking about him. Caleb tried to block out the sounds because he didn't want to hear it.

"I think he's doing better than me," Notley answered. "If that was me, I'd have formed a riot already. I don't care if it'd be against Tristan or not. If Caleb starts one, I'm joining it. I still feel super mad and it's not even me. You don't knock down a guy like that when he's clearly the best thing that's happened to that side for a while."

"What's going on?" one of the teachers was quick to ask, overhearing the conversation. Anything with the word "riot" got people's attention. The gossip became more muted after that but it was buzzing everyone's interest. It wasn't often that a section leader lost his job because he wasn't qualified to have it. Actually, it had probably never happened in the history of the wares. Caleb had just made ware history. He'd be known for the man who was almost extraordinary.

"You're known for your drawing," Warner reminded him.

Well, now he'd be known for two things.

"I have it under good authority," Kayla said, effectively scooting the rider beside him to the side, "that Tristan is too mentally occupied to make it to breakfast. Know what that means?"

She looked around and spotted the other section leaders now engaged with all the teachers in their gossip. No one had announced

Pg. 348

that Charles had died, but it felt like everyone knew already. It was probably the first thing their dragons told them when they woke up.

"It means that I can sit wherever I please."

Kayla scooted in close. Caleb couldn't look at her. He stared at his plate trying to decide how to break the news to her that he was going to miss her.

"I'm not taking it well. I'm not quite at the stage of starting a riot like Notley just said, because I do have some respect for what the king decided, but this isn't my best day," Caleb admitted.

"I thought when Anvil kicked you out of his ware that that was your worst day."

"That was a bad day too," Caleb agreed.

He'd cried that day. That was the ultimate push away from the one person he wanted to be near. It felt like he was losing Kayla all over again, even if she was sitting beside him. Caleb could tell that the whispers were picking up and so were the glances in his direction. Everyone knew that Kayla wasn't sitting at her table, but no one seemed to care. She was so lucky.

"I'm going to really miss that extra freedom," he sighed.

"This is so characteristically Tristan. If there is some way he can be a stickler, he will be the stickler. So I brought you something. He technically can't fire you. He can make you go to class, but he can't fire you for the reason he used. I copied down the list of legitimate reasons to fire a section leader, and not finishing class is not on the list. You could fight him legally if you don't want to take the riot route, because the riot route can get you fired. You can also do nothing about it and

Tristan will soon find out that he can't hire a different section leader, because there is no way to remove your name when you've not done anything wrong. This doesn't apply to teaching though. You can't teach class when you're in one, but that extra freedom you wanted, you still have that."

Kayla passed him the paper, so Caleb looked at it slowly and skimmed over all the bad things he would need to do to get fired. Lucky for him, he'd not done any of them and had no plan to. He hadn't really lost everything. He got less time with Kayla, and Valiant was going to be starting over again on respecting his teacher, but Caleb was still in charge of basic section leader duties.

"Hey, guys!" Caleb called out, grabbing the paper and giving Kayla a quick hug as he dashed over to the huddle of leaders that was getting louder and more mutinous in his favor. Notley had everyone knotted up wanting to stand up for him. There were fumes coming out.

"Kayla has proof that I'm not fired."

Caleb passed around the list and explained. He didn't expect the rowdy cheer that came as a result, or the applause that suddenly started around the mess hall for Kayla's ability to know the legal rules of Aralot. People were patting her on the back, and Mulligan was declaring that Caleb was staying in the job. They still would need to call someone else to watch everything when he was in class, but he was fine with sharing that responsibility.

It was so strange to see everyone this excited for him. He didn't even know these people, and yet they were on his side so strongly that there really could have been a full ware mutiny for what Tristan had done. It was so strange. It had Caleb standing there more in a daze to
Pg. 350

hear that he was keeping his job than when Tristan had tried to demote him.

He looked around the room, his eyes settling onto Kayla's as she smiled back at him. He couldn't help but salute her. Hers was the victory. She had all the answers to standing up to Tristan, no matter what the guy did. Hearing the joyful people around him laughing and cheering for him made it so that taking his classes wasn't that bad of a deal after all. He did need to learn them.

Kayla had found a way to make everything better just as fast as Tristan had made it bad. And all of them won with Kayla's solution. Caleb would get the training he needed, and he'd have the freedom to keep training those dragons in the evening. That would be his class. He really didn't want to lose that class. It was the only time that he was certain Valiant was listening.

Tristan eventually made his way into the mess hall when he realized that no one had left to get to class and classes should have started half an hour ago. The scouts called out the hour and no one moved. They were all too busy talking about Tristan until he came through the door and the conversations dropped off as one.

"You lot are fancy." Tristan rolled his eyes, guessing what they were all chatting about. "I assume that you've heard about Charles. You don't get a vacation because he took one. And I am aware that you are passing around information claiming that Caleb can't be fired. Fine. He's not fired, but he will go to class, and he is not to be pestered about section leader duties during the day. You will be reporting to Javier who is going to be the assistant section leader and will be holding all the section leader keys."

Tristan held his hand out for the other keys that Caleb hadn't turned back in. The room was quiet as everyone stared at him, waiting to see if he would comply. The word riot flashed through Caleb's head again until he remembered that Tristan wanted him to cause a commotion. If he started a mutiny then Tristan had adequate cause to really fire him.

Caleb pulled out the keys and passed them over, which unfortunately included the key to get into his own bunkroom. It didn't matter. He had a lock picking spell in his arsenal. He could magic his bedroom door open every night, and if he ever ran out of magic, there had to be some way to convince Valiant and Bantin to give him more.

"Class," Tristan thumbed the riders to head out the door.

Caleb was the first one sliding outside to get away. He had a year or two of this before he got his job back. It already sounded too long. It felt frustrating too because his new team had trained together for a full year already and he had no idea where he fit in. He scrambled up into the air doing his best to mimic his fellow classmates lead. Notley gave him his position, on the side, but both him and Warner still didn't know where they were supposed to be exactly because they didn't know the formation. He needed to be either beside or in front of the neighboring red dragon. He let Warner guess, and he picked slightly behind but still beside the red to cover both cases.

It didn't help when Sparkle showed up having deposited Queen Tia at the office. The dragon chirped at Valiant, who rose into the air to chase after her, and Caleb knew that Kayla wasn't getting any work done with Mulligan. Caleb glanced toward the rest of his class only to get called out for it.

Pg. 352

"Caleb!" Notley shouted at him. "Kayla isn't your rider. Get your head back in the formation!"

Kayla was his rider! Caleb screamed his thoughts at Warner instead as he glanced away. Not two minutes had gone past before he was being screamed at again.

"Caleb pay attention!" Notley screamed.

Caleb sighed. He was up in the air so he had a great view of how badly his class was doing. Most of them were working for Mulligan, except for Kayla who was curled up asleep on the ground wearing her gray sweater. He was starting to hate that thing. It was her way of hiding from the world and withdrawing when she couldn't find any other way to cope. Why was she down on the ground? He'd not fully figured it out yet.

"Caleb!"

"I'm sorry! I can't help it. Kayla gets really bad nightmares. She shouldn't be left unattended during the day when she should be awake. Brea needs her form improved. Nick needs to shift down. Norrin keeps messing up his knees. Avery needs to improve his sloppy hand signals..."

"Yeah. That's why I said I didn't want you in my class. You're the kind of person who shouts out corrections. Leave them alone. You need to stop thinking like a teacher and focus. That's your fault for the day. Fix yourself before you start worrying about anyone else."

"When do you think Valiant is coming back. He shouldn't leave Kayla like that on the ground!" Caleb complained to Warner.

That was what was really worrying him. Something wasn't right and no one was around to check on her that cared. Valiant had flown off and left her. Him turning his back on Kayla when she was down really got to him.

"Caleb!" Notley shouted at him again.

"I'm paying attention!" Caleb lied.

He looked up just in time to catch a prong that was flying past his face. This was going to be hard. He could catch weapons in the air, but not if he wasn't looking at them. Warner would be happier with him if he didn't get his head cut open in their first class.

Game

Tristan

Tristan didn't need to hear the conversations in order to know the thoughts of the people around him. They were all angry with him and they would have been that way even if he hadn't sent Caleb back to class. The only one who had looked a bit wary back at him was Kayla, which was funny because Riven and told him what she thought about the situation already. She was prepared to take him up to the castle and have a verbal law battle if Caleb asked for it.

Everything felt hinged upon Caleb's word, even if he was the second youngest rider at this ware and one of the least experienced. There was just something about him that had people looking at him and wanting to follow his directions. It was disgusting. In fact, the way Tristan felt about Caleb in the current moment was very similar to the way he usually felt about Kayla Brixton: irritated, cantankerous, indignant, superior.

Of all the people who could cause him problems, Caleb was gratefully the only one not being a rock in his shoe. At least so far. He was mad, sure, but Tristan had seen Caleb mad before and the guy took his anger out in his fists. He'd stopped doing that ever since Kayla looked at him. Caleb had finally gotten what he was after, which interestingly enough, had mellowed him out a great deal. Maybe he had finally realized that Kayla's attention wasn't gained by fighting for it.

In any case, Tristan had already added in a few days on the schedule where riders could sit wherever they wanted in the mess hall. He'd added in team-building field days where the classes intermixed too, all in an effort to keep Caleb in line because he could look forward to seeing Kayla. Not that it would do Caleb any good. Once he learned that Kayla was already married, he was going to walk around depressed. Kayla had left them both for some king that lived across the river.

With her out of the way, Tristan had been reading through Charles's personal secret notes. These ones he had never managed to break into before. Charles was usually pretty good at heading toward his office if Tristan had broken in, so Tristan had never had this much time to search his things. Now that Tristan's time was mostly limitless, he was scanning over titles and he smiled when he found a section about Colts.

Here it was! Charles had collected a lot of rare passages about Ritz. This was the best day ever. A lot of them were things that Tristan already knew. The general age of the man, and speculation about twelve different family lines Ritz could have come from. All of them were probably wrong. There was a list of people he had personally trained and then an interesting poem.

"Your heart held steady. Your heart held firm. It didn't waver through the storm. To you I turn and you I trust when all else fails and turns to dust. Upon the soil you shall dwell, held inside this timeless spell. Your life will stay aflame until the statue ends his game."

Pg. 356

This was incredible. Charles had the answer to what could kill off Ritz! A statue. Ritz was trapped inside a conditional spell, and if Tristan could locate the correct statue and destroy it, he would be able to put the ageless man to rest before Ritz did the same thing to him.

Given the time period in which Ritz had first started the Colts, the only one capable of casting him into such a spell would have been King Gladius Felding himself. A lot of objects from Gladius's rein had been destroyed already. What had survived were hunted for by Colts. Ritz was always setting his people out on special missions trying to get objects. This could prove that he didn't know where Gladius had hidden his special life statue. If it was in Aralot though, the two best people to search were Ian and August.

Tristan would simply cast a truth-telling spell to learn about statues, and he'd be one step closer to taking down Ritz. Tristan pulled the blue magic to his hand, cast the spell, and then jumped from the office heading in the direction of the last known location of Ian and August. They had been hanging around here again, so Tristan hoped that they hadn't wandered off too far.

"Can you do me a favor?" Riven asked. *"See if Kayla's dead?"*

She couldn't be dead. Valiant was not crying out the dragon song of death, but since Riven was sounding concerned, Tristan changed his direction for the field. Kayla wasn't hard to find. She was the only one in a gray sweater curled up on the field not moving. Valiant wasn't anywhere in sight but Riven was close by staring at her.

When Tristan got closer, Mulligan dropped down from the air looking more annoyed than concerned.

"Russel told me that Caleb told him that if Valiant curls up and refuses to work to simply ignore him, but no one said what to do if Kayla decides to take a really long nap on the ground. I know that Caleb needs to do his own training, but what if Kayla is moved to a night class and Caleb teaches that one? Even if it ends up being three hours a night, it would still be more training for that girl than what she's given me."

"Caleb is not qualified to train," Tristan stated again. He bent down and checked on Kayla finding her incredibly warm. "What does Valiant say?" Tristan asked looking at his beautiful bronze dragon who complained that he couldn't communicate with Valiant at all.

"That's the answer then. It's not Kayla. It's Valiant taking a nap on the field. Kayla is being him and she flew off somewhere for the fun of it."

"Valiant flew off after Sparkle," Mulligan informed.

"Even more of a reason to not worry. Tia came to visit. She was in the office perhaps ten minutes before heading away. She must have gone to visit her daughter in dragon form and Kayla copied her. Valiant and Kayla will be back to class in a little while."

"It's been a few hours…" Mulligan complained.

"I'm sure that they're fine. If she's not awake by sunset then you need to get worried. Until then, I'd just leave it alone."

"I'm going to go find them," Riven declared.

He looked into the air and then backed away from Kayla to go find Valiant. It couldn't be that much of a problem. It looked like Kayla was exhausted and she had every right to be with the sort of night

Pg. 358

dragon she had that kept her up at all hours. Maybe moving her to a night class was the best thing that they could do for her. He'd have to think about this, because her current classmates all had day dragons.

"Know any night dragons that would be a good fit for a class with Kayla?" Tristan asked Riven as the dragon took off one way and Tristan took off in the other.

"I can think up a lot of good night dragons, but I don't know if they will be accepting of a dragon that uses spells with his training."

Eh. They were dragons. They could adapt if they needed to. Tristan decided to leave his dragon to the task of handling Kayla and her issues so he could take care of Ritz. That was his greater concern today. He located Ian and August on one of their favorite camping hills. Before they knew what was coming at them, he put on the truth spell. They hid what they were doing from him when he got closer, but he was pretty sure that they were reading a book on magic theory. No matter. They had never cast any spells of their own as far as he knew, and with all the odd trinkets they picked up, magic would be something they would want to know about.

"I need you to tell me where all the small statues that Gladius left behind are located. These will be miniature statues, the kind that could be used for a game piece."

Ian pinched his mouth shut tight. August clamped a hand over his mouth as they both struggled against the confines of the spell that Tristan had placed upon them. They had to tell him where those items were located. It was impressive that it took them as long as it did before they couldn't resist anymore. That's what came with holding ancient artifacts. They probably had some of the best protective spells hovering around them.

"There's a board game hidden near Salka in the dirt beside the city sign. The pieces are not cursed though. The only thing they do is make the white figures win every time. I've been waiting for a good moment to play it against Jack so that I can beat him at something," August told him remorseful as if he could already guess at what Tristan's intentions were. Yes, he was going to destroy everything they told him about.

"There's a bull that's been sitting in the window of the Bull Tavern in Deluth that has stopped brawls from taking place inside the building for years," Ian sighed next. "It's not anything evil either."

"Remember when we found that pet rock?" August laughed deciding not to be too angry over Tristan's current quest. "It was hidden inside the belly of a stuffed animal and it had two jewel eyes. It put me right to sleep. That one right there is evil. We decided it was made to put to sleep crying babies."

"He's very much a baby," Ian grinned at his best friend. "We tossed it into the pond near Arkridge."

"We had a statue of Gladius's wife, Jean, once that when held made hair grow longer. We sold that to the barber on Pickly Street," August told him. "That's all that I can think of. Most of Gladius's things were not statues or small enough to be used as a game piece. He liked gaudy jewelry and functional items."

Tristan glanced at Ian who gave him a shrug as if he couldn't think of anything else to fit the description that he had given them either. That gave him four things to destroy and then he would need to see if he could find Ritz to verify if the man was still alive or not. No time like the present to destroy something that Gladius had left behind.

Pg. 360

Missing Heart

Caleb

Caleb followed Notley into the bunkroom silently. He didn't feel like being on speaking terms with the section leader anymore. He didn't feel like sharing a room with him either, not after the class that he had. He'd never been picked on that much during a class before and it left him feeling horribly inadequate. He wished that he had never transferred here. Then he wished that Tristan had never gotten the ware leader job. He had come up with a plan to tie Tristan up and leave him to rot in a dark pit. He got yelled at for coming up with that plan because it had distracted him away from learning the formation Notley was trying to get through his head.

Notley tossed a section seven book onto the top of Caleb's bed, grabbed a novel to occupy his own mind, and left the bunkroom, not wanting to engage with him anymore either.

"Good riddance," Caleb grumbled as Notley closed the door behind him and Caleb finally got a break. He had two hours to learn this formation before class started back up again. Caleb glanced at Malone who was sleeping in the corner on his bunk and then opened his trunk to pull out paper so he could make a sketch of the formation to learn it that way only to find that all his clothes were neatly washed and folded. His papers were not a complicated mess but were pinned together in sections by content. With his stuff organized this way, it fit into his trunk rather well, but he hadn't been the one to fix his storage problem.

When had this happened? It could have been anytime yesterday or today or last night because he'd not entered his bunkroom for a full day. He smiled about that and took out clean clothes carefully learning the organization of his trunk so that he could keep it this nice forever. If only this current formation was his trunk, he wouldn't have a problem with it. His main problem was moving too soon or not looking the right way or not understanding what his teammates glances meant because he didn't know these guys. He'd never watched them ride before, and it was a great lesson to him on how confusing an enemy could be if he had no experience in their formations.

Caleb reached the bottom of his trunk fingering the paper from Wisteria that had been placed on the bottom. He inhaled sharply and pulled it out because whoever had organized his trunk would have seen this. What he saw had him gripping the edge of the page.

"Hello? I destroyed the orb that kept all rare breed dragons inside of Aralot and cast the spell that will allow your dragons to return home. You should feel honored. That was scary stuff."

The new words had been written on the paper in Kayla's handwriting causing him stomach to turn. That's what she had been doing in that dress he got her. It must have been. Kayla was giving into Wisteria's demands, which was the opposite of everything that Caleb wanted. If only she didn't instantly connect with the darkest sob stories. It wasn't like Wisteria was being nice to her or anything. They were being jerks.

Pg. 362

"Have you changed your mind then?"

"Not at all. My spells allow dragons their own free choices. What you were after was force. I will still send you back home every time you attempt to use force, but you have my curiosity over why you feel so strongly about collecting Valiant. Is it a binding spell that has you trapped? What is trapped?"

"Take a guess."

"A person? Some living thing that means a great deal to your kingdom and every time you see it, you remember that it can't move. How close am I?"

"Farther away than I would like."

"Really? You always want to stay far away from me. If you attempt to steal my dragon, I will curse you worse than Gladius did. What is your problem? Be honest or I shall cast a spell to force the truth from your lying mouth."

"You're always so fun to talk with."

"You too. My spell has been cast. You have no choice but to scribble it out."

"Multiple dragons are trapped inside a binding spell. It took us years to get another spellbinding dragon to fix this and he was stolen away as he hatched."

"I am aware. Lucky for you, he has expressed interest in visiting Wisteria. When he's not super busy, he might stop by."

"Might? Kayla, we need him. He can't be super busy. He's a dragon. They don't have jobs."

"He trains at a ware, thank you."

"My patience is wearing thin."

"I think you should accept what you have already gotten and be grateful. I have already helped you and I would appreciate you to not call me a witch."

"I expect that dragon sometime within the next month. If I don't see him, action will be taken. Until then, this conversation is over."

Kayla had stolen into his room and touched his things! Caleb didn't mind the neatly folded clothes. He was grateful for the clothes and the tip on organization, but he hadn't wanted Kayla to hand over her long fought for dragon to Wisteria, now that she'd finally gotten Valiant out of Vankerdale. Couldn't people stop trying to take the dragon away from her? It was *her* dragon! She shouldn't have agreed to part with him even if she had been vague.

Forgetting all about that formation and changing his clothes, Caleb tucked the paper into his pocket and left the bunkroom to go tell Kayla that she couldn't touch his things.

"She hasn't moved?" Caleb asked Sherman, who was standing around on his two-hour break instead of leaving the field. For that matter, the rest of the class was doing the same thing. They all rushed over to him. Junia gave him a large hug complaining about how unfair it was that he wasn't teaching because his lessons were fun and she was feeling bored. Nick was just about to take up the whining next, but Caleb cut them off with a signal.

"Kayla hasn't moved all day?" he asked again.

"Tristan said not to worry until sunset because he thinks that it's Valiant sleeping instead of Kayla," Brea told him. "I think he's wrong though. Valiant would wake up if we did something like this."

Brea tossed a knife toward Kayla that had Caleb lunging for it to prevent it from slicing her. The knife bonked into an invisible magical shield and bounced away. Caleb wasn't so lucky. He landed on top of Kayla as his fingers missed the knife. Gee! He couldn't catch anything today! That's what had him so mad at his own class.

"That would have Valiant waking up to cast spells at us," Nick agreed. "It has to be Kayla sleeping there on her own. He wakes up when we shout things too. Mulligan had all of us screaming around her in a circle and nothing happened."

"I pushed her," Avery said next. "Nothing happened."

"Take her to the doctor's office," Caleb instructed.

Something wasn't right. Valiant wasn't here probably because he had left in an attempt to find some new spell that would wake up his rider. Valiant wasn't having any luck on this today, and Caleb didn't think the doctors would either, but at least Kayla would be out of the way where people wouldn't throw knives at her to wake her up.

There was no way he could complain to her about writing to Wisteria when she was struggling so much today. He had to figure out what these nightmares were, and for that he needed to go talk to Vermelo. He seemed to know what was going on. Caleb looked toward the castle, gave his old class a nod, and then headed out of the ware regardless of the scout on duty eyeing him, wondering if he should report Caleb's absence. The scout followed him down the roads toward the castle, and if he wasn't mistaken, there were a few Colts doing the same thing.

Just like last time he was here, the castle guards opened the door for him before he reached it. He made it four steps inside the courtyard before Vermelo was running at him with words shouting across the expanse.

"There is no way to change Tristan's mind regarding your position. The decision has been discussed with both Jack and Tia. I know that you're mad—"

"I am way madder at Kayla right now than Tristan," Caleb found himself complaining. She really shouldn't have written what she did. If she slipped into a coma there was no one to tell Valiant not to go to Wisteria. Valiant didn't listen to anyone else that well.

"Kayla?" Vermelo questioned reaching Caleb's side with a frown. "And what is she doing? She knows better than to dive into certain nasty magical practices to get her way."

"Oh no. She's not cursing Tristan," Caleb agreed. "She's all about letting people and dragons have their free will."

Caleb sighed, wishing that Kayla's life wasn't full of these hidden political battles that she tried to conquer all on her own.

"I know she has this mentality that she has to secretly save everyone behind their backs, and she's awfully good at it, but there are some places that she has to draw the line. She was suggesting that she'd let Valiant go to Wisteria to stop them from sending a war at us. I don't care what they say. They won't give him back if they get their hands on him. She'll die all over again. She'll be immobilized just by looking at dragons all over again. Why is she not scared of that? Does she have to always be the hero?"

"Yes," Vermelo answered with a loud sigh.

He looked around the courtyard and then waved for Caleb to follow him to one of the guard towers. Caleb didn't follow him alone. A few of the guards came tumbling after them, and Caleb didn't think they were invited. They stubbornly looked back at Vermelo daring him to do something about them coming along.

"I will admit that I have not heard this news about Wisteria. Is it something we need to get the king and steward involved with or can this be resolved by you talking reason into Kayla's head?"

"She won't listen to me," Caleb complained as they reached the tower. Vermelo opened the door and started up the stairs. The Captain of the Guard paused on the third step and looked backward with a rather thoughtful expression.

"Actually, you may be the only person she *will* listen to. She's stopped listening to me. She did everything I told her not to do and then laughed about it. She joined the King's Ware against my warnings. But you, Caleb, you're the voice in her head that was always there before Valiant was. I never thought about it that way until now. Your words are the ones she listens to."

"Rubbish," Caleb retorted. "She can't hear me now that I'm disgraced. Everything I..." He trailed off before he could admit that everything he had ever wanted out of life had been stolen away from him by Tristan Cluster. The resentment flushed his face, raged over him, made him want to break something apart with enough force to shatter it forever. Vermelo wasn't a Colt, he was born a noble and had always been one, but he picked up on Caleb's missing words anyway.

"You fear she will ignore everything you most want to tell her; because she is locked in a political battle that trumps the battle of her heart."

Caleb shrugged. That was one way to put it. Kayla had to choose the political side of things instead of the side she wanted.

"Wisteria hosts an annual art contest that they invited me to participate in. This was sent back to me for my efforts. I suppose that I should have already handed it over to Jack..."

Caleb trailed off and fished out the offensive magical paper. "I don't understand her," Caleb continued to complain as Vermelo read the words and walked up the stairs at the same time.

Caleb followed along, still not sure why he wasn't giving this evidence to King Klavian or even Jack and Tia. Maybe it was because he didn't want them to do anything about it at all, and Vermelo had said "we" like he might offer up a solution that wouldn't involve starting this war or breaking Kayla apart all over again.

Vermelo was astute with all the castle talk. Caleb had once overheard Jack complain to his wife that Vermelo was more of the king than either him or Klavian. He could help. Plus, Caleb still needed to ask him more questions about those nightmares.

"She's sacrificing herself as if no one else can do anything about this. There are three wares in the way of Wisteria reaching Valiant. There are armies and magical protections, and she's acting like none of that exists. Sure, it's her dragon and all, but she *needs* Valiant. I don't understand why she would say what she did. I'm not losing that dragon. There has to be another way to handle this."

"Caleb Andrade," Vermelo whispered as if contemplating something else entirely. He even paused on the stairs to stare blankly at the paper in his hand. He nodded to himself and took the rest of the steps three at a time forcing everyone else behind him to keep up. When they reached the top of the tower, Vermelo unlocked a door and opened it up waving everyone into his personal bedroom. Caleb hesitated for an instant and then stepped inside, letting the other four guards file in after him. With six of them in the small room, it felt crowded.

"If you could do anything at all to handle this, Caleb, if you had no restrictions at all, what would your heart tell you to do?"

"Defeat the curse on Wisteria before Kayla gets to it," he admitted.

That's what he most wanted to do. It was much harder choosing a path that was against her, but he had to save her. This was probably the first time that he had ever found himself wanting to fight Kayla, and the feeling left him rather angry.

"She can't lose that dragon. Valiant is her and I don't mean that lightly. They might look like two beings, but they are the same thing... to a certain extent," he added, not sure how to express what he really felt about the two of them. "Valiant learned to talk and walk at the same time Kayla did. They are each other so completely that it's amazing. Sometimes I can't tell which one of them is really paying attention to me and which one has decided to take a nap, because they can be in each other's form at any time. To lose one of them would destroy the other."

"And yet someone has been trying to destroy Valiant," Vermelo said, sitting down on his bed. Caleb considered sitting down beside him but decided to lean up against the wall instead. "I agree that we can't allow Wisteria to take him from us. Kayla needs Valiant now more than ever. She needs his help if she is to survive. She needs his love to fight against the emptiness that consumes her."

"She's feeling empty?" Caleb asked. "I really came over here to ask you about those nightmares of hers. Kayla's not waking up today. Valiant took off with Sparkle and hasn't come back. You looked like you knew about the topic, so I'd really appreciate you helping me understand it. She's not going to fall into a coma, is she?"

"No. Not yet," Vermelo answered. The yet part didn't sound very promising. "If she still has the mentality to save then she still has the ability to love and she isn't done fighting. I try not to let people know this, Caleb, and Jack has been searching for years and years only to increase his search recently as if he can tell that the impending moment of Kayla's doom is coming. He's right. Without intervention, Kayla will fall. She has proven before that her heart is stolen."

"What do you mean?" Caleb asked, edging off the wall already. Doom. Fall. Stolen. None of these things sounded good, and if this was something that was also stumping Jack, Caleb had a lot of questions. Why was Vermelo not confiding some cure to Jack? Caleb didn't think that Vermelo was talking about Tristan having Kayla's heart. He'd never had it. This was something else. Some curse that Jack hadn't gotten rid of.

"It's Aralot that has Kayla. She's always had her from the moment that Kayla was born. That girl was born out of magic and she will die from magic unless we can find a way to defeat Aralot. Our only hope to defeat Aralot is Valiant. If he is gone, Aralot wins. No question about it. It was no accident you got invited to that contest or that Wisteria was notified on how they could reach Kayla's dragon. Aralot is trying to consume Kayla. She was involved. She found a way to bring in Wisteria to take Valiant away now that Valiant was released from his lifelong prison in Vankerdale. Aralot wants Valiant gone."

"Will you please make sense?!" Caleb screamed along with his heart. "She's not dying!" Anything but that. "How can a kingdom eat Kayla?"

"Not eat her, Caleb. Consume all her love. Swallow up all her joys. Steal away from her every moment of gladness and happiness, leaving her empty and defeated. Every time Kayla falls down in tears, Aralot sings, because she eats away all the lost happiness."

"I hate you right now," Caleb admitted. He wanted to grab at Vermelo's shirt and strangle the guy. "Kayla cried because her connection to her dragon was broken."

"Yes, and her mother feels responsible for that, but Tia's really not to blame since she was compelled to sacrifice herself, her feelings of happiness, and Kayla's future happiness to the same gripping curse that has Kayla so bound. Tia could never make herself restore the bonds in Vankerdale because she simply *couldn't,* even if her own excuses didn't make sense to herself. Her feelings prevented it. Kayla, on the other hand, fights those feelings with everything she has. She's learned to stand back up in the face of depression. She can smile again after falling down. She can love dragons without ever interacting with them. I'm getting there!" Vermelo cried, because Caleb was about to cut him off and demand the same thing he had just asked.

This man wasn't making any sense! Well, he was making sense, but not in the same way that Caleb wanted to understand what he was talking about. It felt right, this curse of the land that was pulling on the Feldings. Tia felt it and Kayla did too.

"Why have you never brought this to Jack?" Caleb spat out instead.

Vermelo shook his head and looked weary. "I've made it my job to guess what Jack would do if I ever told him the truth of what he is hunting for. He would kill himself over this. He would spill all of his love to save Kayla, and I can't have that. This kingdom needs him. I have to handle Jack in a different way so that he makes a different sacrifice."

This still wasn't sounding good. It really did sound like Vermelo was the king of the land, nudging the two other kings to achieve his goal of …. What? Vermelo had also let Caleb into his room, sharing with him things he kept from Jack as if the kingdom needed Caleb and not Jack. As if Caleb could spill all his love as the sacrifice instead. Could he? If it would save Kayla, then yes, he would do it. After verifying these claims and such first.

"*Did you just… Don't die,*" Warner hesitantly spoke into his head.

"*I will go down fighting.*"

"*I just peed myself,*" Warner admitted.

Caleb tried not to smile, but he just couldn't help it even if he was also tearing up at the same time. He was terrifying his dragon, but there wasn't anything he wouldn't do to save Kayla. If it was a sacrifice that Aralot needed to stop some curse, he would hand it all over just so Kayla could see another sunset, share another smile, lift another fallen heart. This land needed her. Without her, they were all left to Tristan, and he was a face that Caleb cringed over.

"How does one spill all his love to this curse?"

"You can't." Vermelo shook his head and passed back the note from Wisteria. Caleb put the magical paper back in his pocket.

"Which is why I'm now hiding something in my room in case Jack tries to locate it again to take it over to Vankerdale and beg King Tyler to have his dragon destroy it. This is where part of the problem starts."

Vermelo reached underneath the bed and pulled out a box that when pressed in on the corners flung open a lid. From the inside of the box, he pulled out a foul-smelling mess of twisted dried sticks with slugs on them. It was so revolting that Caleb moved to cover his nose. He never completed the gesture because Vermelo tossed the foulness at him. Reflexes kicked in. Caleb caught the revolting circle, and he held his breath even more at how it transformed inside his fingers.

The instant his skin connected, Caleb found himself holding the crown of Aralot. He'd heard tales about this object. It only responded to Aralot's true kings and would not take the shape of the silver crown with circling rubies unless it was in the hands of the king. So this had to mean that Caleb was destined to be the king. The king of Aralot. Was he seeing this right?!

He found himself not only with his back to the wall again, but he slid down until he sat on the floor. He couldn't look away from the simple circlet. It was not anything elaborate or even beautiful, but it was the most powerful thing that Caleb had ever touched. The crown was cursed beyond measure so Herb Felding, Jack Brixton, and King Klavian all refused to wear it even if Klavian had tried to become crowned with it at first. Jack saved him from the fate of its curses. Now this crown was hurting Kayla.

"I have spent my entire life studying this one object," Vermelo told him. "It was created by an ultra-dragon king named Choladon. It has to be destroyed by the same type of dragon. We now have an ultra-dragon king under control that has bonded the king of Vankerdale. The dragon is named Coal. Vankerdale's new king is Tyler Valeron."

Caleb had heard the name Tyler before because Kayla had mentioned who the new king of Vankerdale was. She had also mentioned that she and Tyler were friends despite the man being responsible for both of her previous kidnappings. She hadn't said anything about Coal leaving Aralot for Vankerdale though.

"If Jack even thinks of taking the crown away to destroy it, it will be his death. Anyone with the desire to destroy the crown dies. To get around it, people instead seek to change the nature of the curses on the crown, which is also a deadly task that has killed many a wise man and spellcaster. As far as I can tell, the crown itself does not have the exact curse that kills off queens. It's simply the device that makes a man magically and legally the king which in turn creates a queen. The crown isn't exactly to blame. However, Jack will blame the crown for his daughter's misfortune as many a king has done, and then he will kill himself trying to destroy it. I have to prevent that."

"I hate this thing," Caleb couldn't help but express while he cried tears of relief at the same time. Vermelo shook his head like he understood why.

This crown was controlling Kayla, but at the same time, it had just told Caleb something that Kayla had never told him personally. Kayla loved him. She had been his all along, and there wasn't anything anywhere that would change that. Legally they would have to fight to be together, similar to how Jack had been changing up laws so he could marry Tia, but once that fight was out of the way, Kayla was his.

The most beautiful girl in all the world loved him! All those years Caleb had spent trying and failing to get her to look at him, all those years of drawing pictures when images terrified her due to her dragon, they had all won her over. There had been a million empty nights where he cried himself to sleep trying to come up with the perfect thing to say or sketch to gain her affection, and here was the proof that he'd won. The royal crown declared it. It had done the same thing for Jack, only Jack hadn't known anything about the object to know this. It revealed itself to him because he could be made the legal king for being in love with Tia Felding. Caleb had heard that the crown never lied. Meaning that even if Caleb lost Kayla to something tragic, he could still end up as the king of Aralot one day without her.

"How are you doing Warner?" Caleb asked his dragon.

"Oh, I'm fine with that part. I guessed at that a long time ago with the way you never changed your mind over Kayla Brixton. I'm not scared of the crown. I'm only scared of losing you."

"This crown is known to kill Aralot's queens. The instant you put that on your head, Kayla will die," Vermelo continued. "It is in my best judgment that Tia escaped the curse because her love has always been placed elsewhere. See, she loves dragons more than her own daughter, more than all of Aralot, more than her husband, although she won't admit to that. Her keeper status saves her, since all the other queens before her were not keepers at all. Their husbands were keepers and Aralot claimed its crowning sacrifice from the keeper's wives. Tia has escaped and will continue to escape as long as Jack keeps the crown off his head. But Aralot is patient. She has adapted and found a way to reach queens that were also keepers. Kayla has been suffering from the nightmares for years while Tia has never been touched."

Caleb lightly shoved the crown off his lap, watching it turn into a slug infested wreath once more. He wasn't going to put the crown on his *head,* was he? This thing was said to predict the future. What if he put it on his head and doomed the woman he loved? Why would he do something like that? Would he even do it, or would someone else shove it up there for him killing off the most important thing to him? How was Aralot still eating Kayla?

"Indeed," Vermelo said as Caleb pinched his eyes closed trying to find a way to get around the future he couldn't witness. "Which is also why I've been hiding some news from the general public and the self-proclaimed rulers of our land. As I see it right now, no one is officially crowned the king in Aralot. You're as much of a candidate for that as Jack, only Jack has the power to do something disastrous about this and you don't.

"Kayla is already a queen. Once she got back from Vankerdale, Aralot's spells on her increased. Her nightmares got worse. Once she reaches a certain nightmare where she is searching for something—all her lost love is my best guess—she will die. The spell on her will be complete. Aralot will have sucked the joy out of another queen."

"Kayla can't... die," Caleb said feeling the panic kick in. He wiggled his legs and considered throwing the crown to see if it would

Pg. 376

shatter, then thought better of it because if he wanted to destroy the thing, he would die too, and that would never help him save Kayla from this curse.

"What do you mean that she's already a queen?"

"She's married in Vankerdale." Vermelo moved to a drawer in his room, fiddled with it a bit, and then pulled out a paper. It looked like he was hiding this paper far better than he was hiding that crown. This paper had to be worse, or perhaps it was the thing that would make Kayla's dad flip. Already Caleb was feeling worse. If the crown couldn't lie and it claimed he could be the king, how could it declare that of him if Kayla was married?

"Technically it states engaged, but it means married in Vankerdale. Kayla would know this. I have no idea what stress she was under in Vankerdale during her second kidnapping, but I do know that this is her handwriting and it wasn't forced. She signed a legally binding document to be engaged to Tyler Valeron, which made him the king over there after the Peyton's were defeated."

"I can't breathe," Caleb said as he took the paper from Vermelo's outstretched hand and flicked his eyes to the very bottom. He glanced at the guards in the room next wondering how much of this all of them knew. Judging from their shallow breathing, they were all surprised too. Kayla's signature was on the paper agreeing to be engaged to Tyler so he could be the king. Caleb had no idea when it was that he had inhaled last, but it had been a very very long time. He scrambled to get air into his lungs only the air was short as his body refused to be relaxed. Everything about him was tense.

"Why would she… Tristan."

That's what this was about. It wasn't about the king of Vankerdale. Kayla had said that she and Tyler were friends and that Tyler was good friends with Valiant too. It didn't sound like she was lying about that. Tyler might not have her heart, but she was in a position right now where the only one who could claim her heart was Tristan. Kayla refused to give her love to Tristan and this was her way of fighting back. He couldn't have her. She would rather create a scandal in Vankerdale than marry Tristan.

"You are probably right. Kayla is keeping herself as far away from Tristan Cluster as possible without realizing that the nightmares used to never attack anyone but Aralot's queens. Aralot hasn't seen a real queen in three generations, not since Gladius's wife. Aralot is starving and Kayla is now considered a queen even if she's not a queen of here. Aralot will only devour her faster. There was nothing you could have done, Caleb. No one saw this coming."

Caleb glanced again at the slug covered twigs near his extended legs. The crown saw this coming, only it couldn't talk to tell everyone what sort of disaster was trying to eat them up. It knew though. It had to know. In a way, that made Caleb feel better about himself. He wasn't going to be the cause of Kayla's tragedy by putting that crown on his head. She had already done the damage herself. Now if only he had been bold enough to tell her that he loved her before all of this took place, she might have never signed that paper. Caleb's eyes couldn't hold back the tears. All this talk about Kayla dying on him was making all his joy flee.

"Kayla is probably sleeping so long today because she's sad that you lost your spot. It's that lost happiness she could have found today that is bringing her down. I think that she won't have much time left, and as I mentioned before, the crown was made by an ultra-dragon king. This same dragon king was married to a spellbinding dragon named Aralot. It is a spell from her that we are dealing with all these years later. I've never pinpointed where exactly the spell comes from, but it's in the kingdom someplace. So to defeat Aralot, we first need to defeat Wisteria so that we can keep Valiant. He's the only spellbinding dragon we have that can even begin to understand what kind of spell is attacking his rider."

Caleb gulped and then fought for air again. Kayla's love was being eaten alive, and she loved him, so Caleb would never receive any of that love until Kayla was able to give it out by being free of this curse. Even if he found a way around both Tristan and King Tyler, Kayla would never be able to love him freely. Not feeling loved by the women they had married had to drive the kings of Aralot insane long before that keeper poison reached them. This thing was evil. That dragon named Aralot was evil. What kind of a dragon wanted to devour love? This probably wasn't what Vermelo was thinking, but the first thing that came to Caleb's mind was something that Kayla had mentioned to him once.

"So Kayla was right. King Gladius wasn't as crazy as everyone said he was. He put curses on Vankerdale to constrain their dragons, stop their bonds, and shove them into winter. He cursed the ocean so no one could trade with Wisteria and they couldn't reach us. He was blocking out Wisteria and Vankerdale trying to isolate the problem that killed his wife. He was trying to contain the curse, find the source, and destroy it. Everything he did that had people screaming at him was an effort to take down Aralot's lingering spell."

"Kayla told you that?" Vermelo asked sounding surprised.

Caleb shrugged. It wasn't exactly worded like that, but it meant the same thing. She could feel it. Kayla saw keepers in a much different way than everyone else saw them. To her, they were not the heroes but the ones that pushed the heroes forward. To her, they were the people that got overlooked and forgotten, the ones that gave their hearts to the cause of aiding the dragons and humans in the entire land every day and night. They were the ones being hit with this spell. Gladius had known what it was, and his purpose in life had been to destroy it. He had unfortunately died first.

"You can't find the source of this curse?" Caleb asked to be sure.

Vermelo shook his head. "Jack hasn't found it either. I can't verify for sure if Gladius ever found it, but I do know that he didn't destroy it before his death. Don't tell anyone what Kayla did, please. If people around here see her as a queen, I'd hate to think of how that would affect her. I'm only telling you because you brought this paper from Wisteria. The spell is closing in trying to take away the dragon that could save her. I can't bring that up with Jack or Tia. They would—"

"They are going to be so mad that she got engaged and didn't tell anyone," Caleb cut off.

He felt mad about it, but he couldn't do anything about it just as Vermelo had said. Caleb might have the potential to be the next king, but he would never be one as long as Kayla had to hide her love. It must be really hard for her to be around him sometimes if all her love was eaten up, and yet, with a thing like love, she wouldn't want to stay away. She was still fighting an inner struggle that no one else could see that consumed her and claimed her life, her heart, her everything.

"I have to stop this."

"Don't get your hopes up. Every king has tried. None of them have succeeded yet."

"Don't get preachy," Caleb said standing up ignoring the crown on the floor. "I'm not a king. I have no obligation to uphold kingly laws or rules. I have no time constraints, no magical laws I need to fulfill. King Klavian and King Jack handle those. I'm going to stop this. So…"

He fingered the magical paper that Kayla had written on. He didn't care what Tristan was going to do to him for deserting the King's Ware. He had to get out there. He had to head off Wisteria to safeguard the spellbinding dragon. Then he had to get Valiant to trust him enough to help him save Kayla.

"I need to get into Wisteria, find the curse that started there during Gladius's reign, and shatter it."

Every part of his plan was impossible. He couldn't reach Wisteria. They didn't let people inside, and he had missed the deadline to claim entry to see the king. Go figure. He also was a baby with casting spells.

"Okay maybe just finding out what curse Wisteria is suffering from first would be the wiser plan, and then I can ask the people who know spells to shatter it. Kayla would break it. It looks like a binding spell of some sort."

At least that's what the paper made it sound like after Kayla had asked her followup questions to the Wisterian King.

"If we're trying to not get Jack involved, I could probably get Anvil to break it too. I know he denies it, but everyone knows Anvil does magic."

"I don't think we should get Anvil involved. Kayla is pretty much his daughter. Jack has a deep-seated grudge against Anvil taking away the women in his life. I wouldn't aggravate that by turning to Anvil instead of Jack. No. I will help you stop Wisteria, Caleb. Let me think."

Caleb skimmed Vermelo as the man closed his eyes in thought. Vermelo made it sound like he practiced magic. Caleb had never heard of this before, but he probably shouldn't be surprised all things considered. Caleb found himself looking at the other four guards when Vermelo took his sweet time. These guards now knew all about the spell that was sucking Kayla's life away. Hopefully, these men were very trustworthy. They looked back at him rather morbid as if they felt sorry for the fate he had dropped inside—loving a woman that could never love him back. At least it wasn't because she didn't want to love him back.

"Okay," Vermelo said opening his eyes again. "I'm going out on a limb here, but when I first asked you what you wanted to do, you said you wanted to enter Wisteria. After hearing me out, you still wanted that same thing. I'm going to trust your gut on this because you kings happen to have the best instincts. We need to get you into Wisteria. Entering by sea is out, but since you can hold the crown, I can safely assume that you can travel through the king's portals to reach Wisteria the same way that King Lester Noltman entered the king's magical library. Dwarf dragons killed off Lester's father. It was Kayla who found King Lester and got him back to his own kingdom without anyone else knowing a thing."

Of course it was. That was the sort of thing that she did in silence as she tried to handle everything on her own. Maybe she was so withdrawn from sharing the workload because to divvy it out would prove that she loved another person enough to trust them with a task and trust and love were hard on her.

"Since it's dwarf dragons blocking your way, I'd suggest that you take Merlock with you. I need to give you something before you go through the portal, so once you get your things together come back to see me, and I'll show you where the portal is. Then find the spell that Wisteria needs Valiant for, devise how to stop the spell without losing the dragon, and do all of this as fast as possible before Kayla dies. Sound good?"

"It sounds hard, but you had me the first time you said 'save Kayla.'"

He was going rogue. Caleb had never gone rogue before. He knew a few people who had and they had never been let back into the same ware they ran from. Caleb didn't know how he would ever explain this to Tristan so he wasn't banished.

"How about the truth? You are leaving to save Kayla," Warner answered. *"And I'm coming with you."*

Caleb moved to leave Vermelo's bedroom tower with the intention to leave the entire kingdom. He still had questions about this nightmare thing that Vermelo hadn't answered. There was one person he could think of that might know the answers.

Arsonist

Kayla

The nightmares from past keepers had been repeating themselves over and over again like echoes smashing against the empty cavity of her skull. There were certain spots that Kayla usually fought to stop the chaos around her. Today she didn't fight at all. She'd seen these echoes from the past so many times that they held no meaning, caused no resistance. When she had finally given in to the dreams that's when they all changed.

The sounds of battle had left. She wasn't looking out of dragon eyes or past keeper eyes. She was herself, which was the strangest thing of all. She couldn't remember ever having a dream where she was herself. Kayla wondered at first if she had cracked the code to end the curse by not fighting, but she was wrong. The scary part came in the shape of vast beauty.

There she had been standing in a field of bright blue flowers with no one else around. At first, the break was heavenly, relaxing even, until she realized that the field didn't end. Kayla had just spent the last several hours of being asleep running in a straight line without making any progress. That was scarier than the other nightmares she had gotten used to. She felt trapped and caged even though she was outside and the air was sweet. Every now and then she could swear the air whispered something to her, something that sounded like "Aralot." Kayla wiped away the feeling of being eternally stuck running in search of the exit as she sat up.

"You are finally awake! I spent the time trying to convince Sparkle to help me search for the spell that might be doing this to you since she's so good at finding things with her nose. We hunted for a while but didn't turn up anything other than Riven who was poking around and Tristan who was blasting apart a few old cursed objects from Gladius. Other than that, we didn't find anything."

"I was dreaming about a field of flowers and couldn't get out," Kayla admitted.

Did she need to mention that the field of flowers was all the mystique, indicating that she was now dreaming about being trapped inside of magic? She didn't like the thought of it because she was starting to think that other people had been lying to her. There was nothing new about seeing the dream leading her through the destroyed castle in the south. The flower dream was new. Perhaps it was that dream that really meant something. After all, someone had once drawn the picture of the mystique and it was adopted on Aralot's flag. These flowers meant something and Kayla was pretty sure that it was sinister.

"Is it possible to think happy thoughts today?" Valiant prompted.

"I am fairly certain that this dream has been seen before," Kayla remarked. *"Only I don't know what it means. Is there any information about why Aralot's flag is the way it is?"*

"No," Valiant snapped. *"I don't like that dream. Think of something else."*

Pg. 386

"Okay. Has Caleb been spotted?"

"Something else."

That was a no. She had woken up once inside the doctor's office to hear Notley telling Mulligan that Caleb had gone missing. The scouts had seen him walk toward the castle and he had not come back to class. Mulligan wondered if he was trying to find a way to get his job back. Kayla wasn't sure what he was doing, but she had missed him the second she heard that he wasn't her teacher anymore.

Once Notley and Mulligan left, Kayla had stumbled her way to her own bed where she had slept all over again. She hadn't seen Caleb for hours. She hadn't heard his voice, hadn't listened to the pattern of his shoes walking, or felt his smile aimed in her direction.

"Happy thoughts, Kayla," Valiant redirected. *"You felt sad about Caleb and collapsed. Being sad makes you fall. Please find something happy."*

Okay. She didn't want to ignore how she felt about Caleb, but she'd try. That meant that she had to get up and do something to take her mind off losing one of her best friends. Kayla latched on her weapons belt and entered the mess hall, scowling at the food because there was nothing happy about always needing to trade trays since hers got poisoned. Sometimes this happened five times in a row with no one able to pick out where the poison was coming from. Dinner tonight looked to be soup and salad. Tossing soup was going to be messy.

Kayla trudged into the line hearing the mellow sound that her new shoes created. The sound alone had her smiling already. These boots from Ritz reminded her of Gladius on days he was feeling confident. Since Maslon had been a shoemaker, Kayla was fairly certain that Gladius's favorite boots had been created by his brother. Ritz hadn't sown up boots like this in ages, but he had made her some. Kayla sidestepped to the right and sidestepped to the left simply to hear the sound they made. Oh, she loved these! If she ever got Ritz alone again, she was going to give him the biggest hug he'd ever gotten. On a day that had started out bleak, he had given her sunshine that was going to go everywhere that she did.

On that note, another thing that would make her happy would be to not need to trade her food with anyone else. The riders around here were switching up places, reluctant to be near her when she was close to food in the event that her tray became poisoned. She had spent too long ignoring this. A little problem solving would take her mind off Caleb being gone.

Kayla ended up trading her food around three times before she could lift her food into her mouth without it glowing orange on her. She rambled through suspects as she chewed.

First on the line was Ritz. She had wondered if it was him slipping her the poison so that she would turn insane. Then she would be capable of fighting him off so she could reach the end of the path in her dreams. Now that she was away from him blocking her, the whole idea sounded ludicrous. How could it be Ritz?! He felt the same thing she did when interacting with other keepers. He wouldn't be able to poison her because the magic in his blood screamed at him to protect her. What he had done to keep her away from the end of that path in the old castle was done to keep her safe from whatever it was that could be giving her nightmares.

She really didn't think that it was Gladius that had cursed her. His goal to be the worst lover was still troubling, but he must have known something more about this curse than she did. He had destroyed his entire castle trying to take it down, and that still didn't stop it. Whatever spell he had used, must have been a strong one. He had talked about heart magic so maybe he had started to believe that there was such a thing, like a love could be a magical force.

In any case, her current poisoner could be anyone who didn't love keepers and wanted to kill her off. It could be anyone who was scared of Valiant since he was a spellbinding dragon. A lot of people were scared of magic hitting them. Valiant had not cast any harmful spells, but that didn't stop the fear. If Kayla swallowed the poison she would start fighting with Valiant until she eventually killed him off.

Since Tristan's focus had been on who was after her instead of her dragon, she was going to take the opposite approach. He'd not made any discovery with his sleuthing. So perhaps the reason for the poison wasn't her. No one was scared of her. They were scared of Valiant. To detect who kept slipping in the poison, she had to find out who was scared of spellbinding dragons.

It would be a hidden fear, but one that the person would want to check up on now and again to see if the poison had reached Valiant. That was a harder question because lots of people ventured in and out of the ware. It could be a milkman or a seamstress or a mail runner. However, looking at them couldn't explain how the poison kept getting onto her food so often when they were not here. This was the job of someone who could influence her meals from a distance. Someone who could invent a spell to place the poison right where she would find it. Someone who also would be trying to secretly take down her protection spell once he learned of it.

Tristan wasn't the problem, but his dad? He had never liked dragons. He spent his time in books and could have come across a passage that told him something scary about spellbinding dragons. Both Tristan and Klavian picked castle windows that faced the ware. Klavian gazing out the window to check on the state of Valiant wouldn't have caused anyone alarm. Why had she never considered him before?! He was the perfect person to create some spell that would only put the poison into her food. It had to be magic doing this, because she really didn't think it was any of the riders.

"Here we go again," Kayla sighed, skipping out of the mess hall with a smile over the sound of her boots. She picked out the king's window in the distance and looked at it with distaste. The Clusters were always the ones getting in her way. Aria had been killing off dragons from previous keeper bonds. Tristan had been cursing women so that more keepers couldn't be born, and it was very possible that Klavian was trying to make her kill Valiant.

If Caleb could go venture over to the castle, then she could. Maybe she would see him while she was there. Kayla waved to the dragon scouts that watched her leave, but the guards at the castle refused to tell her anything about Caleb. Normally they would tell her anything she wanted to know, but not today. To try not to be irritated by that since she was trying to stay upbeat, Kayla let it go and asked after Klavian instead. A shrug was the answer, but Kayla knew where to look all the same.

King Klavian usually ate around now and was predictably in the kitchen fixing himself his meal instead of letting the cooks prepare it for him. See? He was picky with food. One point against him.

"Hungry?" he asked her holding out his sandwich as if he knew very well that she wasn't eating much. Not eating well and not sleeping were going to do her in, but she wasn't taking his food. Then again if it became poisoned…

"Oh starving," Kayla pretended. She took his sandwich and took a bite while he made himself another one.

"No spies out of Wisteria yet?" Kayla asked him, leading up to finding her answers. "I've been waiting ages for information on spellbinding dragons. Valiant is so picky. There are times when he won't move at all and times where he wants to conquer the world."

The good thing about Klavian was that he had never been a Colt. He was raised a noble and his expressions showed on his face. He grimaced over the conquering part. Nice.

"Wisteria has caught most of our spies," Klavian admitted. "They've sent us a list of everyone they are holding hostage and refuse to release them until we release *them* from an unknown curse they think we know about. Naturally, Aria has been comparing the captured list against the list of spies we have sent. All but one is on there. One person got away, or never made it, or whatever."

That curse was the one that was trapping a few of their dragons. Kayla didn't bother to mention it to him. She was going to take care of it eventually. It was *her* dragon that they wanted after all. If she told Klavian what Wisteria wanted, he would probably tell her to give Valiant away, which would be another point against him.

"And you haven't read anything here that talks on spellbinding dragons? It's got to say somewhere that they are the stars of the night or some other poetic rubbish."

"Rubbish indeed," Klavian answered. He finished slapping his sandwich together and took a bite of his own. "King Peyton knew what he was doing when he stabbed you with that particular dragon. The only thing we know is that spellbinding dragons are horrible for kings. He must have had his hands and head full of SilverWings bad temperament, and he was passing along the curse to us."

Kayla set down the sandwich and glared at him. Klavian considered himself a king even if he wasn't one exactly. He had just admitted to thinking that Valiant was a curse to him. Here she went.

"Stop trying to kill my dragon or we're going to have issues you and I." Kayla kept her tone cold, the kind of cold that Gladius used. It made most people shiver. It made Klavian cough on his sandwich.

"Kayla I would never—"

"Shall I cast you into a truth-telling spell or would you like to admit it all on your own? You are trying to make me kill my dragon. If I get any more keeper poison put on my food, I am going to start messing up your food too."

"Kayla, I respect you and your family—"

"But not our dragons," Kayla cut him off. "You can cure me after I ingest the poison but there's no cure to the dragon that dies from it. Please stop. This will be war otherwise."

With that, she turned to leave him to his food. She believed that he was fully responsible, but if he wasn't, he was going to find out who was really fast and make it all end.

"From the way the other Clusters have treated your family, I think it's him too," Valiant said.

King Klavian would have to stop now. She had taken down Aria and Tristan and now Klavian. She didn't expect to get any recognition for her work, but she was the worst thing that had ever happened to the Clusters. She was going to keep tearing down their threats, see through their disguises, and bring glory back to keepers again. Beating them at their own game wasn't as satisfying as it could have been, but knowing that she could eat her next meal in peace was a fantastic thought that helped her keep the smile.

Urns

Caleb

When it came to finding answers about the nightmare curse on Kayla, those who watched Kayla had to be the ones that knew what was happening. Apart from Vermelo's incredible watch, Ritz was the other man who spied on her all the time. Caleb considered changing out of his riding gear as he ventured over to the Colt camp, but he didn't want everyone to know that he was defecting so he kept the red leather on.

The Colts near the castle lived in a constant but permanent state of camping. They had nothing but tarps for doors and fire for heat as they bunked inside of shabby wooden A-frames. Other Colt settlements lived better, like the stone homes by The Pits. Then there were still more Colts that didn't live in any collective bubble but lived inside of towns choosing to join up with the organization at various points in their lives when their views aligned with what the Colts taught.

From hearing Kayla talk, Caleb knew that some people who had passed the Colt tests and earned their wild stallion tattoo had since fallen away from the main group. However, once a Colt always a Colt. Those people still joined in with the hardest missions. Being a Colt meant living with a few shared ideas without sharing similar ways of living.

Caleb reached the A-frames feeling off-center. Riders never came here. To do so was asking for trouble, and if he got these Colts mad at him, he was asking for death. Still, he was going to die when Kayla did, so there was more to gain than lose from venturing into the enemy camp.

He never did like the color of the red leather that he was wearing, but wearing it here had him looking like a fresh target. Colts were tumbling in behind him and before him blocking him off before he got too far. Caleb spun around searching for a sympathetic face. Finding not even one, he dismissed with the pleasantries and got straight to the point.

"I was hoping I could speak with someone that would be well versed on Gladius."

"Try Jack," a man with a wicked burn mark down the side of his face answered, "or Tia," he supplied next.

Caleb shook his head. He had a question he was certain they wouldn't know.

"Is Ritz around?"

"He's liable to curse you, cut you, or steal from you as payment if you ask him anything," another Colt told him sincerely. It was strange to hear the guy try to protect him, but Caleb wasn't changing his mind.

"I'll take my chances."

"Actually, Ritz wasn't here at all until rumors started spreading that Kayla was limp on the field today. Then he appeared like a ghost out of nowhere in a very bad mood. Brave him yourself. Don't blame us for your misfortune," the burnt man said.

He pointed to an A-frame, so Caleb gave him a nod and headed toward it, knocking on the side of the building since it didn't have a door. Ritz pushed the tarp over his head to exit looking around with a scowl that would have kept most anyone away from him. He glared at Caleb and turned his sour mood to him.

"You must find yourself incredibly brave to stand in the Colt hive when you're wearing the wrong stripes."

It sounded like Ritz was trying to recruit him again because Caleb couldn't find what his soul craved if Kayla wasn't in the wares. Gee. He'd probably stay away from wares forever if she married King Tyler and moved to Vankerdale. He'd move to Vankerdale with her no matter what it did to his insides to see her married to another man.

Caleb gave Ritz a smile not willing to add fuel to his games. That's how Jack dealt with him. He stood there until Ritz got annoyed enough to mellow out. Knowing that, Caleb stood in silence too, thankful for all the time he had spent spying on Kayla and her family so he had tips like this up his sleeve.

"You're a sorry excuse for a rider, Caleb. You'd make a fine Colt with the way you fooled everyone about your experience level."

That was almost a compliment. Caleb had advanced two levels in a single year up until the point Anvil kicked him out. However, he had done so with the same team of people. Learning how to work in a new team was challenging and he really missed his old one.

Pg. 397

"Kayla is crumbling under your instruction," Ritz tried to insult.

Ritz probably thought he knew everything there was to know about him. Caleb normally jumped at anyone who said anything mean about Kayla, but he expected the insults from Ritz, so he stayed standing there silent not letting anything bother him. This was all a front for the other Colts that were watching.

"She's an even worse excuse for a rider than you are. There's no way she could have gotten into the King's Ware if she wasn't royalty. She belongs in the class before level one. She hardly ever gets on her dragon."

He didn't even flinch. Ritz couldn't rile him up one bit because he wasn't here to fight. He was here to save Kayla.

Ritz frowned at him. "You must be really desperate. You and Kayla both. She spilled all her darkest secrets to me. Care to do the same?"

Sharing his secrets with Ritz wasn't his plan, but the way he had shifted his tone made Caleb believe him about Kayla. She was always running off into the night with Ritz standing around. She could have talked with him. Maybe she was telling him about all the nightmares she couldn't share with anyone else. She had to unload it somewhere.

"What do you want, Caleb?" Ritz asked him.

There. That was his cue. Jack had told Tia that he couldn't ever talk with Ritz on level ground until Ritz pushed aside all his

Pg. 398

slandering and asked him what he was after. Caleb had done it! He had stood there until he got Ritz to ask him the question.

"Did Gladius know that his wife was dying?" Caleb asked. That was it. His one question that had pushed him to seek out the notorious leader to chat.

Ritz turned quiet. They stood there in silence again in what Jack had called "the stare down period." If Caleb talked before Ritz did, Ritz wouldn't tell him a single thing. Caleb waited and waited. He couldn't help but fidget because Ritz was taking forever, testing his patience really well. Caleb was patient. He was very determined to get the answer even if it was one word that Ritz gave him back.

"I think you'd better come with me," Ritz said.

He turned and started to walk out of the camp. Caleb felt Colt eyes staring at him from every angle, silent and curious. Yeah, his question brought up a lot of questions. Most people believed that Gladius's wife, Jean, had died in childbirth. It wasn't common knowledge that she had been dying before that with the same curse that was taking Kayla.

Caleb took off after Ritz keeping his hands near his weapon belt. Following Ritz into the unknown was only done by the bravest of men. Whisperers claimed that there were people he had led away that never came back. It was too late to ask Kayla if those tales were true. Caleb was already heading out behind him.

Ritz took him into the woods directly through a horde of wild dragons that included Norber and Halfax. The two dragons turned their back to him rudely not acknowledging that he was walking among them when he had been training them. If Caleb was a Colt, he'd probably be terrified by the display of blinking dragon eyes watching him.

Ritz led him to the monastery walls, then through a window he busted open, and into the monastery. This was getting worse now. Breaking into the sacred monastery wasn't something Caleb would ever do. It made him question if Ritz was going to give him an answer or simply trick him into Colt tests to make him one.

They snuck behind monks. Ritz stole a holy lamp that Caleb knew was going to be used for a ceremony soon and put it in Caleb's hands. Caleb held the object uncertain if he needed it to get his answer or not. After sneaking down several hallways with it, he set it down.

Ritz pulled him deeper still, unlocking a door with eight locks on it under a few minutes. He opened up a special box and handed a stolen piece of paper to Caleb. Not sure what this was, Caleb started to read it. Written in Tia's handwriting was a copy from a page out of Gladius's journal.

"Mortality is too short for some and too long for others. Who gets to decide when a life is snuffed out? Why wait around for a magical fate when I can make the decision faster? The end result will be the same. Her love will still linger in the air, still get stolen by everyone around me when it should be mine and only mine. She loves me and not the kid down the road she's never met. If her love is to be devoured, it is I that shall devour it. It is I that will have it. I refuse to share her love."

As soon as Caleb's eyes reached the end of the page, Ritz grabbed it from his fingers and locked it back up again silently. It sounded like Gladius had known that Jean was stuck in the curse and he had not liked the lack of love at all.

Pg. 400

Caleb was led down some long stairs deeper into the monastery. It was impressive that Ritz knew where he was going so well. They found a bunch of urns down here with names of the dead kings and queens on them.

"Tia believes that the passage you just read relates to Gladius killing off one of his dragons. It's not. It relates to his wife. See for yourself. All the other urns for queens are empty except for Jean Frizer. She wasn't lost in the same way the other queens were and her ashes are here. Read the inscriptions, Caleb. You'll get the idea."

Gladius was indeed a troubled man who had failed to get revenge. No wonder his writings had been locked up and his items destroyed. Caleb moved toward the urns not liking what he was seeing.

"In loving memory," one claimed. "Whose love will never leave us," another queen had inscribed. "Our love forever," and "who had a love that will never fade," were the next ones. Then there was Jean. Hers was scarier than all the others and simply read, "death to Aralot."

"Now read this one," Ritz directed passing over a paper that Caleb hadn't seen Ritz take.

This was definitely the answer he had come looking for and he had gone to the only man who would be able to sneak him down here to see it. Caleb had no idea where to even start looking without Ritz. He had no idea that the monks had all this information. Gladius was destroyed from the inside out, both in his heart and his mind. Caleb was hesitant to read the next paper.

"Her cries don't bother me anymore. I can't even hear them. Oh, Aralot, thy wings so bright, thy scales so smooth. Your voice like milk and your hum like a summer afternoon. I shall never stop fighting you. Long after I am gone, I shall be the knife in your side, the prong in your eye, the rip in your wing. I shall be your worst lover ever."

That's what Gladius was all right. It was hard to get Gladius out of the land even though he had been dead for three generations, but what if Gladius meant this all literally? With everything that Vermelo had said, it looked all too real that Aralot was a dragon. A living dragon that was still alive feasting on the love of queens that the crown claimed.

With Jean having her remains in the jar, it proved that she wasn't taken by Aralot in the same manner as the other queens. Jean had never lived long enough for the dragon to eat her because someone else had killed her first. It sounded crazy because all the other stories from Tia claimed that Jean died in childbirth after having two sons; Herb and Arvid. Gladius was furious that someone had hidden his kids from him, which would only indicate that he hadn't been the one killing off his wife trying to stop the dragon from eating her first.

Caleb tilted his head at the paper in his hand. It wasn't written in Tia's handwriting so it couldn't be taken from Gladius's journal. This had to be written by the person who had stolen Herb and Arvid. Who would steal the infants and claim to be a horrible lover? It was someone who knew about Aralot who had thought that stopping Jean from giving her love away might also stop the dragon. That hadn't been the answer. Aralot was still devouring Kayla's love anyway. She was still starving because the past three queens had escaped her. No wonder she hit at Kayla so strong.

Pg. 402

"Do you know who wrote…" Caleb started to ask only to find that Ritz was no longer to be found. In his place was someone holier and more frightening. Abbot McLean. Today the man had on robes of white with a yellow sash tied around his waist. He was balding on the back of his head, but that only added to his superior look.

"I didn't…" Caleb started to say. "I was brought down here…"

"You shall atone for your crimes," the abbot told him. He took the paper from Caleb's hand and read it with a puzzled expression.

"Where did you get this?"

"From Ritz," Caleb volunteered the truth.

"This is Maslon's hand," the abbot claimed.

Maslon who was Gladius's younger brother. The guy had been killed off by riders in his own keeper bond. At least that was what the stories said. Seeing how the stories were mixed with lies, anything was possible at this point. It was Gladius's younger brother Maslon who had killed off Gladius's wife and stolen his sons. Herb and Arvid had no proof that they were related to Gladius until they were around the age of twenty-one and someone brought them Gladius's journal.

"You will still make penance for breaking and entering. You broke the law," the abbot said, pocketing the new writing.

Caleb was led back up the stairs by a group of monks and into a room with a book of scripture. Then he was told to write out a few passages. Looking down at the first one already had him groaning.

"No man shall defy the holy sanctuaries of light…"

Nice. This was going to take a while and give the monks a great handwriting sample from him. It was worth it. He had learned things that most people never got to see or know. Aralot was real. She was a living spellbinding dragon trapped in a spell that fed her love, and he had a large hunch that the image that Kayla had drawn was the map that would lead him right to her.

Dust

Tristan

Just the same way he had failed with trying to decide who was poisoning Kayla, Tristan felt like he had failed in making a dent into anything that Ritz cared about. Destroying the objects that Ian and August had told him about had done nothing but make a few people mad at him. Ritz was still alive and whispers circulated that he had taken Caleb Andrade out on a private conquest after Caleb had asked the man if Gladius knew his wife was dying.

It was unheard of that Ritz walked a rider toward information so easily. The monks were complaining that the two of them had broken into the queens' tomb, but the complaints didn't get too far because Caleb and Ritz had also left behind some old writing from Maslon that had never been discovered before. Caleb had gotten in trouble. Ritz, of course, was spared because of that writing. It was his clever ticket to not be held accountable for his actions. He had bartered his way through.

To Tristan, this didn't prove that Ritz was collaborating with riders. It proved that he had spent a great deal of time searching for things that Gladius and Maslon may have left behind. The missing object that Tristan was looking for could be just about anywhere, and if it was buried at the bottom of the ocean, odds were that Ritz hadn't been able to reach it until Jack took the curses off the ocean. That had been done some time ago, but there was another place that no one in Aralot had been able to reach in a very long time—Vankerdale.

Tristan himself had buried things in Vankerdale, which was why he was now crouched down really really low trying to avoid detection by Conner, the old mail runner. Tristan had been heading in the direction of the Vankerdale border wondering if the statue he needed to find was somewhere near the river line. Afterall, Aralot's crown had been kept hidden near there before. That had led him to discover that Conner was meeting with Ritz next. This had Tristan's full attention.

Tristan had kept quiet about what he knew about Conner, but the man had run into Vankerdale trying to save Kayla's dragon from King Peyton and gotten stuck there behind Jack's spells that prevented border crossers. Conner was back. He was a person well versed in Felding ways. He had known that Tia was a keeper long before she herself knew. He had helped Kayla defeat the Peyton's and crown Tyler the king. Conner would know about Kayla's secret engagement and all the other things that no one was talking about regarding that girl. This was going to be a good spying session as long as Tristan didn't blow his cover.

He had spotted Ritz first before he'd seen Conner. The man now had shaggy long blond hair, but he still wore leather pants and thick black boots as he had in his younger years. Standing beside Ritz had the men looking oddly similar. Ritz looked to be trapped in about the same age as Conner was now. For a moment there, Tristan had wondered if Ritz was heading him off before he could enter Vankerdale, but he'd changed his mind now that he was seeing this.

Pg. 406

"Tell me that you brought scrumptious food from Louie's Bistro. Every good spy lord needs to tempt his spies with a good bribe," Conner claimed, causing Ritz to smile at him. Tristan noted the smile with amusement. There was only one other person that Ritz gave that smile to and it was Kayla. Everyone else got his ugly smirk and death threats, even Jack.

"I brought you something better since I know that you're a collector."

Ritz reached into a satchel that he had brought with him and pulled out a large stack of papers. Having seen Caleb drawing on this type of paper recently, Tristan knew exactly what it was that had Conner grinning and reaching for his bribe.

"They'd better be real. I can spot all the replicas of his work and I don't fall for the fake ones."

Ritz laughed. "They're real. I left Caleb with all the fake ones. He probably won't ever notice."

"You ever feel bad for the guy?" Conner asked sifting through the images of some thirty freshly stollen drawings. "His adoration is so visible."

"He's not suffering for it," Ritz answered.

"Really? The guy knows. Just look at this one." Conner flipped back to an early image that Tristan wished he could see.

"I thought you would like that one. It was the first one I picked out, but I'll have you know that when he made that, he had no idea how much his feelings were justified."

"I'm determined to not let him end up like Anvil," Conner said, putting the pictures carefully into a backpack.

"He won't. Anvil was always in love with Tia because he loves being the best, and seeing the best inspires him to love. Caleb has never mimicked that aspect of Anvil's character. His love stems mostly from Kayla secretly helping other people. He loves her for the heart that's hidden, and he believes it his duty to likewise spread such compassion to others. Even if Caleb fails, he will be nothing like Anvil."

Conner raised his eyebrows at Ritz. "Now that is impressive. You like Caleb Andrade."

"I said no such thing."

"I may have been gone for a third of my life, but you didn't change during that time."

"Good. You keep thinking that and we'll continue to get along," Ritz remarked, causing Conner to chuckle. "You've had your bribe. What have you done to deserve it?"

"We've got Tyler taken care of," Conner assured.

"You found Tyler a wife?" Ritz asked.

"Yeah. You were right about who to entice his way. It was super easy. Way easier than dealing with Tristan. Tyler isn't hard to please at all. He will settle for Adelyn Peyton and use her last name to hold him in place quite well. She's a brave girl that will do what needs to be done. I tested her myself."

Tristan frowned. Conner couldn't do that! Tristan had just gotten rid of Kayla to Tyler! Now Conner was sneaking around trying to make everything that Kayla had done obsolete. He was pressing a different wife at King Tyler. Oh, that was just the sort of thing that Ritz would have this long-lost Colt doing for him! Ritz couldn't resist sticking his overly large nose into kingdom affairs.

King Tyler would be better off if he kept Kayla and took her far away from Tristan. It was ever so nice to not need to fret over Kayla all the time. If Conner was right (a Colt never told Ritz something like this and dared to be wrong), Tristan was back to where he had started, trying to figure out how to get along with the shadow that just happened to be far too caring, patient, helpful, and young. Blast! Kayla was probably in on this whole scheme. She hadn't been telling anyone that she was engaged because she was going to make sure that she wasn't.

"And Tristan?" Ritz quizzed. "The brat can't die."

A brat was he? This was all the proof that Tristan needed to point fingers at Ritz for trying to kill him. Ritz had just admitted to his deeds, and he was going to pay for them.

Conner and Ritz stepped closer together to talk so Tristan wasn't able to hear the rest of their conversation. He didn't need to hear it. They were talking like ventriloquists so that he couldn't lip read their words, but his eyes saw everything he needed. Ritz really was trying to head Tristan off from searching Vankerdale for things Gladius may have put there. Conner passed him a small statue about two inches tall that very well could be used as a game piece. That could very well be the thing Tristan was looking for! Ritz put it into his pocket, and if he had the chance to hide that thing himself, no one would ever find it.

Tristan reached for his magic, excited to test his theory. All he had to do was pull toward him any statues that Gladius might have touched. If he got the statue that Ritz had just accepted, he'd have his answer. He worked on drawing up the magic into his hand finding it hard to get the magic's cooperation. This wasn't even large magic. All he wanted to do was steal from Ritz! Stealing was easy magic. It had always worked for him before, but it was resisting him as if the magic was indeed losing all respect for Tristan's wishes as Vermelo had claimed. It had better not. He was going to need to go see Jack about this soon because it was a problem. He still questioned how problematic magic was being for Jack since Vermelo had mentioned the king losing his touch.

There! The gem nearest his hand finally responded. It put blue magic out and miraculously didn't alert the talking men as they leaned forward to whisper. A jade dragon statue flew across the expanse from Ritz's pocket into Tristan's hand. The creature had two jeweled eyes that were deep in color and perfect for holding a long-lasting spell. Tristan propped the statue onto a branch before him and fought even harder with the magic to blast it apart. He was just about to give up and take a hammer to the thing when his spell connected and the jade dragon crumbled into several pieces.

That was another item from Gladius gone. Tristan looked down from the tree back at the conversing men. Ritz wasn't in view anymore. Conner was still there with his head tilted sidewise looking confused as if Ritz had suddenly disappeared.

Tristan found himself looking around as dragon voices started crying out. He had expected to feel a bit different after succeeding in ending Ritz, but instead of feeling relieved or even happy, he felt a little scared.

He had won. He hadn't expected to actually win no matter how long he hunted, but he had won, and that left the Colts without their esteemed leader. If Conner figured out that it was Tristan who had just turned Ritz into a pile of dust, Tristan might end up being disgraced from the Colts and hunted for the rest of his life. He had to get out of here!

He could hear dragon wings coming over. Once the dragons communicated what they had seen with their sharper eyes, Tristan was done for. He climbed down from the tree right as Norber, one of two wild dragons that Valiant had adopted, landed before Conner. The man didn't recoil an inch. Most Colts would have, but Conner had been the mail runner to all the dragon wares and dragons had never bothered him. Norber was singing the death song for Conner to tell him what had happened.

"Who are you?" Conner asked Norber. One minute he was staring at the dragon, and the next, he was down on his knees reaching toward the pile of dust with tears streaming down his face.

It wasn't going to take Conner long to figure out that the dust was missing the jade dragon when it looked like Conner's hands brushed up against other materials like a coin bag and a few keys and such. When he realized that it was gone, he might connect all the dots. Tristan gave Conner and Norber one more glance before he ran for it.

Unbound

Caleb

"The words keep coming spinning in my head, no time to lose because she's almost dead. Feel the heat dripping through my blood, all my tears will make a flood."

Caleb was composing a rather sad song indeed as he continued running. Kayla had woken back up, so his dragon told him, but there was no way to know when she would fall down again. She was used to trying to sleep during the night, so he expected her to become unresponsive. The only way to give her a fighting chance was to leave and fight against Aralot himself. Ritz had said before that the difference between fate and magic was nothing. If that was the case, it was magic that had Caleb meeting Merlock before he needed him, and magic that had Tristan taking over the ware to push Caleb out of it. Caleb felt no responsibility to anyone inside that ware apart from Kayla now that his job was taken away.

Caleb dashed along behind Merlock and Vermelo through a tunnel that had been spelled to look like solid rock in order to reach the hidden portal in the back. He glanced down at his left arm where a thin line of green puss indicated that he had been stabbed by dragon venom for the second time in his life. If the dragon had been alive, he would have been already dead, since humans couldn't survive a double bond even if Kayla mostly handled it. Vermelo had slashed Caleb's arm with ancient ice dragon venom which was the antidote to traveling through portals. Caleb could go through them now without falling over sick. This was knowledge that only belonged to the kings. Despite the added support from the Captain of the Guard that Caleb could be his king one day, Caleb didn't feel royal.

He glanced further down at his light leather pants and then rotated his shoulders inside his green shirt. He'd discarded the red leather of the King's Ware inside a clothing shop feeling like a true renegade while he wondered if Ritz had always known that one day Caleb would find himself standing in opposition to the wares that stopped him from reaching his goals. He had always wondered why trained men could run from dragon wares.

Usually, those men ended up being cast out of the entire kingdom so they didn't start up secret dragon armies. Now Caleb knew what could make him turn his back on everything he had ever stood for. He had a leader he didn't appreciate, a team he didn't know, no Kayla, and an impending problem that needed his immediate attention outside.

Caleb came to a stop as both Vermelo and Merlock did. He recognized the sight of a portal easily. It was a tall gray stone slab with hexagonal bricks that bumped outward. Seeing the portal had his sense of urgency increase. He had to get through this as fast as he could.

"You can't go without me!" Warner whined. This wasn't his first time complaining. He was rather upset to be left behind, and he couldn't decide if he wanted to hang out in the woods with Reed or

stay inside the ware where he'd be pestered over the location of his missing rider.

"Sorry, Warner. Merlock is a lot smaller than you, and I'm not risking you getting stuck in Wisteria. I am taking the dwarf dragon."

"Ready?" Caleb asked looking down at the brown mini dragon at his side. Merlock in answer started tapping at the hexagons on the portal with his tail before he hummed at Caleb and looked at him expectantly. Caleb had to look at Vermelo because he had no idea what he was supposed to be doing.

"You touch your magic to the bottom left block and that turns on the portal," Vermelo told him.

Oh. That's how they worked. Caleb pulled out the fox statue that Kayla had given him and pressed the object to the stone. The purple and blue glow that usually only came to life around the Brixtons roared to life before him.

"Caleb." Vermelo stopped him before he could step through. "Please tell me."

"What?" Caleb asked back.

"You broke into the monastery with Ritz and looked over papers from Gladius. Ritz has never been a man I could talk with. In all honesty, I've never tried, but if he showed you something, you must know what I don't."

"Yeah. Aralot the dragon is still alive. It's not only a spell that I'm facing, it's the actual dragon, and Gladius never found a way to stop her."

Vermelo frowned and then rubbed at his chin. "You think that Aralot is trapped in a time spell that eats love. Without a real queen on the throne, she's starving. Someone must have been feeding her all the years in between queens if she's somewhere in Aralot. Who could keep a secret like that? How are we hiding a fully grown dragon?"

Caleb opened his mouth to answer, but he didn't know the answer, so he shut his mouth to think instead. It was someone good at keeping secrets that knew the dragon was alive. Perhaps the person wanted to stop the dragon enough to give Caleb a hint about what he was facing. As for where it was hiding, it was hiding beneath Gladius's destroyed castle in the south. That's where Kayla's path ended.

"How about Ritz?" Caleb posed. "He knows about the dragon. He's lived long enough to take care of it."

"I thought Ritz hated dragons. He stays alive to care for Aralot?"

"If it's a wicked spellbinding dragon he has to tend, he might just hate dragons," Caleb answered.

He hadn't made that connection when Ritz had him read that paper about fighting off the love of Aralot, but it made perfect sense now. He wasn't scared of dragons, and Kayla wasn't scared of him, as if she felt a strong family connection to the ageless man who had always spied on her.

Caleb was starting to pick out what it was that Kayla knew and had never told him. Ritz was surprisingly good with large numbers of dragons. Norber and Halfax. Those were Ritz's dragons. They had turned their backs when he walked past to pretend like they didn't have any connection to Ritz. And the reason why Ritz had a handwriting sample from Gladius's younger brother Maslon that the monks had never seen was because Ritz was Maslon cursed to stay and face the dragon that Gladius hadn't defeated. That made him related to the Feldings. He could be a keeper. One of the hiding ones that Anvil couldn't find.

Ritz had killed off Gladius's wife and stolen his sons away trying to hide them. He had been trying to fight Aralot his whole life only he had failed so far too. Caleb didn't have exact proof, only large guesses to base all this on, but the truth ran through his chest strong and fierce as he found it. Ritz had shown him what he did because he was asking for help.

Caleb's fate in life felt tied to what he was doing right now; facing off against a timeless animal, because he was the only one who had ever trained a spellbinding dragon. He was the only man in Aralot gifted with the respect of magic, the power of the kings, and the rush to win before Kayla was gone. What made a man fail and a man succeed? So many other stronger kings had failed at this task. Caleb couldn't get this wrong. He had to do this. He had to learn how to stop these spells!

"Let's go!" He ordered before he ran through the portal feeling his head spin on him briefly as he pushed his way through the magic before him. He came out in complete darkness, but the sounds he heard had him skidding to a halt. Dragons. Small ones. He couldn't tell where they all were but Merlock came dashing out behind him, looped his tail around his right leg, and started to guide him through the dark while Merlock chatted with the creatures that Caleb couldn't see. He could make them out when their glowing eyes looked in his direction but that was all. Their sounds came from all directions, even though he was certain that he was walking through tunnels composed of tar whose walls should stop some of those directions.

The smell was strong. The turns were very complicated. He was completely lost without Merlock guiding him, and he would probably be tarred without the dragon as well. Merlock laughed at something another dragon said and his reply had a few other dragons laughing back at him. The sound dropped Caleb's tension down a notch. He was safe among friends because others had been here before him, paving the way for him to show up. He gratefully reached for a hole in the roof when he could make out pale sunlight. Gee, he'd been working on this all day already, and the night had passed him by. Those monks had him writing a long time! Merlock helped to push him up even if he didn't need it, and Caleb had to shut his eyes because the heat and light after such darkness were too much.

Merlock jumped out behind him as did a few other dragons. Several of them rubbed their heads over Caleb, taking an interest in his magical fox as Merlock did. Caleb clamped a hand over his pocket, letting his eyes adjust before he opened them again.

Everything was green. Trees rose taller than any trees he had ever beheld. Vines and plants squished together on the ground, on the trunks, and through the air looping across branches. Welcome to the jungle. It was indeed hot around here and so visually cluttered that Caleb was glad he had not brought Warner. The dragon would have gotten stuck between a tree ten steps in.

Merlock growled beside him, so Caleb spun around pulling a prong out at the same time in case he was to face those dwarf dragons now. What he found was Merlock knocking over a white sign. Caleb

Pg. 418

barely had enough to read what it said before Merlock tarred the thing and tore at it with his claws.

"Here lies the tomb of King Anthony. All who enter or exit shall face immediate death."

Yeah, Caleb didn't like that sign either. He had just come out from that hole which meant that already he was off to a bad start on a death list. There was another sign beside it warning of danger in the hole. That one Merlock left alone, since it was more helpful. Green dwarf dragon eyes were watching from the hole and close to it were those other dragons that had come out with him. Caleb was now with five dwarf dragons. There were two black ones, two dark blue ones, and Merlock who was brown.

"I have no idea where to even start looking," Caleb admitted as he looked out toward the jungle that had no clear path. He could get lost in this for ages and end up facing dangerous creatures he had only ever read about but never seen in real life before.

"Do you know how to smell out poisonous snakes to keep them away from me?" Caleb asked Merlock. "What about finding something or someone that could help me locate Wisteria's curse so we can save Valiant?"

Merlock looked up from the sign he had destroyed but it was one of the black dwarf dragons chirping at Caleb and grabbing at his arm with his tail. The black dragon hummed at Caleb and said something that Caleb couldn't make out. Then the dragon started to pull him through the jungle.

"I have a bit of a time problem and need to do this fast," Caleb said not caring for the slow pace they had going. The dragon was being considerate of his need to jump over vines and logs, but Caleb was still ready to take this whole thing down running. He heard birds scream out warnings that the dwarf dragons were out and the cries sent small critters scrambling out of the way as the dragons picked up the pace for him. The black dragon let go of his arm to run, fly, and jump through the foliage. Caleb was wishing for a long machete after a while, but he shoved his way through the tangles. Merlock burnt apart the narrowest spaces because he was limited to the ground as well.

After an hour, Caleb's sweat had drenched right through his shirt. He had an extra leather one in his bag on his back, but he wasn't about to swap it out when the heat was so intense. He started to reach for his water bottle only to have his arm knocked down as a creature landed on him from above stabbing his head and slicing him down his face. It wasn't a jaguar or panther as he feared he might find. The slice was from a dagger and his foe distinctly human. He had removed his heavier weapon belt so that he wouldn't give himself away as an Aralot rider, but he was probably being hunted down for being here all the same. The dwarf dragons screamed out their furry over his attack, but they didn't charge in because the person with the knife was too close to him already and sending out tar would only hit Caleb.

Caleb turned to his training, expecting more of a struggle considering the rather good silent direct attack at first. He had his assailant pinned down in a few minutes, and despite the waste it probably was, he used magic on his face to stop the blood from oozing everywhere.

The person that had been captured was a woman with curly black hair, sharp green eyes, and a quick tongue. She hadn't said anything at all during the fight, but now that she couldn't move, she was ready for that chat.

Pg. 420

"Filthy snake hide. You can't treat a Wisterian citizen like this."

"You're Wisterian?" Caleb asked her taking in the state of her clothes that had holes all over the place. Since Ian dressed with holes, Caleb guessed it was fashionable for Wisterian's. Either that or necessary for heat resistance. All the same, Caleb hadn't expected a girl from Wisteria to have the accent of a person from Vankerdale. He might not know Wisteria, but he had fought against Vankerdale before, and he heard lots of those people screaming insults.

"Yes I am, and you're a cold bottle of cod liver oil dipped in frog eyes."

"It was you who was jumping at me. Not the other way around."

"It was you leading tar spitters right at me!"

"Dwarf dragons. That's what they are. You can stop with the lies. I know you're from Vankerdale. I can pick out the accent. I also know that if you're in Wisteria that you're a spy most likely sent to find information on spellbinding dragons."

He only knew the name of one of those spies, so Caleb took a gamble just to see what the lady would do if he said something like: "Your dragon named Reed happens to love me."

Beneath him the woman shivered. Her breathing turned ragged as if the name meant a great deal to her. She came back at him with a mouth full of bad language, accusing him of bonding her dragon. She told him that Reed had promised to stay with her forever and she was horribly upset that he had broken his word. She was so mad at Caleb that she was going to cut him up and feed him to a baby wolf.

He'd gotten it right? Out of all the spies that had been sent over, he just happened to find the only one he sort of knew? This was too strange, too much like magic pushing on him that he couldn't see. Jack sometimes complained about magic like this when odd things happened, like the time he felt inspired to pack the right sandwich to give a certain person to gain information. It was magic like this that followed kings of Aralot around. Caleb wondered if such magic would still work if that crown was busted.

"Lena Sherman, I assure you that I did not take your dragon from you. I'm bonded to Warner. I just happen to know the light green Reed because he came into Aralot looking for you, and since Kayla Brixton can understand all dragon speech, he asked her for help."

"You came to save me?" Lena asked dropping the act now that he sounded like a friend instead of a leader of tar spitting dwarf dragons or a stealer of the dragon she loved.

"Actually, I came over here to stop a spell that is plaguing Wisteria so that we don't have to send over Valiant. Would you happen to know what Wisteria is in a tizzy about? And in case you haven't heard, King Peyton and his son are dead. A guy named Tyler is the new king of Vankerdale and the border between Aralot and Vankerdale is open. The curse on your dragons is gone. Reed would love to bond you once he can find you again."

"I heard about Vankerdale. I've heard about the spell that Kayla cast allowing dragons to return to Wisteria. The catch with her spell is that it's not a round trip. Dragons can enter if they have the intention of staying, but they will struggle with leaving if they change their mind. I'm not sure how many dragons will decide to come back. It's too hard to leave. I've tried escaping from everywhere only all the

Pg. 422

people and dragons know my face and I'm dead on sight. I thought you'd found me to kill me."

Vermelo hadn't talked about the spell that Kayla had cast, although they both had read about it on that magical paper. This irritated Caleb all over again. Kayla shouldn't be weakening toward Wisteria when she needed to stand strong.

"Just so you know, there aren't any other spies left alive. The Wisterian's caught five of us and the others tried to break them out. It was a losing battle right from the start. I might have joined except right before they headed out for the attack, I heard a dragon crying. It was a bronze one with a ripped wing so I talked it into letting me wrap the wing and missed the fight. At least that part of it. I saw everyone get hanged in the square afterward. How did you get here? You have a plan to get out, right? I'll make you a deal. You promise to get me back to my dragon, and I'll show you why Wisteria is trying to get into Aralot. I know where that spell is that you came to stop."

"Deal," Caleb agreed, freeing the woman and holding his hand out to shake hers. Lena Sherman. The dwarf dragons had led him to the only spy left alive, and her life had been saved by her love of dragons. That would make Reed happy with her when he saw her again.

Lena pulled to her feet but didn't take his hand. Instead, she looked at him untrusting even when he smiled at her and then laughed at her reaction. She couldn't hurt him again because she needed him to escape. However, she didn't fully believe him.

"Reed's really bright. Give me a second and I'll prove to you that he's on my side."

Caleb looked around to find Merlock. He didn't see him at first until Lena pointed up to a tree. When he looked, after taking a step away from her to make sure she couldn't slug him when he wasn't watching her, he saw Merlock happily swinging from the tree branch with his tail like he was a monkey.

"Merlock can you ask Valiant to ask Reed what Lena's favorite color is please." Caleb didn't know too many dragon words, but Warner had taught him the basic colors before, so he thought he could make this trust exercise work.

Lena crossed her arms as she looked between him and the other swinging dwarf dragons. From an attack position, it was interesting to watch this technique. The dragons hadn't jumped into his fight but if he looked like he might have needed help, any one of those small dragons could have dropped down on top of Lena the same way she had done to him. He was going to have Merlock practice swinging from dragon tails in the air the next time they got back to their illegal class.

"Is this a keeper bond at work here? Did Reed get snagged into a keeper bond?" Lena asked picking up on everything really fast and not expressing the fear and anger that usually came along with such an assumption. Caleb found himself smiling at her again.

"Not that I've picked out," he answered. "He's been hanging around Kayla's keeper dragons and training a bit with them, but I don't think he's mentally linked."

He decided it was best not to mention that Reed was flying Kayla around in class. That was only going to get Lena mad and Caleb was trying to build upon a shaky sense of trust right now. Merlock chirped out an answer that he could interpret but in case he couldn't, Warner was already thinking the answer to him at the same time.

"You like black?" Caleb asked Lena. He would have taken her for a green or even a navy-blue kind of person. It was a good thing that he wasn't guessing here.

"Where's Reed?" Lena asked back instead of telling him if the dragons had passed along the correct answer.

"He's at the King's Ware in Aralot," Caleb answered.

"Are you on the field or in the woods?" Caleb asked Warner.

"I'm in the air trying to escape the glare of section leaders asking where you are. Reed is sitting beside Valiant who is pretending to be a rock. Kayla is pacing."

He was guessing then that she may have had another nightmare or two and was refusing to go back sleep.

"Correct. She keeps falling over so she's got all her gear stacked up beside Valiant and she is refusing to work. I think she's going to start biting her nails soon."

She was scared. She couldn't control her ability to be awake and her emotions were all running away from her. He had to get through Wisteria so he could make it back to Aralot!

"Come on. I haven't time to waste. I can get you back. Just stick with Merlock and me."

Lena looked at the correct dwarf dragon as he named him. Merlock flipped down from the tree gliding down to the ground. As he landed, Lena gasped as if she was quick to pick up on Merlock's real flightless nature.

"He was tortured by Gladius," Caleb whispered. "Show me where to go to stop this thing. Will there be guards we need to push out of the way?"

"It shouldn't be hard considering that you have magic and none of them do," Lena pointed out, scanning the side of his face that she had lacerated and he had healed.

"That depends on what I need to do with that magic. I'm not a master spellcaster by any means."

"Okay. Who are you?" Lena asked him. "You have to be from Aralot, and you have to know the Brixtons, but everyone knows the Brixtons over there. Somehow that family seems to have a personal relationship with everybody."

"Caleb Andrade," he told her, holding out his hand to try this again. She didn't take it from him for a second time. Instead, she sized him up and then must have recognized him from his artwork because she started laughing.

"They thought they had you tricked to keep you from showing up to collect the art prize but you double-crossed them!" Lena giggled. "You've been in Wisteria this whole time! Oh, that's great."

She laughed a little bit more before checking on the state of a new hole in her shirt. She shrugged at it and got herself focused.

"Wisteria is upset because there are two spellbinding dragons trapped in time along with the girl King Lester is supposed to marry. Even though Erana was born like three generations ago, it's been every

Pg. 426

king's duty to free her and marry the woman. Any king who fails is seen as a disaster and their picture gets torn down from Wisteria's hall of kings. Lester was getting anxious to find a solution because he doesn't want to be erased.

"This girl is stuck at the age of twenty-two. She was supposed to get married to the ancient Prince Armond only the girl didn't love him so she became friends with spellbinding dragons and asked them to trap the prince in time so she could escape him. They trapped her instead. I kind of pity the man who has to marry her. That's got to be nerve-wracking, considering that she's liable to not like him either."

It was magic laced with politics that had King Lester and his now deceased father stumbling into the magic library where Kayla had been. Caleb wished that politics didn't have to be so harsh all the time, or magic so backstabbing. If he was ever made the king, he was going to simplify everything. Lena claimed that Erana was trapped to escape her royal fate. However, that magical paper he had been talking with had told him that the binding spell was planned to thwart Gladius. They were probably trying to stop him from obtaining their spellbinding dragons. Gladius wanted one of those so he could learn how to kill it in an effort to kill Aralot. Wisteria had succeeded in stopping Gladius, but Vankerdale had managed to steal an egg years later.

"Lead the way," Caleb directed as he pulled at his shirt trying to break through the heat.

"You never get used to this weather. It's horrible for my hair!" Lena shook her black frizzy curls and tried to mat them down some. Her hair sprang back up right away.

"Can you tell Reed something for me?" Lena asked wiping at her nose. "He asked me not to go into Aralot and I promised that I'd be back by the end of the month only I learned that spies were needed in Wisteria, and it was just too tempting to see if I could find a way to break through to get information that no one else had. Both Aralot and Vankerdale would pay heavily for this information. I was hoping it would give me a new start, a way to break out of this same old life. I can do so much more than this! However, Wisteria only gave me more problems."

"What do you want to tell Reed?" Caleb asked as he started to follow her through the jungle next.

She was even slower than the pace of the dwarf dragons and he wanted to urge her to speed up, but he didn't know if she was going slow because she was avoiding traps that he didn't know about. He was careful to step where she was stepping just in case.

"Tell Reed that I'll figure things out soon."

"We have been following this conversation," Warner told Caleb. *"Reed has been asking me what Lena is saying because he's so excited that she's not lost anymore. Reed wants to ask Lena to consider moving to Aralot."*

Caleb rubbed at his arm at the answer. Warner had to verbalize the conversation to Reed. Any other dragon around could know that Caleb was in Wisteria talking with a spy from Vankerdale. Hopefully, they were not tattling on him.

"Is he mad at me?" Lena questioned.

"He wanted you to consider moving to Aralot. I think he really likes hanging out with Valiant."

Pg. 428

"And you?" Lena quizzed. "You seem like the kind of person that dragons like. I don't trust those people."

Caleb looked at the dwarf dragons that were slowly plodding along behind him still and had to laugh. He had no idea why the other four dwarf dragons were trailing along other than that they were curious to know what he was doing.

"You should have seen Reed doing formations with Mr. Grumpy and Merlock. That is super fun to watch, although it keeps getting more and more illegal for me to teach them."

"You were teaching Reed?" Lena had to stop to look at him like he was crazy.

"Yeah, because Valiant won't work with a lot of other dragons. He's really picky so I was letting him pick his own teammates and he happens to like Reed. A lot."

Reed was the only other dragon that had been allowed to fly Kayla around so far. That was a lot of trust right there.

"You were teaching Reed how to fly Aralot formations along with an ice dragon, a spellbinding dragon, and a dwarf dragon?" Lena blinked at him not sure she should believe him. It only had him laughing again.

"Don't forget to add in the two wild dragons that have joined the night class. I'm under the impression that those dragons have ties to Colts."

Rather one Colt, but he wasn't going to share that information.

"Reed must have loved that. You're going to get in so much trouble teaching that class."

"Yeah… but it was worth it."

"You already got in trouble for it I see."

Caleb shrugged at Lena who turned back around and kept going. "I was banned from teaching but not directly for that," Caleb continued. "I've got the section leaders speaking up for me because none of them want to take on Valiant so that night class is probably all I'll get. You should come. I'll sneak you in and train you to ride your dragon."

"And then you will be fired," Lena stated.

"How? The new ware leader already did that. I can't be fired twice."

"They're going to kick you out, Caleb, especially if you start training Vankerdale women."

"I thought you were moving to Aralot," he replied.

"Funny." Lena cast a look over her shoulder at him but she was grinning. Caleb didn't know if she really believed him, but it felt easier between them so he had no problem in asking her if they could pick up the pace. He had dragons to get back to and a person to save.

Lena Sherman. She was funny and attractive, and she came with a dragon, and she knew how to be a really good spy.

"Meaning?" Warner asked him. *"You're not starting to like her, are you?"*

Pg. 430

"I'll always love Kayla. I was simply thinking that if I get Lena to meet Tristan, there might be some sparks flying there."

"Oh! You found Tristan a new love interest. I'll suggest it to Reed to have the two of them meet."

If it worked out, that was one prince out of his way. Tyler was still in the picture, but maybe something would magically work out for him there as well. It wasn't like Kayla was standing around acting like she wanted to go see her fiancé. She was too busy trying to not love anything at all.

"We're not that far from the spellbound trap. I was sticking close in case Valiant showed up. I had this plan to convince him to take me back with him," Lena told him.

Riding on Valiant. Now that was something that Caleb hadn't tried out yet. He wondered how that would go if he asked the dragon to give him a lift. Valiant would probably sit down and refuse to move. There was still so much work left to do with him that it was sad. Caleb looked out at the future bleakly. Even if he defeated Aralot, Kayla was still going to move away from him for Vankerdale.

"Is Tyler the kind of person that accepts outsiders?" Caleb questioned.

"Tyler as in the new king? I don't know. It depends on what the outsider is there for. I've heard that King Tyler is rather reasonable."

Maybe Caleb really would consider moving into Vankerdale even if he knew it would make Warner cry at him on a constant basis. It all depended on if he managed to keep Kayla alive. If she died, there was no sense in moving. She was far too young to die. It was a good thing that Kayla couldn't hear his thoughts because they were verging on despair, and that lapsed his conversation with Lena into a deep silence.

They trudged through the jungle avoiding mushy spots and certain plants that looked mean. They didn't slow down until Caleb could make out voices talking about some play a few men had seen. It had been a long time since Caleb had gone to see a play. He frowned because hearing these men talk only reminded him of all the stipulations he had to follow at the wares. He couldn't take breaks to do fun things unless he invented the fun things himself. There were a lot of after-work activities that happened at Anvil's Ware, but Caleb hadn't seen the same kind of joyful play at the King's Ware. People never transferred back to a ware after being transferred away, but maybe he could get Anvil to make an exception. Even that sounded unlikely. Why couldn't he be in a place that made him happy?

"You're worrying about something," Lena whispered at him. "I can distract the guards if you really need me to. If I run out through the trees, they'll chase me."

"With the intention to kill you." Caleb shook his head. "Not to worry. I've got a link to a spellbinding dragon. Warner can tell me what to use on the guards."

Caleb didn't have to wait long. Warner advised him on how to put the guards to sleep from a distance. It was such an easy solution that Caleb shrugged as he cast the spell and heard the guards stop talking. Lena looked at him terrified before crawling forward to see what he had done. He followed after her but instead of looking at the guards asleep on the ground, his eyes found themselves stuck on what they had been guarding.

Pg. 432

There it was. Two spellbinding dragons sat staring at each other hiding their tails with their wings tucked down. The look was one that spoke of fear. These two had been very scared to do what they had done, freezing themselves for an unknown time. Between them was the trapped noble holding her hands out between them as if to stop them from casting the spell. She looked scared too.

Caleb dashed into the area, noticing how this part of the jungle had been kept clear of vines. It even had a path that led up to it to help the guards find the spot. The spellbinding dragon on his right was a dark blue while the one on his left was a rather light gray. Caleb had never heard of a dragon of this color before. He couldn't help but reach out and touch it, feeling the warmth of the dragon that couldn't move, couldn't die, couldn't break free of the fear that had once caused this mess. Lena came up beside him slowly inching forward as if the dragons were going to growl at her for being so close.

The woman in the middle, Erana, had about as many holes in the top layer of her dress as Lena did. Only on her, she had a white layer beneath. Caleb blew on the trapped princess's dark brown hair not seeing a single one of her hairs move out of place. He reached in and flicked the hair next which caused it to shift. That was scary. How did Erana know that no one would kill her while she stood here defenseless? How did the dragons know that they would be all right? Erana was wearing a jeweled bracelet that Caleb unlatched and held in his hand.

"Caleb!" Lena opened her eyes wide, glancing around at the guards as if they would wake up and shoot him for stealing from this woman.

"What? Spellbinding dragons have to suck up their magic in order to use it. This is how they did it. They took the magic out of this bracelet after they enticed Erana to bring it to them. I'm not going to leave it in their face for when they wake up. They still think that bad things are going on. They could shoot anything at us when I bring them back."

Lena circled the dragons and then walked toward the path looking out toward it trying to decide if they were going to be safe or not. Caleb left her to it because his was the harder task. How was he going to break this spell?

"Is Valiant in a mood to talk?" Caleb asked Warner. *"What would he do? How do I do this?"*

While he waited for his dragon to break through Valiant's moods, he climbed up on the gray spellbinding dragon. Lena spun around looking like she wanted to tell him to get off. He knew he was trespassing upon sacred beasts, but he'd never been up on a spellbinding dragon before. He skimmed the length from head to tail and compared the narrow seat to other dragons that were better suited for larger men. Caleb climbed up on the dark-blue dragon next before moving on to their hidden wings barely making out the silver on their folded wingtips.

The ends of the tails he couldn't see at all which left him rather curious. Valiant sat on his tail too. Why? Most dragons were rather proud of their tails. Ice dragons were especially vain about them. He had thought that Valiant was simply reacting to being held in captivity in Vankerdale for so long, but he really wasn't. This was normal behavior.

Pg. 434

"If he's not talking tell him that I could be looking at his parents right now. Doesn't he want to save his parents?"

"You are so good at this," Warner finally answered. *"That did the trick."*

At least on Warner's end. Caleb had it tougher. Warner told him that it was going to be very very hard magic to get right because the caster had to get lost in time first. Then he had to call time to him and command it to harken to his wishes. If he did it right, the spell was supposed to look green instead of blue. Yeah, that sounded tough, because Caleb had never pulled up anything but blue magic from this fox thing. Maybe he would use the bracelet in his hand instead. Then he wouldn't be wasting his own magic on a mistake he had never made.

Getting lost in time wouldn't be too difficult. Whenever he got a good drawing session going, he had no idea what time was passing around him. He'd set himself up to draw on every single paper in his stack, and on the last page he would tell himself to cast the spell.

The really hard part was calling upon time. How to do that? The only thing Caleb could think to do was create a sundial on the ground and try to create different shadows with it from a light source so that time swirled in a circle. Some spells required drawing things out first, but he was pretty sure it was advanced magic. After that, all he needed to do was wish that the stuck dragons got put back into his current time frame. That was a large wish, one that would require a very clear mental focus after feeling so aloof to time beforehand.

"I could use your help on this," Caleb said looking at Lena. "I'm going to get myself lost in time and when I start casting the spell,

I need you to tell me what time it actually is. Can you do that? Don't tell me anything until the spell has started."

"You're what?" Lena asked, moving to take a sleeping guard's weapon.

"Getting lost in time so I can cast this spell," Caleb repeated setting his bag down and pulling out his paper. "When you see magic come up, tell me what time it is."

"I'll try," Lena replied while Merlock entered the area and hummed that it was time for a snack.

Caleb tossed him a treat that he had thought to bring along, which required him to toss snacks at the other four dwarf dragons too. They did tricks for their snacks. One stood on his back legs. Another curled his tail into the shape of a dragon. The other two used their tails to fling each other into the trees. Snacks completed (Caleb tossed a field snack to Lena while he was at it), his team moved to guard the perimeter so he could forget all about where he was and what he was doing. This was going to be hard, because he still felt that sense of urgency ticking down his back, and he had to lose that in order to get lost in his artwork.

Caleb took in a deep breath and found himself drawing Kayla in the mess hall when she had handed him the paper to help him keep his job. She had looked at ease, but he could see the hidden worry in her expression now that he drew it. He moved the paper to the back of the stack and tried to find something else to draw that wouldn't make him feel anxious. What about the dragons before him? He'd draw them curled up looking like a rock. Then he could draw them with their wings spread out looking happy and glorious once they were free.

Pg. 436

He could draw the dragons meeting Valiant even if these dragons couldn't really be his parents given the time they were trapped. They could be his grandparents unless of course they had trapped their unhatched egg in a spell as well, hoping that the creature would be born during a time of civil rest so they could be set free. It was possible. Caleb had no idea how to create a spellbinding dragon. Breeding rare dragons was exceptionally difficult. He drew the plight of the trapped egg next sitting in a dusty corner until he could hatch.

"Valiant was born alone in a greenhouse," Warner told him. *"He saw one person holding meat before he met King Peyton."*

Caleb drew that next. There was baby Valiant shining and bright before he was trapped. He started to draw Valiant trapped in a dungeon in Vankerdale waiting to break free only to notice how unfair it was for spellbinding dragons to find themselves victims of time when they themselves could spin it around so easily.

He kept drawing until he reached the paper telling him to cast the spell. He drew a picture of a sundial and stabbed a knife down through the center of it before he looked up at Lena and used the bracelet to cast a magical light down on his paper so he could create a shadow. She told him an approximate time that was corrected by both Merlock and Warner who gave him more exact details.

Then came the hard part. He had to make his wish, which really meant that he had to set his focus and have an iron resolve to bring those three trapped beings back to the time they were missing. It was actually easier to make the wish than he thought it would be. He did want them free. He wanted Wisteria to leave Valiant alone because he refused to let anything make Kayla sad when she was already fighting for her life. He needed these spellbinding dragons back in the present so that Valiant wasn't the only one of his kind and others could learn how these rare dragons behaved. He needed time to return to normal, to stop being so controlling and teach him how to take down Aralot when he faced her next.

Woosh! Green magic shot out of his hands crashing into the tragic scene before him that picked up right where it had left off.

"Wait! I didn't tell my mom!" Erana yelled while the two dragons coughed testing to see if either one had magic to spit. The dark blue one started to inhale to pick some up.

"Stop!" Caleb commanded. "You've already done it. You've already been stuck in time for ages. I'm pretty sure everyone's mom found out about it."

"How long?" Erana asked him keeping her hands in the air while she looked at Caleb rather interested in his group of trailing dwarf dragons that came around to chirp hello.

"Gladius is now survived his great-granddaughter. That's how long you've been stuck here. Wisteria's current king is King Lester. I heard that he's supposed to marry you."

"You are not Wisterian," Erana decided. "Who are you? How did you tamper with the magic? Only a spellbinding dragon can do that and I don't see one of those with you."

"I happen to be friends with a spellbinding dragon," Caleb answered, feeling awkward to be talking with the really old woman even if her given physical age was only three years older than him. It made him wonder what age Aralot was trapped at. For that matter, was it Aralot that was Valiant's mother or these two other dragons that were here?

"My name is Caleb. I'm from Aralot. I came to release you from being stuck in this spell that was cast to either smite Gladius or help you escape marriage to King Armond. I think the exact reason has been twisted over the years."

"King Armond took the spellbinding dragon egg and cast it into a spell so that it wouldn't hatch until Gladius's ocean curse was lifted."

"King Jack lifted that curse," Caleb nodded.

"I have no idea who that is," Erana sighed. "But we couldn't get the spellbinding dragons to stay in Wisteria without cursing them. All the rare dragons were being summoned into Aralot by something Gladius did. We couldn't stop it. We lost all the water dragons. We couldn't lose these ones too."

Caleb looked between the motionless talking woman and the still unmoving dragons and frowned.

"Why aren't you moving? What did I miss?" he asked. "Valiant, my spellbinding dragon friend, told me how to bring you back to the current time, but you're not moving."

Erana giggled at him. The two dragons snorted like he was cute for asking. He crossed his arms trying to figure it out on his own.

"You forgot to take away the binding part," Erana laughed. "I thought you did it on purpose so we wouldn't try to attack you for trespassing. Those are Wisterian soldiers you've knocked over. I know a break-in when I see it."

"They're only sleeping." Caleb shrugged at her. "It's easy to fix, but that will happen from a distance because I don't need them shooting at me. How does one create and take apart a binding spell? I will finish freeing you."

"Why?" Erana asked him. "After all this time why you?"

"Because I need to save someone from Aralot and to do that I need Wisteria out of the way. I need you to stop trying to get Valiant over here. He's the only thing saving my friend from Aralot right now."

"So Aralot has another nasty king?"

"No. Aralot's king is fanstastic. I meant the real Aralot. The ancient spellbinding dragon is eating my friend from the inside out, devouring her love to sustain the dragon's own life. That Aralot."

"I do believe that you've figured out the queen's curse. Are you a king then? I'd bow, but I'm stuck."

"I'm not a king. If I was, perhaps I would have remembered my manners."

Kayla had taught him how to bow at least. He pulled off the move as best he could by putting his arm to his head and bending at the waist.

"You got time magic to work," Erana noted. "You must be a king of Aralot. You can't move time without great authority. Are you from Vankerdale?"

"No. I was born and raised in Aralot's dragon wares. There isn't one true king of Aralot. We know the crown is cursed so none of us will wear it. Aralot technically has three kings at the moment who are all not real kings."

"You're a king?" Lena asked causing Erana to try to turn her head to see Lena and fail.

"Your magic and kingdom still sound really messed up," Erana blinked at him. "I hope Wisteria isn't doing as poorly."

"Your previous King Anthony just died, but the prince has taken over the role. That's all I know about it. I'm not large on the state of your political affairs."

"King Lester, my next intended. I didn't forget," Erana sighed. "I shall tell you what I can about binding spells but it's really hard to understand. It's all very much a feeling."

Caleb found himself smiling at the word. That was a spellbinding dragon's forte. They were very good at being emotion based.

"I've tried to do binding magic before and couldn't do it. You might need to allow the dragons at my sides to cast the freeing spell themselves."

"I'd rather not. There's only one spellbinding dragon that I trust. I'll give this a try. I managed to get the time part right. What do I do?"

"Well as far as I can tell," Erana said while the dark-blue dragon snorted at her. Caleb guessed that she had to be bonded to that one, and it was trying to describe in words an impossible feeling so it wouldn't stay trapped. "To create a binding spell, you need to feel something that is always permanent."

"Like the stars?" Caleb asked.

Erana shook her head. "No. Stars move and change. Something that doesn't ever go away. I don't know. It's a feeling. You find the thing that doesn't ever change and you use it as a condition to the spell. In any case, you're not binding but unbinding. You need to find the spot the spell was bound and unlink it with something that changes constantly. It doesn't really make sense when you compare it to how other magical rules work. Hand back my magic and we shall sort it out ourselves."

Caleb placed her jeweled bracelet into his pocket instead of giving it back. That got the two dragons to growl at him, but he had his protection. Valiant couldn't harm him through the charms that Kayla had given him so he wasn't worried. He was going to figure this out. The other things he could think of that didn't really go away were air, or perhaps light, or maybe even true love. It had to be something that he could grasp a concept over.

"*Space,*" Warner told him. "*Valiant's guess is that he feels the infinite expanse of space. He can sense a timeless, ageless vast chamber of nothing and everything all at once.*"

Space. Binding spells were bound to space. He couldn't feel this as a dragon could and he sort of doubted that he would be able to unless he could move his consciousness into a spellbinding dragon for the task. In order to bind and unbind magic, one had to be previously bound to such a thing. How was he going to defeat Aralot if he couldn't get inside of Valiant's head?

Just to make sure he had this right, he pulled out the bracelet again, sat down, and attempted to cast the spell to unbind from space. He saw the blue glow rise around him getting brighter and brighter

Pg. 442

trying to obey his directions but it couldn't take hold of anything because he didn't have the right frame of mind.

"Fine," Caleb said placing the bracelet back on Erana. "But don't attempt to hurt me or my friends."

"Of course not!" Erana agreed. "I thought I was talking to a dragon in human form for a while, but you're just a man. You're not bonded to a spellbinding dragon."

"That would be Kayla Brixton. She's the person I'm trying to save," Caleb replied. "I have a fire-breathing dragon. He's magnificent."

"I don't doubt it. Kings happen to attract rather special dragons," Erana smiled at him and then she held her breath as the spellbinding dragons sucked in the magic from her wrist and freed themselves from the spell. For them, it took less than a minute to get the magic to work. The dragons whipped their tails out from beneath them and spread their wings revealing their silver-winged edges. They hooted into the air and were answered by the voices of startled dragons answering them from all over the place.

"We're going to go," Caleb told Erana. "King Lester has had different ideas on how to set you free and he's not happy with either of us." Caleb looked at Lena who nodded that she was ready to leave. "I'll wake up the soldiers in a minute."

"I can do it," Erana answered. "But a question first. Has Wisteria any ice dragons?"

Caleb shook his head. "There's currently one living magical ice dragon."

"And it lives in Aralot?" Erana guessed. "I suppose I need to catch up on my history. Perhaps I will come visit to thank you for your generosity."

"That would be something. Wisteria is very closed to everyone." Caleb gave her another bow as he started to back away. He didn't think that she would be allowed to visit because she would be coming over with two spellbinding dragons who wanted magic from Bantin. That wasn't going to go over well.

On that note, he cast the spell to wake up the guards himself. He didn't want Erana lying to Aralot pretending that he had left sleeping men in his wake that she needed magic to cure. That would give her an excuse to obtain magic, and he wasn't about to start that war. His purpose in coming here was to prevent it.

Caleb got back into the thick of the trees only to find that Lena was way ahead of him running behind one of the dwarf dragons that she had asked to show her how to get home. She wasn't going to enjoy the process. Caleb was going to be pulling her from the portal while she cried and felt like she was dying.

Anyway, that wouldn't be too hard on his part. He had a battle ahead of him, and now that he was done with Wisteria, he set his mind on his next goals. He had to do something about that crown that was linked to the process of this binding spell on Kayla. It was the thing picking who to devour and it passed the energy into Aralot, who was trapped.

"Quick recap on the royal crown," Warner thought to him. "It was created by an ultra-dragon king and so an ultra-dragon king has to be the animal to destroy it. If you think about destroying it, you will die or so the rumor says. You thought about it once, and you're still here, so maybe it only

counts if you take action on that thought. Gladius cast a lot of spells at it trying to change the nature of the crown and so have many other spellcasters without succeeding. There can be strange unseen effects on the object that no one knows about. It chooses who the queen is when it finds a king."

Only in his case, Kayla was always stuck in the crown trap from the moment she was born. Caleb needed to go see King Tyler after first finding a way to keep *himself* safe from dying when he tried to destroy the crown. How would he do that? He would need to keep himself stuck in time unable to die like Ritz. What had Ritz stuck?

"Are you sure you want to know the answer to that?" Warner asked him. *"Because I know the answer. It's a very sad answer."*

"Why?" Caleb asked as he ran.

"Ritz was defeated, and if he was the person keeping Aralot happy as you suspect, I fear Aralot is going to get worse for the rest of us."

"He died?!"

"Don't tell Kayla. She doesn't know yet. She was asleep when the news started to spread through the dragons. Valiant thinks that if she finds out, she might never wake up again. She loved Ritz very much. This is going to be her undoing. In any case, Ritz was time-bound to the life of an object. That object was destroyed. Valiant is willing to cast you into such a spell if that's what it takes to save Kayla. He's going to time-bound Kayla too, because he doesn't want her to die."

It sounded like Warner had updated Valiant on everything that was going on. Nice. Caleb was going to be trusting Valiant with his entire life. When he said that he trusted only one spellbinding dragon, he didn't mean that he trusted him that much. Valiant was going to stick him to the life of an object. The life of...

"We've got to get that crown!" Caleb shouted.

Gee! He was going to let a dragon curse him and the woman he loved at the same time. The crown had to be the answer though. Gladius had trapped his brother to the life of an object because he was trying to mimic the spell he needed to defeat, only he couldn't destroy the royal crown! Aralot was trapped not only to this time spell but also to the life of the crown. That's how she was still alive.

If Caleb destroyed the crown, then he could stop Aralot! Vermelo was right. They had a tamed ultra-dragon king now. That same dragon was born from dragons that had been in Herb Felding's keeper bond. Herb had tried to further his father's work and destroy the crown too. Kayla was also right. The keepers that everyone thought were tyrants had been trying to save them all. Magic had brought together all the dragons they needed. Caleb just had to get them all to cooperate after he made it back to Aralot.

Stunning

Kayla

Caleb wasn't back yet! Kayla glanced up into the air where Warner, Valiant, and Reed were specks. They were so high up, so much like accomplices, that Kayla was fuming down below them. Valiant had to know where Caleb had gone because he had done nothing but talk with Warner for hours. He wasn't telling her anything, and his silence to anything she thought or said to him only proved that he was hiding things from her in the only way he could. He couldn't lie to her so he said nothing at all.

"Valiant!" Kayla complained again.

What she got wasn't Valiant. It was Reed. The dragon dashed down to dance on his toes like he was excited and happy. Something good must have happened but that didn't mean that Reed would tell her anything. She looked at him debating with herself if she wanted to steal into his thoughts to get him to talk, but Reed was rather good at reading human facial expressions and didn't keep her waiting long.

"Lena is coming!"

The sentence hit Kayla in the chest and she pulled over her sweater hood to avoid interacting with anyone even if everyone had stopped interacting with her. Lena Sherman. The spy was found. The people in the castle would be happy if she had brought back information, Kayla was feeling only sadness over Reed's joy. Reed was the dragon she had been depending on, and now he was going to leave her. She couldn't ask him to help her anymore. His rider was back.

"That's great, Reed," Kayla said with false cheer in her voice. She had to fight this sadness. The second it hit her, her weariness came back threatening to drag her under. Another person's achievement shouldn't be her defeat. Lena would have a long story of her struggles, and Kayla should be feeling happy that she had found a way back to her dragon.

"Do you need to go?" Kayla asked in dragon speech not trusting her human words at the moment that might betray her feelings. She was going to crumble if she spoke the human tongue right now.

"No. Lena is really coming!"

As in into a dragon ware? How was a spy going to walk right into a dragon ware? She'd be surrounded and tied up. Kayla pulled the hood back off and scanned the area only to find her heart leap, stealing away the sudden sadness in a much-needed sigh of relief. Caleb! Lena was a woman with dark curls and she was entering the ware right beside Caleb! The afternoon scouts were dropping down from their dragons, demanding that Caleb vouch for the stranger beside him, and go see his section leader for punishment for running away. Caleb was ignoring them.

Kayla ran to them with Reed bouncing along behind her. She ignored the scouts too, and her only reaction to Lena was a short nice to meet you before she jumped at Caleb and hugged him. She had no idea that she could be so worried about him before. He had taken off

Pg. 448

without a word and somehow found a missing spy and who knew what else.

"You give out hugs now?" Caleb asked, pulling her directly in and holding her just firmly enough that her fears and sadness cascaded down to her feet and became her shadow behind her, hidden and ignored for a while but still present for when Caleb left her sight again.

"Where did you go?"

"How are you feeling?" was his answer.

She couldn't accurately tell him, so she let her head hang into his shoulder. He smelled like sweat and he was out of his rider clothes which only indicated that he had gone someplace where he needed to hide his rider status. Wisteria probably. That's where Lena was supposed to be, and for Caleb and her to get back here so fast would point fingers at portals. Caleb must have noticed the additional writing on Lester's paper and his version of her peace was defiance.

Kayla shoved away from him watching his face flash through worry and then hurt over her own expression.

"You turned on me," she accused.

Caleb opened his mouth to answer and then shut it again, tilting his head to the side trying to find something to say to redeem himself against her thoughts that he couldn't hear.

"In what way?" he decided to ask, not sharing his version of his thoughts.

Kayla glanced up at Valiant with a glare wishing he could ask Warner to tell her. Silence. She could think of several ways. Caleb had fetched back Lena to take Reed away. He hadn't fought against Tristan to keep his job. He had left the ware and had returned without ware colors like he was going rogue. He had done something in Wisteria and he wasn't telling anyone what.

Ugh. Kayla took in a deep breath and turned back to her Colt teaching, trying to see the situation not from her perspective but perhaps from Caleb's. He would have seen her crumbled to the ground unable to do anything with Wisteria. In his mind perhaps this wasn't a betrayal, but a bold step of turning against the wares that he loved in order to help something he loved greater. No betrayal to her at all only to himself. He had given up his life trying to help hers.

"Never mind. I'm an emotional wreck. You're fine. What happened in Wisteria?"

"I saved Valiant by freeing two spellbinding dragons that I assume are his parents. The spell also untrapped princess Erana who had also been stuck in time since Gladius was alive. Valiant won't need to go over there anymore. He can stay here with you. In the process, I found Lena Sherman. Lena said that the other spies didn't make it."

"Did she get information on spellbinding dragons?" Kayla asked looking at the woman who was gazing up at Reed with a large lump in her throat. Reed was being horribly quiet. He should be charging toward her getting that bond he had been waiting for. Why wait? Kayla glanced at him next. He greeted her with a sentence.

"Can your emotions handle sharing me?"

"You're not mine," Kayla replied in dragon speech which caused Lena to nudge Caleb as if he could translate. He gave her a shrug.

Pg. 450

"I know," Reed answered. "But I know you well enough to see that you are sad about this."

"Get it over with Reed. She's waiting."

"No!" Reed spat at her and that was a sound that everyone could interpret. Kayla glared at him for defying her too and making her emotional pain even worse. Why was this happening? She knew this was coming and should have been able to handle this! If only Valiant wasn't being so quiet!

"You want my interpretation? You are incapable of being nice right now. The only emotions you can produce on your own are sadness and anger. Therefore, the rest of us tiptoe around you not sure how to help."

"I am not incapable!" Kayla screamed in the air and then she frowned. Valiant couldn't lie to her. He had been her enough times to know her ever-shifting emotions. So he was right. This next part of her curse was to keep her trapped inside only two emotions. She had to break out of it. She was going to start by accepting what she currently was and pretending to be otherwise.

"Sorry," Kayla sighed at Valiant talking normally again. "And I'm sorry to you too, Reed. Don't skirt around me. Your best course of action is to ignore me because I can't get out of this spell. My emotions should not influence your own. Please be happy. You got Lena back. On any other day, I would be extremely thrilled for you. Honestly. Valiant says I am incapable of producing positive emotions today. I will be fine if you ignore me. Everyone else already is."

"That is not… no," Caleb stammered. "That isn't the way to help you. I know how to fix this, Kayla. Ignoring you isn't the answer, although you may still feel that it should be. When you're sad, you hide. You expect everyone else to want to leave you hiding. You might not be able to feel the hope, but I don't want you to mentally give it up. I'm going to save you, although I will need to borrow Valiant for the task. You'll probably feel abandoned but you won't be. I promise. Now first things first," Caleb said glancing at the scouts who had given up on demanding anything from him. It was strange that they were simply standing there doing nothing about Caleb bringing a spy into the middle of the ware while he was out of his work clothes.

"I want you to think about the day you got Valiant's bond back."

"It was a really bad day. Sparkle attacked us."

"Not that part." Caleb gave her a short smile. "The other part."

"You were telling Valiant stories without me and I was jealous."

"The other part!" Caleb insisted, twisting his mouth upward at her declaration that she was jealous over him. She'd not told him that yet, but it seemed like she was determined to find all the negative things and none of the good.

"Valiant's wings glowed," Caleb reminded her.

He pulled her to face him while he talked her through the event of the night and how at peace she had felt. He must have given a hand signal to Reed and Lena because Kayla heard them moving behind her and she knew the instant that Reed fanged his rider. They were going to be happy after all this time of waiting and being true to each other. There's was a rather beautiful story that Kayla wished she could partake in better.

Pg. 452

"You did fine. You helped to take away Reed's anxiety by being his friend. You make a very good friend, Kayla. Hey! I wasn't ready!"

At the sharp cry, Kayla started to jolt as a green glow spread outward all around her only to realize what it was that had Valiant shrieking. Sound stopped! Kayla looked at Caleb to see if he had noticed or if it was only something strange happening to her own ears. He blinked back at her but no one behind him did. It wasn't just sound halted in its tracks. Everyone was stopped except for her and Caleb. Dragons were frozen in the air not moving as if time suddenly held no meaning. Caleb had figured out time magic and a person really could use it!

"How...?" Kayla trailed off looking at it all again before looking back at Caleb. "Is it them or us that are stuck in time?"

"Neither. No one is stuck. I'm extending this moment," Caleb answered. "I uh... wanted to give you a special bit of hope before... well... I didn't think I would be this bad at this."

"Bad? Caleb no one has figured out how to use time magic before! You're not bad."

"Correction. Gladius knew how to use it. He cursed Maslon with it."

Kayla blinked at him. Caleb knew! He knew that Ritz was her great-granfather's younger brother. So he'd know that he was a keeper as well. She didn't know how he knew, but he knew everything. He even knew more than she did making her wonder...

"Have you been talking with Maslon?"

"He told me that you have. I was rather proud of myself for knowing all the tricks of talking to him. He didn't manage to rile me up once, and he answered my one question better than I expected him to. If I think about it, his trust is incredible considering how long he's kept his secrets hidden. That's a real smile right there."

Caleb pointed to her face and it only made the smile larger. She was smiling! See? She could produce the emotion. It was impossible to not be impressed with Caleb for figuring out time magic, handling Wisteria so effectively, and saving Lena. He made it sound so easy. Those were the things she was supposed to do, and he had done them all in a day as if the forces of magic had passed to him the rights of acting in her name. He was incredibly effective with magic all of a sudden.

"Has anyone ever told you that your smile is compelling?" he asked her.

She felt confused and then smiled wider about that because it was yet another emotion as if being stuck in a moment of time could block out the spell that was upon her. Perhaps her spell had to deal with time magic. She was going to have to ask Valiant although he was ignoring her questions. Maybe he already knew the answer to that and she had to be patient for him and Caleb to fix it because it wasn't the "time" for her to know.

"That was a dumb pick-up line. I am really bad at this. It's a good thing that no one else can watch me," Caleb fidgeted. "Okay let's back up. I would like to give you a spark of special hope in the form of something that you won't be able to deny because obviously, you can see how real it is to me... Nope. How about...? Kayla, I have always...

Gee. I face dragons for a living. You'd think that people, especially you, wouldn't be this hard!"

She had to laugh at him and wonder what it was that he was rambling around. Something that he wanted to tell her had brought him to freeze time, so it had to be rather important.

"What is it?" Kayla asked him.

"I love you," Caleb told her, looking more awkward than in love at the moment. That was until he decided he had better back up his words. He stepped up to her and brought his face close only to bonk her nose with his. His whole face was turning red and it was a shame because the only thing Kayla could think to do was laugh at him.

He was so cute! A special something. He was going to kiss her! Her first kiss from the one person she actually wanted to kiss! Even more exciting was that he wasn't aiming for the side of her face in an obligatory way. This was the real thing!

Caleb shut his eyes as if that would help him better with his aim even if it wouldn't, and wrapped his arms around her, which only revealed that they were slightly shaking from his nerves. He was perfect! Caleb was all the awkwardness that she had dreamed about from a first kiss. He was probably wishing that he wasn't blundering, but Kayla was loving this. She loved it even more when she wrapped him into her own arms and let their mouths meet.

Time was already standing still or it might have done it again. Neither of them had any idea what they were supposed to really do, so they sort of stood there with their hearts pounding and their faces flushed taking in the slow breathing and the perfect sense of everything finally lining up. Stress evaporated. Anger and sadness vanished. There were only the two of them paused in time.

"I love you too," Kayla whispered when she couldn't take the awkwardness any longer. She was finding it really funny that she had even wanted this to be clumsy because now she was thinking that once they got a bit more practice, the kissing could turn from uncoordinated to seamless. Every moment longer she could spend with Caleb was a special present indeed. Near him, her greatest struggles vanished. Her hope came alive.

"Nothing will ever change my love for you. Not your mood, or dragons, or time, or other people. Not the fact that you're engaged — Don't pull away!" Caleb cried when she started to do that.

He really did know everything! People were starting to learn about Tyler, and while Tristan had laughed at her for it, Caleb was the opposite, standing beside her even if it must have hurt him. She thought that once he found out that he would back away, but he wasn't. He was still here, and finding him being so stalwart had her love for him grow even stronger.

"Kayla, please. I love you. Whatever it is you have to do to make it through this life, I will support you. Your path is not easy, but all the best rewards come after the hardest work. We will not give up. We will not back down. We're going to win this battle of magic because nothing, not one thing, can take our love away."

He looked so certain. Caleb's brown eyes had lost the shyness now that she had admitted to being equally in love with him. His boldness was back; his spark of fire that had often gotten him trouble for expressing how strongly he felt. It was a warm fire. A safe fire instead of a dangerous one that destroyed without caution. Caleb's passion was the glow that thawed away the icy cold from her heart.

"You have marvelous feelings," Kayla mused. In a world that could make her feel numb, Caleb would be the one standing tall for everyone. Only admiration could express that.

"I need to have Valiant put a spell on you, on the both of us, to get through this. I can't tell you what it is yet. I need you to trust me."

"Oh, I do," Kayla answered and at that moment the time returned back to normal and she gripped her hand into a fist wishing that the wedding ring she had wasn't from Tyler but came from Caleb. The anger was back. There was a rage there wishing evil on Tyler so that she could have Caleb beside her instead. It was an unfair rage because Tyler was her fault.

Kayla wished that she could have stayed inside that time bubble with Caleb and then found herself jumping away from Caleb as Valiant came charging down from the sky with his eyes swirls of anger that matched her current mood. His normally brown eyes mixed with yellow and green in a rather dizzying force that Kayla tried to ignore.

"I couldn't hear you!" Valiant screamed. *"I can't reach you when you fall into dreams either and Caleb was stealing you away from me in the same way! He won't get away with it."*

"Stop Valiant!" Kayla ordered, wishing that her bad mood hadn't transferred over to him and that his fears didn't manifest themselves like this. Valiant flicked his tail at Caleb causing her to scream. The tail didn't hit him, but he stood there stunned and unmoving even without a spell being cast while Valiant jumped over his back and prepared to hit him from behind.

"No!"

This couldn't be happening! Her dragon couldn't attack Caleb! She had never seen a spellbinding dragon fight like this before not even in her dreams. They usually cast spells and hid their tails, but their tails were just as deadly as their heads. Valiant had clearly stunned Caleb by using the tail, because she was certain that Caleb had also been avoiding those eyes.

Warner plopped down from out of the air taking the harsh stabbing blow that Valiant aimed at Caleb. It was a good thing too, because one more second and Kayla was going to be tormented to fight against her own dragon to defend Caleb. Valiant was being horrible for making her choose like this. Him or Caleb. Valiant's scales were tougher. She'd have to fight against her own dragon, forcing herself to turn against the bond that held them together.

"Please stop," she whimpered as Caleb came back to himself. He grabbed at his tools and spun around to fight his foe. Valiant screamed at him. Warner cried, and then Valiant shrieked as her current thoughts of her turning against him finally broke through the barrier of his own emotions and he realized that he was forcing her to hate him.

"Valiant!" Caleb scaled his bleeding dragon bravely facing a beast that could immobilize him even without magic. Valiant was really really scary. Kayla started to back away not wanting these emotions to turn against her bonded dragon even as they plunged over her without her being poisoned. This was wrong. Everything was wrong. Valiant stood there panting and gasping as if he was caught inside a demonic force he couldn't break free from. She had that same feeling all the time when she couldn't wake up from the nightmares.

Pg. 458

"It's okay," Caleb soothed granting instant forgiveness that Kayla wasn't about to bestow. Her dragon had attacked the man she loved. She was still seething.

"It's the spells. They're going to get worse and stronger. I'm sorry if I scared you by using time magic. I wouldn't hurt her. I swear. You know me better than that."

Valiant stood there working himself into a sweat until they both heard Norber chirping from the distance asking if there was anything he could do to help. Norber's voice made Kayla start crying, and she didn't even know why she was crying this time. There was something sadly special about thinking about Ritz's dragons today. Valiant chirped back to him, a simple hello, instead of a real answer, but at least his eyes stopped swirling and his anger vanished. He adopted her sadness, sinking to the ground after he healed Warner from the stab he had given the dragon for protecting his rider.

"Can you still help me defeat this spell or is it getting to you too?" Caleb asked Valiant. "I don't know what to do if it reaches you, Valiant. I've just been trying to take this one step at a time."

"You need to be stepping off this field," Tristan ordered dropping down beside their chaos with Riven. Kayla didn't look at either of them. Her eyes adhered to her dragon trying to make herself forgive him for stabbing Warner and trying to slash Caleb. It was very slow going.

"Not you Lena Sherman," Tristan said as Lena started to inch away. "Only Caleb. He deserted the ware knowing exactly what he was doing. He can't come back in here riling up fights. Get out."

Kayla found both her hands gripping weapons as she looked away from Valiant toward Tristan and Riven. If she could contemplate getting in the way of her dragon, she most certainly could contemplate attacking Riven to reach Tristan. Caleb couldn't let Tristan kick him out! He had just saved them from Wisteria. Caleb should be the one fighting this lousy prince only he still wasn't raising a single weapon toward him. She would do it. She'd take Tristan down.

"You are too good at fighting off the sadness," Caleb said looking at her still and not at Tristan's threat. "The spell on you is adapting and turning your struggle to anger instead. Both you and Valiant don't know what to do against the anger. My advice. Don't let it win. You are not angry. What would you normally think about all of this? Separate your emotions from your thoughts and actions."

"That's Colt teaching. I was never good at that part," Kayla complained.

"So practice," Caleb replied before laughing at himself. "Hey. I just told a rider to be a Colt. Good thing it was you or there'd be complaints about my teaching practices."

"Your teaching practices are—"

"Perfectly suited for their intended target," Caleb cut off Tristan. "May I introduce to you Lena Sherman? She has a dragon."

Caleb winked at Tristan, which caused the prince to look confused and Kayla to lower her fight response. It wasn't so much about what Caleb said, but his manner of talking that took her anger back away. It was horrible that she couldn't spend her full day around him soaking up the tones of Caleb's voice that sucked away the poison from her veins. Tristan was taking Caleb away again. Kicking him out.

Pg. 460

She needed him! It was going to be hard to stay cheerful when her cheer ran away.

As she contemplated that thought, she realized what Caleb had already discovered. The spell was getting worse—stronger. It could tell that the linchpin holding her together was Caleb so it was Caleb that was under pressure to stay away. It could tell that it was Caleb that she had just put her love toward so it was shoving that at Valiant making him jealous and scared and angry. Whatever spell Caleb was working on to fix this, she hoped it went over smoothly, because with him gone things would look bleak.

"Here," Valiant squeaked. He puffed out his chest and then shot a spell that first hit at Caleb and then hit at her. This had to be the spell that Caleb had told her about, the one Valiant needed to cast without explaining what it was. It came out green.

"You know how to stop the nightmares?" Kayla asked Caleb as he plunged his hand into his pocket to grip at his magical fox that had glowed briefly from Valiant's spell.

"I will stop this," Caleb answered. He was already standing on Warner so he sat down and Warner stood up. Hope. Caleb was leaving and it felt like he was taking with him all of her hope.

"Don't you stop fighting those emotions!" he called down to her while Tristan gave him the look to leave already. Kayla found herself inching toward Valiant and then leaning up against his head for support as Caleb and Warner got a running start and launched away. She fought for the desperate, the lonely, the broken, and the shattered, but today the fight had fled.

"Come back!" Valiant shouted for her as if he could feel the same thing and he didn't want it gone. Kayla hugged Valiant's face refusing to let him leave her too. It was just them fighting against the unknown curse. For a moment it had felt wonderful that Caleb knew how to win that fight.

"Did you discover what curse gives Kayla nightmares?" Tristan asked Lena, slipping off Riven now that Caleb wasn't around. He waved at Lena to join him in his office while he pulled out a bandage to wrap up her new fang wound. "I'm Tristan Cluster by the way."

"I know who you are," Lena answered. "And yes, I do know what Caleb has gone out to fight, but if you want the information, you'll have to pay for it."

"I'll be more than happy to accommodate your needs," Tristan answered.

"*Gag,*" Valiant thought to her. "*Tristan found a girl who likes bribery. Caleb thinks that Lena and Tristan would make a good couple. Do you ever find it odd that we're more connected to our enemies than our friends?*"

She was trying to ignore everyone else actually, because with Caleb gone she was back to trying to decide how Valiant had stunned him by using his tail.

"Perfect," Lena replied to Tristan. "Answer me this. Was Caleb Andrade, *the* Caleb Andrade, really training my dragon with a spellbinding dragon, an ice dragon, and a dwarf dragon or was he making that up?"

Tristan had to chuckle over the question even if it was his fault that Caleb wasn't training anything right now.

"I don't think I've ever heard Caleb lie," Tristan answered. "He was telling you the truth. My dragon Riven joined the class too, along with two random wild dragons."

"Caleb said they were Colt dragons," Lena provided which caused Kayla to pick up a rock on the ground and chuck it at Lena's back. Those were Ritz's dragons! She didn't need Tristan looking into it. Lena gave Kayla a shrug over her glare, but she didn't make a further comment although the damage would already be done. Tristan would get nosy.

"Don't you touch those dragons," Kayla demanded when Tristan turned to look at her next. He also gave her a shrug.

"I don't need to," he replied. Tristan kept one eye on her throwing arms as he started talked to Lena again. "Lena, it is really fun to sit on the sidelines and watch Caleb train those dragons. Once he gets his act back together, you'll see it for yourself. Charles, he was the ware leader here previously, wrote that Caleb is going to be one of the best dragon trainers of all time because of the way he clicks so well with them. He was getting that ice dragon to cooperate, and it's incredibly hard to gain an ice dragon's respect. He was getting the dwarf dragon humming out joy. Let me tell you, those dwarf dragons hardly ever do that. He's good. Really good."

Kayla scowled at them. Tristan was trying to make her feel better, but it wasn't working. She still blamed him.

"What did he get in trouble for then?" Lena asked while Kayla tried to block out the conversation by plugging her ears.

"I told Caleb he had to finish his own training before he could be training others. He's not completed his own coursework. Now everyone sees me as the enemy around here for giving the kid the training he needs. It's remarkable the glares I can get for having an unpopular opinion. I never said Caleb was bad at his job, only that he needs to learn his stuff before he can teach it."

"He didn't sound mad about it when he mentioned that he'd gotten in trouble," Lena's voice was finally starting to get harder to hear as they started to walk away again, but she still wasn't far enough away. "And yet you had him leave."

"Did you see him? Clearly, the guy has some issues he needs to work through. That and I'm fairly certain that he's the only person still alive that knows how to rescue Kayla. Everything I tried ran me into walls. Caleb needs the excuse to get out of the ware and rescue her. If I don't have to be the one worrying about Kayla all day long, I am extremely happy about that. Caleb can do it and have the pain of losing her to another guy. I'm so done with it."

"Losing her to..."

Kayla clamped her arms over her head. Word about Caleb showing back up and then leaving again was starting to spread. She could hear Notley and his dragon winging closer no doubt wondering if he needed to do anything about his missing rider. She could still hear Lena too. Nothing was blocking out this conversation! She didn't need everyone to know what she had done! Couldn't Tristan whisper or walk faster so that he was in a private room already? It was strange that Tristan was unloading all of this to a Vankerdale spy so quickly. He should know better than this.

"Ah. For that information, you'll have to pay for it," Tristan said, causing Lena to giggle at him. Kayla pulled down her arms to glare at their backs as they finally reached the office door. The one thing Tristan wasn't telling Lena was the one thing she would learn remarkably easy as soon as she went back to Vankerdale. Reed could probably tell her quickly enough. He probably already had and that was why she was laughing.

"Anyone ever tell you that you're ridiculous?" Lena asked Tristan as he looked up at Notley and decided not to engage with him. He dashed for the office door finally to put in that distance Kayla wanted. Lena ran right after him.

Kayla sat down on the ground glad to be rid of them. She didn't want to hear the gossip about her and Caleb and Tyler. What she still wanted to know was how Valiant used his tail. She gave him a meaningful look to produce the answer, but he had since shut his eyes and curled up trying to ignore her moods. Maybe it wasn't the tail. Maybe Caleb had looked at Valiant's swirling eyes and gotten dizzy. Spellbinding dragons could make people dizzy if they didn't want to use magic to fight.

"I don't make people dizzy," Valiant finally answered. *"I stun them and take away their consciousness. I use it on you all the time. It's what used to help you sleep when your nightmares got too bad. All I had to do is flash you an image of my tail and down you went. Now I have the opposite problem and can't keep you awake. It's part of the reason I don't like you dreaming about the mystique. You are seeing the image of my tail everywhere you look and being stunned into unconsciousness so I can't reach you."*

Completely spooky. She was being stunned to sleep. On that note, she fell into dreams again, and the despair with which they hit told her that she was going to have a very very hard time breaking out.

Crown

Tyler

"Someone from Aralot to see you, sire," General Reis interrupted Tyler as Tyler brought the spoon to his mouth for his second bite of very very late lunch. It might as well be supper time. Tyler glanced toward the window to check the time of day wishing that he hadn't been getting these interruptions. Five minutes to eat couldn't be too hard to ask for.

"Is it Kayla?" That was probably too much to hope. Kayla was ignoring him. It was obvious to everyone and he still hadn't found a way to get her to willingly come see him. He had planned out four more kidnapping attempts that all would work and tossed each idea aside, unable to bring her over by force for the third time.

"It is not Kayla." General Reis shook his head like he wished it was her too.

"Any news on Narl?" Tyler asked equally hopeful.

His brother had bonded a dragon and was having the time of his life out there pampering the thing. Tyler had written to his brother asking him to come help at the castle, but so far Narl was ignoring all his requests and had only sent back a brief note saying he would think about it.

Narl was too smart for Tyler. Tyler wanted his brother around so he could verify that the man wasn't turning against him, but Narl wasn't about to have that. He didn't want to live his life by being spied on, but staying away forced Tyler to spy on him so there was no good solution yet. Maybe time. Narl was still trying to figure out where he fit. He was happy with a wife and a team of dragons, and a cozy house, but the dragon thing was new.

"Nothing has changed with Narl. Your visitor is a dragon rider of a brown dragon. The man wouldn't say his name. He wouldn't say his dragon's name either, but we got the name out of another dragon. If it helps, his dragon is named Warner. The rider refused to state his business, but he handed over all his weapons for the chance to speak to you. He made no protest when we tied his hands. He made no protest when we chained up his dragon. He said it was urgent."

"Thank you, General Reis," Tyler said standing up and giving up on his food yet again to see who had come to visit him. That was a lot of concessions that the general had this rider making. No rider wanted to see their dragon chained down. No dragon wanted to see their rider tired up, weaponless, defenseless, and in the hands of an unknown king that could very well be his deepest enemy. Tyler wasn't going to do anything mean to the rider, but with the ease that he had surrendered everything, Tyler felt that it was indeed an urgent visit.

General Reis led Tyler into the entryway where Tyler could make out a large crowd of soldiers all grouped around the strange man. One look at the man and Tyler was already smiling. The stranger hadn't noticed him yet, but there was an ease in his stance, a cheer in his voice, and an honest look in his eye that could make anyone instantly comfortable. That was probably why the general had so many soldiers around this intruder. It looked like the guards were all feeling

Pg. 468

the same thing because they were chatting with him and laughing as if they were all great friends.

Tyler could make out the rider's weapon belt set down by the door along with his dragon's saddle and headgear. Tyler wanted that saddle. He wanted that headgear. So he walked up with his smile and asked for it.

"Vankerdale doesn't have any dragon wares and I'll be the first to admit I have no idea how to properly ride my own dragon. I'll let you speak to me in exchange for your saddle and headgear."

The rider laughed at him. "You must be King Tyler. It shows. I've heard way too many things about the give and tug that comes along with unexpected visits into Vankerdale. I knew I'd be losing something. Unfortunately, I already know that the saddle and headgear won't fit on Coal. He's larger than my dragon. If you like, I can teach you how to measure a dragon and craft a correct saddle and bridle."

"And after that, you will explain to me the V4 formation. I don't get it," Tyler said making the rider laugh at him again.

"You've come to the right man. I've been itching to teach again after Tristan knocked me down. Tell you what, I know what you're really after. I'll come over here and give you personal dragon training lessons if you answer my questions without hesitation and without lying."

Tyler tucked in his bottom lip trying to decide if this was a good idea or not. He still had no idea who he was talking to. He still didn't know what he was getting into, but the rider was right. Every time Aralot and Vankerdale got together there was that give and take where each side gave more than they wanted in order to get what they wanted more. It had been like that for generations. The larger question was if Tyler trusted this stranger to not turn around and use what he learned against him.

"What's your name?" Tyler asked trying to pick it out by looking at the guy's brown hair, his easy brown eyes, and his solid stature. For a man, this guy was a good looking one.

"I try not to say that. My reputation proceeds me and it gets in the way. You've heard of me. I swear. It seems that everyone has heard of me. It was a bit of a surprise when I found out I was famous. People use it against me, so you won't be getting my name from me."

Tyler shoved his hands into his pockets. The rider had smiled at him through all of that, and despite feeling irritated, Tyler still happened to like him. Well, the guy knew Coal, so there was a chance that Coal knew him too. There were too many riders in Aralot for Coal to know all of them, but he would probably know the ones that would be bold enough to travel into a neighboring kingdom without getting an invitation. This guy was here on his own and that right there made Tyler a little nervous. The last person who had ventured to the castle like this had been Jack when he was after a spell to save Tia.

"Coal wake up."

"No," Coal snapped at him. *"Figure out your problem yourself."*

Tyler rolled his eyes at his dragon. Coal was probably in a deep part of his sleep cycle. He still had a few hours before he was supposed to be waking for the night, but Tyler didn't have any other way to get this information. It was written all over this rider's face that he wouldn't say his name even if they tortured him.

"Wake up! Do you know a rider that rides a brown dragon named Warner?"

"Caleb Andrade. Go to bed."

Caleb. This was the guy who drew all those pictures of Kayla. Caleb really did have a large reputation, and if it was Caleb that was over here, Tyler could guess exactly what he was come around to ask. He had some questions relating to Kayla. Tyler wasn't sure if he would have the answer that the guy was after, because he hadn't been able to settle King Jack's questions either.

"I might not know—"

"You know what I'm looking for. I assure you. If not you, Coal knows," Caleb provided.

Coal was being grumpy though.

"I'm awake. Caleb is here? I'm coming. Did you know that there are very few people who smell good to the large majority of dragons? Caleb smells great to everybody and it's not because Pyro splashed him with his dragon king protective magic. I've not met a dragon yet that doesn't like Caleb. I'll wake up to smell him. He's fabulous."

Tyler wasn't sure what face he made due to Coal's comment, but whatever it was, it had Caleb smiling at him again. He probably looked slightly annoyed because Coal had never told him before that he liked the smell of some other man.

"You're the kind of guy that breezes through dragon thought," Caleb told him. "Newly bonded people split their sentences talking half in their heads and half out loud. Oh, I bet you've never slipped your focus once. I find that admirable. You've got a good strong head on your shoulders, Tyler. I can see why Kayla likes you so much."

Yup. There it was. Caleb was here because of Kayla, and with the way those words came out, Tyler found everything he had been trying to squeak out of Kayla standing right in front him. Caleb Andrade. As invested as this man was in her life, Tyler knew it with every breath he took that this was the man that Kayla refused to leave.

Caleb was the reason she wouldn't come back to Vankerdale. This man was stealing his wife from him. Tyler wanted to hate Caleb. If only Caleb didn't still look at him so kindly. If only Caleb hadn't offered to give Tyler the very thing Tyler needed more than anything. Personal dragon training lessons. Tyler really wanted that, but to get it, he had to knowingly give up the last hope he had that Kayla would ever come live with him.

"Just what exactly do I say to a guy who is stealing my wife?" Tyler asked Coal. Caleb had to be the spellcaster that Kayla wanted to teach too. This was Tyler's rival in every single way, and the man was here bound before him, his dragon chained down, his life in Tyler's hands.

"Treat her well," Coal answered. *"You can't steal wives from Aralot. The magic over there would never stand for it. You never had her, Tyler. I think she was only engaged to you so that she could unknowingly bring you Caleb. Kayla won't answer your dragon questions or your magic questions. Caleb would, and his skill is breathtaking."*

"You sure about that?" Tyler questioned.

"Absolutely."

Pg. 472

"I'll accept your lessons and dragon knowledge. What do you want to know from me?" Tyler asked.

"Don't get scared. It's a bit of a nasty topic but I think you'll understand it," Caleb started. Tyler saw General Reis reach for the sword by his side not wanting to trust Caleb as quickly as Tyler was. "Aralot was founded in conjunction with two dragons. One was a spellbinding dragon named Aralot. The other one was an ultra-dragon king."

"His name was Choladon," Tyler provided.

"Well, Choladon died, but I've found the answer to what is killing Kayla."

"You did?! Let him go," Tyler ordered stepping in closer to Caleb and pointing to his hands. "Where did you find the answer. I've looked everywhere. Jack's looked everywhere. Where did you look?"

"I talked with Vermelo, who is our Captain of the Guard, and with Ritz, the leader of the Colts. Those two know a lot. Thank you," Caleb added as the ropes on his hands were released. The soldiers around him drew weapons now that Caleb was free to be as incredible as Coal claimed him to be.

"Aralot lives. She's in a spell that has her staying alive by devouring the love out of Aralot's queens. What I need from you is information on how to destroy an object made by an ultra-dragon king."

"That object being…." Tyler trailed off already feeling nervous about this whole thing all over again.

"Aralot's crown," Caleb stated. "Aralot and the crown are interlinked. They both have to go. It's the crown that declares the kings of the land and the crown that decides what queens Aralot can devour. Aralot is bound to the life of the crown and can't die if it can't."

"Caleb," Tyler flinched. At the sound of Caleb's name, the soldiers all looked at each other as if they wanted to lower their weapons because they all knew who he was suddenly. Even General Reis wavered before he decided to pull out his sword and aim at Caleb's heart out of duty.

"King Jack will come kill you. He won't let his kingdom fall."

"I won't let Kayla die," Caleb said. "Whether that means she marries you or not. Whether that means I'm disgraced from my birthland or not. I'll come live over here and teach your dragons. Jack won't be the only one wanting me dead. I know exactly what I just asked for. I'm asking you to help me destroy the kingdom of Aralot. I'm asking you to help me break the spell that makes it what it is. I want to cast off the magic that separates Aralot from Vankerdale. I am asking you to help me do something that no other king has ever done before, because they refused to bow to Vankerdale. I will serve you, Tyler. I'll be the traitor if it keeps her alive."

His eyes were tearing up. Tyler almost expected Caleb to drop to his knees and beg next. Caleb had found the answer to what ate Kayla, and he was going to destroy the lives of everyone he knew to save her. Aralot's crown kept Aralot stronger than any other kingdom around. Caleb was the absolute worst rebel that Aralot had ever known, and he had turned on his kingdom. He was tearing his heart out in front of Tyler, handing Kayla back over to him right when Tyler had finally decided to give up on her so Caleb could keep her.

Pg. 474

If that wasn't hard enough to watch, the thought of Aralot's kingdom realizing what had happened was. Vankerdale wasn't prepared to handle the smaller kingdom's war dragons launching out against them in fury when their kingdoms joined up again. Aralot was geographically smaller, but it was still the strongest force, and if Tyler angered King Jack, he was going to lose his keeper status. Jack would take it from him. Both Tyler and Caleb would die. Aralot would gain control of both kingdoms and they would do a smashing job at running it all. They had two very capable kings already.

"Jack will kill me," Tyler said next.

"Oh please!" Caleb let the tears fall from his eyes. "I know you like her, Tyler. You'd really let Kayla die? You'd let Aralot eat her from the inside out? Don't say no. I can't live like this. Death is the answer that all the other kings chose. They let Aralot eat their wives, all except for Gladius whose wife was murdered after childbirth in an attempt to stop Aralot from having her. Letting Aralot get away with this can't be the solution.

"Jack won't know anything about the crown. Vermelo handed it to me already, and I have the location of the dragon Aralot because Kayla dreams up the exact route to reach her regularly. Aralot is calling Kayla to her so the girl can walk herself down there and die. Kayla doesn't want to be that sacrifice. She's been fighting her own death ever since she was born. There has to be something we can do that will both save Kayla's life and not make everyone want to kill us for doing so."

Caleb was sounding like Tyler had already agreed to help him destroy his neighboring kingdom. Tyler had done no such thing. King Peyton would have loved this. He would have used Caleb up, strung him out, taken everything out of him already. That wasn't how Tyler did things. He respected Aralot. He quite liked them having their own kingdom, even if the thought of gaining access to everything they had was appealing from a kingly perspective. Still, acquiring Aralot didn't feel right. Saving Kayla though, that was still something that burned through his soul too.

"Vermelo gave you the crown?" Tyler asked catching the meaning behind what Caleb had just said. The Captain of the Guard wouldn't give the crown over to anyone but a magically claimed king of Aralot. Caleb was a king of Aralot. He was magically bound to Kayla and would remain that way as long as that crown existed. Breaking the crown would free up Tyler to have the girl. Caleb had come over here to destroy his own life. That took guts. There was no way that Tyler would ever be able to do the same thing, even if he was in love with a girl.

Then again, Aralot, if the old dragon really was still alive and trapped, had been around for hundreds of years. What dragon wanted to keep living when her rider was long dead and her only purpose was to torment the king's wives? This had to be a curse that Vankerdale had put on Aralot. Tyler could see that. Choladon had crafted Aralot's crown and been forced to live in Aralot when Choladon would have loved to stay in Vankerdale across the river. He had spent his life trying to make his dragon wife agree to not split the kingdom but to keep it all together. Then when he died, there was nothing left to take away his curse and no one else understood what the curse even was.

That was the basis of the queen's nightmares. The dragon Aralot sought after people who had strong love. She had been giving the queens nightmares telling them how to reach her so she could harness the queen's love throughout her kingdom keeping everyone

Pg. 476

there. The fight to keep Aralot and Vankerdale apart was still happening. Any king who learned this would refuse to destroy their entire kingdom, harming the lives of thousands of subjects for the life of one queen. Every king except for Caleb.

Tyler looked over at General Reis who shook his head that Tyler shouldn't do it. The man's firm jaw testified the general's opinion. Lock Caleb up. Keep him contained so that Aralot wasn't the one starting the war with them. Stop Caleb from being the traitor and giving Vankerdale everything. It was kind of funny that General Reis didn't want to merge with Aralot either when Vankerdale had been trying to achieve this for hundreds of years.

"If the magic falls inside of Aralot, the only thing keeping us apart is a river," Tyler told General Reis. "That and hundreds of years of paperwork that I've already hunted through. I assure you that King Klavian will write a lengthy document citing examples of why we should remain apart. There's nothing to enforce his words except for their war dragons because they won't have any magic. It will evaporate from their kingdom and come over here as soon as that crown and dragon are destroyed."

"Jack will kill you," General Reis assured him.

"Unless we provide him with an alternative. Jack didn't want to be the king when he first got started, but he wouldn't drop the title now for anything. We formulate a magically binding document that allows Aralot to remain on their side of the river. We get the legal papers all ready so that Jack has no time to contemplate fighting with us. We hand those papers to Jack. Make him the legal king. He will no doubt keep Klavian as his steward and they can handle the terms of their family feud as they were doing before. This doesn't have to be a war for anyone except for Kayla and Caleb, who are the only two people brave enough to fight what the rest of us could never look in the face. We do this and we gain more than we lose. Vankerdale gets magic back. We can't regain magic until this curse in Aralot is gone. You said that you'd stand beside me as king so long as I found a way to restore our broken dragons and regain our lost magic. Let me introduce you to Caleb Andrade. He's agreed to give you everything you wanted."

"You have no idea how to destroy an ancient crown or kill off a spellbinding dragon," General Reis noted.

Tyler shrugged. So he had no idea. Coal might know. He had watched Valiant kill off SilverWings. As for the other part, it had to be mostly intuitive right?

"Find me some other artifact made by an ultra-dragon king and I will work on figuring it out," Coal offered. *"Valiant sucked away all of SilverWings magic and then I tore his head off. I doubt Caleb is capable of doing that."*

"Coal is willing to try to destroy the crown. Caleb might need to see Valiant for tips on that spellbinding dragon part. All we know is that the dragon needs to be devoid of magic first."

"I have Valiant on my side," Caleb agreed.

A second later magic shot in through the walls of the castle, similar to the way that Kayla had once shoved it out and away from Prince Evan. Caleb pulled it toward him. The blue substance danced around his fingers and Tyler snorted oddly not feeling scared by the sudden show of force.

Pg. 478

Caleb hadn't surrendered himself one-hundred percent. He was holding magic. He could break away from all of them whenever he wanted to. He could use magic against them if they refused him. He hadn't come over here to beg but to give Tyler the choice to agree with his decision. Caleb's desperate desires could very easily lead him to destroy Vankerdale before he destroyed all of Aralot in his attempt to save Kayla.

Tyler was doing the right thing here. Caleb was not to be messed with. He was going to fight everything just as hard as Kayla did. Unlike Kayla who acted more reserved with magic, Caleb didn't have that problem. It pooled around his hands and when the magic left, it did everything he asked of it. Tyler wasn't certain what spell it was that Caleb was looking for in the entryway, but he found it. He found them all.

Spells that had been previously cast inside the walls of the castle lit up in yellow. Caleb looked at them and laughed at a few.

"Broken only if wearing a blue shirt," Caleb giggled. "You were funny. Whoever that spellcaster was is highly amusing," Caleb chuckled. "You have a good strong entryway, Tyler. I approve."

He left behind a spell of his own that covered up all the other ones. "There. Probably self-defeating but if you're standing in this room no king of Aralot can kill the king of Vankerdale."

Tyler hoped that's what the spell was that Caleb had cast. It could very well be the opposite. He looked at General Reis who was thinking the same thing and fidgeting to get out of the entryway. Tyler really needed to learn magic. He was so far behind on this topic it was pathetic.

"I thought you were doing fine," Coal said.

"I'm not as good as that," Tyler sighed.

"Once Caleb destroys Aralot, he won't be as good as that either. He won't have any magic at all remember? It will all come to you."

"And go where?" Tyler questioned. Magic had to have a physical location to sit inside. It was rather happy resting inside of gems.

"The throne room is full of gems on every surface. The room will be your strongest."

Having cast his spell, Caleb walked past the soldiers that backed away from him like he wasn't the nice man he appeared to be. They treated him the same way they had Prince Evan. They retreated, terrified of the magic that Caleb could control. Caleb put back on his weapon belt and riders backpack. He tossed his dragons headgear over one shoulder and slung the large heavy saddle over the other. He left a box on the ground in the process.

"Aralot's crown is in there," Caleb stated. "I expect that thing to be destroyed as soon as possible."

"You knew I would agree?" Tyler questioned moving to pick up the crown before anyone else could run off with the priceless treasure. He'd never expected to be given Aralot's crown. If either King Jack or King Klavian found out that he had it, he was going to be paying the price for Caleb's betrayal.

"I expected you to be a keeper who couldn't refuse my idiotic plan of saving Kayla Brixton," Caleb responded. "And if you refused, I was going to find something that you couldn't."

Yuck. Caleb might team up with Jack and cut Tyler off from being a keeper again. Maybe Caleb would discover who had been previously possessing Coal. He'd take possession of his dragon, or have the previous spellcaster do so, and together they would force Coal to destroy the crown. It was such an unsettling thought that Tyler shivered.

"Not anything that would hurt you, Tyler. Kayla would be hard-pressed to forgive me if I hurt you. I don't want her to hate me. I'm going to be miserable enough to lose her to you. Come on. I'll show you how to saddle a dragon."

"I'll see it later. I should put this away," Tyler said clutching the box in close. "You can go. Safe journey to you."

"Thank you for your understanding," Caleb replied before he somehow opened the door with his hands super full and stepped outside having won what he came for.

"I just…" General Reis let out a heavy sigh. Not one of the soldiers followed Caleb outside to tell anyone that he was allowed to release his dragon. "This is bad. People love Caleb from the most devious miscreant to the highest of kings. He's known in all three kingdoms. He's going to be a really hard king to take down."

"He won't fall," Tyler shook his head. "But I agree that it's bad. Once he's done with Aralot, he won't have the heart to watch the woman he saved be married to someone else. I've got to get myself another wife before he builds up resentment and it's him coming to kill me next. Caleb will give us the dragon knowledge we need if we handle this right. Start spreading the word that Kayla is cursed so she can't marry me. That shouldn't come as a shock to anyone who has followed the path of her life so far. Find out if there is any opposition to the idea of Adelyn Peyton sitting on the throne. Get the councilors together so we can start drafting a document that both Klavian and Jack can't refuse. I need an object made by an ultra-dragon king so Coal can practice destroying it before he tackles this crown."

"All those past relics are in Aralot," General Reis stated. "And Queen Tia guards them."

"Okay, find a way to get around Tia and her ice dragon…" Nope. General Reis wouldn't be able to handle that one. "I will try to find a way to get an object away from them. It'd be helpful if Kayla liked me enough to just give me something but she won't. I know!" Tyler cried out coming up with a much easier solution. "Bring me Conner the merchant. We'll send him into Aralot to steal an ancient artifact. If he knows that it will save Kayla's life, he won't protest."

"It will be done, sire," General Reis agreed, looking worried still.

"I can do this," Tyler told him. "I can help defeat Aralot and then build it up again."

He had to do this. There would be no rest for any of them until it was done, because it wasn't going to take a man like Jack forever to realize what was going on.

"*Something to note, Tyler,*" Coal cut back into his thoughts. "*If anyone tries to destroy the crown or even thinks about destroying it this strongly, their wife dies. Warner told me. Caleb will risk it because Kayla is dying anyway. Don't go claiming any other wife but Kayla until this crown is gone or you'll be hurting yourself. You need a perfect resolution to keep that woman as your wife.*"

"Don't bring me Adelyn," Tyler amended.

He looked at the box in his hand and wanted to back down. He couldn't destroy the crown. He couldn't ask for it to be torn apart if it would kill Adelyn. This meant that he couldn't break the crown at all because he'd already given up on Kayla and no amount of telling himself that he hadn't would change that. He couldn't give up on Vankerdale either. This crown was magical. It knew the desires of his heart past, present, and future. If he did this, Adelyn was going to die. That was why no other king had let this happen before. Someone had to die from it. Kayla was dying anyway. There was no stopping her death. Tyler wondered if Caleb realized that or if he was skipping over that part at the moment.

Tyler broke open the box and grabbed at the slug infested wreath that awaited him there. He ran the item out of the castle into the courtyard where Caleb's brown dragon Warner was out of the chains. He was already saddled, and true to his word, Caleb was walking a young lad through the steps of how to gear up a dragon. Coal was in the courtyard sitting nearby so he could watch and inhale the smell of this tragic king of Aralot.

"Caleb!" Tyler screamed.

He threw the crown at him. Caleb's face turned dark and stormy as he caught it, probably expecting Tyler to back down from everything he had just agreed to do. As the crown connected with Caleb's hand it changed form. No longer was it hideous, but it became a silver circlet with rubies. An instant hush fell across the courtyard as the nobles and dragons that were there realized what it was they were looking at. Caleb Andrade was the third uncrowned king of Aralot.

"I'm sorry," Tyler said into the silence. Since everyone was watching him and was going to talk about this no matter what he did, he decided to get his subjects comfortable with the idea of Kayla not being their queen himself. "I appreciate you coming to tell me that this crown has cursed Kayla. She will not be joining our kingdom. We cannot accept the ancient curses of Aralot upon our soil."

"What are you doing?" Caleb asked him in a voice that chilled Tyler through his bones. Caleb was fantastic, but if mad, he was lethal.

"I am declaring a cancellation of my engagement to Kayla Brixton. I will be marrying a native to Vankerdale and will always be in your debt for bringing it to my attention the additional curses you have identified upon the princess. Kayla will always be very dear to me, and this does not in any way affect the relationship we will uphold with Aralot."

Yes, it did. Tyler could see the anger now burning through Caleb's face.

"Tristan will pound her if you do this," Caleb growled. So he would, but Tyler couldn't kill off Adelyn! Kayla was going to die either way. There was nothing any of them could do about it.

"It will not be my will dealing with the nature of the curses on that crown," Tyler continued. "You have my permission to converse with my dragon over its properties, but it won't be my will touching that thing. I won't watch my wife die to it either. I still stand behind everything else we discussed earlier and will keep my part of our bargain."

"What part?!" Caleb screamed at him. "I asked you to destroy the crown. It's cowards like you, Tyler, that leave the rest of us

Pg. 484

wanting to cut your heads off. We don't have any bargain. I'm not teaching you anything."

Coal growled over the threat but one look from Caleb had the dragon inching backward in fear. It left Tyler feeling scared too. He was making Caleb mad, but he had every intention of writing up a document stating that Aralot would not join with Vankerdale once Caleb destroyed it. He wasn't going to tell King Jack or King Klavian what Caleb was planning. He was going to let the man have his way and that was his bargain.

"I will not be cursed by that crown," Tyler said again. "Do with it as you will. I won't stop you."

Caleb pulled out a prong and Tyler wished that he had asked Caleb to step back into the castle entryway before he gave him his cursed item back. There was a good chance that Caleb really had given him a spell to withstand death as he said. Out in the open Tyler wasn't as protected.

"Especially since Caleb has been training with Mr. Grumpy and the dragon is here too," Coal said right before the ice dragon dropped into the courtyard causing people and dragons to scatter in all directions.

"You're spying on me, aren't you?" Caleb asked the ice dragon. He tossed the crown at the dragon who caught it in his mouth. "Take it back then. You'll get no more support out of me until you get Coal to destroy that thing. If you come to see me before that thing is gone, I will do my best to hurt you."

With that additional threat, Caleb mounted Warner who was flattened to the ground terrified of Caleb's mood. Tyler looked at Coal as did Mr. Grumpy as Caleb directed his dragon to take off. The courtyard was still dead silent as if they had all witnessed the ravings of a madman broken by the stab of keeper poison. But Caleb wasn't a keeper so he couldn't be poisoned. It was the torment of watching the love of his life die that was eating at him.

"Caleb just threatened us," Tyler expressed to Coal.

"As a true king of Aralot, they all seek our destruction if we can't solve their crown problem. Typical. But I don't think Caleb was talking about us. He was looking at Mr. Grumpy. I think Mr. Grumpy has a secret rider," Coal answered. *"I'll explain to him about the crown. We'll get it destroyed, Tyler. It's not your destruction order. It's Caleb's. You did fine. The only man who will suffer here is him."*

Coal started whispering to Mr. Grumpy about what was taking place. It was a shame about Caleb. He was going to lose no matter what he did, and his wrath could stretch all over the place with curses and evil deeds. Yes, he was a king of Aralot all right. All the real kings of Aralot went mad from the death of their wives. Hopefully, Caleb would be the last one and with Jack on Tyler's side, they could hold back the young man's rage.

Tyler looked around the courtyard searching for a dragon that could speak directly to Conner's thoughts. Forget the general summoning him. Tyler was going to take care of that too. Tyler found what he was looking for without trying very hard. Tempest himself was sitting in the courtyard looking after the way that Caleb had stormed off.

"I'll be needing Conner. I have got a job for him. We've got more information pertaining to the quest he's after."

Pg. 486

Tempest didn't say anything to acknowledge that he'd heard Tyler. He didn't even look at him, but he did jump into the air and head in the direction of his home, so Tyler knew that Conner would be there soon.

"Is he going mad?" a concerned voice asked from behind Tyler.

"Caleb?" Tyler replied, spinning around to see a group of nobles who would not hold back their tongues over what they saw. They had to do this fast. Jack was going to know that the crown was in Vankerdale waiting to be destroyed. The spies and Colts were going to be whispering about it all over the place. They had no doubt already started with the way that dragon and man could send thought across the river right now.

"Caleb is not mad. He's suffering from a broken heart due to the curses on his kingdom. We have no need to panic. His actions will not tear us down. I've got everything worked out already."

Or he would. Really soon. With that Tyler gave a grateful smile to his dragon who took the crown from Mr. Grumpy and plopped it into his own mouth. They had the crown of Aralot. Walking felt way too slow. Tyler ran back into the castle screaming for the documents he was going to need to calm down Jack and Klavian. He no longer felt hungry at all.

Farewell

Kayla

"I know you don't want to hear this, but I wish that Caleb was here. He'd know what to do," Mulligan's voice filled up the air above the endless field of blue mystique flowers. Kayla had stopped trying to walk through them to escape. Since Valiant had told her that it stole away her consciousness, she was taking a new approach to handle the flowers and not looking at them at all. Her eyes were shut within the dream as she lay on her back facing the sky after having ripped out all the nearest flowers around her to squish them.

Maybe it was working because she got the sense that she was coming back to herself. It felt like she'd slept a full day away.

"I hate to tell you this, but Caleb is already out there doing what needs to be done. He's not coming back here," Tristan's voice answered.

"He took Valiant!" Mulligan cried. "I don't know what he's doing but he's pushing it."

Kayla wasn't sure what Caleb was doing either, but Valiant had stopped talking to her. She suspected that he knew what the problem was, and he refused to say anything at all in case he accidentally gave away the answers. He had spent sixteen years not saying a word to her. Valiant could keep this up a long long time if he felt like it.

"Yup," Tristan answered.

"Don't worry. His arms are ripped. He's good at pushing things," Lena's voice said next.

"He took Warner with him this time, so he can fly around before he pushes things." Tristan chuckled. "Got to love the guys that do your dirty work for you."

"You two are making me sick," Mulligan complained. "Do something! You're supposed to have all the answers to get Kayla up. What good was going into Wisteria if you brought back nothing?" Mulligan asked Lena.

"I happen to like everything Lena brought back," Tristan defended her. Kayla wanted to roll her eyes at him for how quickly Tristan was stepping up for Lena. So what if Reed had worked beside Riven during a night class? Lena was still a citizen of Vankerdale and shouldn't be allowed to be walking around the ware like this.

"There isn't anything I can do," Tristan kept talking. "You want me to do something magical and amazing. I get it, Mulligan, but magic is being super weird and not working properly. If I start casting complicated spells, they're going to get all screwy. I suspected that Vermelo had something to do with it since he was the one who brought it to my attention, but he said that Jack was having trouble with magic too. Since Jack hasn't come charging over here to use magic, I'm starting to think that Vermelo wasn't lying but right. The only one who can fix the magic, and therefore Kayla, is Valiant. That's what we learned from Wisteria. This is a problem with a binding spell. Caleb and Valiant are taking care of it."

"Don't you have anything better to do than clog down this room with conversation?" a voice asked.

Kayla heard the shifting feet of Mulligan, Tristan, and Lena leave the room and silence fill the air instead. She let herself smile because that meant she got to wake up without Tristan in her face and find out where she was. She let her fingers shift on the sheets trying to figure it out.

"You're stuck in a binding spell?" The voice with her changed.

"Conner!" Kayla cheered elated.

She forgot all about waking up slow and jumped from the bed to find herself in the doctor's office again. Conner had used his super good acting skills to get the room all to himself and sneak into the ware. He had proved before that he could change the sound of his voice, although Kayla had never seen him use that trick for his own personal gain before. Conner really did look like one of the doctors that worked at the King's Ware, although Kayla wasn't sure of the name of the guy since she'd only interacted with Dr. Weber.

"You're back in Aralot!"

If it wasn't for Conner talking to her with his own voice, she would have been completely fooled too. That, and she was certain that the real doctor wouldn't hug her back when she tightly wrapped her arms around him.

"You came by to see me," Kayla noted.

She glanced around wondering if her parents had stopped by at all. Seeing Conner only made her think of the last time she had been kidnapped into Vankerdale. It was Ritz charging out to save her instead of her parents. Now Ritz's son had shown up as if he still felt strongly that he might save her when her parents were absent.

Yet again, Kayla had that strange feeling like her parents had given up on her now that they had the promise of some other new baby on the way. Kayla pushed the feeling aside because that would only make her scared, and she wasn't going to give in to her feelings. She was going to do what Caleb suggested and think with her thoughts, not her emotions. Her parents had probably stopped by to see her. She was simply asleep when they came.

"I felt like I needed to slip in. You're worth the effort, and the wait," Conner added as Kayla failed to keep away the short stab of sadness that her parents were not here. She fought with the emotions but it was a lost cause. She felt herself falling into Conner's arms taken by dreams again. Voices of past keepers screamed across her mind as if calling out to her. They whipped around her until she found the voice she was trying to find. Conner's.

"We've got Tyler taken care of," Conner's voice hit against Kayla's ears drawing her instantly toward this new dream even if she realized it was going to be a nightmare. It took a moment longer before the image of him came to focus.

Conner was standing in Aralot with Ritz before him. Kayla was looking out of dragon eyes that she had never been before and it was her best guess that she was in the form of a night dragon, probably Ritz's dragon Norber. It was dreams like this that made her question all her other nightmares. If she was seeing this, was her brain making it up, or was it something real? How had she gotten the image from Norber? Something else had to be able to grab the thoughts from him and reconstruct them enough to turn them into a dream. No. Not a dream. It would be a nightmare. It was going to be bad.

"You found Tyler a wife?" Ritz asked.

"Yeah. You were right about who to entice his way. It was super easy. Way easier than dealing with Tristan. Tyler isn't hard to please at all. He will settle for Adelyn Peyton and use her last name to hold him in place quite well. She's a brave girl that will do what needs to be done. I tested her myself."

"And Tristan?" Ritz quizzed. "The brat can't die."

"You know how certain things just click into place after everyone else has tried everything they can think of? We all give up or at least realize that we're failing, and some bloke comes along and sees the empty hole. Well, I am fairly certain that the bloke to tackle Tristan is Caleb Andrade," Conner replied keeping his lips perfectly still as he spoke to avoid anyone around that might be a Colt overlooking their conversation. Perhaps that was because he passed Ritz a small jade dragon while he talked of something completely different. That thing had to be important, but Kayla didn't know why. It was important enough for them to communicate about it beforehand and not say anything about it after. Kayla wanted a better look at it. In dragon eyes, she may have had a chance to get a close-up, but Ritz put it into his pocket rather fast.

"Can you feel it on him?" Ritz asked, causing Conner to turn confused. "Figure out how to sense that feeling, Conner. What you found on Caleb is deep-seated magic. Most people don't like the topic of magic—"

"I'm fine with it," Conner cut off. "I think I know what you mean."

"Caleb is the force we all need to respect right now. I saw it too."

"Wait you *saw* it?" Conner questioned taking a step back. "Saw it like...?"

"I need to tell you something, Conner. I—"

That was as far as Ritz got because he burst into a pile of dust.

"Uh..." Conner looked at the pile not sure what this new trick was.

Kayla was doing the same thing. Dust. It wasn't a tall pile at all, but her current dragon eyes blinked and then she heard several dragons screaming. It wasn't a good scream, and there was a cold hand squeezing shut the dragon brain she was being. Since she had felt the death of a keeper on a dragon before, it didn't bother her this time around. Kayla still suspected that she was being Norber, and her guess proved correct when Norber's voice rose not in a scream, but in the song of death.

Weird. She had seen Ritz dying before and had spent a whole day fretting over it until she saw him and proved that he was still very much alive. She was doing it again; making up nightmares that showed her the things she didn't want to lose. It was interesting though that her dream depicted Ritz almost telling Conner that he was his father.

As if it was something vital for Conner to finally know, Norber dropped before the man and commanded the keeper to hear him.

Pg. 494

"Who are you?" Conner asked. "I've got all the dragons I need, but I appreciate your faith in me."

Norber growled and looked at Tempest hiding in the air above them. He screamed at Tempest and a new sensation came to Kayla that she'd not felt since the dream of Valiant bonding her. A brand new connection. The cold hand vanished from Norber's head as his thoughts joined a new keeper bond.

"Ritz was going to tell you that he was your father," Norber's voice cast itself out. *"And I was his bonded dragon. Who did you tell about that dragon statue? That was Ritz's life. Did you figure out why he asked you to bring it?"*

Conner jumped back and then plopped to the ground trying to find the statue in the pile of dust. Kayla could sense the panic about him for not being able to find it, and then his face turned toward the trees while it took on the look of communicating with his other dragons. He turned back to the pile of dust and started to cry.

Perhaps it was the sound of tears that helped break her free this time because Kayla was really good about fighting against tears. She shoved the sound away and found herself waking up on the bed again. Conner was still acting like the doctor checking over sheets to see who had been sick or hurt last.

"I'm back again," Kayla said causing him to sit beside her on the bed.

"I heard that you were falling into dreams quickly but that was rather sharp," Conner frowned. "If I hadn't overheard that Caleb is out there doing something about this, I think I'd be really troubled."

"You came to see me," Kayla reverted back to the start of their first conversation, because she couldn't let herself think about Caleb and Valiant being gone from her. That would pull her under.

"Yes. I did come to see you even if I have a few dragons telling me that it's a bad idea. It's not even an idea really, but this compelling need to… see you before anything bad happens. You've only been pictures to me for most of your life until you showed up at my doorstep. I needed a better memory of you. Not that I think anything bad is going to happen," Conner was quick to cover up.

Kayla gripped at the edge of the blanket with her hand. Conner did think that something bad was coming. Keepers were often the first to feel like they needed to act on a threat. Conner simply didn't know what the threat was so he was here instead of outside searching for the force of it. That's where her parents would be. Outside. They hadn't come to—Kayla refused to think the words because she very much wanted to stay awake.

"It's a really odd moment when you think that you have all the dragons you're ever going to have in life and another one or two or twenty suddenly come into your head," Conner told her.

"Yeah, I don't have that problem," Kayla replied.

She was grateful for that. She only had her small group of dragons, most of which were not connected to her even. She didn't have this large host that Conner had to care for all on his own. Maybe one day when her head wasn't such a battleground, she would consider caring for more than just Valiant, Riven, Bantin, Merlock, and Sparkle. She couldn't handle all of them right now as it was.

"Kayla, I need to tell you something." Conner slipped off the weapon belt that he had stolen, not liking the feel of it against his waist. "I know who my father is."

Kayla pushed the blanket away from her with a frown. It was all a dream, right? She saw horrifying events from keepers that happened far away in the past. She didn't see events that were current. No. She had made the dream up.

"Isn't it great? I know he's not the most compassionate person, but he did what he had to do to protect you. He loves you so much Conner—"

"Don't make me cry again," Conner cut her off breathing in and out deeply to hold back his emotions. "Ritz died. That's what I came to tell you. His dragon, Norber, came to tell me. Norber asked me to... well..." Conner fiddled with his hands so Kayla scooted away from him.

Her dreams couldn't be this real. They simply *couldn't!* Not this time.

Kayla felt the air in her lungs leave her. Conner was lying. It was all a bad dream. It hadn't really happened. Nothing could make Ritz explode, particularly not a dragon statue. Norber hadn't turned to Ritz's son to ask him to link him back to human thought. The dragons Conner had just referred to joining his keeper bond were not all the ones that used to be with Ritz.

"I'm taking over the Colts. My wife will be furious with me, but I have to. I've always felt like there was a place I needed to be where I was commanding some sort of troop. The Colts need a king again. They'll be horrendous without someone keeping them in line. I'm going to change things a bit though. No more hiding that it's been keepers all along commanding them. They're going to know the truth because I'm going to tell them."

"I don't believe you," Kayla said keeping her despair away at the tip of anger. "Ritz can't die. I need him."

She really did. Ritz had made her believe that he was going to be there to help her. He couldn't let her down like this. Of all the stupid Colt things to do, he had to die?!

"Who is responsible?!" she demanded.

"A bunch of people," Conner sighed. "First it was Ritz himself. He told Norber that he had watched too many queens die and he couldn't do it anymore. He loved you way too much to outlive you, so Ritz came to visit me and had me fetch something for him. I didn't know what it was, but the item was a jade dragon with a curse on it that kept him alive. Ritz was going to get it from me and destroy himself in a few days, thereby ending his own life, but he'd been trying to snuff out Tristan so Tristan was trying to snuff him back. Tristan used a spell on the jade to take it from us, and when he destroyed the item, Ritz turned into a pile of dust just like that. It was a very painless death so I'm told."

"Tristan..." She was never ever going to like Tristan Cluster. This was the last time he was going to shatter her heart. He would never have it. If only she'd not saved him from that tar, she could have been done with Tristan already. Why was she so nice? Why did she let Ritz fail? Now Ritz was gone and Tristan was left.

"You are probably mad, but give it a bit of time. Ritz knew what he was doing when he asked for that cursed artifact. He was prepared in case one day you lost him," Conner told her as he wiped away a tear. "He left this for you. Norber had me fetch it before we stopped over."

Conner handed her a crisp piece of paper and a small box. "I made a copy of your letter. Not going to lie. It's one of those things that I couldn't let leave my sight without keeping around."

"He's not…!" Kayla trailed off as she took the letter and the box and felt her heart drop below her toes. Ritz. She could not feel sad about Ritz and yet it was the one thing she wanted to be right now. It was going to be really hard to keep away a feeling that she suddenly *wanted*.

To distract herself, Kayla opened up the box first and nearly flung the item inside away from her. His necklace. Ritz had left her the replica of the flower necklace that he had always worn. It was this necklace, well actually the real one that Ian and August had, that had gotten her grandfather Herb Felding taking a large interest in dragons again. One could almost say that it was this necklace first crafted by Gladius that had been the start of changing keepers from hidden and feared to recognized and respected again. Kayla didn't want it. She shut the box and shoved it into her pocket to deal with later.

Maybe the letter was better. She pulled out the paper to see that it was a list of lost keepers. Among the names were Troy, Shane, Gladius, and her parents. Both of them. Jack's name was a recent addition in much fresher ink. Ritz had been holding onto the names of keepers. He hadn't let them live in vain but had found them. They had lived on inside of Ritz, and now he was passing the information along to her with a personal message at the bottom.

"Remember that box that Jack has in his yard that claims to grant wishes?" Kayla knew the spot really well. She'd met Ritz there a couple of times. "Well whenever you left it, I would drop in a coin and wish for something too. I'd wish that you would love me as much as I loved you. You came at me during a time when I'd lost my only son. You were quite the stubborn baby crying all the time, refusing to look at dragons and most people, but if I snuck into your house and picked you up, you would smile at me and laugh for breaking in. Your parents caught me a time or two, but they never made me leave you. They just watched me—closely—until I put you back down and you started crying again.

"Then you got older and I had to stop holding you. You found other arms to silence your fears. Other faces to smile at, but I believed that you'd never forgotten about me. You proved that to me recently. Out of all the queens of Aralot, yours is the deepest love, the most precious love, the most perfect love that could always look at a man's heart instead of his actions."

Kayla glared at the words. She wanted to scream. Why was Ritz telling her this? She didn't want to look at hearts. She wanted to look at Tristan's actions and destroy him for what he had done to her. She was going to destroy him. She was going to take all his magic orbs away and toss them into the ocean. If they ended up being swept into Wisteria so be it. They wouldn't be with Tristan any more. Only she didn't act on her feelings because she was trying to get rid of them. She kept reading.

"You see beneath the surface of our hidden lies and make people believe that they can have another chance to be happy again. Yours is a love that I will miss greatly when I'm gone. If you are reading this, it's because I have finally passed on. I was honored that I lived long enough to know you. May your love be all the fight you need to win."

Pg. 500

Win against her nightmares. How was she supposed to win when her love was gone? Ritz had died! This couldn't be right. She wasn't going to let it be right.

"There has to be some way he can come back!" Kayla cried.

"Kayla," Conner said reaching in to hug her. "With the number of gray hairs Ritz should have had, he was well past his time. One simply can't outlive time forever. He lived long enough to find those who could win his battle for him. He found you."

"Well, he failed because I haven't won anything!" Kayla shouted.

"You broke Gladius's orb. You broke curses on keepers and dragons. You're still here instead of... not here." Conner shrugged.

Kayla realized now that Ritz was gone just like he wanted, that he wouldn't be around to block off the entrance to what he was guarding, but she was too tired to even try to reach the old castle. Him dying hadn't done anything good unless Valiant was charging at the castle right now. Either way, Conner was holding back on her. He knew what her curse was too, and he wasn't saying! Why could no one tell her? What would happen if someone told her what the curse was? Would she decide to stop fighting the nightmares or something? That was ridiculous. When she got back to that field of dream flowers, she was going to tear all of them up from the ground refusing to be put into a stupor.

"Ritz wrote me a letter too. A long one. He wrote that he was worried it was his fault that I vanished from Aralot because he blocked me from keeping the crown. He didn't want my life to include battling against my most trusted friends which would be the legacy I left behind if I had run off with the real crown on your parent's wedding night. I would have compounded the war for the crown. Ritz feared that he had pushed away his son, the one person he delighted in. Then he found you, and you calmed the ache inside him. He felt whole again when you helped him find me and proved that I hadn't run from the crown but instead had chosen to stand beside you when you were too young to stand up for yourself. After I read everything, I wasn't so mad that he had died anymore. He was ready, Kayla. He had gotten everything he needed put in motion before he left us. His life's work will save millions."

Kayla shoved away from Conner's arms. She was still mad. Life's work or not, she didn't want to sit there and talk about all the good that Ritz had done. She wasn't privy to most of it, and any other time she would love to hear it, but right now she was too mad.

"Tristan is horrible!"

"Tristan is a Cluster prince. It's in his veins to maintain the balance of keepers. He did what he felt compelled to do with the magic that attacks his head. He was doing his job. It's all in that letter."

"I still hate him. Tristan does things for all the wrong reasons," Kayla glowered.

"He was stopping Ritz from killing him off. Ritz was trying to kill Tristan to keep him away from you. Perhaps if Ritz had collaborated more with Caleb, he would have realized that he didn't need to take action himself."

"What are you talking about?" Kayla asked.

"While the rest of us have never been good at nudging Tristan Cluster anywhere, I completely believe that Caleb Andrade will be. He'll do it in a way that Tristan respects, and your problems with the prince will vanish."

"I don't have problems…!" Kayla started to scream but that sentence, and the one referring to Caleb being taken away from her, pushed her back into the dreams again. She couldn't tell if she was seeing the present, the past, or the future with what came charging at her next.

The only thing she knew was that she wished she was making it up because she didn't like the way Caleb was standing in front of her father at Anvil's Ware. For him to be there had to mean that he had taken another portal, but even then, it proved that he had left her at least two days ago because he hadn't left with Valiant initially. He'd come back and gotten him. She was sleeping too much! She wished Caleb was back with her. Then she wished that her father wasn't at Anvil's Ware either. He should be over here trying to stop her from falling asleep every ten minutes!

Behind Caleb stood his family. Kayla had never paid them much attention before, but she could pick out the similarities. There were his two parents, both dragon riders, and his three brothers, Mikka, Brandon, and Grant. It looked like Caleb had swung by to say farewell to them or something because they were all looking pale clutching at each other.

"I can't have you doing what you've done," Jack said.

Kayla stiffened at her father's tone. That was his patient "I want to kill you" tone. Kayla felt fear slice right through her at the sound of it, especially since the recipient was her friend. First Valiant had turned on Caleb and now her father was doing the same thing as if they couldn't fight off the pressure to keep away from the only thing set on saving her. They just had to attack him.

"Well, I've already done it. Going to take a swing at me? I'm dying for a fight, Jack," Caleb goaded. "I haven't gotten into a fistfight since I left here. Why not keep the tradition going for me, huh?"

Kayla wanted to shake her head, except that she was looking at the scene from the eyes of a dragon (no surprise there), and she wasn't controlling the animal. She was simply stuck here spectating or (hopefully) making this all up because she had a good imagination.

Her father wasn't standing on the field alone. Kayla could make out Pyro and Sparkle and her mother's most lethal connected keeper dragons all sneaking over to get in the way of the fight. This was not going to be a fair fight if Caleb got himself into it. He couldn't do this! He was right. He *had* stopped fighting everyone when he was at the King's Ware. Why did he feel the need to fight against all authority if he wasn't beside the castle?

"You'll get a fight alright," Jack agreed. Then he stood there while the dragons jumped at Caleb. The dragon she was being screeched and tried several times to lunge forward to help Caleb only to be blocked from all directions. She was being Warner. She didn't want to be Warner.

"No!" Kayla screamed. She could make out the sound of her own voice pleading only she was asleep and not able to do anything to make herself wake up. That's right. She was sleeping. This was another nightmare and not real. Not. Real. At. All.

"Dad, no!"

Pg. 504

Kayla couldn't even see Caleb through all the dragon hides. His family was likewise struggling to jump in to save Caleb only they kept getting outsmarted by Tia's keeper dragon team that sent them onto the ground or flying backward with hard landings. Even their dragons were being swatted nastily in the head.

First Ritz and now Caleb. She couldn't lose them both on the same day! Tears were already falling down her face and there was nothing she could do to wipe them away. The world was broken and wrong and she was helpless to fix it. The despair continued to haunt her even as the dragons jumped away to reveal Caleb still alive standing in the middle. Instead of crying or fighting, he was staring down at a large blue gash that ran from the top of his right arm down to his elbow. That was the gash of a recently made keeper.

Caleb! No, it was taking Caleb! He couldn't become a keeper to have all the torment that she had gone through with the condition. He'd have to be protected from keeper poison or he might attack his bonded dragon and slowly lose his mind. It couldn't have him!

"That's your grand plan?" Caleb asked looking up at Kayla since she was being his dragon. Warner whimpered as the pressure on his head started to change. This wasn't fair to Warner at all. He should have been able to live his whole life without needing this curse stealing his joy.

"Turn me into one of you so I can't go through with it all?" Caleb asked, correctly guessing what had just happened to him. "You think that if I'm a keeper I won't take Aralot down because I'll be forced to love her like all the other kings. It won't make a difference, Jack. You can slash me with the best controlling spells you've got. You won't change me. There's not anything you can do that will change my mind. Aralot is going to lose because she has no place in my heart. That's already taken."

"You'll see," Jack answered him. "This isn't about Aralot. This is about what you did in Vankerdale. You can't destroy other keepers when you're like that. Your body won't let you."

This wasn't making complete sense. How was Caleb planning to take down Aralot? What had he done in Vankerdale, and why did her father feel like he needed to defend himself by forcing Caleb to gain a keeper affinity? A keeper couldn't kill off another keeper. This was a very cruel way to prevent Caleb from turning on him. Caleb wouldn't turn on Jack!

"Your trick to control me is only going to work against yourself," Caleb claimed. "You can't stop me now. You can't order your dragons to kill me off. I know how keepers work."

"But you don't know how Aralot's magic works," Jack said with his voice wobbling. "You're one step closer to being the real king. All the magic in the land is conspiring against your head instead of mine."

Dad no. He couldn't shove his magical problems onto Caleb. Caleb was glorious with magic, but he wasn't ready for this. If only she wasn't so tired, she would tell her dad to keep the magic longer.

"Kayla was legally a queen as soon as she was tricked in Vankerdale to be one. You were tricked into being the king as soon as you took that crown from Vermelo. I knew what he was doing the whole time. He would never hand over my crown, Caleb. I told him that he could tempt you with it and you fell for it. It is you, Caleb, that can't turn on *me* when she dies. That is why you are now a keeper. That is why you have lost."

"I'm not against you, Jack, only against Aralot," Caleb declared.

"You interfered with Wisteria. You went to Vankerdale to talk with the king. You took my crown. I don't care what your intentions were, that puts you against me."

"Jack, I'm trying to save your daughter's life!"

"You can't," Jack whispered while Kayla whimpered, fighting even harder to push against the feeling that her dad was giving up on her. He couldn't do that! She was still here! Not dead. She wasn't dead!

"No matter what you do, she dies. I've talked with Vermelo too."

"You didn't talk with Ritz," Caleb declared. "You didn't talk with Valiant. I know where Aralot is. I came here to say goodbye to my folks in case I never saw them again, but I have no intention of losing. Kayla won't die."

He got that right! She wasn't dying! Kayla refused to die and burn out like so many other people had done before her. She refused to die and leave Caleb to the pressures of being a keeper alone. She was going to stay alive.

"I'm speeding this up," Jack continued to talk softly. "I'm tired of watching her die. Now that you're the stronger case for the king of the land, Kayla will vanish in a few hours."

What!? This wasn't right! This had to be another of her nightmares proving her fear that her parents would be fine without her now that they had another kid coming. That's all this was. She was projecting her fears about her parents into her dreams.

"You can't!" Caleb screamed. "I won't let her die!" He jumped toward Jack, and Kayla could see all his anger bursting through, wanting to punch her dad really really hard. Caleb stopped himself just in time.

"You can't turn against me remember? A keeper can't kill another keeper," Jack pointed out.

"Punching you won't kill you," Caleb spat. "But it doesn't help me right now either. You're the one who will lose Jack, because you could never look beyond Kayla's curse to her spirit within. Kayla doesn't fall quietly no matter how silently she tunnels beneath the hood. She screams. She fights. Kayla loves keepers no matter what torment their hearts have put upon them. Your heart failing will not be the fall of hers. You'll see. She's not going anywhere."

Except perhaps back to the field of flowers. Kayla dropped out of Warner's eyes, finding herself back among the long field of the mystique. True to her earlier thoughts, she tormented the field, pulling up flowers and tearing them to pieces as soon as her fingers brushed them. She wasn't done with this fight. Nothing was going to kill her off like this. Nothing.

Aralot
Caleb

If he didn't already have a fail-safe plan sitting in his pocket in the form of that fox, Caleb would have been screaming quite different words into Jack Brixton's face. How dare the man make him the king?! How dare he?! This only proved that Jack wanted the crown destroyed just as much as Caleb did. The difference was that Jack had taken the cowards path to let someone else risk death at the hands of it instead of himself. Jack was standing there trembling from his own fear; from the path of the king that couldn't lose himself because he felt too needed by all his subjects.

Caleb wanted to hold up the binding magic in his pocket and declare to everyone gathering on the field that he wasn't dying or going insane. His life was fixated to a fox statue along with Kayla's life because they knew a spellbinding dragon.

Okay. So that did sound a bit maniacal.

If he lost this statue, he could wither in the blink of an eye. If it was busted, Kayla was done for. He should take it out of his pocket because he was going to be charging directly at Aralot as soon as he left Anvil's Ware. Caleb left it where it was, but he was going to attach it to Warner to keep safe while he was fighting that evil spellbinding dragon with Valiant. It was going to be strange leaving the ware this time because there was no way to take back anything Jack had just said. Caleb was the magical king. No one took that lightly around here.

"Guys stop!" Tia screamed as she ran to the field along with a bunch of other people who hadn't been in the right spot today to see all the action firsthand. Caleb had been hoping to slip inside the ware quietly. His bribe on the scouts he knew would have worked if it wasn't for Jack spotting him. Now riders and dragons from every field were dashing over.

"Have you both lost your minds?!" Tia screamed as riders and dragons converged around them, staring not sure what to do about Jack letting his authority go when all of them trained to serve the king and their king was suddenly the banished kid.

"I get it alright. You both love her to death. Fighting won't change her fate. Indigo said... You can't change it," Tia declared.

"Indigo doesn't know everything," Jack blurted back suddenly showing that he did still have a backbone and wasn't losing all his love as Caleb had first thought. "I don't care if Indigo is a dragon queen and sees points in the future. Every future can be changed. Kayla will die, but the rest of us can still be saved from her sacrifice. Kayla knew lost souls and saved them even if she could never save herself. Her heart was showing us secrets about keepers that we could never see before. Just ask Sparkle to tell you all about it. Kayla's found loads of information."

"But Jack!" Tia pointed to the blue line running along Caleb's arm. There was no way to cover the thing. Caleb was always going to have this gash showing everyone exactly what Jack Brixton had done to him. Keeper. He had felt his head shifting on him the instant Pyro cut his arm, and he didn't need an explanation walking him through what he now was.

"I love Kayla more than anything," Jack continued. "You know I'd give up everything I have to save her. There is nothing left that I can do but hand over my entire kingdom on blind faith. I've finished giving it to Caleb. He's been garnering in all the magic for some time now anyway. He went into Wisteria and vanquished the last of their curses. I bet none of you knew that. He's been to Vankerdale and gotten King Tyler to draw up plans to grant us our kingdom without us ever worrying about merging with Vankderdale again. I had Vermelo plant these ideas in his head, and Caleb did them. Caleb has been guiding us, and as the king, he will have the power to finish what he started. Feel free to hand that force back without killing me when you're done with it," Jack said giving Caleb a commanding look.

Caleb rolled his eyes at the way that Jack made it sound like he was still in charge when he had just admitted to giving everything up because he couldn't find the way to destroy it all. Everyone was still staring at Caleb, but it was Anvil's voice breaking through the tension of his men.

"I knew I always liked Caleb," Anvil spoke cheerfully.

He made the riders laugh because everyone here had seen Anvil lecturing Caleb pretty much every single day of his life. That was Anvil for you. He could let a man have it, but if he felt like he needed to ease the anger away, he would do so. That had to be one of the many reasons that Kayla loved him. Anvil found the things to say that brought out joy, and that was the emotion she struggled with. He was indeed a good person for her to be around. Caleb gave Anvil a nod of appreciation, something he was certain he had never given Anvil before.

"Let's go," Caleb ordered looking at Warner as he took a few steps toward him.

"Just a second," Anvil spoke. "You're doing what?"

"The only thing left to do," Jack replied, but his voice was breaking and he was starting to shake unable to hold back his fear again.

Caleb turned his back on Jack so he didn't have to watch the man cry. He heard the sobs starting up and it had everyone holding their breath. Caleb couldn't think of a single time that any of them had seen Jack cry.

"Caleb is going to face Kayla's curse," Tia told Anvil. "Kayla was born of magic and is going to die from magic. The best we could do was give her our love and protection until her time came. I've always known," Tia said.

Anvil couldn't hold himself together at the thought of Kayla dying on him. He broke down into a fit of sobs himself. They were all breaking! The path of a king was hard. Caleb had to keep going when everyone else failed. He couldn't stop.

Wouldn't stop.

"You realize, Caleb," Jack said, gaining his voice back for a moment, "that if you succeed, we lose all our magic. Our kingdom merges with Vankerdale until King Tyler hands us that paper he drafted to remain segregated. If you succeed, we're going to know the moment it happens."

Pg. 512

Jack didn't bother to mention what was going to happen if he failed. In Jack's mind that meant instant death for Caleb and for Kayla. Yeah, it was best to not reveal to anyone else that their lives were bound to a statue.

"Any news on the nature of that crown being destroyed?" Caleb asked Warner as he mounted the dragon and they looked for a way to push through the crowd so they could go join Valiant where they had left him.

The crown was the part of the plan that still felt tricky. Caleb could walk himself before Aralot, but he couldn't make her vanish if the crown was still around. Not only that, but he didn't have any way of really knowing what was going on with the crown unless Valiant asked Bantin to give him the information.

Bantin had better get Coal to destroy that thing. Caleb hadn't really meant what he said about trying to hurt Bantin and Vermelo for failing him in the destruction of the crown. Vermelo had hidden his information from everyone too long. Caleb really didn't like the way that people felt they had to hide their bonded dragons or conceal magic if they didn't want to join dragon wares, or if they didn't fit the perfect stereotype of being a rider. When he was king, he was going to change the mentality of riding dragons.

"When you're the king?" Warner questioned jolting him a bit before he started running to launch into the air.

"No one sees me as the king, Warner," Caleb answered. *"Jack will see to that. He'll talk everyone around to thinking that he's still in charge and King Tyler will agree with him. I already agree with him."*

"How about a prince then? When we finish this, you can find ways to get everyone seeing riders in a new light."

"Something tells me that I won't be the only one feeling the need to bring to light hidden bonds," Caleb thought.

Kayla had been keeping quiet about it, but she knew about Colt riders long before Caleb did. Once the keepers were free of this curse, she would need a new project, and she would no doubt end up wanting to aid Colt dragons. Next up would be helping Vankerdale some. King Tyler was right that his people needed to learn how to mount and care for their own dragons, or he was going to be losing good people as they attempted moving to Aralot to tap into that information. Aralot needed to send a few teachers over there and hold a few week-long day camps. That would help to keep Vanderdale people in their own kingdom.

"It's kind of funny to hear you thinking like a king," Warner expressed. "This is strange pressure indeed."

"Do you feel different?" Caleb asked as they left the ware below them escaping the dragon and rider gossip that was mounting.

"Yes, but it's hard to explain," Warner replied.

They dropped down on the other side of the mountain where Anvil's scouts didn't venture as much. Valiant was there pacing himself in circles. He didn't look at all surprised to see them, and he didn't make any attempt to ask for information because he would have heard what happened from Sparkle.

"I need to know how close Coal is with that crown," Caleb said as Warner landed beside the anxious slate-colored dragon. He wanted

Pg. 514

to ask how Kayla was doing, but he held off on that question because Valiant already looked anxious enough, and Caleb didn't want the dragon to sit down and refuse to move. He needed Valiant up.

"Coal is still working on it," Warner told Caleb when Valiant answered. "He was able to destroy an ever-sharp dagger that Conner brought to him, but the crown has different spells in the way. They've gone to see a monolith left behind by Choladon trying to get additional answers. It was the place that Pyro learned how to make keepers so they have high hopes."

Great. Caleb was going to be ready for when Coal got his answer. He signaled for Valiant to take him to the portal with trust that Valiant would correctly link him to the portal that came out by the old castle just as Valiant had linked him to reach Anvil's Ware. Dashing back through the portal didn't take long at all since Caleb had already bribed the scouts here to let him back through when he first exited. He wasn't being followed by angry riders from Anvil's Ware so none of the scouts knew what had occurred between him and Jack, but they were going to learn of it the instant their shift ended.

It still sounded strange that he was the king of the land right now. He had never been this special before. He was always the kid in trouble or the kid who drew pictures or simply another ware born rider. That's who he used to be. Now he was suddenly much larger and it came at him really fast.

As Caleb and Warner came out of the portal on the other side to look at the destroyed castle, his eyes were instantly drawn in the direction of Aralot. There was a group of wild dragons lazily sitting in front of the entrance watching him. Caleb pulled out the map and tucked the fox statue into Warner's saddle before he winced and glanced at Valiant. That statue had all his protections on it. If he left the fox behind, he didn't have anything.

"What's your vote?" Caleb asked Valiant who started conversing with the sitting dragons in their way. "Leave my magic here and lose my protection or take it with me and risk this thing getting busted?"

Valiant looked away from the sitting dragons as they stood up and scooted over to the side. The dragon's brown eyes put themselves onto Caleb, and he started to answer before he gave a short growl and shot a spell at him.

"Was that new protection?" Caleb asked.

"No," Valiant answered causing Caleb to shake his head since sound suddenly sounded odd. "I put a spell on you to understand me. It's faster than making Warner translate. Leave your magic behind. Aralot will suck it all up and render it useless if you take magic before her. The last thing we should do is give her any chance to put a spell on you."

Right. "So now we wait for that crown to disappear," Caleb replied as he came down from Warner and looked at the cooperating wild dragons with new eyes.

He had looked at dragons tons of times, but this time, he couldn't help but pick out the dragon's dirt and problem areas. A young green dragon chirped back at him and hummed. While Caleb had no idea what words that dragon said with his ears, he could feel them all echoing against his heart. It was something like, "Hello, Caleb. Want to wash my claws?"

Pg. 516

This was going to be weird being a keeper. Dragons could already sense what he had become and were already asking him for personal care as if they instantly trusted him. Notley wasn't going to like this. Being a keeper was going to make Caleb more distracted in class.

"Not fair," Warner snorted. "I didn't get to say your dragon name first. Caleb, Caleb, Caleb. All hail CJ, the magical king of Aralot for the next few hours, before magic ceases to exist."

"Don't be so loud," Caleb chided his dragon while he rubbed at his ears for understanding Warner talking back to him. Valiant's spell had to be conditional to work on dragons that were standing close to him because he really hadn't understood the wild dragon in the distance apart from feeling that magical pull.

"Don't feel obligated to help those ones," Warner thought to him. *"I was listening to Valiant's conversation with them and they joined up with Conner Felding now that Ritz is gone. They will be fine."*

Conner. That was Kayla's lost uncle that no one ever talked about. There was yet another bonded Colt that was in hiding. Even larger of a thing to note, Conner was a keeper.

"Male keeper directly related to the ruling line of kings," Warner provided. *"Conner Felding could be the king of Aralot just as easily as you."*

They had too many kings of Aralot. There had been Conner and Ritz, Jack and Klavian, and now Caleb all living at the same time. That would make it confusing indeed for Aralot to find a girl to devour, especially since none of the kings had put on the crown.

Valiant's eyes swirled with anger and he growled in the direction of ancient Aralot. Caleb looked toward her too, wondering if she was going to show up after all this time in hiding. Nothing came toward him except for Valiant's alarming words.

"Coal destroyed the crown, but I still can't hear Kayla! She would talk to me if she could because she misses me when I'm away from her. When Ritz's jade dragon was destroyed, he became a pile of dust instantly. Aralot must not be using the same spellbinding spell after all. Her life isn't bound to the crown. The crown was simply used to feed her. She's still alive in there, and she's still killing Kayla because she has already picked her queen to eat!"

Hopefully, this didn't mean that Kayla had to die before Aralot could. It wouldn't make sense to bind Aralot to Kayla when Kayla was already on the brink of death. No that was silly. Aralot was still alive because Kayla nearly wasn't. Aralot's life may have been bound to the crown, but she had more than one spell keeping her alive. The loss of the crown didn't stop her life because Aralot had found a way to devour other lives instead. Killing off the dragon would still save Kayla.

"I had the feeling that it wouldn't be easy," Caleb answered.

He glanced toward the fox statue hiding in Warner's saddlebag, double checked his shoelaces, and then glanced at the state of his weapons. He had to go in there and take down the dragon himself. He'd never killed a dragon before, even if he had gone over techniques on how it could be done. Now he was a keeper and the thought of killing off a dragon sat wrongly in his gut, but if Kayla could shove aside all emotion to fight this thing, he could too.

Pg. 518

"Do I know enough to kill a spellbinding dragon?" Caleb asked Valiant. "King Tyler didn't have tips, and Warner told me that it was both you and Coal that took down SilverWings. I know enough to not give her magic."

Caleb started to go through everything else he had picked up from Valiant.

He had seen Valiant shooting spells and he could interpret by the shift of his claws or the expanse of his stomach when he was going to cast a spell. He had seen Valiant stun him. Well, he didn't see it exactly, but Warner had seen it so that was helpful. Caleb couldn't look at Aralot's tail, and he couldn't look at her eyes because that could make him dizzy. He couldn't fight with spells.

"How do I kill off a dragon that I can't look at?" Caleb whined. "I have to avoid the eyes and the tail. I have to make sure she has no magic to work with. This is a job for Kayla. She could do this with her eyes shut."

"You have to make her happy, Caleb," Valiant answered. "Swirling eyes proves she is mad and glowing wings proves she is happy. Get her to glow, and then when she trusts you, stab her through the eyes as deeply as you can. Also, don't let her into your thoughts. If she gets in there, you're going to be stuck."

"Are you helping me fight that part, Warner?" Caleb asked keeping his gaze on his bonded dragon who nodded to him.

"It's easier to say than do," Valiant spoke. "Aralot is a dragon queen. She slips beneath my mental grip. Do not let anything break your concentration on keeping her out, Warner."

Warner sat down and stared at the ground doing his best to focus. He would probably do an excellent job as long as Caleb didn't start thinking anything alarming to distract him. In that regard, Valiant was right. Caleb had to keep Aralot happy up until the moment of her death so she wouldn't start fighting him too soon and break Warner's concentration.

"How do I make a spellbinding dragon happy?" Caleb questioned. "I don't have anything to tell her that she's not heard before."

"That doesn't matter. You don't have to have magic to make her excited that you're there. All you need to do is talk about magic. Even if she knows more about it than you do, it will make her smile."

There it was. Valiant was admitting to Caleb how to break beneath his own defenses. Caleb looked at Valiant and decided to give the dragon a short bow for all his help. Valiant finally bowed back! However, he then tucked his head down growling like he was fighting his own mental war. Then he curled up into a rock and Caleb sighed. He had planned on taking Valiant with him to face Aralot. This looked like he was going to be seeing the dragon all on his own. Once Valiant was in that curled up position nothing got him to move.

Caleb took one last look at the dragons that had helped him get this far, and then headed toward the spot on the map that had been calling his name. Time to face it. He walked between the wild guard dragons that all whispered him words of fortification before their words were stolen away from Caleb's understanding as Valiant behind him sucked his spell back.

Caleb had spent most of his life not needing magic to feel protected, but he suddenly felt a little helpless without it. He reached

Pg. 520

his hand into his empty pocket and nearly turned around to retrieve his fox before he remembered that he couldn't take magic down with him. The pressure to bring some down was probably a spell on the ruins. He squished himself through the hole of a narrow gap and found himself looking at a door with a gold-lettered stamped sign.

"King's only."

He now fit that category. Caleb reached for the door before he noticed the locks blocking the way. If he had magic, he could open the door without much effort. He pushed the thought aside to turn to Warner.

"Shall I pick this or do we know where the keys are?"

Warner didn't say anything back to him, so Caleb shrugged and started to pick his way through the locks one at a time until he had them all off. He gave the door a tug and frowned when it still wouldn't move. That's when he saw a muddy footprint on the ground leading away from the door. The door was a distraction.

Caleb followed the footprint directly into a wall. If he had never gone through the portal by the castle, he would have thought that the wall here was solid stone and not tried to walk through it. He passed through the secret doorway in the wall easily enough and found himself instantly intrigued.

There were portraits hanging on both sides of a stone hallway. He was suddenly inside a part of the old castle that had never been smashed. There were kings and queens and children and beloved pets in the pictures. There were dragon faces and sports trophies. At the end of the hallway, Caleb found a podium where a metal book sat along with a sharp stylus. The book claimed that it held the names of the caretakers of Aralot. Caleb could make out Gladius and Maslon's names as the last two. Beside the book was a fading paper that Caleb carefully unfolded to read.

"You rotten keepers! I shall find the hiding keepers of this land and destroy you for holding us inside your curses. You have been warned."

The note was signed from King Virgil Cluster IV who was Klavian's father and indeed a king who had tried and failed to kill off keepers. It looked like he had found this room and had been unable to write to his name upon the magical metal book. These were keeper names then. This was a list of all the keepers that had seen the dragon Aralot for themselves.

Caleb looked behind the podium instinctively knowing what he needed to do. In order to get through the next set of curses to see Aralot, he had to be able to sign this book. Caleb had thought that Jack was being a jerk to make him a keeper, but here was proof that the always lucky man knew what he was doing even if he didn't really know why. Caleb wouldn't have been able to get through without being a king and a keeper at the same time. He also had no way to take Valiant through with him because the dragon would never qualify.

He picked up the stylus and before he could even touch the metal pen to the surface of the book, his name appeared before him in his own handwriting, and a magical doorway in front of him opened up. The first thing he heard was the sound of birds. Birds. Inside the castle. It was a strange sound to hear and even stranger was that when he took a step around the podium to find the sound, papers fluttered up in front of his face written by past kings.

"Do not forget. She's the ugliest thing you've ever seen," was written in large bold letters as a warning from one dead man to the
Pg. 522

next. "Her soul is so cold that it will never be warmed by the love of anything," another hand had written. "Behold, the devil awaits," was another message. Caleb kind of liked the last one. It simply read, "Don't let me down," and was clearly written by Gladius Felding. Anyone who recognized that handwriting would get the shivers over words like that. Caleb found himself nodding. He had this. He knew what to do.

With bold steps, he entered into the magical cage of Aralot and looked around flummoxed. This wasn't a cage. There were plants and trees and real birds and a pond and a cave to sleep in. It looked like a personal dragon oasis, complete with piles of treasure flattening down the grass in several locations. He didn't see Aralot as he was too busy trying to make out how large of a pen this dragon had. He couldn't make out the walls so there was enough room for the dragon to fly comfortably. She could be anywhere.

Caleb glanced behind him to note the spot he had entered. It was marked with a large golden pole that had a brass bell attached to it. Finding the dragon looked simple. Ring the bell and it would come, but why ring? Aralot would be able to smell him and hear him.

"Hello?" Caleb called out. "Quite the place you have here," he spoke trying to come up with a good way to bring up the topic of magic so he could make Aralot trust him enough to lower her head toward him in a bow. Then he could reach her eyes.

The angry dragon growl right beside him had Caleb jumping away from the door reaching for a weapon on instinct. He saw a flash of gray that he dodged thinking it would be a tail but it was really Aralot's leg stomping outward to push him away from his one point of escape. Round one to the dragon. She was already in his way and growling as if she knew what he had come there to do. Then again, all the kings wanted to kill her once they learned what she was doing to the women they loved.

Caleb ran a good distance away from the dragon to get out of reach of her tail and risked looking at his foe when he heard Aralot snort at him and sit down, no longer in any stance to attack. He took in the bright gray of her legs at first and couldn't help himself but take another few steps backward in surprise. Valiant was a dark blue color close to one of his parents who were blue and gray. Aralot couldn't be called gray. She was silver. Her scales glistened like the silver on the royal crown, bright and gorgeous.

Who had called this dragon ugly? She was the prettiest dragon that Caleb had ever seen! Her claws were black as obsidian. Each of her scales looked like the shape of a jewel. Despite being caged forever, she looked strong and healthy with strong muscles and folded wings and a tucked under tail. Aralot had blue eyes like the Felding blue that had always been a temptation for Caleb. She shifted slightly and then yawned when Caleb found himself lowering his prong and sliding it back into his weapon belt.

"Just stay right there. You're too good to be real." Caleb grinned as he reached for his drawing supplies and frantically started to draw Aralot. Her head had perfect proportions, all triangles beneath her curves and large eyes that spoke of innocence.

"Did you already forget what you went in there for?" Warner interrupted Caleb's drawing. Caleb felt irritated by the sudden voice in his head. Warner knew better than to interrupt him when he was drawing!

Pg. 524

"I interrupt you drawing all the time!" Warner declared. *"Did you look at her eyes? Did she mesmerize you that fast? I agree. She's an ugly dragon."*

Caleb had to laugh. There was nothing ugly about this dragon. She was the most perfect dragon in all of existence. Sleek, yet strong. Gleaming, yet not blaring. She was patient and watchful. Warner was simply jealous.

"Kayla needs you!" Warner shouted causing Caleb to mess up a line on his page and scowl at it. Now he'd have to start all over again. He grabbed out a new sheet of paper and started again.

"You probably hear this all the time, but you are fabulous," Caleb spoke to Aralot.

"By golly," Warner complained. *"Do me a favor. Close your eyes for two seconds and try to remember what you went in there for."*

He knew what he had come in here for. He had entered this area to meet Aralot so he could make her happy.

"No! Close your eyes and try again!"

The pest. Caleb was going to finish his drawing first. He scribbled it out, nodded at it that it was a great likeness, and then put it into his bag. He looked back at Aralot and got started on that happy part. He was going to tell her how beautiful she was with her moon-kissed scales.

"Oh no," Warner whimpered into his head.

"Now we can do this properly. Sorry about that distraction. I happen to be an aspiring side artist. I'm Caleb and you must be Aralot.

It's a pleasure to meet you. I've never seen a dragon with your coloring before. Would it be okay if I..."

She was sooo pretty. Caleb reached his hand out and watched in fascination as Aralot scooted over to meet him. Valiant didn't do that. He was far more cautious with strangers and even with friends. Aralot's nose touched his hand and the hum she produced was a cute adorable girlish sound that made him want to cuddle her face. He hugged her nose, running his hands along her smooth surface while he traced the curves of her head that he had drawn with his hands.

"Great. Now close your eyes and see if you can still see the lines," Warner told him.

Warner was being unwise. It was one of the first rules a rider ever learned to never take his eyes off a dragon he didn't know. The beast could surprise him.

"You know this dragon. It's Aralot," Warner told him. *"You've felt her presence ever since you were born. Close your eyes and tell me what she's like."*

Well, that was true. He did feel like he had known this dragon forever. What would two seconds of shutting his eyes cost him? Caleb hugged the dragon's head letting his eyes close. That's when the reminders that the kings had left in their spell flashed before him.

Not beautiful. Ugly soul. Devil. No love strong enough to satisfy her.

Caleb flinched and pulled backward stumbling over his own feet so that his eye's flashed back open and he found himself looking

Pg. 526

directly into Aralot's sweet face again. She gave him a bow with such grace that it made his heart sore just to see it.

"How's her stomach looking?" Warner asked.

"Flat," Caleb answered, looking down from her face to her stomach. She didn't have any magic in there that he could tell so there wasn't any kind of spell that she could use on him.

"Then why are you not remembering about Kayla?" Warner asked. *"Ask Aralot if she's hungry."*

Nothing could make Caleb forget about Kayla, but she was fine. She was trapped to that fox statue and couldn't die. There wasn't a rush to do anything for her, but Aralot could be hungry. It was sweet of Warner to ask her.

"Do you need any food or water or anything?" Caleb asked getting up on his feet and checking over the state of the scales on Aralot's legs next. They were just as smooth as her head. Every inch of her was perfection sliding beneath Caleb's hands.

"No," Aralot answered him spreading out her wings finally as she yawned again. Caleb couldn't help but glance at the wings to catch sight of the additional silver on her wingtips. It glimmered even more than the rest of her. Breathtaking.

He backed up and gave Aralot a smile. She would be tired during this part of the day because she was a night dragon. Valiant was usually napping right now too and Caleb was keeping Aralot awake. Perhaps he should go and let her rest.

"Remember what Valiant said?" Warner asked him. *"He only sleeps around his friends. Aralot doesn't trust you which is why she is not*

sleeping. The reason she's not hungry is because she's eating Kayla, and the longer you put Kayla out of your mind, the weaker Kayla grows. She might not die, but you're dooming her to live nearly dead for the rest of this fox's life if you don't remember why you went into that room. Shut your eyes and remember."

He was in the room so he could impress Aralot enough to reach her eyes. He did remember, but he had forgotten to talk to her about magic.

"I just started learning about magic," Caleb said. "I find it particularly interesting how some people mix up fate with magic and magic with fate as if they are the same thing. I've heard that Gladius thought that magic was fate and it was his special ability to control them both. Maslon said that they have moments of being the same thing too. Do you agree with that?"

"Caleb!" Warner screamed at him. *"Don't ask her questions! She's shoving at my head! I think I've felt this before right after Jack made you a keeper."*

Oops. He had no idea what that would feel like, but it probably wasn't nice. The thought caused him to frown. Aralot was supposed to be sweet, not nasty. What was she doing messing around with Warner's head? That wasn't right. She already had all of Kayla, she wasn't getting Warner too.

"Great!" Warner cheered. *"If you won't fight her off for Kayla, then fight Aralot off for me. Don't let her destroy our bond."*

Destroying dragon bonds was impossible unless Aralot was to use poison or magic on Caleb. She didn't have either because she was a trapped dragon, doomed to live alone while she devoured love. How did she convert the love into usable energy anyway?

Caleb looked around the room taking in the birds and the gold and silver piles of treasure. Now that he was looking harder, he noticed something unique about the treasure. Not one item had a jewel on it. That had to mean something. Maybe Aralot had asked for treasure, and once the kings managed to get out of this room, they remembered what they had gone into it for and decided not to bring Aralot back magic that she could use. She hadn't asked Caleb for anything yet, but now that he wasn't looking at her, she was shifting again.

Eyes on the dragon! Caleb spun back around to make Aralot stop advancing. She smiled at him and hummed and spread out her wings as if she was trying to impress him. Caleb wasn't fooled. That was not how a spellbinding dragon tried to impress people. That was how regular dragons behaved. Not Aralot. She was trying to distract him because he had looked away from her for too long. She might not have magic to cast additional spells, but she was still trapped in this room, and she had spells placed upon her because of it.

Maybe it was the room! If the room was destroyed... Ah. Caleb understood why Gladius had destroyed this castle. He was trying to destroy the room where Aralot lived thinking that if he got rid of the walls or the treasure or the trees or whatever it was that held the spell on her, he could get rid of the dragon. Gladius got every other room destroyed in the castle except for this one. That had to be frustrating. No wonder the man was so mad all the time.

"I suppose it doesn't matter too much if fate is magic or magic fate. If you think about the essence of moving magic, it really comes down to having a strong will and it is desire mixed with action that moves both fate and magic. It's our actions that make us who we are and our thoughts that lead to our desires."

Oh. He got it! There was some spell around Aralot that caused her to scramble his thoughts and that was messing up his desires. He really should be fighting this thing, not standing around giving her time to work out her charm on him.

"I can teach you all about magic," a melodic voice tempted directly into his thoughts. *"You can be greater than Gladius. He was a brute of a man, consumed with his own legacy and scared of himself. You are nothing like that, Caleb. You're not scared of anything."*

He had been scared of things before, and he didn't trust anything telling him that he shouldn't be cautious.

"Caution is not fear. It's wisdom," the voice continued.

Caleb reached for his prong pulling it out and holding it up. Aralot was in his head. This had to be why only keepers could come in here because only keepers could be trapped like this and turned into slaves for the dragon. It was all those keeper names on the list that lost time and love and magic to this beast.

"Silly Caleb. Those other keepers didn't lose anything. They shared their time so that I could teach them fantastic things and they could keep the kingdom running strong. King Tyler might be a keeper, but he will never be as great as you without me to teach him. The poor dear. You shouldn't believe anything he's told you. He will never help you and will only stab you in the back."

Caleb clutched his prong even tighter. He had no real ties with King Tyler, but he'd rather put his trust in an unknown man that was Kayla's friend then put his faith in a spellbinding dragon that was eating Kayla alive. He was going to stop listening.

"Warner!" Caleb cried out trying to reach his dragon. He felt his head struggling with the task and he wanted to back down which was the easier path, but he refused to let his thoughts be gobbled up by Aralot. If she could hear him, she would know everything he was planning!

"Warner!"

"Did you close your eyes yet?" Warner asked.

No because he didn't know how to fight a dragon blind. He needed his eyes open.

"If I fail at this, it's up to you to finish destroying this traitor," Caleb thought.

Warner was incredibly silent which made Caleb sigh. Caleb was the one being the traitor to the kingdom by seeking to blow it up. This land belonged to Aralot, but she was an old creature and had killed off many a woman by stealing away the love they held. She was done sucking them dry and scattering queens through the dirt. He refused to think otherwise.

Caleb rubbed the chills from his arms. Growing up he heard tales of magic being embedded into the ground of Aralot. What it had always been was the love of queens that entered the subject's hearts and helped them to continue onward when all other hope failed.

Once Caleb reached Aralot's eyes, he would be stealing away that hope. He was going to take away the fortification that lived in everyone's hearts whether they were a Colt, noble, rider, or farmer. It was a somewhat beautiful thought to know that even after Kayla died her strength wouldn't leave the land. She would still be around, holding them all up, sending out her confidence and light. No. He couldn't think like that! Kayla was dying!

"It's a crutch," Warner finally spoke. *"We expect something else, some magical force, to give us courage. The Colts are the only ones that have got it right. They fight on regardless of their feelings. They push past the feelings in the ground as if they have always known that they were resisting the love of dead women."*

"Ritz did know," Caleb said. Ritz had taught people how to fight it. Everyone who was a Colt was going to have a much easier time adjusting after Caleb killed off Aralot. Non-Colts were all going to need to take the strength of Colts in order to carry on. That would be a hard thing to swallow for a lot of riders.

Caleb shook his head. Normally when he thought of Colts versus riders, he thought of how it was the Colts that needed to learn to respect riders better. It was the other way around. Riders needed to learn how to bend their pride. They were all brothers, all sisters, all friends who just happened to live in different locations and trained in a different way. They didn't need Aralot providing the love for them. They could figure out how to love each other without her. They could keep going, keep thriving, without forced love holding them all back.

Kayla had already started paving the way for that. Aralot had never had good relations with Vankerdale until now. This peace that Kayla had brought about was the closest the two kingdoms had ever been. She had become friends with Vankerdale's ruler. Kayla hadn't known that this would be the end result, but she fought against the fake love stronger than anyone.

It was Kayla's soul feeling the truth. Her heart guiding them all out of the darkness that had fooled kings and queens for years. Kayla gave her life to Vankerdale, gave her life to the people of Aralot so that they could all survive. Caleb was going to make sure that Kayla was the one surviving this. Not Aralot. The dragon wasn't going to break through his defenses. He was going to break through hers.

"So there's this spell," Caleb said hoping that Warner was strong enough to keep Aralot out of his head still, "that talks about transforming one object for another." Caleb pulled out a knife next. "I've not quite figured out how to do it, but it mentioned being very familiar with both objects and sort of swapping them around…"

Caleb tossed the prong and knife into the air to switch hands before he tried his luck at throwing them at the dragon's head. Aralot didn't waste a single second on his trick. Her tail lashed up so fast that he had no time to react. Caleb wasn't sure how much time he was standing there stunned, but when he woke back up, his weapon belt had vanished along with the knife and prong. It could have been put anywhere, buried in a hill, in the cave, under the piles of treasure, or shoved into a tree. He should have stabbed Aralot when she let him hug her head! Now he had to play dumb.

"Did that scare you? Sorry about that. I'll use something else," Caleb spoke to the air since he couldn't see where Aralot was. He spun around and found two different rocks that he started talking about instead. He rambled on about what it might be like to switch the places of the rocks, and when that didn't bring Aralot back into view, he started to walk toward the cave. He might be without his weapon belt, but every good rider carried an extra knife in his boot. He could still do this if he could reach those dragon eyes. However, he needed to come up with a new way to entice Aralot.

"Hey, did you know that there were spellbinding dragons trapped in Wisteria? There was this dark blue one and this gray one that had cast a spell on themselves to be trapped in time."

The sound of dragon wings whooshing toward him from above had Caleb wanting to roll out of the way, but he had to give off fake trust, so he stood his ground and let Aralot land right in front of him flashing him with her brilliant blue eyes again while her tail was kept looped behind her. He didn't let his eyes tell him that she was pretty. He made sure to tell himself that she was a rather ugly dragon so he could keep up with his plan. He expected that any spellbinding dragon would be interested in hearing about others of their rare kind. This could get Aralot thinking he was on her side again, especially if he looked at her while he talked.

"They were there since the time of Gladius and their friend Erana laughed at me when I figured out time magic but not binding magic."

Aralot sat down and chirped a curious sound interested in this story that she'd not heard before. Perfect! He could get close to her with this story and hold her interest because not many people could use time magic. He knew just the right place in the story to reach for those eyes. He had climbed up on the other spellbinding dragons and he could climb up on Aralot during that part of his story. He backed up a bit so he could set the scene keeping his tone light and playful so that Aralot was put at ease.

Pg. 534

He managed to get his voice right, but his thoughts were all over the place as he told the story. He shouldn't want to hurt Aralot. It would ruin everything. Furthermore, he was a keeper! It was in his blood to protect dragonkind. Thinking about harming a rare dragon made his stomach physically recoil.

The other side of his mental battle was just as fierce screaming at him to save Kayla before anything bad happened to that fox that was sitting outside with Warner. If Aralot learned about that fox and got magic, she would stop at nothing to destroy it so she could finish taking Kayla for herself. She was a greedy, evil, dragon and aspects of his story were starting to reveal that about her.

She growled about the dwarf dragons being nice as if she wanted them to be wicked and would have planted the idea in their heads to spit tar at Lena. She scratched her claws into the ground when Caleb didn't kill off the guards but only put them to sleep. She laughed at his description of Lena standing in the middle frozen in fear.

"So there I was looking at this amazing moment trapped in time, and I thought to myself wouldn't it be fantastic to ride on a spellbinding dragon," Caleb continued. He had already circled around Aralot acting out his previous actions. He'd even pretended to jump over logs and cut through plants too. Now he was directly at Aralot's side, and while she was looking at him still interested in the story, he wasn't looking at her face. She hadn't shifted yet to correct that.

"I went up to the gray dragon and climbed up on its back noticing the narrower seat in comparison to fire breathing dragons," Caleb spoke placing his feet against Aralot and hoping that his fast breathing wouldn't betray his stomach roiling on him for what he was about to do. His body was screaming at him. There was a pressure pounding against his head causing his ears to pulse with his own heartbeat. He had to get both of the dragon's eyes and he only had one knife and no prongs to hold on. Not only that, but Aralot's scales were far too slippery. They looked amazing, but they were horrible for his grip. The first stabbed eye could render him in pieces as Aralot fought back. He might not be able to die, but as Warner had just mentioned, he could live in agony for the rest of his life rather well.

"Both of the dragons were like that," Caleb forced his voice to keep talking when he really wanted to fall over. He couldn't hear anything anymore. He couldn't feel anything other than the angry nausea of his stomach. He wanted to curl up or cradle his midsection, but thoughts of Kayla pushing herself back off the ground over and over again for years and years had him keeping his stance wide.

"That's when I saw it," Caleb said feeling Aralot shift beneath him so she could look over her shoulder. He felt her chirp out a question beneath his boots, but he still couldn't hear anything with that buzzing in his ears. "Erana had a jeweled bracelet on her wrist that held the magic the spellbinding dragons were using."

"Can you bring it to me?" Aralot's voice suddenly broke into his thoughts bringing the sound of the birds back instantly.

All at once Caleb wondered if the odd pressure against his head wasn't because he was a keeper, but because Warner had been fighting to keep Aralot away from him. And if Warner had failed to block the dragon out, the only time that Caleb had was now.

He pulled the knife from his boot without thinking about it and lunged toward the closest dragon eye connecting with the squishy substance that burst beneath his pressure. Aralot screamed, and he was wrong that she didn't have any magic in the room because she started

Pg. 536

to inhale and he felt the pulse of blue magic racing toward her mouth so that she could cast it out at him to kill him off.

Aralot was screaming into his head making him lose his focus. A rider with no focus was absolutely done for. It was the many different ways that spellbinding dragons could break a focus that made them so deadly. That and the spells. Aralot spat out her spell just as soon as she got the magic while she flipped onto her back and smashed her head against the ground, slamming Caleb down. He heard his back crunch and his ribs scream.

He had no air with which to breathe, but his muscles had practiced enough to know better than to take his arm out of her eye. If he lost his one grip on the dragon, he was dead. Aralot's spell wasn't one to hurt him, but to heal her eye only he wasn't out of it. She growled and started shaking her head back and forth trying to break him off. She rolled, tumbling him over again so hard that he felt his right leg snap as it hit the earth at a bad angle.

Now he was screaming while Aralot kept yelling into his head to let go so she could eat him just like she was going to eat Kayla when she stunned her well enough to walk the young queen down here to take her life away. He was not going to let that happen. Caleb reached for something his left arm could grip onto like an eyelid so he could move to the other eye and end this.

Aralot was too fast for him. Her tail smashed him off her head ripping at his right arm that hadn't moved which fractured his bones. Air gasped in and out of his lungs with short painful bursts as he crashed to the ground miserable and in pain. He needed more weapons! He needed his prongs to help him stay on and a good team at his side to distract the demon. He needed to be able to anticipate

Aralot's moves, because her head was coming down toward him to bite him apart now that his right side was already broken and he couldn't move. He needed to be Kayla who would never have failed this badly. Caleb shut his eyes tight not willing to see the moment that his body split in half while his mind was unable to die. This was going to be the worst torture he had ever given himself. Even worse, he had let Kayla down.

"Don't let me down."

The words that Gladius had written appeared into his thoughts now that Caleb's eyes were closed again. He didn't want to let Gladius down. He didn't want to let Aralot's head get down either. It was interesting that out of all the words Gladius could have chosen to write, it was those four that he had picked.

Gladius may not have been talking about himself at all. He could have been talking about his wife Jean or all the other queens that had died in this coffin. Don't let them down. At the very last moment, Caleb used his abs to roll himself away from the ivory-white teeth of Aralot so that her face hit the ground without him. She had great teeth. He tried not to notice as he screamed out the pain, refusing to let himself pass out. The pulsing was back in his head. His broken arm and leg burned. His back and lungs ached.

"You're done eating us all!" Caleb shouted feeling like an idiot.

He should have brought magic into the room. Sure, Aralot would have used it against him, but she was using magic anyway. Keeping magic away from her was what all the other kings had decided to do. In order to win, Caleb had to do the opposite of what they did.

Aralot started to pull herself up to use her tail to smash him apart next, and he let himself search for the pulse of magic drawing it into his hand quicker than he expected. It came rushing at him from the ground and then rushing toward Aralot's greedy mouth as she sucked it up trying to keep it away from him.

Caleb pulled harder while he focused on breathing. He could see Aralot's stomach expanding from the magic in her body while her wings spread out glowing with the pleasure of gaining magic again. He didn't doubt that she would do something horrible with it if he let her.

She was so enticed by her greed of the substance that all she could do was continue to draw it in while she ignored the knife in her eye. Caleb didn't know if there were rules in magic that said a person couldn't cast two spells at once since he had never heard of anyone doing it, but he was doing it. He let his right hand—that he couldn't feel beneath the pain of the broken arm—keep summoning the magic to distract Aralot's desires, while his left hand used magic to yank out the knife from one eye and plunge it into the other one.

He expected an explosion but what he got was silence. The birds stopped. Aralot stopped sucking in magic. Her body stood there as if frozen while the piles of gold started to disappear and the grass beneath him turned into the hard stone floor. Walls and a roof suddenly sprung up where there had been sky. Trees turned into piles of dust as if they had been real living things.

Caleb gasped as he remembered what Valiant had said about Ritz turning into a pile of dust. The trees *had* been alive! They were the queens of Aralot, stuck to the demon spellbinding dragon unable to find rest as they fed their love to the dragon and the rest of the kingdom forever. As the last tree fell, that's when Aralot exploded. Green time magic shoved outward from the center of the room and pushed with it Caleb who had no ability to grab anything with his busted body. The last thing he heard was Warner screaming.

Devious

Tristan

If it wasn't for the sound of the castle creaking as blue flashes of magic flung upward from all directions, or the sound of his father screaming for everyone to get out, or the sound of the guards running, or the sudden sound of hundreds of trees falling over outside, it would have been the sound of Riven that had Tristan jumping from his bedroom window without any gear at all and no shoes.

Tristan grabbed at the guide rope that Riven was wearing noticing how the dragon didn't have a saddle because Tristan hadn't planned on riding him anywhere today. His day was going to be filled with showing Lena around the town because he was trying to avoid the ware now that it wasn't working for him. His plans to stay away from the revolting riders had vanished because chunks of the castle were exploding outward and smashing everywhere.

Riven landed on the ground trying to shield Tristan from the worst of the blows by rolling, attempting to knock Tristan off his back and beneath him. Tristan held to the rope refusing to land even if he was already on the ground. There was a green glow that had shoved past them that was continuing the destruction of the trees. He wanted to see it.

Magic was running away. The gems on his clothes were hot inside his seams and even though the green spell had passed, his gems struggled to keep their protective charms. They failed all at the same time bursting apart so that Tristan ripped out the hottest ones and watched as their blue glows pushed into the air and away from him. His once beautiful gems were pieces of rubble now, too small to hold any good-sized amount of magic.

He would have loved to blame Ritz for his loss of magic, only Ritz was dead, and Tristan knew of only one thing that would cause all the magic in Aralot to run away. The royal crown was destroyed. Where was Vermelo?

"Screaming at his men," Riven pointed the direction with his tail. Vermelo was indeed screaming, ordering people to retrieve certain documents from the castle that was still blowing up into the air before the papers were lost to the destructive forces around them. The soldiers scrambled back into the fray doing their best, and Tristan gave up on blaming Vermelo. If the Captain of the Guard had been the one breaking the crown, he would have been prepared for the sudden loss of magic and guessed that the castle would burst. This wasn't him. It was probably Jack.

Tristan looked around once more and shrugged. He couldn't do anything about Jack. He had always been wary of the man ever since Jack proved that he could hold a good lie, but Jack was also the magical king, so if he felt it the right thing to clear out the magic of the land it was his job to do so. Tristan could only hope that Jack had further plans to bring it all back. Magic was too much a part of Tristan's life to see it leave forever, and he was certain that Jack would feel the same way.

Pg. 542

"Tristan!" King Klavian ran up to him incredibly climbing up onto Riven's back which was a place he had never been before. Seeing his father had Tristan glancing around for his mom, hoping that she had made it out of the castle and to a safer location.

"No sign of your mom yet," Riven answered. *"Your dad's shoulder is interesting."*

It was wounded and Tristan didn't have any magic to heal his dad. He started to reach for bandages to do the job the slow way with the intention to clean the wound, stop the bleed, and wrap it up. His arms never made it to Riven's saddlebag, because Riven wasn't wearing it.

"You have to fix this! Klavian shouted pointing to his shoulder.

King Klavian had a gaping wound filled with green puss. The entire castle that Gladius had built with magic was rubble. The trees were all down. The town had holes, and there would be citizens in need of medical care, yet here was King Klavian complaining about a fang wound.

Who had done this? Tristan scanned the area and it didn't take him long to spot the culprit. The blue night dragon Norber, that had snuck his way into ware classes with Valiant, was licking at his fangs while he laughed himself silly. It was bad, but Tristan had to chuckle too. Now there was a dragon that knew how to keep himself in class. Bonded to the steward no one would tell him to leave. Norber was probably reacting to the rider's recent protest.

Kayla was immobile and both Caleb and Warner were missing. For some reason that was enough to make the section leaders stand together and refuse to work. Once the section leaders stood up in the mess hall and stated their demands, all the other riders decided it was a nice time to turn lazy and copy them. They demanded that Tristan send for Caleb to come back even if he had told them that Caleb was busy and not banished for life.

Mulligan, Notley, Russel and Malone treated Tristan like he had kicked Caleb out even if it was Caleb ditching the ware all by himself. It was like a spell had been placed upon the rider's heads and they couldn't pick up a single piece of gear unless they had the princess and her eternal lover both back alive and under their watch.

The worst of Mulligan's claims still shoved against Tristan's ears painfully. "If my princess and future king don't work, I don't either."

They were so annoying. Caleb wasn't anything but a good teacher. Just because he had been in love with Kayla forever and had started carrying magic didn't make him a king. Tristan had considered putting his own spell on the section leaders to make them all work, but he hadn't because magic was acting strangely, and now he knew why. It was anticipating not working at all.

"Do something!" Klavian screamed grabbing at Tristan's arm. "Kayla is behind this!"

Tristan looked over at the ware to find that someone, probably Mulligan, had gotten all the riders to gear up and stand on the field. They were not doing anything to help but stood there watching the continued destruction. Tristan had no idea if they would move if he asked them to help care for the town. In any case, the only flying dragons were a group of seasoned scouts circling the doctor's office where Kayla slept.

Pg. 544

"Dad, Kayla can't wake up. She's not cognizant enough to tell a dragon to fang you."

"It's her I'm telling you! Norber can't lie to me. He admitted to being inside a keeper bond, and there is no other keeper that would do this to me. Kayla is getting back at me for trying to poison her so that we could get rid of Valiant."

Tristan lost his smile. He started to reach for a knife to aim it at his dad's head. He changed his mind for a rope and then changed his mind again. His *dad* had been the one trying to destroy Kayla! Tristan had spent hours trying to solve this mystery blaming Colts, especially Ritz, for the death threats.

"You were trying to kill Valiant?!" Tristan cried, reaching for his weapons and dropping his hands over and over again. This was his dad! As Kayla's ware leader, it was his job to hold him to justice, but how did he hold his dad responsible when he was the steward? He loved his dad!

"My father told me personally that spellbinding dragons are the death of kings. Kayla can't control that monster. Everyone knows it. Valiant is going to be the death of us all. I'm sorry if that makes her sad but she's dying anyway. The least we could do is make sure that her monster wasn't alive to kill us off after she fades. But the poison wasn't working, and Kayla figured me out before I got a better plan, so we'll need to find something else—"

"No!" Tristan screamed. "Your father was wrong about spellbinding dragons. What would he know about them when he'd never met one?"

"Don't talk about my dad like that!" Klavian said turning to glare at Norber who was still laughing so hard that he was now on his side unable to help himself. Looking at Norber was like looking at a baby giggle for seeing a ball bouncing for the first time. It was one of those ridiculous things that tugged the smile back on Tristan's face and he couldn't keep it off this time when he looked back at his dad.

"King Virgil Cluster IV was wrong," Tristan repeated.

"Well, you don't see Valiant here, do you? Kayla gets closer to death and what does he do? He blows up everything that has ever held magic! I was in that castle. Valiant was trying to kill me! Once it's possible to move her, we are shipping Kayla off to Vankerdale and that's that. I don't care what her parents will say. We'll find some way to banish the child. Right now, I need you to get me that anti-bonding stuff so I can get this dragon out of my head. Kayla will not be in my thoughts to control me."

Norber stopped laughing. He got to his feet and silently looked at Tristan, waiting to hear what Tristan was going to do—protect the dragon bond or shatter it. Tristan sighed. He still didn't feel it his place to tell Klavian that Kayla was engaged in Vankerdale even if it sounded like he already knew. There was no need to bring it up now that Conner was changing that. Kayla was too busy to consider dragon sabotage. Klavian was the first person to suspect it. He once had Misty the ice dragon in his head, and the ware leader Rogan had broken the bond. Klavian had always claimed that Misty sought to control him too, but what he never wanted to admit to was that an ice dragon, as devious as they were, were incredibly picky about who they bonded. They only respected the best. It was an honor that Misty had fanged him. Not a curse.

Pg. 546

"Dad. I'm not going to break your bond," Tristan told him, crossing his arms to enforce his message. "Maybe your father told you that dragons are horrible for kings, but they like you. They want to share their lives with you. That is a privilege. And need I point out, you're not the king."

"You horrible dragon lover. I will make the doctors do it," Klavian declared. He slipped off Riven and Norber started shouting into the air telling all the other dragons what Tristan had said so that no one inside the ware would break the bond.

"Why would Valiant shatter the magic?" Tristan called out to his departing father. "He loves magic. If anything, he would try to keep it around. Dad, use your head here. Magic leaving means that the crown was destroyed. The person we need to find is Jack."

"Would Jack really kill himself to break a crown? I think he put Valiant up to it," Klavian declared, still storming toward the riders that were refusing to work for them. Yeah, Klavian wasn't going to meet with anything but resistance over there because Mulligan had gotten it into his head that Caleb was the king.

Tristan looked down at Riven to commiserate. Norber knew that Klavian didn't like dragons in his thoughts. He was asking for trouble on this, but Tristan still didn't feel it was the right choice to always break bonds.

"Are you connected to Kayla?" Tristan inquired looking toward Norber and noticing how dirty the dragon's scales were. Kayla would have kept him cleaner. She would have seen to that chip in his scale near his left side. If not her, then Valiant would have.

"No," Norber answered. He grinned again and looked toward the south. What he said next had Tristan rethinking that broken bond thing. Riven was quick with the translation telling him that Norber was claiming to be with Conner Felding, Ritz's son.

Puzzle pieces started clicking together inside of Tristan's mind and Norber returned to laughing as he watched. This was Conner sneaking his way into the castle, not Kayla. It was Conner setting a trap to keep Klavian from further picking on Kayla, because it was Conner who had been secretly defending her for years. Tristan knew that Conner was somehow a Felding, but Ritz's son?!

"Who was Ritz then?" Tristan asked shaking his head. Riven shrugged. Norber chuckled at him. Tristan sighed and started to look around for Lena. She'd help him sort this out. Either her or Kayla. Yes, this would be something that Kayla knew already, and she wouldn't laugh at him for being slow on the uptake. She'd explain it to him nicely.

"Don't ask Kayla. She's going to want to cut your head off. She loved Ritz remember?" Riven prompted.

Oh yeah. She was the only one in the entire kingdom who had ever liked the guy. That was probably why she liked him. Ritz was a Felding and therefore a keeper and now that it was revealed what Ritz had been, Tristan smacked himself on the head not needing to find Lena, although he looked for her too to make sure she wasn't hurt. He scanned for his mom again and then jumped off Riven to rush to Vermelo.

"The crown?" Tristan asked. "Did Jack have it?"

"Caleb had it," Vermelo answered in such an offhanded manner that Tristan felt his jaw drop. It was Vermelo that had told Mulligan that Caleb was the king and that was why no one wanted to work for Tristan! The stinker!

"What do you mean that Caleb had it? It worked for him?"

"Obviously," Vermelo retorted. "Are you going to stand there and gawk or get in there and help?"

"So Jack got Caleb to blow himself up to destroy the crown? I thought Caleb was doing something to save Kayla…" Oh. He was. Everything really was falling into place even as the castle gave a horrible grinding sound and collapsed inward. The blue magic stopped lifting from it and Vermelo stood there in horror at the number of soldiers that hadn't come back out.

"They're smart men," Tristan stated. "They'd have found a pocket to hide beneath. I'll see if I can get help in clearing through the stone."

He looked toward the riders and then he gave up on them and looked at Norber instead.

"Can you help find survivors?"

"Yes," Norber answered, and without needing to say more than that, wild dragons that had been dodging the spell whipped trees swooped upon the castle and started to help dig.

"Norber just bonded my dad," Tristan explained as Vermelo squinted at the dragons trying to figure out why they were so helpful. "And these ones aren't exactly wild. They're in Conner Felding's keeper bond."

"That one's not," Vermelo pointed into the air at a mature red dragon. "That one belongs to a different Colt that I've been tracking. This shall be interesting. The Colts have always been good at restoring what magic destroys. I think we're going to be working rather closely with them."

Tristan shrugged. That didn't bother *him* any. He scanned the air to memorize the dragons and smiled when he made out Reed. Lena was on his back, safe from the magical storm. Seeing her up there had Tristan changing his mind suddenly about everything. Lena was so fun to be around. She was smart and adventurous and in the perfect place in her life, looking for something new. She was debating about staying here and Tristan quite liked the idea.

Kayla had once told him that he could keep the castle, but there was no castle left to keep. Now that there wasn't any magical pressure anywhere to tell people what to do or what to think or what part in life they had to play, Tristan felt a strange release of his former obligations.

Why had he felt so strongly before that he needed to be in charge of Aralot, follow after his father and continuously bash against the Brixtons for control? His father was stubbornly trying to keep his control as he faced off with Mulligan, who stood before him with his full ware army refusing to move or hand over poison that would break Norber's bond. That wasn't the legacy that Tristan wanted. He didn't want to be in opposition to his friends all the time. He had actually rather enjoyed being on Kayla's side while it lasted.

Tristan smiled at the way she had laughed at him in the restaurant and her trick to use Sparkle so she could talk about Valiant. Kayla wasn't his enemy here. She had been doing the same thing he was this whole time, trying to sort out why the magic of the land was so confusing and busted. It looked like Vermelo had known and given the crown to Caleb, which was now destroyed, so…

Tristan ran toward the ware skipping around his arguing father and glaring at riders that attempted to block his path. He shoved a few out of his way and yanked open the door to the doctor's office to see if Kayla was alive or dead. Dr. Weber was in there pacing and he answered before Tristan could ask a thing.

"Still breathing."

That was good news, but if the crown was destroyed did that mean that Caleb was? Caleb had been Kayla's magically eternal lover ever since he had first seen the girl. That's what magic had made him. So with magic gone, was it still that way or had Caleb sacrificed his life for Kayla's? No one got away with destroying the crown without death unless Caleb had found some way to cheat death and that was why he had taken Valiant with him.

"Riven!" Tristan cried as he stepped out of the doctor's office and smiled at a few riders who likewise wanted to know the answer about Kayla's wellness.

"Valiant claims that Caleb made it," Riven answered. *"Bantin survived too because he's been in Vankderale with Coal. Valiant is heading toward them because the spell that took the magic away burned at his scales. He left, but he'll come back when Kayla asks him too."*

It was magical foresight that had placed Bantin out of the way of the curse. Tristan hated to think what would have happened to him if he had magic in his belly and it suddenly burst. They would have lost him, but the ice dragon hadn't been inside of Aralot at all, so everyone was spared the tragedy.

"Why did he go to Vankerdale?" Tristan asked.

"He was following the path of the crown," Riven answered. *"He chased Caleb there when he took the crown to Coal to destroy it."*

Ice dragons loved magical treasures so it wasn't very surprising that Bantin had noticed the crown leaving the kingdom. He would have smelled it with Caleb. Tristan returned through the group of riders back to his dad who had a good argument going but not one that was going to make Mulligan move.

"You don't see me as your king but the portals are gone. Jack can't reach us for days. You have to listen to somebody. Without order, this ware turns to chaos. We will sort something out with Vankerdale to maintain our rights. We will not be merging with them, and even if we do, King Tyler can't reach us for days either. You need order."

"They're all lined up. They look pretty organized, Dad," Tristan said as he asked to borrow some bandages from a rider near him. He took them and started to wrap his dad's shoulder. "Don't worry. Kayla will straighten it out. They're worried about her and Caleb who I hear is fine."

Tristan gave Mulligan a smile because while the man was still being stubborn, he wasn't listening to the decree to break Norber's new bond. It only showed that there were things that Mulligan agreed with Tristan on, and if they could agree on things like this, they could get the ware functioning together. Mulligan had his moments, but the magical pressure holding him down was gone. There were only his own commitments and his own honor which was set on serving the king.

Pg. 552

"Dad," Tristan smiled tying up the fang wound. "Think of it this way. We're finally free. There is no magic to dictate that we fight with the Brixtons. There's no magic to make dragons dangerous to kings. We can start over and do everything right this time. Stop being scared. Norber has to love you which is highly amusing from any angle considering who he was bonded to right before you."

"Who?" Klavian asked, turning away from Mulligan and the riders that now disregarded his authority.

"Ritz," Tristan answered hearing the surprised inhales from riders who could hear them. "Norber used to be bonded to Ritz. Mind boggling huh?"

Klavian opened his mouth in horror for a second before he shut it and turned thoughtful. "Well, I suppose there would be lots of information that Ritz had that I could learn…"

"Norber was probably thinking the same thing about you," Tristan laughed. That was going to be one smart dragon. Norber had ties to the Colts, the castle, Valiant, Kayla, and Conner. He knew how to stack it up. Tristan shook his head at the way Norber wanted to know everything, although, oddly enough, Tristan felt no threat by it.

"I bet I can talk with Kayla without her wanting to spar with my words," Tristan grinned, anticipating the release of their mutual animosity. "This is going to be good."

"Particularly if your words haven't gotten any better," Kayla's voice piped up from behind a group of riders. How she snuck through them all without them knowing was impressive. The riders turned to see her, and they may have lost their willingness to act, but they hadn't lost their heart. A loud cheer rang up from the ware, causing Kayla to cover her ears while she squished on through.

"I was so mad at you!" Kayla hissed at Tristan through her smile to everyone else. Tristan had to laugh at her for her continued tricks. This was her trying not to show everyone that she was upset.

"Mad for..."

"Ritz! Gosh, Tristan! He meant so much to me. I was totally going to kill you off myself or else destroy all your magic spheres in the desert to make you hurt, but Conner was against my anger and it looks like he's all about helping you."

Kayla looked toward the castle where the "wild" dragons were being the only useful ones. That was indeed how it looked right now. Conner was on his side which was unusual since Tristan had never really talked with Conner back when the man was a mail runner.

"Now that I have the capacity to pick my own emotions again, I have decided that I am *still* mad at you."

"Ritz was trying to kill me. He nearly succeeded twice if you remember. If I left him alone, I'd be dead."

"Sounds good to me," Kayla mumbled.

"Are we always going to be like this? It's a Cluster and Felding curse that our families clash this much. I thought those curses were gone. Kayla, I'm very sorry. I know you liked Ritz, but I think you were the only one... one of the only ones... who liked him. Look. I'm sorry. I was defending myself. Can you really look me in the face and tell me that if there was something trying to kill you that you wouldn't fight back? I thought your whole life was one large battle of you fighting to keep it."

Kayla shut her eyes on him and he wasn't sure if she was drifting off to sleep again until she opened them back up and gave him a sad nod.

"I'm sorry too. You're right. Ritz nearly had you and that was my fault. I told him that I felt pestered by you."

That's why Ritz had come at him! Kayla had felt threatened by him and put him on her worst enemy list despite everything Tristan had done to stay off it. He had failed at being her friend when it mattered, and Ritz had somehow succeeded. Tristan had to fix this feeling of always being a nemesis because while the riders may still be celebrating Kayla being awake, the dragons would pick up on her terse whispered conversation and know her true feelings. No one would respect him again if they thought Kayla hated him.

Everything Tristan had ever feared was right here before him. The riders had Kayla Brixton in their hearts. They had spent so much time worrying about her and trying to save her from Vankerdale and herself that every small victory of hers felt like their own victory. He was done for. No one would accept him on the throne if they had Kayla to cheer on instead. At one time that would have felt like the largest blow to him in all the world. It didn't feel like it anymore. He didn't enjoy the political battle. It had always been a forced thing on his part where he tried to remain in the spot he felt his parents had placed him. It wasn't what he really wanted to be. Kayla felt he was a threat to her position as a princess, so it was high time he shared what he really was.

"Kayla, I don't want the castle anymore." She laughed at him for the statement. "Not because it's broken, but because I don't feel like I have to conform to all those weird rules if Aralot is being rewritten. I can be free to be who I want to be for once! I never liked fighting with you over it. Not once did it bring me any happiness, only misery. I really like being a ware leader so I would love for you to do me one favor. Let me die slowly the long hard way: overworked, wrung out, in the service of man and dragon. The section leaders claim they'll only respect you and Caleb at present so a little faith in me would be nice if you have the notion to forgive me yet again. You can totally keep me away from the castle by letting me have this job. I don't want to be your competition anymore."

"Yeah," Kayla answered and then she jumped into his arms surprising him. "Caleb got hurt!" she wailed.

Tristan blinked stupidly at the top of her auburn head and then turned his stupor toward his dad. This was the second time that Kayla had hugged him when she was scared, and it was startling that Tristan still felt the same way about it as he had the first time. He didn't hate Kayla. He wouldn't claim to love her like a wife, but a close sister would suffice. They would fight, but they would always be friends; near siblings. He hugged her back glad that he could put a name to the sort of love he felt for Kayla Brixton.

"Is he hurt bad, little sister?"

"I don't know! Valiant didn't stay around, but he heard Warner screaming about it," Kayla whimpered, clutching at Tristan tighter as if he could help her feel better. Tristan had no idea where Caleb was or what he had been doing. Riven provided the answers for him making Tristan feel grateful that he was part of Kayla's keeper bond. He was changing his mind about keepers. They weren't servants to dragons. They were caretakers, with lots of love waiting to be spread around. With those portals knocked out, it was these keeper connections that would tell them what was happening across the kingdom.

"You know what? Caleb had Warner with him. Warner is an incredibly smart dragon. He'll take care of Caleb. It's going to be fine."

Kayla clutched at him again and then wiped at her eyes, giving him a brave nod.

"And you're going to be fine being bonded to a dragon," Tristan told his dad. He looked at Mulligan next. "And you're going to get this place together and help Vermelo clear up the rubble and dig out soldiers and help the town get stone blocks out of their homes and shops."

Mulligan looked at Kayla for a nod, and then his "yes, sir," was all Tristan needed to hear before he grabbed his dad's arm and started to lead him to the ware leader office.

"Dad! Did you hear about the dragon Aralot!?"

Riven had said that Caleb had destroyed her after destroying the crown. There had been a super old spellbinding dragon living inside of their kingdom and none of them knew about it except for Ritz!

"Yes," Klavian spoke back now able to get information from Norber. "And it was horrible! It would get inside keeper's heads and make them love her. Every time they looked at her, they became confused and no other creature or person could compare. Ritz hated that beast. He was determined to never love anything because he

Pg. 557

didn't want Aralot taking his love away. Only he failed to not love Kayla because she loved him. I have no idea how Caleb killed Aralot when the spells on the room dictated that only a king and a keeper could enter the realm of Aralot. We're still missing a few things, but we'll figure it out soon. I *knew* there were hidden male keepers in Aralot! It was Ritz and Conner. They were supposed to be bound to the care of Aralot, only Conner was kept out of the kingdom, and Ritz was the greatest Colt of all time, so he'd never squeal. You know, hearing Norber isn't so bad. I never knew these things about Ritz before."

Tristan hadn't either and he suspected that if Ritz was still alive, none of them would be hearing anything about him still. Some people's legacy grew greater after they died and that was the case with Ritz. Once feared, he was going to be deeply respected for the service he gave them all, holding back Aralot, the ancient spellbinding dragon.

Tristan unlocked the ware leader office door and found himself feeling relieved as he stepped inside after his dad.

"I knew the two of you would end up in here," Aria said glancing at a small brown sack at her feet. "I thought that perhaps the most important thing to grab from the castle was the extra ice dragon venom. Never mind that we don't have working portals right now. Mr. Grumpy knows how to reconstruct more. They'll be back. I didn't want everyone finding the venom and becoming immune to portals. There's only one vial that I need you to look at."

Aria pulled a vial from the sack onto the table as Tristan shut the door. It was Bantin's vial and the vial was completely empty. Someone had either dumped this or bonded their magical ice dragon.

"You think he's bonded?" Tristan asked his mom.

Pg. 558

She nodded her head yes. Klavian disagreed thinking that one of the Brixtons had dumped it to prevent him from being bonded. Tristan gave his parents a smile, determined to figure it out one day. After all, Bantin was training with Valiant. Being bonded would make an appearance eventually. There were mysteries inside of Aralot still to be discovered and that made his job of ware leader super fun.

Broken

Caleb

"**O**uch!" Caleb cried out, as he tried to roll over and remembered that his arm and leg had snapped. His arm wasn't dangling off him at a bad angle anymore, but it still hurt, and he was scared to look at it in case it wasn't there at all.

"Caleb," Warner hummed into his head. *"You did it! You are the most amazing king and worst lover that Aralot has ever known."*

Caleb smiled about being Aralot's worst lover because that meant that he was Kayla's best one.

"Looks like he's awake!" Ian's voice had Caleb opening his eyes to see August running into a tent. Ian was already in there reading a book that he tossed to the side without marking his place.

"What are you doing here?" Caleb asked them, trying to calculate the amount of time it should have taken for the two treasure hunters to travel on foot from the castle up north to this location in the south. Caleb had taken portals. These two must have done the same thing or there was no way they could be here.

"A little bird told us that we would want to be here to see if any new relics popped out of the ground," August grinned. "You were not quite the relic we expected."

"Bird?" Caleb questioned. "You're bonded to a secret dragon?"

"Who us?" Ian laughed. "No. We don't talk with dragons. Only birds." Ian gave August a special look that had August laughing back at him. Caleb wasn't so sure about these two. They either had dragons of their own, or they knew of a magical artifact that told them things.

"You took a portal?" Caleb asked.

"About those," August stopped chuckling. "You destroyed them, Caleb. We found Warner dragging you out of the castle with this large blasting green spell chasing after you, and when that spell struck, everything magical blew up. I don't know what you did, but if your aim was to destroy magic, you succeeded."

"We were going to tie you up and take you to Jack for some great ransom money since you're going to be the most wanted man in the land, but then we realized that the portals are gone," Ian added. "It's the slow way for all of us now. Why tie you up when you can hardly run anyway? Now that you're awake you can explain what happened."

"I saved Kayla. I think." Caleb said. "Did you see Valiant?"

Caleb took in a deep breath and got the courage to glance down at his legs. They were both there! His right one was splinted and he could already tell it was going to cause him a limp for the rest of his life if he didn't get magic to heal this thing. He took in another breath and looked at his right arm. Also there. It was wrapped tightly down to his side, but his fingers couldn't move. This was the sort of injury that had doctors cutting off the break before it could get infected. His arm was gone. He couldn't be an effective dragon rider or teacher with his arm gone. He stared at it. Warner stayed silent.

"We saw Valiant," August spoke keeping his voice calm in the face of Caleb's shock. "He screamed at the spell and then charged upward into the air to get away from it, running for Vankerdale. I guess he doesn't like spells that take magic away."

Caleb forced himself to gaze away from his arm into August's face instead. He inhaled deeply so he wouldn't put himself into shock or send his mind into a panic about his missing and broken limbs. There would be time to relearn how to use a broken body later. He was okay for now. Being broken didn't mean that he had failed anything. It didn't mean that Kayla would love him any less because he couldn't jet stream.

He shouldn't have thought that. His heart screamed at him as if missing the connection of Kayla's love that it had always felt. It was gone. Was Kayla gone? Would she still love him now that she had no magical pressure to do so? Had he doomed himself completely? Was she even still alive?!

"Warner!" Caleb screamed struggling to get himself up as his leg shot pain into him and nearly caused him to black out. Both Ian and August ran to catch him, and then true to their kind natures, they carried him outside so he could see his dragon.

"Warner is fine," August continued talking in a calm manner even if Warner wasn't fine. The dragon was lying on the ground crying.

"I can't answer you, Caleb," Warner whimpered. *"I don't know Kayla's state unless Valiant is here to tell me."*

"Well am I not a keeper anymore?" Caleb asked, looking down at his right arm again where he used to be able to see the blue line of Jack's foresight. If he was still a keeper, then he wouldn't need Valiant. He could add some other dragon to his thoughts that would be able to tell him about Kayla, although from Tia's stories he did have to be near the dragon to make a connection happen so it wasn't helpful right now when the dragons he wanted were at the King's Ware. His blue keeper line was covered by the bandages hiding what he was, but he hadn't wanted to get rid of his keeper line by cutting his whole arm off.

"A what?" Ian asked. "You blew up magic to make yourself a keeper? Are you mad?"

"I didn't do it," Caleb panted leaning against Ian to hold him up. "Pyro and Jack made me a keeper so I could go in and defeat the demon that was killing Kayla. I defeated the demon that all the other kings couldn't kill off, but we knew the consequences would be the loss of Aralot's magic. Does that also mean that Aralot no longer has any keepers because that is a magical connection and the magic is gone?"

"How do we get the magic back?" August asked.

"Find the ice dragon," Ian pointed out.

"I don't know if you're still a keeper," Warner sniffled. *"I'm too sad to think about other dragons when you can't ride me."*

"Hey, I still have a good side *left*," Caleb attempted to cheer up his dragon by making a pun about his functioning left side. Warner only cried harder.

"I can answer your question about keepers," Ian declared looking up into the air. "Right there is one of Tia's spies. It can tell us. Are you still hearing keeper thoughts?!" Ian shouted upward even if the dragon's ears could hear them without screaming. Yeah, perhaps Ian and August weren't bonded. They just used to have special magical trinkets. Now those would be broken.

"Yes," the spying dragon answered. It rambled off some other words that Caleb pouted about, not because he didn't like them, but because August was able to squint at the creature and determine what it said while Caleb couldn't understand the dragon speech.

"She," August shrugged, "is telling us to go to the King's Ware to meet Jack."

"Never heard that order before," Ian smiled as he looked behind him at the tent. "We might have to drag Caleb…"

"Warner can drag all of us," August decided. "We'll tie Warner up to the wagon. Jack always did say that dragons made the best horse."

"He also said that he would pay us for our bird," Ian added. "I think now is the best time to sell it to him."

"Now that it's busted?" August laughed. "Think he'll fall for it?"

"I'm surprised it wasn't something that Tristan thought to destroy," Ian continued to chat as he led Caleb over to a wagon and both treasure hunters carefully put him inside. Caleb felt his tears picking up next. He was useless! Even worse, he was looking at nearly two weeks of sitting in a wagon driving himself crazy with questions about Kayla now that they all had to walk to the other side of Aralot.

"I have long legs. I'll walk us really fast."

Warner shook the tears from his eyes as he stood up, determined to be brave and get Caleb to where he wanted to be. Caleb let himself slump into the wagon and the tears started to come out. He hurt both physically and emotionally. He was right to think that everyone who wasn't a Colt and hadn't trained to resist the queen's love of the land would be feeling a great loss in their souls when it vanished.

"The bird wasn't exactly a statue or a game piece," August kept chatting. "It was more like a bookmark."

Ian started laughing. "You got around Tristan's spell by calling it a bookmark? I thought of it as a suncatcher."

"It's not a suncatcher."

"Well, it's not thin enough for a bookmark."

"It could fit nicely inside of a cloth book," August insisted.

"It could fit nicely dangling in a window," Ian replied still laughing.

Caleb used his good arm to shield his face from the sun as he tried to not think about what he could fit nicely inside. There was a certain oblong wooden box that he could have been buried in if he hadn't had Valiant bind his life to that fox. Thinking of which…

Pg. 566

"*The fox is still with me,*" Warner answered. "*I didn't notice it shattering, but it did glow brightly as the green spell hit and then it glowed again a few minutes later. You will glow again, Caleb. I have decided to not be sad about you. You will stand again and you will be magnificent.*"

Magnificent felt a long way off, so Caleb focused on breathing in the present, only smiling when Warner had chatted with Tia's spy and gotten the information that Kayla had lived.

Scale

Kayla

"**K**ayla! He is doing it again!" Russel screamed as he burst into the mess hall where the current discussion revolved around if the new castle should have a secret entrance into the throne room or not.

Klavian, Aria, Jack, and Tia went quiet as Kayla stood up and gave them a shrug happier than not that Merlock was acting up. They had cleared the rubble off the castle, but that only opened up the hole into Merlock's home beneath it, so he had taken to popping up during the day and covering the ground with tar. At night he would be out there building his underground tunnels above the ground. Everyone was getting tired of knocking those back down.

"Hehe," Merlock laughed into her head. *"You should see their faces! I thought that you'd want out of there anyway. Sparkle claims that she can smell Caleb getting close."*

She was so out of this discussion! Kayla dashed from the room grateful that Sparkle had a dragon nose better than any of the other ones, and that she would think to tell Kayla about Caleb when he finally got back.

"Is being a dragon rider always like being an acrobat?" Tyler asked her as she exited the mess hall. He had been kicked out of the discussion hours ago, but he didn't mind at all. He was more than happy to sit around and watch dragon training. Coal was sleeping out among the trees that Tyler himself had brought back up. Yeah, he was loving his vacation into Aralot so far. Tyler was learning spells and all about dragons.

Kayla gave Tyler a smile and a nod, glad that they were done with all their awkward discussions. He was going to marry Adelyn Peyton. Whoever that girl was, Kayla loved her. Even better, Tyler had told her that he wasn't mad at her for never coming back. He was simply glad that Vankerdale and Aralot had a strong foundation to build upon.

She didn't have to marry Tristan either. They both had already silently agreed upon that, but Tristan had made it public before both of their parents so she didn't have to say anything. Glorious!

"Kayla can we just agree that we should never marry each other and get it over with? You're great and all, but not for me. We've always been a puzzle with all the wrong pieces. Let's be fake siblings instead. You need some of those to compete with all your fake uncles," Tristan had said.

Aria had shrugged and stated that at least the both of them had given it an honest effort. Kayla had felt instant relief over the way Tristan was stepping down from things lately. She had expected to need to perform some sort of complicated trickery to keep Tristan at bay, or else talk her Uncle Conner into taking over the throne to appease Aralot's magical laws since Uncle Conner fit all the descriptions of being noble born, a male keeper, and capable of using magic even if her dad had made himself a keeper trying to keep the peace. Now that the laws could be rewritten, none of those hard things had to happen. They could all live the way they wanted to. Kayla knew exactly how Tristan had felt when he said he was finally free. They were! They didn't have to bash against each other anymore. It was so nice!

Jack had been a bit more direct with his newest ideas for her. *"No more getting engaged without telling me about it first,"* her father had ordered.

She felt too young to get married or engaged, but she wasn't too young to run toward the castle, and if she was running, the busy body Tyler was going to run along after her.

"Merlock is splattering tar," she told him, although she already suspected that Merlock had stopped now that he had gotten her out of her meeting.

"Me? Nope. Sparkle doesn't think that I can make a tar sculpture. She made an ice sculpture of you and I'm trying to copy it. This stuff is hard, but don't you stop me. I've got to try."

The ice sculpture was placed far away from the tar, but even at its distance, it wasn't hard to see because it was so huge! Why did Sparkle make her the size of a house?! There was no way Kayla could let Merlock make a tar sculpture that same height.

Valiant's dragon laughter wafted down toward her and he shot out a spell toward the ice that made it even larger.

Pg. 570

"Valiant!" Kayla laughed at him, trying not to find his part in this funny. "I'm a bit shorter than that! Merlock, don't you dare make it that tall! Sparkle, no more dares."

She heard Sparkle laughing next and Kayla knew it was going to take more than that to make Valiant and Sparkle cooperate. She'd do better against Merlock. All he needed was a bright light shining his direction instead of this cloudy sky they had going on, and he'd pop back beneath the ground.

Kayla looked toward the monastery and then over at Tyler before she scanned outward trying to spot Caleb laying in the back of a wagon. From Tia's sources, Caleb hadn't moved much, but he had good timing in arriving. Today was the day that they were holding services for Ritz at the monastery. Everyone was invited and they expected a large crowd mostly because they were going to give Ritz an empty grave beside all the other kings, and because they were going to reveal his true name. He was going to go down in history as one of the uncrowned kings of Aralot. Jack had already commissioned a safer, prettier crown created.

"You know from all this time being over here, I still can't get over how pretty Sparkle is even if she is a pain to work with," Tyler said watching Sparkle loop over Merlock's current pile of lumpy tar so she could snigger at his progress. Sparkle had been instigating trouble a lot lately, but most of it was to tease Valiant and he was all about teasing her back.

"Come on. I'll talk you through how to use a healing spell," Kayla said turning away from the sight of her overly large ice self to head in the direction that Caleb would be coming. Tyler became the attentive listener beside her. She hadn't personally taught him any spells yet, so she knew that Tyler saw this as a victory on his part. She had told him several times in the past that she would never reveal magic to him. Well, she had finally changed her mind. She was going to need him knowing a thing or two so that he could help her.

Kayla squealed when she caught sight of Warner's dusty brown scales coming toward her. A week and a half without Caleb was just too long. She felt his absence even from half a day let alone twenty half days. Kayla raced to the wagon as Warner came to a weary stop.

Caleb was laying in the back of the wagon covered in sweat as his body tried to fight with the brokenness. His brown hair was matted, his eyes were shut in pain, his mouth was a grim line. She had heard that Caleb had broken a few things, but this wasn't what she had in mind. Seeing Caleb like this made her whimper and then think about all the other broken people in Aralot that didn't have access to quick healing as Caleb did right now.

"We've done our best," August sighed. "But we're not doctors, and when we stopped at a doctor none of us could say what the blue line on his arm was and if it was affecting him or not."

Kayla wished that she could bring greater healing to their people, but most of the time the doctors were fine. It was when they came up across magically caused illness that their finest men became stumped.

"Blue line?" Tyler questioned. "Pyro made Caleb a keeper? You tell Caleb to watch out for that. If Jack gets mad, he can threaten a guy to take that keeper status away. Let me tell you, that's a scary threat. No one knows how it would affect a human brain to suddenly stop hearing multiple dragon thoughts by destroying the keeper magic.

Pg. 572

Speaking of which, I am under the impression that that magic didn't leave you guys only because the keeper monolith is stationed in Vankerdale."

"You get his leg, I'll get his arm," Kayla instructed Tyler as she started to climb into the wagon and Warner sent her a hum for her help. "The blue line can't be the reason for this. Jack has one too and he's not got a fever."

"Jack is a keeper?!" Ian hissed. "Do I even want to know what kind of trouble he's been getting himself into?"

"Just that," Kayla answered. "Oh and handing all his magical king powers to Caleb so that Caleb could be the one ending up like this and not him."

Kayla rolled her eyes on the sentence. She was ever so grateful for what Caleb had done, but she still wished that her parents had taken a larger responsibility in taking care of the evil dragon Aralot and Vankerdale. They had left it all to her as if those problems were supposed to be her legacy or something. It was now. She hadn't a choice but to solve the puzzle, and Caleb's only option was to pitch in or watch her die. Eh. Maybe it was her job after all. She was the one being affected by Aralot's nightmare curse.

Since the dragon's death, Kayla hadn't had a single bad dream apart from the one of Ritz dying, but she was pretty sure that the dream had come from her and not from the dragon, because she had been able to wake herself up before anything scary happened at all. Control. She finally had control of herself. It was fantastic!

"How are you doing?" Kayla asked Caleb as she ran her hand along his forehead to check his temperature and commiserate with her wounded friend. No not friend. She hadn't been thinking about it too hard because she didn't want to get her hopes up, but Caleb had said that he loved her. They were more than friends.

He didn't say anything back. He didn't even try to smile, and when she picked up his good arm and let it drop, it fell limp and heavy. He was lethargic and hot and while there was no visible sign of infection from his breaks once she unwrapped them, there had to be something wrong with him.

Kayla pulled magic from her keychain, grateful that Bantin was so helpful in handing it out to her, and started to search for what was stopping Caleb from healing. The magic pulsed over him and then he yelled in agony as a silver dragon scale shot out of his left side. It wasn't even the side where he was broken, but sometime before Aralot had died, she had put a curse on this scale and it had been stuck inside of Caleb, causing him all sorts of problems. The devil dragon! She was trying to kill him—still! Caleb had been festering from the inside out which was the same thing that the dragon had been doing to her.

"That's really pretty even if what you did is gross," Tyler commented as he looked up from the broken leg he was healing to the scale in her hand and the bloody hole Kayla had created by pulling it out.

The scale did have a fantastic gem shape to it and it glistened in her hand as she turned it over. It was like finding a piece of buried treasure, or a fantastic new rock that she'd never seen before. It would make a great addition to her rock collection.

Pg. 574

"Destroy that thing!" August prompted causing Kayla to flinch and blast the scale to pieces. Yes, that scale was dangerous. Even without magic, it was distracting her from what she really needed to do. Caleb was bleeding and broken beside her and she was getting caught up in the beauty of a silver contraption.

Kayla focused herself again moving the magic over the wounds to restore the break and take away any lurking evil that Aralot may have left behind. Then she moved to the fever, and cleared that away glad that Caleb wasn't already dead from that scale being placed inside his body. He could have died days ago.

"There have been so many times that I didn't help creatures when I had the power to do what they could not." Kayla sighed thinking over the course of her life. "I'm going to do better. I'm not going to leave creatures whimpering in pain behind me. I'm going to change the way everyone thinks about magic and prove that it does more good than bad."

Caleb's mouth twitched at a smile, causing Kayla to look at his face earnestly waiting for him to be alright again. She reached for his hand taking it in hers, wishing a little bit that she could hear what he was thinking. He was being very quiet about it so he was probably talking with Warner. Kayla glanced at the brown dragon trying to pick out the signs of conversation. Warner was still looking over his shoulder at them, but he wasn't making any other indication that he was chatting.

Caleb squirmed, breaking their hands apart and pulling his fingers into his chest as if they were cold and he needed to coddle them. He examined his right hand and then his arm. He tested out his right leg by bending the knee and putting a little weight on it. Kayla got the sinking suspicion that he was looking at himself instead of them because he was still struggling with something large.

"You never know how grateful you are for a body that can work until it stops working," Caleb mumbled. "I couldn't feel my hand. My arm was completely done for. Thanks a lot."

"You're welcome," Tyler answered. "It's incredible how you survived actually. We had quite a discussion about it while you were still traveling. What it came down to was that you and Kayla would not have made it at all except for that magical fox Kayla stole from me and gave to you. You can keep it by the way. Since the fox was crafted in Vankderdale, the binding spell from Valiant took longer to be affected by the magical destruction spell, since the fox counted as Vankerdale magic. If you had used any other device to bind your life to, you and Kayla would have both failed. That's Brixton luck for you. Kayla said that she gave you the fox because you impressed her with magic and she felt like you would do really well with it. She had no idea that it was going to save anything."

"It really was quite something," Kayla agreed.

It was the largest piece of luck she had ever been part of. It was a rather spur of the moment decision to take the fox from Tyler in the first place and another unconscious decision to give it to Caleb. However, there was still something upsetting Caleb and it wasn't his snapped limbs or the magic that had wonderfully worked.

"I've killed something before too so if you need to talk about it…" Kayla offered. She trailed off because she suspected it felt different to kill off a four-hundred-year-old dragon versus a young prince. It was probably her that still needed to talk about it. She had
Pg. 576

been keeping quiet about her dreams, but she really wanted to reveal them so that she could process them without them being so frightening. They were lessons of the past, and she couldn't think of a better person to help her create something beautiful from the tragic lessons besides Caleb.

Finally, Caleb looked back up, but it wasn't to tell her that he was healed or to talk about the silver spellbinding dragon. It was to talk with King Tyler. Kayla slumped against the side of the wagon wishing for a more exciting reunion than what she got. Later. She would tell Caleb how much he meant to her later.

"I didn't mean to lose my temper and if there's any way to go back to our previous agreement, I'll take it. Just promise me that you won't kiss her in front of me or I'll wish that I hadn't survived this."

Despite being healed, Caleb looked hollow. He had won against an ancient beast that had left others stumped and wailing, and yet here he was stone-faced and still broken. Kayla sucked in her breath. Caleb still thought that she was engaged, and he probably expected that Tyler would take her back to Vankerdale. In his mind, this was goodbye. He was physically whole, but there was still a cut in his soul.

Kayla looked at Tyler waiting to see his reaction. If he wasn't going to say anything, she would. There was no way she was going to live in Vankerdale and leave Caleb behind.

"I hear that you still have your own training to do—"

"No!" Caleb cut Tyler off. "I don't care about the extra training. I know enough to get your people up on their dragons. I'm coming with you. Please don't make me live without her, Tyler. Please," Caleb begged as he wiped at his eyes still refusing to look Kayla in the face. Ian and August both leaned up against the side of the wagon looking between the three of them, interested to watch the drama. Kayla tried to reach for Caleb to tell him the truth only he scooted away from her again as if this pleading was something that he had to do on his own.

"I'm marrying Adelyn Peyton," Tyler stated.

"I love Kayla. I'm not sure if you've figured that out yet but everything I just did was for her. I left the dragon wares. I traveled to Wisteria. I traveled to Vankerdale. I faced death magically and physically so that she could have the chance to go out there and prove to everyone that magic isn't evil and keepers have large hearts and all the other impossibly large tasks she sets her mind to. This world needs Kayla."

"It needs you too," Tyler stated.

"Thank you," Caleb said as he took in another deep breath and kept going. "But the sun would stop rising for me if there wasn't a chance that I could just *see* her on a regular basis. I'll—"

"Caleb!" Tyler couldn't help but laugh at him.

Ian and August were both smiling. Kayla was still waiting for the moment it sunk in that she wasn't getting married so that Caleb would look at her again.

"Everybody, and I mean everybody, knows how you feel about Kayla Brixton. A man would have to hold a devil's heart and then some to get in the way of that. Tristan and I have already released ourselves from any contract to marry her. She's free to pick for herself so treat her nicely because she's got this beautiful red hair and dazzling blue eyes and a heart so strong that she drew up a map to Aralot and helped you break apart your entire kingdom in her attempt to likewise stay with you."

"Beautiful red-brown hair?" Caleb questioned wiping at his eyes again as the words slowly sunk in.

"Yup," Tyler agreed.

"Eyes that vanish puddles?" Caleb asked.

"Sure," Tyler shrugged trying not to laugh.

"You go look at something else," Caleb told him getting defensive.

He scooted himself between Tyler and Kayla and they all had to laugh at him for finally getting it. Kayla wrapped her arms around Caleb's back and let her head rest against the back of his shoulder. She didn't know what Caleb was thinking exactly, but it was warm enough of a thought that Warner purred.

Tyler ruined it. "Aralot put one of her scales in you. It was silver. That would have been a remarkable color to find on a dragon."

"There was nothing good about that dragon," Caleb stated. "Too many people told Aralot that she was beautiful. She was vain and cruel and self-centered."

"She was holding magic inside of Aralot so the rest of us could be safe," Kayla said. She felt Caleb stiffen and then he pushed away from her again so he could see her face.

"You're the only one that would try to find something good about her. One look at that dragon had me forgetting everything except to cater to her wishes, and she was wishing for us to die. I drew a picture of her, but I think I might burn it..."

"I'll do it," Kayla volunteered. "I have lots of practice at burning pictures. I won't feel tempted to look. I promise."

"Part of me still doesn't believe she was real. She was deceptively beautiful as if she used her magic to trick and lie and hold all power under her talons because she refused to share her most brilliant treasure—magic. I'm so glad that's over with. The best treasures are the ones we can share with others. You taught me that," Caleb told her, "and I'll share you as long as you're not too far away."

Kayla jumped at him again wrapping her arms back around him so she wasn't very far away at all. He was so fabulous! It was hard to find a person like this so willing to sacrifice everything for his friends and still able to let those he loved learn and grow and be themselves. Caleb was pretty much the opposite of the spellbinding dragon Aralot. No wonder she had tried to get rid of him so fast while all the other kings she hung on to and used.

"I stayed because of you," Kayla told Caleb feeling her entire body relax just by being this close to him. Caleb didn't even need to say anything and she felt like she had found the best treasure in the world too. Peace of mind and peace of soul. There wasn't anything better.

"You know, I think tonight I just want to sit," Caleb voiced. "Pretty boring guy, huh?"

"Sitting sounds fabulous," Kayla agreed.

Pg. 580

She shared a look with Caleb that spoke of more than just sitting and he chuckled at her before putting an appropriate distance between them so he wasn't tempted to kiss her. At least that's what Kayla thought the look was. Maybe he was simply reading the emotions in her own eyes. She could kiss him again and she wouldn't feel awkward doing it.

"I have to ask Anvil if I can date you before I ask you out," Caleb said jumping from the wagon and checking over the state of his dragon that had just walked for over a week. "He will lay into me if I don't, because he's forbidden me from asking. Let's not forget about your dad either. You know he'll add on some ridiculous rules like I have to keep my feet four inches away from yours at all times. Then he will enforce those rules with a spell because he loves you greatly. Then there's Vermelo. He's going to start eyeing me and passing me boring rule books about how to run a kingdom. And then there's Tristan."

"Tristan abdicated," Kayla informed him.

"Really?" Caleb spun around not believing her.

"Yeah. He abdicated in favor of keeping the job of ware leader."

"Oh!" Caleb chuckled. "He likes to boss everyone around and spy on everyone else's business so that's reasonable. Ware leader is right next to king anyway. It's one step down from Captain of the Guard. Have you ever realized before how much Vermelo is the king?"

"Vermelo?" Kayla asked, wiping some dust off of Warner's brown scales as she helped Caleb circle him. He looked fine although tired.

"Yup. Vermelo is very much the king at times, holding together the Clusters and Brixtons who are his strongest supporters."

Kayla couldn't help but laugh at the way Caleb saw everything. It was usually her that had strange alternate views on how the world worked.

"What does that make you then?"

"Still in trouble," Caleb remarked.

He glanced toward the wagon and the people they had just conveniently put out of sight. With a move that Kayla didn't see coming, he dashed forward and gave her a five-second kiss that left her glowing from head to toe. Then he had the audacity to snicker about it and run away!

"Hey!" Kayla cried out.

"Race you!" Conner said dropping down from Tempest.

Kayla blinked in surprise. She had been so distracted by everything to do with Caleb that she hadn't heard Tempest show up. Normally dragon wings were the first things she heard. But in any case, she wasn't going to lose this race. She had been waiting too long for it. Kayla gave Conner a nod and ran for all she was worth after Caleb. Conner unfortunately won.

Laceration

Caleb

It was like seeing her for the first time in his life. She was so beautiful. Her red-brown hair was let down and pulled over one shoulder as she ruffled through a bag in the doctor's office for tweezers to pull the splinters out of a random rider's arm. The rider had a lot of them from the tree that had been accidentally dropped on top of him while they were helping to repair the town. Kayla had set herself up in the doctor's office at first light determined to read through as many medical books as she could in a day now that King Tyler was gone and her parents were on a long trip with Bantin to restore their broken portals. Kayla hadn't come back out, so Caleb was heading in. He thought the rider's splinters looked painful. Then he looked down at his own self-inflicted wound and grinned.

Kayla hadn't noticed him yet. She wasn't wearing her riding gear but no one had called her out for the infraction. She was back to the hooded sweater and hiking pants. Her special riding boots she kept on, making her the cutest thing this doctor's office had ever seen.

Caleb felt slightly stupid to be standing where he was. He had never cut himself on purpose in order to see a girl before. But when Warner told him that Kayla wasn't ever coming out to help rebuild the town because she was fixing everyone that went into the office, his mind had started to spin with the possibilities. At first, he thought he would get in a sword fight with Mulligan and let the man accidentally slice him except they had no swords. An ax fight sounded far more dangerous and Caleb didn't want to see Mulligan wield one at him. So Caleb had pulled out his knife and cut his own arm. Mulligan had caught him at it and gave him a concerned look.

"Would you look at that? I best get that taken care of," Caleb had smiled at Mulligan.

Mulligan called him several names as he walked off with his minor cut. Lazy was the nicest one. It didn't put a dent in Caleb's mood. If anything, Mulligan had only added to it. He was going to see Kayla today no matter what, and he was rather happy about it.

The sun filtered through the window as Kayla located the tweezers and started in on the splinters. She had the sharpest eyes, the gentlest hands, and the kindest expression. He couldn't wait until she looked his direction and noticed him. But she was taking a really long time intent on the arm before her. She didn't look up when he cleared his throat and Caleb sighed as he went to grab a bandage for himself. Maybe she had spotted him out of the corner of her eye and noticed the non-threatening cut. Perhaps what he should do was come back covered in splinters.

He stepped from the doctor's room with a frown. Then he pulled out his knife and gave himself a larger cut, one that she couldn't ignore, before he stepped back inside. That did the trick. She met his eyes that time and his heart started hammering at the accusing look she sent him that quickly turned into concern.

Pg. 584

"Caleb, what are you doing?" Kayla asked abandoning the tweezers to grab at his twice injured arm. He let her see it as his eyes scanned over the smoothness of her face, the warmness of her downcast blue eyes, and the glint of a chain about her neck. Was she wearing a necklace? He had never seen her wear one before. Curious, he reached out to grab it trailing his fingers down her neck as he went. He grinned as her face turned red and she looked at him. He didn't return her blush. If he did, he was likely to come undone. Had anyone ever told her that she could steal a man's heart like that?

"What did you do with your arm?" she asked him as he pulled the necklace out and smiled amused. The pendant on the necklace featured Valiant with his tail curled around him and his head cocked to the side in his most charming adoring state. Kayla rolled her eyes at it.

"Valiant swapped the flower from Ritz with this dragon that he created. He says his is better, and it is, but it was the sentiment that counted. I now have to go on a treasure hunt to find my lost item which makes me think that this whole thing was a dare from Sparkle. Now what did you do with your arm, CJ4?"

"My arm?" Caleb asked as he tucked the necklace back inside Kayla's sweater causing her to blush even deeper. Caleb felt his chest start to warm up with fire. It wasn't just from the nickname. He had never dared to do anything like this before. He'd ditched class to spy on her hundreds of times, and he'd held her hand and given her two kisses, but this just felt different. This time he was sneaking away because he knew that Kayla would acknowledge that he existed. That made all the difference.

"My arm got a cut on it," he shrugged meeting her gaze. Kayla was looking at him worried but she burst out a smile at how ridiculous he was being.

"Whatever for? What was wrong with the last cut?"

"The last cut didn't get you to look at me," he replied biting his lip.

Now she really would know how much of a fool he was today but what other way did he have to see her? She opened her mouth trying to come up with a reply but shut it again speechless. The confusion across her face was priceless. How could she still not know that she thrilled him just by looking at him?

Kayla had to look away as her neck took on the heat of her face. He couldn't help but laugh at her. She faced demons and terrors that he could only imagine, but when it came to endearing words, she was lost. He pulled her face back around to look at him and wasn't prepared for what he noticed. She wasn't lost. But he might be soon if she didn't look away again. The fire wasn't only in his own chest. He could see it burning within her eyes and suddenly he became more aware of himself than he had ever been before. His arms felt alive with nervousness wanting to reach out and bring her closer. He'd bring her in close and spin her around just to hear her giggle.

Not only did his arms want her closer but his legs begged him to step closer too. They nearly bridged the gap all by themselves and one of them wanted to bump against her scarred left leg that she always hid to tell her that he still found her to be beautiful.

Then there was his chest hammering away with such a force that it imprinted her blush into his mind, and he knew he'd have to

Pg. 586

draw it just to get her out of his head. Perhaps if he never drew her on paper again, he could get her to stay in his thoughts forever.

He could feel his own cheeks start to flush and he never blushed. His mouth was starting to get into the action too, filling up with liquid that would horrify him if she was the one to step closer and kiss him. He swallowed before that happened and strangled her reaction to him. He had no intention of disgusting her right now.

They were hardly touching. She only had one hand holding his arm and her other hand was holding the bandage close by. Really they had been much closer to each other before, but she had never looked at him like this. The tension in the room was probably too thick because the splintered rider cleared his throat and broke Kayla out of their trance.

"It's stupid to cut yourself," Kayla told him wrapping the cut with a swift motion and yanking on the knot just enough that it stung.

"I thought we'd already established that you're the smarter one in this relationship. Me? I'll go do stupid things if it gets your attention."

"You are so weird," Kayla laughed at him. "What project did you just ditch to sneak in here?"

"I was fixing a roof with Mulligan. He swore at me when I walked off on him."

She was going to be a bad influence on his ability to stop himself from doing something like this again because she didn't tell him to go back to the roof. Kayla started laughing.

"Mulligan is going to get you for that."

"Chores or something," Caleb shrugged.

"Are you kidding? Mulligan places squirrels into people's beds."

"How do you know that?" Caleb asked. He had once kicked a pet squirrel out of a bunkroom that had a ton of other issues wrong with it. He had never figured out where that squirrel had come from.

"I have large ears! He was telling his dragon about the squirrels he had captured as soon as the trees started falling. They made themselves rather easy to scoop up into his traps because they ran right into them."

Mulligan! The man had noticed the problems inside the bunkroom before Caleb had, and it was him taking action against them. He was pretty funny. Thanks to Kayla, Caleb knew to check his bed really well before he lay down tonight.

Kayla pulled her bag around from her back and fetched out a folded piece of paper. "You can have this if you look at it on your way back to work," she bribed.

Caleb looked at the paper curiously. The edges had some black around them so he could tell it was a drawing. This was a tough call. Take a drawing from Kayla and go back to work or stay in here and watch her get frustrated. He was going to pick the staying around option.

"Get out, Caleb." Kayla grinned at him already guessing what he really wanted. "I'll see you after work." She shoved the paper into his chest so that he had to take it along with him as she pushed him out the door.

Caleb held the paper in close wishing that he could mess up time just a tiny bit so that work got over really fast today. Nah. He'd better not. He knew that messing around with time caused other problems that he didn't want to have to correct.

"I want to see it," Warner hooted, swooping over Caleb likewise in a good mood. That was because Warner had overheard one of Tia's dragons talking about transfers for the upcoming year and on the list was Warner's good friend Jewel who might transfer over to be with him. He was understandably excited.

Caleb pulled open the paper carefully and he couldn't help but stare. This was way better than the stick figure that Kayla had made for him before. She was remarkable. Then again, she had drawn his favorite subject. There she was up on the top of a mountain with her hiking gear at her feet and the sun pressing in upon her face as it rose. Caleb had spied on her hiking a lot, but he always thought that she never saw him. He had been wrong, because instead of her usual shadow standing behind her, he was her shadow.

"Shadows are always connected to the light," Kayla had written at the bottom. "They shift and move when the light changes. Sometimes they are larger and more important than the light and sometimes they are smaller. You taught me that. The greatest echo of one's soul is found where the heart looks. If echoes could be seen, mine would look like this."

Kayla could change his mood up in an instant. Gone was the desire to sneak around to flirt, and in its place was the strong desire to be incredibly marvelous. Like the kind of amazing that everyone else looked up to. The kind of man that didn't break the rules (too much), and the kind of man that finished his training so he could get back to the prize of having Kayla in his class again. He'd be the kind of man that deserved sharing the same light Kayla saw. Gee. That girl could get him back to fixing a roof in an instant!

She had just told him that she loved him in one of the most beautiful ways he had ever heard of before. Kayla saw them as connected through the heart, taking turns being equal, smaller, and larger. They were an ebb and flow of balance; a force so strong that it was never going to be erased, because wherever there was light, shadows would come, and he was never going to fade from her soul.

Caleb put the folded paper into his own bag to protect it. He was going to draw the two of them as shadows later tonight and then post his pictures all over the ware for Kayla to find. The smile tugged at his mouth for turning back to his old ways. He suddenly didn't care that the images were going to end up spread throughout three different kingdoms. Let them all know that he got to stay with Kayla forever. He could make the magic happen between them even without the blue force dictating their actions. The spells across the kingdom were all gone, but there was no denying that he and Kayla were both still in one.

Name Bank

Kingdoms:

Aralot	-current location
Vankerdale	-east of Aralot
Wisteria	-north of Aralot across the ocean

Brixtons and Feldings:

Kayla Brixton	-secret princess	Dragon: Valiant
Jack Brixton	-Kayla's father; the king	Dragon: Pyro
Tia (Felding) Brixton	Kayla's mother; the queen	Dragon: Sparkle
Conner Felding	-Kayla's missing uncle	Dragon: Tempest
Esmay Felding	-Conner's Wife	Children: Sashi, Ruth, Tova
Herb Felding	-Kayla's grandfather	
Alice Felding	-Kayla's grandmother	
Gladius Felding	-Kayla's great-grandfather	
Jean (Frizer) Felding	-Gladius's wife	
Maslon Felding	Gladius's younger brother	
Shane Felding	-Kayla's great-great-grandfather	Dragon: Tang
Troy Felding	-Kayla's third great-grandfather	Dragon: Bandit

Mentionable dragons:

Tia's keeper dragons:	-Clawson, Pyro, Midnight, Fang, Duchess, Hemp, Darkwing, Lightning, Slasher, and Fern
Nebula	-Conner's water dragon
Luna	-a wild dragon and Pyro's sister
Gastron	Herb Felding's fourth dragon

Aralot Castle:

King Klavian Cluster	-steward and son of King Virgil Cluster IV
Queen Aria	-wife of Klavian Cluster
Prince Tristan	-son of Klavian and Aria
King Virgil Cluster IV	-Klavian's crowned father
Vermelo	-Captain of the Guard
Merlock	-a dwarf dragon
Bantin	-also called Mr. Grumpy; the magical ice dragon

Monastery:

Abbot McLean	-the current abbot

Colts:

Ritz (Maslon)	-ageless leader of the Colts Dragons: Norber; Halfax
Fenix, Steve, Bret, and Kyle	- Kayla's uncles on her father's side
Joss	-Jack's best friend
Halfax	- a dragon in Ritz's keeper bond
Norber	-Ritz's bonded dragon

Vankerdale:

Tyler Valeron	-The new king	Dragon: Coal; Flare
Adelyn Peyton	-Tyler's former pen pal	
Bate Peyton	-Adelyn's father	
Narl Valeron	-Tyler's brother	
Jess Valeron	-the woman Narl married	
Prince Evan Peyton	-former prince of Vankerdale	
King Peyton	-former king of Vankerdale	Dragon: SilverWings
General Reis	-the general	
Choladon	-the ulta-dragon king that made the keeper monolith	

| **Mentionable Dragons:** | Choladon | -the ulta-dragon king that made the keeper monolith |
| | Aralot | -Choladon's spellbinding dragon mate |

Anvil's Ware:

Anvil	-ware leader	Dragon: Clawson
Annaliese	-Anvil's wife	
Rosa Cluster	-Kayla's Aunt	Dragon: Pewter
Clark Cluster	-Kayla's Uncle	Dragon: Midnight
Achilles	-a rider in Tia's keeper bond	Dragon: Fang
Caleb Andrade	-a rider and artist	Dragon: Warner
Aiden	-a rider that fights Caleb	

The King's Ware:

Charles	-the oldest ware leader	Dragon: Clipshire
Caleb Andrade	- section leader over levels 2 and 6	Dragon: Warner
Mulligan	-section leader over level 8 and up	
Russel	-section leader over level 4 and rider's kids	

| Notley | -section leader over levels 3 and 7 |
| Malone | -night section leader over levels 1 and 5 |

Kayla's Teammates

Avery	Dragon: Fisher
Davis	Dragon: Summit
Nick	Dragon: Flint
Norrin	Dragon: Mordred
Sherman	Dragon: Cuprite
Brea	Dragon: Sulphur
Keran	Dragon: Umber
Junia	Dragon: Forge

Mentionable people and dragons

Shirley	-a night scout	
Dr. Weber	-a doctor	
Brandon Sloan	-lost his ware books	
Javier	-Caleb's assistant section leader	
Reed	-a light green dragon	Rider: Lena Sherman

Wisteria:

King Anthony Nolteman	-an eaten king
King Lester Nolteman	-the new king of Wisteria
Erana	-a trapped princess in time

Treasure Hunters:

Ian	-old street urchin in Wisteria
August	-used to be a baker in Wisteria

Other Wares:

Vincent's Ware:	-led by Vincent	
	Shilo	- ice dragon trainer
Vladimir	-past ware leader	Dragon: Giselle
Desert Ware:	-training ware in the desert	
	Dani	-Tristan's past girlfriend
Turid's Ware:	-led by Turid	female ware leader
Rogan's Ware:	-led by Rogan	Dragon: Indigo
Niles's Ware:	-led by Niles	-training ware in the west

Towns and Places:

The Pits	-a stone quarry owned by the Colts
Troni	-the town by the castle
Salka	-a city below the castle
Deluth	-a city where Jack's uncle lives
Arkridge	-a city in the north
Louie's Bistro	-near the castle
The Castle	
Old Castle	Gladius's destroyed castle in the south

Don't fly off yet!

There is magic lingering in the air encouraging you to leave a **Spoiler Free** review on Amazon or Goodreads. This is an excellent way to spark the flames of another person's fire so they can enjoy the book as you have. I thank you for your time.

For more exciting stories and content please visit my website at:

amandaheit.com

Or my author page at

https://www.amazon.com/author/amanda.heit

Special Thanks

A very large thank-you to my reviewers Amy Fowler and Adam Morse who have gone through a ton of versions of this story and have encouraged me through every flight.

About the Author

Finding meaning in life—feeling like you're contributing to all of humanity in a good way—is a large undertaking. When I write, it's the task I take on. Sometimes, that task is daunting. Sometimes, it's full of laughter, joy, and fear. Reaching the end of a book can put me on top of the world or cause me endless frustration. But I can't stop myself from trying. I can't stop the inner clock that ticks and tells me that writing is something I enjoy the heck out of and there is nothing that will stop me from writing for long. As one of the quiet people in the universe, my best joy and flow in life comes when I'm creating new worlds and exploring characters. For me, each book I create finds new friends that share with me the intimate tangles of their lives. They cheer and I cheer. They succeed and I rejoice. They fall and I'm there hoping for that happy ending right along with them. I hope that you can find something in the stories I create that will bring you the same type of thrill. Thanks for sticking to the end!

Amanda Heit

www.ingramcontent.com/pod-product-compliance
Lightning Source LLC
Chambersburg PA
CBHW022232020726
47496CB00004B/864